Wal[illegible]
the
Dark Angel

B.D. Edkins

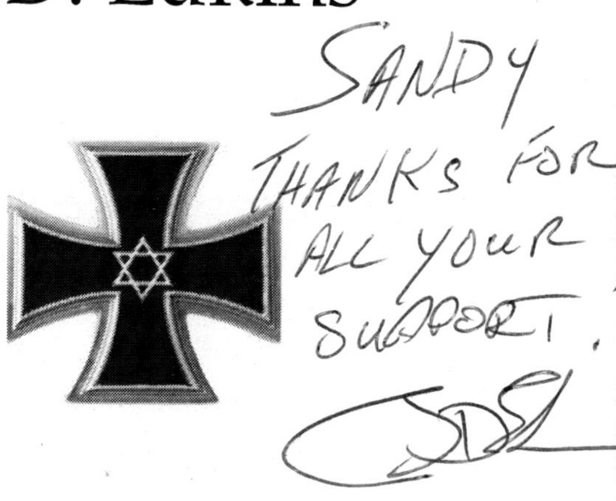

This is a work of fiction and all of the names, places, incidents, and characters portrayed in this novel are the product of the author's imagination or are either fictitious or are used fictitiously.

Waltzing with the Dark Angel

ISBN - 13: 978-1463760410

ISBN – 10: 1463760418

First Edition: November 2011

To my children:
Brandy and Lowell

Chapter 1

Tel Aviv, Israel - 1959

The air conditioner in the window labored as it tried to pump temperate air into Aaron's office. On one corner of his desk sat an oscillating fan buzzing back and forth tempting him with a cool breeze once every cycle. He had tried to set the fan so that it would stop oscillating and blow continuously in his direction but, like the window unit, it didn't work either. On the other corner sat an inbox jammed with papers assembled in no conceivable order other than first in, still there. He had long ago removed the outbox and deposited it in the storage room at the end of the hall where all of the useless or broken equipment seemed to end up. The burnt electrical smell coming from the motor of the fan told him he would be making another trip to the storage room soon. Lately he had thoughts of just moving his entire office into the storage area to save time.

Aaron Singer was thirty-five years old, five feet, eight inches tall and weighed 154 pounds. He had never thought himself very athletic looking but rather considered himself well proportioned for his height and weight. His features were lean and smooth; his skin had been tanned by the desert sun to a light molasses color and whenever there was a sweltering day like today, soaked with perspiration, his hair turned into masses of dark looping curls, the kind mothers prayed their babies would have. His face would be considered angelic if it weren't betrayed by the haunted look of a man who held too many secrets.

Aaron stared at the report in front of him and mechanically went through the motions of reading it. Most of the reports were the same. With thousands of former concentration camp Jews scattered all over the world came thousands of sightings of wanted German war criminals. Some provided good information; others just helped to confuse an imperfect system of hunting these men down. Aaron's eyes glided along the paper in front of him taking in every word that had been pounded onto the paper until his eyes caught a glimpse of his forearm. A flash of irritation flew across his face as he stared at the numbers. After twenty-one years of carrying the tattoo he thought that by now it would not bother him any more than the calluses on his hands or the small scar peeking out from under his bushy eyebrow, but the tattoo, while visible on the surface, imprisoned a part of his soul that may never be free again.

Aaron had thought about having it removed several times. One time he even went as far as to make an appointment with a plastic surgeon, but by the time he got to the front door of the hospital, his hair was once again a mass of dark looping curls and he was physically weakened by the bout of emotional gymnastics he had performed on the ride over. No, he had thought, the tattoo was more a part of him today than the day he had received it. It carried with it the memories of his grandfather's smile, David's devious giggling, Bella's relentless beatings and Heinrich's thoughtless act of murder.

Aaron had accepted the fact that the tattoo would be with him for the rest of his life; the part he couldn't accept was that the terrible memories were just as much a part of the number as were the pigments in the ink.

"Thinking of your grandfather?"

Aaron's eyes shot from the paper in front of him and focused directly on his assistant, Mrs. Levy. Only Levy would dare to burst into his office without knocking; only Levy would ever dare ask about his grandfather.

"Yes."

"And Anna?" she added.

Aaron looked down at the report in front of him. "Yes, and Anna," he said nervously shuffling the papers. "and David, and I was even thinking about Von Reichman." He added as an afterthought.

"Von Reichmann? You mean Klas?"

"Yes, Klas."

"Whatever for?"

Aaron looked down at the papers again. "I don't know. I start thinking about one of them, usually my grandfather, and then it leads to another and then another." Aaron looked up at Levy, "Don't you ever do that?"

Levy thought for several seconds before answering. "They're all gone now, Aaron. I've put them behind me as much as anyone can, I guess. But you still can't let them go, can you?"

"Does it show that badly?"

Levy's left eyebrow raised slightly above the other giving her face an inquisitive look. "Do I need to answer that?"

"You just did." He said, noticing for the first time, the large courier bag she was carrying. "Do I need to ask what's in the pouch?"

Levy looked at Aaron for several seconds before answering, her eyes haunted by inner misgivings about the information she carried.

"Aaron, we might have found Heinrich."

"Heinrich, where? When did they see him? Do they still have contact?" the words rattled out of his mouth like machine gun fire.

"Slow down! I said we might have found Heinrich."

Aaron's shoulders slumped slightly as he looked down at the papers in front of him again. "Might have found him?" he said, not bothering to look up, "Let me guess, he's disappeared again, vanished."

Levy frowned and held the large canvas bag she was carrying closer to her chest. "Well. . . yes, they aren't sure, Aaron, but it's the first piece of solid information we have received on him in almost three years."

"Solid? Are ghosts solid now?" He quipped.

"Aaron, are you going to listen?" She asked raising her tone slightly.

Aaron looked up at her and waved his hand for her to continue.

"Our operatives in Buenos Aries were tracking down a lead on Eichmann.

"Eichmann!, now it's Eichmann?"

"Aaron, shut up!"

Aaron sat there with his mouth hanging open, nothing coming out. As the Commander in charge of the Gabriel Project no one had ever told him to shut up before. Levy was the only person in his whole department that could ever get away with telling him such a thing; she had earned that privilege a thousand times over.

She waited for him to close his mouth before she continued. "They were following up on the Eichmann lead when a man who they thought might be Heinrich showed up instead. The team continued to watch the room for several more hours, hoping that Eichmann would turn up. When it was obvious that no one else was coming, they entered the building. Somehow the man was alerted to their approach and had gone down the fire escape and into another room. Where he went from there they don't know. He. . ." Levy paused for a moment, "vanished."

"And why did they think it was Heinrich?"

"The man's facial features were close to one of the composites we have out in the field."

It had been Levy's idea to have a sketch of each of the most wanted men created from available photographs and the memories of the camp survivors. The composite pictures were then altered to allow for ageing and cosmetic changes.

Usually five or six different sketches were produced of each criminal to give the agents in the field some points of possible reference.
Levy held out the canvas bag. "Here's the courier pouch from Buenos Aries."

Aaron looked at the bag for several seconds and then at Levy. The woman was just a shadow of her former self. Her hair, once the color of autumn acorns was now listless and graying quickly. At one time, her skin had reminded him of flowering magnolias, now it was sallow and weathered. It was only her eyes that remained unchanged from their time together in Auschwitz. They still held their intense cobalt color, their sharpness and passion for life.
As they had a thousand times before, Aaron's eyes traced the thin line of her shoulder blades down her left arm and stopped upon reaching her forearm. There, as it was everyday, was her registration number clearly tattooed in plain sight. Aaron had seen her number a million times before and could recite the number by heart. After all, it was only forty-seven numbers different from his.He often wondered what private memories the tattoo burdened her with. It was something he had always wanted to ask her, but never could find a way to broach the subject. The truth of the matter was he was afraid that she would be all too willing to tell him in exchange for a peek into that dark portion of his memory and that was a frightening thought to him.

He and Levy had arrived at Auschwitz six weeks apart, she being the first to arrive and he and his grandfather followed later. They had spent their entire time in the same camp and even remained together with the same group of survivors for a few weeks after their release, but eventually, as all the survivors did, they went their separate ways. Aaron returned to Berlin for a year in hopes of finding some of his family, but soon gave up the idea. With the ghastly memories of his imprisonment following him wherever he went, Aaron decided he could no longer stay in Germany and with the help of friends in Palestine was smuggled into the country. It was then that Aaron's life took on some meaning. He felt that he was finally going to be able to put the past behind him and get on with his life. He joined the Israeli forces fighting for a free Jewish state in 1947 and moved up through the ranks quickly. Finally, on May 14th 1949, the United Nations reorganized the region of Palestine into two separate states, one Arab and one Jewish.

One day later, on May 15th 1949, the combined forces of Egypt, Syria, Lebanon, Transjordan, and Iraq attacked the new state of Israel. Aaron and his group had become involved in some of the fiercest fighting of the war. Aaron soon gained the reputation of being able to remain calm and in control when faced with a combat situation, traits admired in combat leaders. Other soldiers often remarked openly about Aaron's ability to face death. The truth be known, Aaron had as great a fear of dying as the next man. In fact he probably had a greater zeal for life than most. Auschwitz had taught him that, but he also had learned about death and accepted it for what it was.

In the winter of 1949 a cease-fire was finally arranged between the Israeli's and the Arab nations. It was sometime after the cease-fire took place that the ghost of his past took hold of his life again. At one point the nightmares were so bad that he was only managing a few hours sleep at night and that was with the help of large doses of alcohol.

Aaron's life took another turn for the better in February 1950 when he was approached by a short stocky man in civilian clothing and was asked if he would be interested in serving his country again. Aaron later found out that he had caught the attention of his superiors during the war and his name was one of the few that were being circulated throughout the inner circle of the government, as someone who would lay down his life for the new state. He was quickly approached and asked to take on a new job within the government. In March 1950, Aaron entered into one of the many fledgling agencies in charge of Israeli security. Aaron knew within himself that this opportunity was the sole reason he had not ended his life at the bottom of a liquor bottle. He quit drinking altogether the day he went for training.

In September 1951, the bureau Aaron worked for was combined with several other intelligence and special operations groups to form the single group known as "Ha Mossad, le Modiyn ve le Tafkidim Mayuhadim", The Institute for Intelligence and Special Operations, or better known as the Mossad. The new group was to be the backbone of Israeli intelligence operations and would cover all aspect of security for the State of Israel. It was during the reorganization that Aaron asked for and received command of the special group that was to become known as "The Gabriel Project". It was then he met up with his old friend Mrs. Levy who had also moved to Israel in 1950 with her family and began working for Israeli

Intelligence. Together, they were to lead the group of special agents throughout the world whose sole task was to locate and apprehend Nazi war criminals to be brought back to Israel for trial.

Aaron blinked several times and finally looked into Levy's eyes and then back at her tattoo. What always caught his attention was the small icon, which followed directly behind the number. It was clearly the outline of the German Totenkoph or death head. As far as Aaron knew, he and Levy were possibly the only two remaining survivors who had that special designation after their serial numbers. He had never heard of it used in any other camp other than the one in which he and Levy had spent so many years. Aaron took the bag and rested it on the desk.

"Have you seen what is inside?"

Levy turned and started out the door. "It's addressed to you, Commander. My name doesn't appear anywhere on the bag."

"You probably erased it." He whispered under his breath as he loosened the flap and Levy left the room.

The bag was the standard diplomatic courier bag used by the Israeli Government for transferring important papers from one embassy to another or from an embassy to government departments within Israel. Aaron would get bi-monthly updates from their embassies around the world.

Back in 1951 Aaron had jumped at the chance to help track down war criminals. During the early years it had been much easier. Most of the war criminals caught during the late forties and early fifties were too careless to have remained hidden for very long. But now, eighteen years after the war, there were very few left and it made sense that those remaining were the more devious ones. Now there were fewer and fewer confirmed sightings and more shadow figures haunting Aaron's department and his memories.

Aaron removed the smaller leather pouch and envelope from the courier bag and placed the larger bag on the floor. He opened the envelope and read the short report from his man in Buenos Aries.

Aaron read and re-read the last few lines of the report. "Contents of this pouch were removed from a hotel room in central Buenos Aries. Items were left behind when the subject fled. Subject believed to be Heinrich Oust, former Camp Commander, Nazi concentration camp 117."

There was a copy of the evidence transfer log attached, which was used to help keep track of the pouch on its way to Aaron. Aaron smiled as he noticed that Levy had signed for it before handing it over to him.

Aaron finally was able to loosen the last knot in the leather strap and carefully poured the contents out onto his desktop. There were only three items in the bag. The first was a silver lighter worn from use and obviously missing an emblem on the one side. Aaron recognized the outline of the missing emblem as that of the SS Eagle. He turned the lighter over and read the inscription written in German.

"Gott mit uns"

Aaron had to smile; God is with us, how ironic he thought to himself. The second item was of more interest to him. It was a gold money clip, also missing an emblem. Aaron looked closer at it and could see where someone had used a sharp metal object to remove the SS insignia that had once decorated the clip. He reached into his desk drawer and pushed the revolver out of the way in order to remove the jeweler's glass located there. Aaron held the glass in place and studied the clip. A huge smile filled his face as he turned the clip over.

"Eric's work." he said out loud and then studied the Yiddish inscription hidden on the inside, tucked deep into the fold of the clip. The inscription was very small and purposefully hidden within the inside of the clip. The words were even hard to view under the jeweler's glass, but Aaron knew what he was looking for. The inscription read:

"Es iz nit oyf eybik"

"It's not for an eternity" he whispered aloud.

Aaron placed the clip on the table and removed the glass from his eye. The third item was a cross-town bus pass validated the day of the sighting and was of no value. While the items could certainly have belonged to Heinrich Oust they were still items that could have belonged to anyone. The owner didn't even have to be German let alone a Nazi. Without a doubt his friend and co-worker in the camp, Eric, had made the clip but Jewish slave labor had produced hundreds if not thousands of these items. Just because Eric had made this particular one Aaron couldn't assume that it was at one time in the possession of Heinrich. Nothing remotely tied the items back to Heinrich.

Aaron picked up the items and started to pour them back into the bag when he noticed that there was yet another item in the bottom of the bag that he had failed to dislodge the first time.

Aaron still held the other items in his right hand as he picked up the pouch from the bottom with his left hand and shook it. Quickly the leather folds released the last item and it fell free from the pouch and hit the desktop. The gold orb bounced several times on its edge and began to spin around in circles like a child's top. Aaron watched it spin for what seemed an eternity before the band finally began to lose momentum and start to wobble. Within a few seconds it had come to rest just in front of his hand.

While the ring had stopped, Aaron's head was still spinning. He just stared at the gold cylindrical object and didn't move. Aaron hadn't even noticed that he had dropped the other items onto the floor. Finally, he lifted his right hand to reach out for the ring and stopped short. He waited for what seemed a lifetime then reached out a second time. Again he failed to retrieve the object. This time he was shocked to see how uncontrollably his hand shook. Feelings that he thought long dead shot to the surface, a wave of soaring fear coupled with disbelief and, at the same time, a rush of habitual excitement consumed him. He could almost feel the shaking starting in the tips of his fingers working its way up his hand and into the arm and shoulder. The spasms continued through his neck and other shoulder until his entire body quivered. He tried a third time, pushing his hand across the desktop for support until he reached the ring. Slowly he picked it up between his thumb and forefinger and ever so carefully lifted it from the surface of the desk.

He held it in his right hand and used his left to steady the object enough for him to look inside at the inscription he hoped was still there. Aaron tried to calm his breathing and recapture the breath that had been sucked out of his lungs. His eyes began to tear as a small sob passed his lips. He stared at the inscription, blinking away the tears. As he closed his eyes he gently closed his hand around the ring and continued to weep.

"Go ahead, Aaron." He heard his mother say, "Give it to your grandfather."

Ever since Samuel's son, Aaron's father, had died at a very young age, Samuel had been the masculine figure in Aaron's life. Aaron had been around his grandfather's jewelry shop almost before he could walk. When old enough, Aaron had begun helping Samuel around the shop. He was very quickly learning the trade at the elbow of the world's greatest jeweler, or at least that's what Aaron thought. They would spend hours working together, Samuel laboring on a piece, Aaron watching closely, asking questions whenever he thought he could without distracting the man too much. Soon, Samuel started allowing Aaron to handle smaller jobs, less expensive pieces having a low degree of difficulty. As Aaron grew out of bigger and bigger pairs of trousers; his skills increased. He was schooled in all of the arts of a jeweler, but gold-smithing is where he excelled. Now at the age of fourteen he had better skills than most apprentices five or six years his elder.

Aaron walked over to where his grandfather was sitting. Samuel's eyes shimmered like matched diamonds; his admiration for his grandson was mirrored in his scholarly face. The man's warm smile spread across his face, ending in gleeful crinkles around the corners of his eyes.

Samuel's reassuring nod helped to melt away most of the fear Aaron was feeling. Aaron had worked hard for months to complete the ring and with the help of the other craftsmen in his grandfather's shop, had been able to keep it a secret. Now that it was time to give it to his grandfather for his 50th birthday, Aaron was afraid that it wasn't going to be good enough. He held out the ring to Samuel.

"Happy birthday, Papa. May you always be healthy."

Samuel took the ring from him and held it up into the light coming in from the living room window. Multi-colored points of light danced across his face as he turned the ring from side to side.

The ring was actually three bands, each constructed out of a different color of gold. The three bands had been interwoven into the single large band much like a basket weave. It was a beautiful blend of materials as it was, but Aaron had taken the ring and etched a deep 'V' shape cut between the areas where the bands met. It was these cuts which gave the ring a quality all its own. The diamond cuts seemed to reach out and draw in any available light.

"Why Aaron, it's beautiful." he said while giving Saul a conspiratorial wink. "How did Saul find time to make such an exquisite piece of jewelry?"

"Papa!" Aaron said, taking the bait, "I made it!"

Samuel looked at Aaron with an expression of surprise, "You, Aaron, you made this?"

"Yes, Papa." he beamed.

Samuel looked across the room at his Master Craftsman, Saul, and winked again. "Saul, surely you helped young Aaron make such a fine ring, yes?"

Saul waved both of his hands in response. "I could never take credit for such a piece as that, Samuel. The hands of a true craftsman made that ring. I only helped the boy hide it long enough to surprise you with it today."

Samuel started to put the ring on his finger.

"Papa," Aaron almost shouted, "the inscription. There is an inscription, read it."

"An inscription! I never taught you how to do inscriptions. Samuel said, truly being surprised.

"Saul taught me while you were out on errands, Papa." Aaron beamed. It took forever!" he added as an after-thought.

Everyone in the room laughed. Aaron didn't understand why, but laughed along with them.

Samuel held the ring out and looked down the end of his nose and through his glasses at the inside of the ring. "Let's see now..."

"Father," Aaron's mother said after a few moments of silence, "Read it out loud. Aaron wouldn't let any of us read it until you had a chance."

Samuel looked up over his glasses at his daughter-in-law and then around the room at all of his friends who had gathered for his birthday. Finally, his eyes landed on Aaron as if to look for permission.

"Go ahead, Grandfather." Aaron whispered.

Samuel cleared his throat. "To my Father and best friend, love, Aaron."

It wasn't unusual for Aaron to call Samuel, father. He had done it for years, never really

knowing his true father and Samuel often treated Aaron more as a son than grandson. It would be Aaron who would one day step into his shoes and carry on the family business. Aaron would make a wonderful jeweler one day soon.
It wasn't only the feeling of his grandfather. The other men in the shop were amazed at the amount of skill the young boy exhibited. Saul, Samuel's head Jeweler began helping Aaron also. The more they poured into the boys' head, the faster it seemed he would soak it up.

Aaron had come up with the idea for the ring on a day when his mother was talking with Saul about the plans for Samuel's birthday. He quickly got the approval of his mother and Saul to start the project. Aaron had asked for almost no help designing the ring, and then with the construction. It wasn't until Aaron had decided to put the inscription on the ring that he required any real help from Saul.

Samuel slid the ring onto his finger as though the act was a solemn ceremony reserved for nobility. Again he held his hand up into the light, letting the sun dance across the design of the band. He was so focused on the gift that he did not hear the murmurs of approval and praise from the other guests at the celebration. Nor did anyone in the room hear the two Nazi men beating a poor man senseless on the street just in front of the house.

Chapter 2

Berlin, September 1, 1939

Aaron walked slowly along the avenue leading to the family shop. He had left school a little early and was enjoying the fall weather. He would still make it on time, but the thought of playing outside interested him more at the moment than sitting behind a bench working on someone's broken bracelet or resizing some woman's wedding ring because of an inexplicable weight gain. Sometimes he wished that he could stop by the park and play soccer with the other boys. Aaron frowned at the thought. He knew how he and the other Jewish boys were being treated now. Being asked to play soccer was an invitation for a fight. He had seen other children in his neighborhood come home, clothing torn, bruises and cuts from fights that had broken out in the park. Samuel had warned him to stay clear of such invitations.

Aaron began kicking a small stone along the walkway imagining he was a famous player on the national team. There was no racism in his mind and none translated into his imaginary game. On his team all of the players were equal, even though none of them were as good as he was. He continued to kick the stone down the sidewalk, racing for the goal, all the time hearing the crowds cheer him on. The outcome of the game was squarely in his hands now as the time ran down and he had but one last chance to score. As he squared up with the goalpost, in reality, two small wooden pegs holding a young sapling in place by several length of string, Aaron released the final shot. The rock held true to it course, screaming past the imaginary goalkeeper and into the net for the game's winning point. Aaron raised his hands in victory as the tiny tree shook from the impact of the rock.

Aaron nearly ran into the back of the German soldier standing directly in front of him. It was very fortunate that the man was occupied with his friends and hadn't noticed Aaron's approach. It was also fortunate that he had time to back up and take up a position behind a small bronze statue of a mother bear and her two cubs at the edge of the park. He could hear the soldiers laughing and carrying on. They were the dark soldiers, the ones in the all black uniforms. These men were the most frightening of them all to Aaron. Their black uniforms were accented with black leather boots, black leather belts holding the matching black leather holster concealing the black pistol inside. He knew nothing about their insignias of rank or duties other than the arm patch with the letter "Z". Samuel had told him that the patch with the letter "Z" in the middle stood for the Military Polizei.

He crouched lower behind the statue as the laughter grew among the men. He could clearly make out five of them now and for the first time he could make out their focus of attention. The five men had stopped two young Orthodox Jews and were having a good laugh at their expense. They had already removed the two men's hats. One hat was now resting under the foot of one soldier while the other had been turned upside down and replaced on the owner's head. If it hadn't been for the terror Aaron was feeling he might have thought it funny. The hat had been pushed down on the man's head in an awkward position with the brim sitting high in the air. Both men stood motionless as they were shoved, taunted and ridiculed by the soldiers. One soldier removed a long knife from his belt and held it in front of the smaller of the two men. The other soldiers began to laugh even louder as they knew what their friend was about to do.

Aaron was horrified as the soldiers took the long locks of hair alongside the young man's head and lifted them out until they were perpendicular with his head. Slowly, the soldier lifted the dagger and placed it alongside the young man's head, gradually raising the blade while the others laughed. The blade must have been very sharp as the lock of hair fell away effortlessly. Then for several seconds the man waved it in the young man's face looking for some type of reaction. The young Jew was very brave and showed no sign of allowing the incident to escalate. The soldier returned the dagger back to it sheath and now used his free hand to unbutton the fly of his pants.

The others must have known what was coming because the laughing became louder. The soldier then placed the one end of the lock of hair in his trousers with the majority still hanging out in front.

"Look," he said turning to the others, "Now I have a Jewish penis!"

The others began to join in the taunting.

"It looks mighty limp to me, Werner."

"No wonder the Jewish women are so cold to their men," another man laughed.

Tears began to well up in Aaron's eyes as the taunting continued. He wished the men would leave. He didn't understand why they had to be so mean to everyone.

Aaron jumped several inches as the huge hand fell lightly, yet firmly on his shoulder. He could only suck in a deep breath of air as the hand began to turn him around. He knew that one of the dark soldiers had found him and now he was going to join their cruel games. His first thoughts were to run, but the man had a good grip on him and he doubted that he would get very far. His second thought was to close his eyes and hope the person would release him. It was through wide, frightened eyes that Aaron saw that the man holding him was his grandfather.

Samuel held Aaron with the one hand and motioned with the other for Aaron to remain quite. For Aaron that would be no problem, he was still trying to fill his lungs with air. Together they backed away from the soldiers, keeping the statue between them and the other men. They had walked for several minutes before either spoke.

"Grandfather," Aaron asked, "Why were those soldiers so cruel to those two men?"

"There are a lot of people asking that very question each day, Aaron. I don't think there is a good answer."

Aaron thought about it for several seconds. "Is there a bad answer for it, Papa?"

Samuel smiled for a brief second at Aaron's question, and then the frown returned to his face. "Aaron, those men work for the Dark Angel."

"Like in the Bible?"

"Yes," Samuel answered, "Very much like in the Bible. They are the Angels of Death, Aaron. If ever you fall into the Dark Angel's cold embrace it is only suffering and death that you have to look forward to. You should stay as far away from them as possible."

"I wasn't trying to find them, Grandfather. I was just walking to the shop. I didn't see them until I was almost on top of them."

"I know that Aaron, but you should still be more careful these days." Samuel said as he put his arm around Aaron's shoulder. "Now, let's get to the shop and finish our work for the day. We have to be home for the Sabbath."

"Today's Friday!"

"Yes, Friday." Samuel repeated amused at how easily Aaron could loose track of time, "It's also the first day of September in case you didn't remember that either.

"Papa, I know that."

"Well, I'm just making sure. You do lose track of time now and again." Samuel smiled. "Do you need me to tell you what year it is?"

"Papa!" Aaron squealed, "1939, I'm not that bad."

Well, I'm glad to see that you can remember some things. Did you remember that Sunday is your Mother's birthday?"

Aaron slipped his hand into his grandfather's. "Of course I remembered."

Aaron continued to hold his grandfather's hand as they walked toward the shop. He thought about the soldiers taunting the two men. He was glad his grandfather had been there.

"How did you find me?" Aaron asked after a few minutes.

"I had been behind you for quite a long time, son."

Aaron continued to walk at his grandfathers hurried pace. "How long were you behind me, Papa?"

Samuel looked down at Aaron and gave him a warm smile. It was the type of smile that always made Aaron feel that there was nothing that his grandfather couldn't fix. "I was there," he answered, "long enough to see you score that winning goal."

A sheepish grin crosses Aaron's face as he moved closer to his grandfather and slid his hand around the man's waist. His thoughts return to the game and his winning score.

"Papa."

"What is it, Aaron."

"Papa, some day I'm going to make you proud of me."

Samuel held the boy closer. He looked up at the buildings looming over them as if searching for something to say. He did not want Aaron to see his eyes tearing.

"You already do, son." He managed to get out without choking too badly.

Neither Aaron nor Samuel noticed the man unbundling the newspapers on the street corner. Neither saw the man stand up, paper stretched out over his head as he began to yell.

"Poland invaded! German forces rush on to victory!"

Chapter 3

German - Polish Border September 1, 1939

First Lieutenant Klas Von Reichmann, Waffen SS, stood in the open turret and scanned the area around his Panzer III tank. Two identical tanks were in easy view. His friend, Lieutenant Zimmermen, commanded the one fifty meters directly to his left. Their platoon commander, Captain Strasser, also to his left but in the lead position, commanded the other. Klas looked over his shoulder to check the position of the other two tanks in their platoon. The Panzers were barely visible in the early-morning fog that hung over the formation like a ghostly shroud. Both tanks had joined their platoon last night and he couldn't remember the names of either of the two new tank commanders. Klas looked to his right, but couldn't see any of the tanks of the 2nd Platoon through the dense fog covering the Polish countryside.

All five of the tanks in his platoon had shut down their engines in order to conserve fuel. They would not restart their tanks until they had confirmation that the JU87 Stuka's were airborne. The planes were still grounded by the heavy fog and since they played an important role in the Blitzkrieg concept of battle, the tanks would not begin their advance until the Stuka's started their attack. Once the planes were airborne and the attack was launched, the Panzers would drive straight through to their objective, regardless of the opposition or cost.

He was dressed in the standard wool-rayon black tank uniform worn by all of the tank personnel. While the uniform had become popular with the SS-Toten-kopfverbände, Death's-Head Formations, it was much more a matter of functionality with the tank platoons. The black color hid most of the damage to their uniforms caused by the constant assault of the dirt and grease associated with being around the tanks.

Klas was the typical active army officer. At eighteen, he had been selected for training with the SS because of his racial purity. The fact that the Von Reichmann family had produced a great lineage of military figures for the German Army hadn't hurt either. Klas had attended the preparatory Vorbereitungs-Lehrgänge Courses and then continued through the Kriegjunker-Lehrgänge War-Officer Candidate Courses until his graduation. Based on the recommendation of his regimental commander, two months after being assigned to his field unit, he was appointed to 2nd Lieutenant by the RF-SS.

Klas heard the single "click" in his headset informing him that someone had depressed and released the talk button on one of the radios in the command without speaking into the microphone. The clicking sound was a near silent signal from his Commander to look at him for a hand signal. Klas' heart began to race, the blood pounding in his ears as he looked up in the direction of Captain Strasser. The anticipation of beginning their attack sent waves of excitement through him like small electrical charges. Klas waited for the command. He quickly glanced over at Zimmermen who was intently watching for the order also. When Klas turned his attention back to Captain Strasser, his shoulder sank as Strasser gave the signal to allow a close dismount. This meant that he and his crew could leave the tank, but had to be ready to move out within seconds when given the order.

Klas removed his headset and leaned his head down to where he could speak into the open turret to the other four members of the crew. "Alright my little sweethearts, you can leave the vehicle, but it is an order for close dismount, understood?"

A number of moans and sighs filtered up through the tank to tell Klas that the crew had heard him and were no happier than he was. In live combat a soldier was stupid not to be scared, but waiting for combat put real fear into any man. A man's mind could do terrible things to him if he had the time to think about it.

As the members of his crew began to dismount the vehicle Klas suddenly remembered something.

"Edel," Klas said in a soft tone but it still rang with authority.

"Yes, Lieutenant." The man grunted as he squeezed out of the forward hatch.

"When you relieve yourself, don't piss on my tank this time."

There was a smothering of laughter from all over the tank at Klas' command.

"Yes, Lieutenant." Edel replied as he jumped to the ground.

The thought of Edel pissing on his tank upset Klas greatly. It was as if the man had no respect for the very machine that protected him from enemy fire and, for the next few months, would be his home. "If you have to piss on someone's tank," Klas continued, "Go piss on Captain Strasser's tank."

Again there was suppressed laughter from the rest of the crew. They all knew that Captain Strasser would have Edel repainting his entire tank in short order if he ever caught the man relieving himself on it.

Edel walked a few meters in front of the tank, stretched widely and the spread his legs enough to get a good footing. Then unfastening the metal buttons on his trousers he began to urinate. Klas could not see the man pissing from his vantage point, but he could see the steam rising in front of the man as he did so.

"Good man, Edel" he taunted.

Edel waved his right hand in the air in recognition of the false praise.

"Edel," another crewmen added, "You better hold on with both hands. I've seen how you drive with only one hand. You'll end up pissing on yourself."

Edel did a short jig and re-buttoned his trousers. "At least I don't have to pull up my dress and squat when I go, like you Otto."

Again there was laughter throughout the crew. Klas knew it was the only way for his men to release some of the tension that was building. Waiting was bad.

Klas removed his throat microphone, hung it on the turret and then slid down the side of the turret, pushed off with both hands and jumped to the ground in one smooth motion. His legs buckled slightly as his boots hit the solid earth beneath them. He had been standing too long in the turret waiting for the order to advance. His legs had become weak from being in one position without moving. When the tank was under way it was a constant battle to maintain ones position. The jolting about was enough to keep your circulation going. But when standing still there was little to do other than shift your weight from one foot to the other. Yes, he thought, waiting is very bad.

Klas removed his black beret and ran his fingers through his short sandy colored hair in a characteristic gesture of someone having a much longer mane. The combination of his short hair and aristocratic features had earned him the nickname of Thor among his men. They had often teased that he should have been on recruitment posters instead of a tank. But for Klas Von Reichmann, god of thunder, the thought of being anywhere but on top of his tank was unimaginable. He could never earn his place along-side the Von Reichmann military men by adorning some recruiting poster. The Von Reichmann's were combat soldiers, leaders of fighting men, not actors or some other façade.

Klas began to move around the tank inspecting it for the. . . how many times today, he thought, fourth, fifth? It didn't matter, another inspection never hurt. His mind began to drift as he scanned the wheels and return rollers of the tracks.

Klas understood that he would have to make his mark here and now if he were going to uphold the family tradition. The Von Reichmann family could trace back their participation in the German army to the reign of Frederick the Great in 1786. Few German families could claim such an honor and Klas knew of no other soldier that had to bear such a burden. Klas had been raised from birth with a family intent on adding his name to the family lineage. It wasn't enough that he was predestined to serve; his ancestors had served as Officers and Gentlemen. Klas was constantly reminded that all were well decorated in their time and all had risen into the rank of the General Officers. There was no doubt what his father and mother expected of him and nothing less would be acceptable.

This didn't bother Klas at all because there was nothing he wanted more either. He had always loved to listen to the stories told by family members of how the Von Reichmann's had served with honor. He remembered that as a young boy he and his friends would often reenact the countless battles, always serving with pride, always upholding the family honor. Klas knew what he had to do. The real trick was staying alive long enough to do it. The face of combat was much more distorted and crueler than any face his father and grandfather were able to make when recounting the stories.

Klas instantly became alert at hearing the short whistling sound coming from Captain Strasser. Strasser signaled for the crews to remount their vehicles. He and his crew silently climbed up the side of their Panzer and took their assigned position for battle. Klas fastened his throat mike and re-adjusted the headset to fit comfortably over his black beret. Strasser raised his hand and paused for several beats of Klas' heart before giving the signal for the tanks to start their engines. Klas lightly tapped Edel on the shoulder with his foot and the 296 HP Maybach engine roared to life. Klas smiled. Edel must have had his fingers on the ignition switch anticipating the command. Strasser signaled again and the five tanks leapt forward.

Instantaneously Klas' headphones thundered to life. Now he was busy listening to the chatter on the company net, filtering out the unwanted hissing and static, deciphering pertinent information and acting accordingly. Now he could also hear the sounds of ordnance explosions getting closer, muffled by his headset and the chatter, but not erased. Now the fear was gone.

Chapter 4

Frankfurt, Germany September 1, 1939

Anna looked down at the sheet of music in front of her and could hear the notes in her head a half a breath before her hand would draw the bow across the strings of the violin, replicating them. It was Tchaikovsky's Serenade for Strings, one of Anna's favorite pieces and her fingers were light upon the bow, her touch perfect.

Although she would not look up from the music, she knew her mother was somewhere in the audience smiling. Anna smiled at the thought. She knew that very few things brought joy to her mother's face as much as her handling of the violin and nothing brought more joy to Anna than seeing her mother smile.

Her eyes sparkled as she thought about how surprised her mother must have been seeing Anna at first chair. She had been awarded the position several weeks before, but had decided to keep it a secret until this week's recital. Anna had wanted to tell her mother as soon as she had received the notification from Frau Klibe, her music teacher, but when she thought about how much it would mean to her mother to have her walk out onto the stage and take the first chair position, she held the surprise back. It was one of the hardest things Anna had ever had to do. She and her mother shared everything and holding back such a wonderful piece of news was extremely difficult. For weeks she had been flitting around the house like a spring honey-bee dancing from one flower to another. Her happiness had been so intoxicating that her mother even started to sing during their daily chores. If the concert had been any later in the month she would have burst.

Anna was not disappointed. Sigrid Mayer had already taken up a position close to the front of the small auditorium when Anna and the others walked on to the stage. Anna did not look out into the audience trying to find her mother as some of the other children were doing. Instead, she acted very professionally, in her mind, gracefully walking toward the violin section; her violin tucked under her left arm, her bow held in place by her left hand against the neck of the instrument; her face relaxed although her smile was beaming from ear to ear just beneath her mask of indifference.

Now, as the short concert was drawing to an end, she was having a lot more difficulty hiding her obvious joy. As the last note still vibrated on the violin's strings, the applause from the proud parents and grandparents began to fill the tiny hall. Frau Klibe turned and took the first bow then turned back to the orchestra and motioned for the children to stand. The applause became even louder this time as every person with a child in the orchestra attempted to clap louder so that in doing so their own child would be able to hear them and understand that no one in the room was more proud than they. Anna's mother was no exception. The children were allowed to take a second bow and then were lead off the stage by Frau Klibe so they could be reunited with their family at the small reception afterwards.

Anna wove her way through the small pockets of attendees and occasionally stopped to accept praise from friends and their families, but although she was very polite and well mannered, her eyes never stopped scanning the room for her own mother. After several minutes of searching she began to wonder what could have happened to make her mother disappear.

"Miss. Mayer?" Frau Klibe asked.

Anna turned to face the woman. "Yes, Frau Klibe."

"I believe this is who you are looking for, is it not?"

Anna looked just beyond where Frau Klibe was standing. "Mother!" Anna shouted as she ran into her arms.

"Anna." Her mother was able to side-step slightly before the full force of Anna's dash had made contact with her; their embrace passing the surge of elation from one to the other.

"You were wonderful today."

"Did you really like the concert, Mother?" she asked, already knowing the answer.

"Well, I think the word 'like' would be the wrong one to use darling. Incredible, would be more fitting."

"I was very proud of you today." Frau Klibe added, "I had no doubt that you could handle the responsibility of first chair, but you even went beyond my expectations child."

Anna's eyes danced with pride. "Thank you, Frau Klibe."

"Why didn't you tell me you were first chair now?" Her mother interjected. "Frau Klibe has told me that you were promoted to the position weeks ago."

Anna hugged her mother tighter. "Oh, Mother, I wanted to surprise you."

"Well, you certainly managed to do that young lady." Frau Klibe smiled. "I thought we were going to have to call in a doctor when your mother saw you take first chair. I wish you had let me in on the secret Anna. I could have had the school nurse standing by."

"Was I that bad?" Frau Mayer asked.

Frau Klibe could see where Anna got her beauty. She was an exact duplicate of her mother.

"I have seen worse cases of parent pride, but none recently." Frau Klibe grinned, "Anna is the youngest person to ever fill the position in the school history, Frau Mayer. Which brings us to another issue."

"Issue?" Anna and her mother asked together.

"Yes, issue." Frau Klibe answered very sternly, "Anna is only thirteen years old and is too young to be accepted into the Frankfurt Conservatory. She still has to finish school and. . .

"Con. . .Conservatory?" Frau Mayer asked.

Now it was Frau Klibe's turn to beam. "Yes, Frau Mayer, Anna has not only caught my ear, but that of Professor Guttmann at the Frankfurt Conservatory for Music. He would like to talk with you and your husband about a special program for Anna."

"Where is Father?" Anna managed to pout.

"Oh, Anna, your father will be so hurt that he missed this." Her mother sighed, "If we had known, he would have certainly put off his trip to Hanau this morning." Frau Mayer focused her attention back to Frau Klibe. "What type of special program?"

"I'm not sure of the details, but I would imagine that it would be some type of after school tutoring or working at the Conservatory during your free time. Then once Anna had graduated from school, she would continue her studies full time as a student of the Conservatory."

"Oh, my head is spinning." Frau Mayer said holding her head in mock pain, "We never thought Anna would go so far."

"Let me assure you, Frau Mayer. I have been teaching music now for twenty-two years and Anna is one of the best. . .no, no that's not quite right. She's one of the most gifted children I have ever had the pleasure of working with. Her ear for music and her understanding of the craft goes well beyond her age."

"Oh, you don't know how it pleases me to hear you say so, Frau Klibe. My husband. . ."

"Excuse me Frau Klibe," the man interrupted, "I need to speak with you."

Both Frau Klibe and Frau Mayer looked at the gentleman. It was Frau Klibe who recognized him.

"Yes, Her Rahn," Frau Klibe answered politely. "I'm almost finished here and. . ."

"I want to talk with you about my son's position in the orchestra." He continued without letting Frau Klibe finish, "Why has he lost his position to this Jew." He spat pointing to Anna.

"Her Rahn, Eugene lost his position because of his performance over the last several months." Frau Klibe explained, trying to maintain her composure.

"To a Jew!" He said caustically, his voice rising an octave.

"Her Rahn," Klibe continued trying to ignore the last comment, "have you asked Eugene why he lost the position?"

"It's bad enough that you wouldn't help my son when he needed it, but to waste your time on this, this Jew is insulting."

Anna held tightly onto her mother's dress, her face taking on a deepening hue of shame as she attempted to hide behind her.

"Frau Klibe," Frau Mayer interrupted, "Anna and I will be going now, thank you for your time."

Before Frau Klibe could answer, Frau Mayer had taken Anna's hand and led her to the exit. They could still hear Her Rahn ranting on about the virtues of his son's performance when they cleared the room.

"Mother, why was Her Rahn so upset?"

"I'm sure he is as proud of his son as I am of you, Anna. Losing the first chair must have been very disappointing to him."

"But Eugene hasn't been playing very well. He likes to make noise and laugh more than he likes to play."

"That doesn't change the fact that Eugene has lost his position."

"If he played well he could get it back."

Frau Mayer loosened her grip on Anna's hand. "Do you think so?"

Anna contemplated the question for several seconds as they continued down the hall toward the door. "No, Eugene doesn't really care about his music. He only plays because his parents make him." Anna thought again about the conversation between Frau Klibe and Her Rahn. "Mother?"

"Yes."

"Is Her Rahn upset because Eugene lost the position or is he angry because I'm Jewish?"

Frau Mayer stopped and looked down at her daughter. Anna's face was a swirling sea of emotion being tossed between the rocks of self-doubt and the softer shores of innocence. Tears formed in the corner of Frau Mayer's eyes as she knelt down to look at Anna eye to eye. She wet her lips and smiled not wanting Anne to see the pain she was feeling at this moment.

"He is irritated because his son was lazy and didn't want to work for the position, Anna. I don't think your being Jewish had anything to do with it."

"But, Mother, the way he said Jew, was very mean."

"He is upset with his son, Anna, not at our being Jewish. He doesn't want to blame his own son for his laziness so he found something else to blame the problem on. There are a lot of people doing that these days."

"I could help Eugene, Mother. Then his father wouldn't be so cross at him or us."

A broad smile grew across Frau Mayer's troubled face. The simplicity of Anna's love had been one of her mother's greatest treasures. She reached out and lightly ran her fingers through Anna's hair.

"You would do that, Anna? Help Eugene gain back his position as first chair even if it meant your losing it?"

Anna reacted to her mother's touch by tilting her head toward the woman's opened hand.

"If it would make everyone happy again."

Frau Mayer stood and reached out for her daughter's hand. Anna moved closer, locking her arm around her mother's. Together they pushed on the door leading out of the building and Frau Mayer allowed Anna through first and then she followed her. Frau Mayer was startled to see the two men in the black uniforms standing just outside the door. She quickly grabbed Anna's hand and led her down the stairs away from the two SS Officers.

"Would that make everyone happy, Mother? Giving Eugene back his position?" Anna asked, continuing the conversation.

Frau Mayer kept her head down and only glanced at the two soldiers out of the corner of her eye. The two SS men talked softly between themselves as they watched Frau Mayer and Anna leaving. After a few more seconds the two turned away and continued their conversation. For that Frau Mayer was glad.

"I don't think so, liebling." She answered quickening their pace away from the school.

Chapter 5

Polish Countryside, September 21, 1939

When the transport passed Klas he noticed that it contained another platoon of the SS Einsatzgruppen[1] . Twenty days into the invasion of Poland and they had suffered heavy casualties, but the army had been extremely successful with its battle plan in Poland. He knew they would continue with the attacks until Poland was under the control of the 3rd Reich. Poland was falling

[1] German SS Military term for a Mobile Kill Squad. A group of soldiers assigned the task of killing remaining survivors after a battle. Also used to round up or eliminate the Jewish population.

much quicker than most had thought and the kill squads were very busy.

"Another kill squad" Edel said, climbing up onto the tank.

"Yes, another one." Klas answered.

Klas had now added the silver Panzer Battle Badge to the lower left front of his Panzer jacket. Above the Panzer Badge sat the Iron Cross, 2nd Class. Very soon he might be able to add the Iron Cross 1st class or even the Knights Cross, that is, if you listened to the gossip around the company. The first twenty days of the campaign were a blur. Klas and his men had spent most of their time racing across Poland stopping only to get enough food and rest while their tank was refueled and munitions replenished. The word throughout the Division was that Poland would fall by the end of October. Then what? There were wild rumors of advancing on Belgium and even France, but many thought that the war would come to an end with the surrender of Poland.

His performance in yesterday's battle gave Klas his first taste of command. Their Platoon had been assigned to the first wave of the attack and things proceeded nicely until Captain Strasser's tank took a hit to the treads, bringing his vehicle to a complete stop. Captain Strasser's driver was killed instantly and Strasser received minor leg wounds. Klas assumed command of the platoon as they increased the rate of attack.

Klas had thought about the attack several times since yesterday and still could not understand what he had done. He had convinced himself that it had been a mixture of his training, good instinct and just plain good luck that had kept him and his crew alive.

As they approached the enemy's' front line defenses, the infantry zone began to crumble immediately. He had seen this happen before but nothing so obvious. The troops were all moving off to his right, retreating away from a swampy area off to the left that he and the other tank commanders had been warned about during the morning briefing. The swampy ground would not be friendly to the twenty-five tons of metal he was pushing forward at a speed of fifteen to twenty miles per hour. It would slow the tank advance greatly or may even stop it completely if it were the true quagmire they had been led to believe. If it had been him trying to out run a Panzer tank, he would have headed straight into the swamp hoping to lose the pursuer.

In a split second Klas acted, calling for both the first and second platoon to follow his lead toward the swamp while informing the second wave consisting of the 3rd platoon and the HQ Company to increase their rate of advance and now spearhead the attack toward its original target. It was an unusual maneuver, but each tank followed the orders given.

The ground was not nearly as bad as they had been led to believe and within seconds of entering the swampy area Klas and the two platoons now under his command engaged several Polish tank platoons consisting of twenty-five Polish TP light-weight tanks. The Polish Commander was caught by surprise as Klas' tanks came face-to-face so unexpectedly.

Otto, his gunner and Ralph, the tank's loader didn't wait for the command to fire. They had knocked out three of the tanks before either side had really had a chance to understand what was happening. While the twenty-five ton tanks were slowed down, their 37-mm gun made quick work of the Polish tanks lying in ambush. Klas' own tank was credited with seven kills and received only light damage.

"Lieutenant?"

"Yes, Edel?" Klas answered not bothering to look up from the map he was studying.

"Have you seen one of these squads in action?"

"The Kill Squads? No I haven't. The only persons I'm interested in Edel are those with guns pointed in my direction."

"Do the Jews have guns?"

"I don't stop to ask if he's Jewish or Protestant, if he has a gun and he's not German I shoot him."

"But all Jews are enemies of the Reich, Lieutenant."

"Yes, Edel, that's true." Klas began to fold the map and tucked it into his service jacket. "What would you have me to do about it, Edel?"

Edel looked down at the plate of food that he had brought with him. He began to push the items in the tray around with his fork. "Nothing, I guess, Lieutenant." He mumbled with a mouth full of meat. "I just think that it's interesting."

"You find the Jews interesting? We have to find more for you to do, Edel."

"No, what I mean is, who is our enemy in Poland?"

"In Poland, everyone who is not in a German uniform is your enemy, Edel. You remember that and you will stay alive."

"But who is the bigger enemy?"

"I've already told you; the one with the gun."

Klas had always known that Edel was somewhat simplistic in his thoughts and questions, but he was one of the best tank drivers he had ever seen. Edel could get his tank out of trouble faster than he had gotten into it. That kept people alive and for that reason Klas always had time for Edel's constant questions.

"Lieutenant?" he asked through a mouth full of potatoes this time. It seemed that Edel always had the urge to speak when he had mouth full of food.

"Yes."

"Have you ever killed a Jew?"

"I don't know."

"I mean up close, with a pistol or rifle."

The line of questioning was beginning to get on Klas' nerves. "Edel, I have been here in Poland for twenty days now. Every one of them has been spent with you. When I go to sleep at night you are there. When I wake up in the morning you are there. When we are not sleeping or eating, we are in the tank together. Have you seen me shoot a Jew?"

Edel hesitated as if pondering the answer. "No, I don't think so."

Klas looked down at the man stirring his meal in circles. He decided it was time to end this line of questioning before he lost his patience with Edel and said something he would regret later. For such a hard fighting man, Edel could be very sensitive at times. Not good in a war. "Edel, when you finish, help Otto with the engine. I didn't like the way it was performing this morning."

"emmmph." He answered with a full mouth.

"I don't want anything going wrong when we are in battle." Klas knew that failing to properly maintain your vehicle could be devastating to an Officer's career. Having one's tank taken off the battle line for repairs because of poor maintenance was akin to an Infantry Officer getting a foot fungus. Klas would not let a stupid thing like that stand between him and his chances for promotion.

"It was a bit sluggish this morning." Edel chewed. "I had to goose it a few times. It might be some dirt in the carburetor or worse. Should we have a mechanic look at it?"

"You and Otto take a look. If Otto doesn't like what he sees then you can go and find a mechanic."

Private Radecka had watched the German tank for several hours now waiting for the right moment to fire. When that opportunity might come Radecka was unsure. The tank had been sitting alongside the road, the crew coming and going at their leisure. Actually, there were several tanks parked alongside the road, but this one was the closest to his hiding place in the collapsed farmhouse and gave him the cleanest line of fire. The farmhouse must have taken a direct hit from one of the German tanks earlier in the day. Its walls had buckled when the main support beam had been shattered, causing the structure to crumble inward. The farmhouse had been a modest, three room structure sitting adjacent to a one-hectare plot of average farmland. It had been a good farm producing a stable living for the owners and even allowed them to take some of their goods to market for some extra money. The farm had managed to support three generations of Poles before it became a temporary tank park for the Germans. Radecka knew this because it had belonged to his family. He closed his eyes and the aroma of fresh baked bread filled his nostrils. Visions of his pregnant wife leaning over the freshly baked loaves, coating the tops with warm butter enveloped his memory. From where he sat he could gaze down the front of her blouse admiring her full cleavage. He would look up and meet his wife's eyes; exchanging adoring glances, until she walked over to him, allowing him to bury his face in her breast. She always smelled of fresh lilacs.

The odor of charred timbers quickly crushed the memory and forced him to return to the reality of the ruined home. Private Radecka reached down and placed his hand on the German made 44-mm recoilless antitank weapon. It wasn't much, but it was what he had to work with. He pulled the weapon up and prepared to fire. He had never used one before or even seen one used, but from the looks of the weapon it was just an aim and shoot. That's what Radecka was planning to do with it.

The Polish private brought the weapon up to his cheek and took sight along the side of the weapon. The stench of gun oil was overpowering and smothered the last lingering morsel of the baked bread and lilacs.

"For you, Edyta." He whispered as he pulled the trigger, launching the grenade toward the tank.

Radecka could actually see the grenade moving toward the tank. It crossed the fifty or sixty meters that separated the farmhouse and the tank very quickly. It made contact with the tank closer to the rear than the center where Radecka thought he had aimed it.

Klas heard the weapon being fired, but did not see the grenade being launched or even see it hit his tank. The grenade had entered the side of the tank, just ahead of the gasoline tank and exploded into several large pieces of molten hot metal. Only one piece actually pierced the gasoline tank, but that was enough. The tank erupted into a huge fireball setting off the munitions stored inside the vehicle. The tank literally tore itself apart from the inside out.

The next few seconds were a blur for Klas. He felt himself being lifted up into the air, an extreme blast of heat covering his body as he and the turret were being pushed off the top of the tank. At some point he knew that he and the turret were no longer traveling together, but he was flying through the air, arms grasping for support, his vision splattered with snap shots of blue sky, black smoke, bright light, sharp pain then nothing.

"Lieutenant," a voice asked, "can you hear me?"

Klas just wanted to sleep, he was tired and it felt good to let his body relax. He slipped deeper into the arms of slumber.

Lieutenant!" The voice asked louder this time, "Open your eyes, Lieutenant."

Klas forced his eyes to open just a little. The light hurt.

"Come on, Lieutenant. Look at me, now."

Klas blinked several times. He was able to focus on the Medic that was bent over him. The man smiled at him.

"That's better." He said, "Lieutenant, you are going to be alright. Can you hear me?"

Klas tried to shake his head. The pain shot up through his neck and exploded throughout his brain.

"No, no, try not to move, Sir. Can you speak?"

"Yes," Klas answered weakly.

"That's good." I'm going to check you over a little. The ambulance is on its way. We'll have you out of here quickly."

Klas managed a smile. He felt the man's hands working their way across his body, stopping every so often, probing. Twice he jumped reflexively, gritting his teeth when the medic's hand touched the wrong spot. Klas figured there were more medics than the one he had spoken to. He could hear mixed fragments of a conversation.

"Yes, there, you see. . ."

"I'll cut the pant leg right here."

"Good. His pulse is good, steady.

"Did you see this?" I don't know. . ."

"Yes, yes, we'll just have to bind. . .yes, just like that."

Klas opened his eyes to see the Medic over him again. The man still smiled.

"Hello again Lieutenant. I'm going to give you a shot of morphine now. It will help with the pain."

Klas jumped at the sound of the small arms fire. At first there were one or two small popping sounds that he didn't recognize followed by the sound of several 7.9 mm Mausers' firing in rapid succession. Several more rounds were fired before Private Radecka's life came to an end.

"Easy, Lieutenant." The Medic said placing his hand firmly on Klas' shoulder. "They're just finishing off that bastard that destroyed your tank."

"Ready?" The other Medic asked holding up the syringe filled with morphine.

"Yes, it's fine."

Klas slowly moved his head to one side. He was lying in the mud; several large pieces of burning metal lay strewn about.

Klas' eye widened, as he was able to focus on a severed arm just a meter from where he lay. His mouth gaped open as a sickening wave of panic gripped him deep in his belly. A bile taste filled his mouth as he tried to scream.

"My-my-" Klas tried to form the words, his mind and mouth no longer working together.

"Easy, Lieutenant!" The medic shouted, seeing what was frightening Klas while at the same time pinning him to the ground. "It's not yours! It's not your arm!" "You still have both of your arms." The medic added in a calmer voice. "It's okay now. You're going to be fine."

No matter how hard he tried to catch his breath his lungs felt as if they were being deprived of air. He tried to gulp down large amounts of air, but always felt he could use twice as much.

The medic wiped his face with a cool cloth. Klas found some comfort in the steady expression of the Medic.

"Lieutenant, try and breathe normally," he said with a reassuring smile. "I know you think that's impossible, but it will help."

Klas concentrated on what the Medic had told him and made a conscious effort to slow his breathing. Within a few seconds he found it easier to breathe."

"That's much better." The Medic said while nodding to his assistant.

Klas felt the sharp prick of the needle and then a burning sensation as the drug entered his body. Soon the burning feeling turned to a warm mellow sensation of relaxation followed by Klas' impression that he was sinking deeper into the mud. His eyes fluttered and he was gone.

Chapter 6

The weekend had gone extremely well for Anna. While the family observed the Sabbath at home, Sunday was filled with visitors to the house. And with each new visitor, Anna's mother would retell the story of how she had been surprised by Anna at the recital. Of course everyone was proud of Anna's new position as first chair and would heap praise upon the young woman. Occasionally there was the demand for a small private recital, but this was usually requested by one of her aunts or uncles. Of course all requests were graciously fulfilled.

Then, at some point, the conversation would always turn to the more serious concerns of the day. The talk was always the same. The adults started talking about Heir Hitler or the SS, and things became sullen while the children were ushered outside to play.

This past weekend was no different, there seemed to be more playtime now than ever before, Anna thought as she walked toward the front of the school building. She wished that whatever was bothering everyone about the government and Heir Hitler would just go away. Things were so much better before all of the talk about the Nazi Party filled her home with whispers and gloomy conversations.

Anna walked up the stone stairs that led to the main entrance to the building. Other children were also making their way toward the door and would shout out greetings to each other and wave. Anna was no different. At thirteen years old she was a popular young woman in school and attracted her fair share of young male suitors. As for being Jewish, it would be hard for anyone to pick her and her family out as Jews. Anna, like her mother had long, light brown hair accented by a pair of dove gray eyes. Her features looked more like the posters of the young Arian children than those of the Jewish ones she had seen around town. Even her own classmates would forget that Anna was Jewish and talk or make fun of the Jews in front of her. It usually wasn't until they were all laughing and Anna remained quiet that they would remember that she was in fact Jewish.

Anna noticed that the cruel comments had increased as the school year went on. Lately, the comments had become more frightening. Everywhere she walked in their town, rude comments were being plastered on walls and doors. There had even been bricks thrown through some of the windows of the shops in her neighbourhood. Her mother had taught her not to make eye contact with any of the men who wandered the streets in groups now looking for trouble and usually finding it in the Jewish areas of town.

"Anna."

Anna jumped as she looked up,"Frau Klibe, you startled me."

Frau Klibe smiled weakly at her. "I'm sorry dear. It's just that I wanted to catch you before you came into the building."

Anna was taken back by the ashen look she saw on the face of her favourite teacher. Her fingers, which were normally long and delicate, now looked arthritic and gnarled as they tightly clutched a large canvas bag. Anna's brow wrinkled with concern. "Frau Klibe, what's wrong?"

Frau Klibe cleared her throat as she looked over her shoulder. "Anna dear, let's walk over here," she said pointing to the small landing off to the side of the main doorway.

Anna quietly followed her teacher.

"Anna, I wanted to catch you before you went inside and were subjected to the..." Frau Klibe searched for the correct word, "situation in there."

"Mam?"

Frau Klibe had placed the bag at her feet and was now rubbing her hands together as if she was washing them under running water. "Anna, things are changing around the school. Things are different now."

Anna stared at her Teacher trustingly not knowing what to say. An expression of pain flashed across Frau Klibe's face as she realized that there would be no easy way of telling Anna

"Anna, you can no longer come to school here." She blurted.

Anna's face blushed as the blood raced to her face. "But, I thought. . . Did I do something wrong?"

"No, Anna, not at all." She gestured emphatically, "You've done nothing child. It's just that. . ."

The large wooden doors to the school burst open as several children made their way back out onto the front lawn. Most were crying, huddling close together as they scurried away from the building like field mice chased from the house by the farmer's cat. Anna recognized two of them as brother and sister. Their names escaped her but their faces were familiar. She had seen them several times at the synagogue, but did not know their family. Just when things began to quiet down and Anna was about to question Frau Klibe again, books began to rain down on the front lawn, several coming within inches of the children.

"Go home, Jew!" she heard someone cry from an upstairs window. Anna looked up in time to witness several students fill the windows. From there they began casting books and other items at the group like soldiers might, flinging missiles down upon intruders from their parapet.

"Stay home, Jew!" taunted another student.

"Jews!" shouted others.

"It's Eugen, isn't it?" Anna said returning to her own problem.

"Eugen? I don't understand." Her teacher asked.

"Eugen Rahn- his father. You have to give the position back to Eugen because his father was so upset last Friday."

Frau Klibe's face twisted in anguish. "No child, it's not because of Eugen."

"I. . .don't understand."

"Anna, you cannot come to school here and you are no longer in the orchestra."

Anna still couldn't comprehend what was happening, but it didn't stop the tears from running down her face. "But why, Frau Klibe? What have I done?"

"Nothing, Anna, it's nothing you've done." Now the tears started to well up in her eyes also.

"But Frau Klibe," she cried, "I only want to play the violin and go to school with my friends. I love playing in the orchestra."

"I know, child."

"Can't I at least still play with the orchestra?" Tears were running freely down her pale cheeks, splashing onto the bib of her dress. I'll. . .I'll give the first chair position back to Eugen. No one has to know. I'll sit in the back, I promise." She quivered. Frau. . .Klibe. . .I, I love. . .the. . .the music." She added between sobs. "Please!"

Frau Klibe now took on a wounded look. Her heart was being torn apart by the very thing she had spent so much time building. Anna was her best. Frau Klibe reached down and picked up the canvas sack. "Here, Anna. It's your things. I didn't want you to have to go inside to get them. It'. . ." she paused, "The children aren't being very kind as you can see."

Anna looked up at the windows again. Some of the children had gone, growing tired of the sport, but a large group still remained and was now chanting Nazi slogans, most having to do with hating Jews. Anna wiped her eyes before shifting her violin case to one hand and accepting the sack with her other. It was heavier than she expected and the weight jerked it out of her hand. Both she and Frau Klibe went down for it.

"Hold it tighter dear."

"Frau Klibe." Anna sniffled.

"You should go now, dear. Frau Klibe interrupted as they both stood up.

"But. . .I... I want to say something."

"Yes, dear?"

Anna looked up at the woman, tears freely rolling down both cheeks. "I wanted to. . ."

"Yes, Anna?" Frau Klibe sniffled herself.

"I. . .I love you." She blurted out as she abandoned everything in her arms and ran up to the woman. "Thank you for letting me play." She added holding onto the woman's waist.

"Oh, Anna." She cried. "I know child. I love you too."

Anna continued to bury her face in the woman's dress sobbing uncontrollably.

"Anna." Frau Klibe said pulling Anna away after regaining some of her own composure. "Anna you must not stop playing. You must play at home or wherever you may go. It is your special gift. A gift that others, away from here, will love you for."

Anna shook her head in understanding.

"Now gather your things up and I'll walk you to the corner, away from this." She added pointing with her eyes to the students in the windows.

The walk home had been stressful for Anna. Carrying her violin as well as the large sack of books and personal items had been burdensome. Now she stood outside the huge house feeling isolated from all that she knew. Her school and classmates had rejected her because of her religion, Frau Klibe had abandoned her because of the Nazis and now she stood in front of her own home, wondering how her mother and father would feel about her expulsion from school and the orchestra.

Anna had even thought about lying to her parents, not telling them of the problems at school. She even had gone as far as to prepare a scheme where she would go to school each morning as if nothing had happened, hide in the park all day, then return in the afternoon when school let out and the other children would be returning home. After some more thought, she recognized the flaws in the scheme and abandoned the notion. Anna even tried to think of a place to run away to and hide from everything that was happening to her. When she came to the conclusion that there was no place for her to go, she broke down and cried again.

Now she stood in front of the family home with no other ideas to act on. The house looked cold and unfriendly. The distance from the street to the door seemed like a trek that could take a lifetime to make. She remembered how she had often bounced up the walk, skipping steps, almost tripping when she had good news to tell her Mother about the day in school. The gate looked old and rusty, the walk cracked and worn, small weeds sprouting up through the cobblestone. Even the smell was different. In the afternoons when she walked up to the house she could always count on the smell of fresh baked goods just out of the oven, the aroma of butter warming in the air and pastries tempting her pallet. The thought reminded her of afternoons when she and her mother would sit in the kitchen eating warm cookies, her other still covered with flour and dough, and the two of them laughing and talking about her day at school. Sometimes she would make her mother listen to a new piece she had learned. Violin music and laughter would fill the room until the two of them remembered that father would be home soon and then there would be a rush of activities preparing the evening meal.

Anna stared up at the house and tears welled up in her eyes once again. How could she tell them of her failure?

"Anna!" she heard her mother's voice cry from a distance. Anna looked at the house trying to figure out which room her mother was calling from.

"Anna!" she heard and turned to look up the street away from the house.

"Oh Anna!" her mother shouted again as she ran up the street toward her.

Anna turned to face her mother still unsure what to tell her. Time was quickly running out and Anna could not think of anything.

"Liebling, are you alright?"

The look on her mother's face melted away any fears that she had been creating on the walk home. Anna dropped the canvas bag on the ground and began to run toward her mother's outstretched arms.

"Mother!" she shouted as she began to cry again.

Her mother scooped her up holding her close to her chest. "Oh, Anna. I was so worried about you."

"Mother, I. . ." the words failed her.

"Frau Schmidt at the butcher shop told me of the terrible things that were going on at your school this morning and I rushed right down there to get you. I was so frightened when you weren't there. I feared something had happened to you."

Anna felt a wave of joy washing over her body, cleansing her of all that had troubled her. She held her mother tighter, closer, inhaling the familiar safety she had so often found in her mother's arms.

"Mother?"

"Yes, liebling."

"They won't let me play anymore." She sniffled.

"Anna, darling, they will never be able to stop you."

"But they won't let me play in the orchestra anymore."

"Liebling, they did that because we are Jewish, not for your playing. Not for your playing."

"Mother, does everyone hate us?"

Frau Mayer thought about all the work her husband had been doing, trying to arrange for their visas out of the country. She spent most of her time now working on the paperwork that would allow their family to leave Germany. It was the Americas that would be their new home now. The immigration papers were very difficult to obtain. They had been jubilant when they received official medical certificates confirming that none of the family was mentally or physically defective in any way as well as stating that none had been afflicted with any "infectious, loathsome or contagious disease". Frau Mayer also had been able to have their synagogue write letters of recommendation for the family. The German Jewish Aid Committee, based in Washington D.C. had written to the Mayer's advising them that a visa application had been made on their behalf. If they were lucky they would be leaving Germany in about thirty days.

"Not everyone hates us, Anna." She said remembering her daughter's question.

Why can't I just play in the orchestra a while longer? I told Frau Klibe that I wouldn't be any trouble. I would sit in the back." Anna began to cry again. "Mother I don't want to be Jewish anymore. I just want to play."

"Don't say that child. That's exactly what they want you to say. We have to remember that these terrible men do not come before God, Anna. And you have to remember that it was God that gave you the gift to play the violin."

"Yes, mama." She mumbled into her mothers skirt.

"Come on now, Anna. You can help me in the kitchen. We can work on your cooking talents. They need more work than your violin playing."

Chapter 7

Aaron picked up the last few pieces of glass still remaining on the floor. Most of it had been picked up as soon as the "incident" had occurred, but Aaron was doing his final sweeping before he and his grandfather locked up the shop and headed home. Aaron still shook as he recalled the young boy running toward the door of the shop, yelling the word "Jews" at the top of his lungs then throwing the large brick right through the window and unfortunately, directly into the glass front of the main counter in the shop.

Aaron was shocked at how much noise the brick made when it hit the glass panel causing it to explode into thousands of splinters. The long oak case had received little damage from the incident. There were a few scratches in the wood where the brick had come to rest, but since the cabinet had been empty for some time, there were no other items in the projectile's path after it crashed through the glass.

Samuel had simply walked over to the counter looked over the damage in silence before asking Aaron if he wouldn't mind getting the broom and dustpan. While Aaron retrieved the broom, Samuel carefully removed the brick from the unit and carried it out the back door where he deposited it with the other bricks that had been thrown through some of the other windows the day before.

"At this rate," Samuel gestured, "we will have enough brick to build an extra room onto the shop in no time."

Aaron knew he and the others were expected to laugh and did so quite solemnly, but the hurt in Samuel's eyes did not escape Aaron's attention.

Aaron had been there when his grandfather had received notice that he could no longer own the business because of his being Jewish and that the shop would be put into receivership until it could be returned to the rightful German owner.

He had helped his grandfather remove all of the glass pieces from the old cabinet, polished the area where the brick had landed to remove the scars and then returned to what little work there was to do. Most of the good pieces of jewelry had been hidden away weeks ago. Samuel had left enough items in the shop to appease the Nazi men when they had come to confiscate all of the personal property. Even then they were not happy with what they had taken and took their displeasure out on Saul until the man lay on the ground, hurt and bleeding. Then, in a final act of arrogance, the man in charge had given Samuel a receipt for the items and left.

Aaron looked up at the boards covering the opening where the glass window had been and looked back at the counter. Somehow the two scenes were quite different to him. The jewelry case looked much more. . . peaceful, yes peaceful he thought. The cabinet was old but had been well maintained. The workmanship was excellent and the grain in the wood was well defined. The smooth finish was pleasant to the touch. Aaron had spent many hours polishing the oak being careful not to smudge the glass with the oil. Then he would wipe the glass until it sparkled almost as brilliantly as some of the items that had been on display.

The boards they had nailed across the window opening were much different. They were dingy and mismatched. It was a filthy bandage covering a deep, grisly wound on the face of the shop. Even the afternoon light that seeped through the cracks in the boards cast harsh, pointed shards of light across his chest, punctuating the yellow Star of David sewn to his jacket.

"Aaron," his grandfather said snapping him out of his trance, "If you're finished leaning on that broom, put it away so that we can go home. It's late and I am hungry."

Aaron picked up the remaining rubbish off the floor and headed for the back of the shop with the broom. "Papa?"

"Yes," he answered putting on his overcoat.

"Why do we keep the shop open if all we do now is clean up broken glass?"

Samuel was now standing in front of the full-length mirror, which was the only remaining piece of glass in the shop that wasn't broken. He buttoned his coat, smoothed the material and lightly touched the yellow star on his chest. "We keep the shop open because our customers expect us to be open."

"But we have nothing to sell them, Papa. And so few people come in for repairs anymore."

"We help those who ask for our services, Aaron."

Aaron walked up next to his grandfather and the two of them stood looking in the mirror. From the acorn colored eyes, his grandfather's being softer and somehow looking much wiser, to the coal black hair, Samuel's now peppered with gray, Aaron was always amazed at how much alike the two of them looked. While Samuel still had several inches on him, it wouldn't be long before Aaron would catch up and eventually pass his grandfather by. At fifteen, Aaron was still quite willowy, mostly arms and legs where Samuel had gained weight over the years and had settled into his thicker shape.

"It's late." His grandfather said putting on his hat, "your mother will be serving us a cold plate if we don't hurry."

"Papa, mother has never served us cold food for being late." Aaron insisted.

Samuel turned the lights off and walked to the front of the shop with Aaron. "I know, I know, but saying it just makes me feel better."

Aaron walked outside and waited for his grandfather to lock the door.

"Your papers?" the man said startling Aaron.

Aaron turned to face the man who had walked up from behind him.

"Your papers, Jew." The man insisted, holding out his hand.

"Can I help you?" Samuel asked, as he approached Aaron and the man. The man was not in uniform, but neither did he wear the yellow cross of David on his outer garment. This told Samuel to be firm, but cautious.

"Are you with this boy?"

"Yes, he is my grandson. We are on our way home."

"Why are you out after the curfew?" the man asked.

"I told you." Samuel said, "We are on our way home. Besides, the curfew doesn't start for another half an hour," Samuel stated looking at his watch. We have plenty of time to make it home before then."

"I will need to see your papers." The man insisted, ignoring Samuel's statement.

"Why?" Aaron asked.

Samuel placed his hand on the back of Aaron's arm silencing him.

"Have we done something wrong?"

The man removed a small medallion from his pocket and showed it to Samuel.

"Gestapo." He hissed, "I will need to see your papers, now."

Samuel's heart sank as he looked at the medallion confirming the man's identity. The Gestapo was never kind to Jews.

"Aaron." Samuel prompted, as he dug out his own papers and handed them to the man. "We are on our way home now." He reiterated.

"And I told you that you were out after curfew, Jew."

The man briefly reviewed the papers and looked past Samuel towards the shop. "This is your shop?"

"It was. It is now in receivership." Samuel added.

"Yes, of course." He said waving another man over.

"May we have our papers now, so that we can go home?" Samuel asked again.

"You don't hear so well, Jew." He said, "It is after curfew. You will be detained until we say otherwise."

"It's not the boy's fault," Samuel pleaded "At least let him go home."

The second man approached and immediately gave the other man a Nazi salute. "Yes, Major."

"Take these two Jews with you and put them in the truck. They have violated the curfew. Here are their papers"

"Yes, sir." He answered taking the papers. He then turned to Aaron and his grandfather. "Come with me, both of you."

Samuel put his hand on Aaron's shoulder and the two of them followed the second man now.

"But, Grandfather. . ." Aaron protested.

"No talking!" the man from the Gestapo commanded.

Samuel gave Aaron a sign to remain quiet. Aaron was frightened, but the look in his grandfather's eyes did plenty to comfort him. Aaron knew that if he stuck close to his grandfather and followed his lead, everything would work out.

Aaron followed Samuel around the corner where a large military type truck was waiting for them. Standing at the back of the vehicle were two men in uniform, both were armed with rifles. Neither looked happy to see Aaron and his grandfather. The man in plain clothes pointed up at the truck as he handed Samuel their identity papers.

"Get in. Remember no talking." He commanded.

Aaron helped Samuel up onto the back of the truck while the armed men watched in silence. The truck was higher off the ground than either Aaron or Samuel had figured. Samuel caught his foot on the rear of the truck bed and fell forward into the vehicle.

"Papa!" Aaron said helping Samuel up from the bed of the truck and onto one of the benches along the sides. "Are you alright?"

Samuel nodded and smiled at Aaron that everything was okay.

"They ought to just shoot the old ones now." smirked one of the soldiers, "It would save us some time."

"Yes? And who would have to remove the dead ones?" the other asked.

"More Jews of course." The first soldier answered laughing.

Aaron sat next to his grandfather and looked at the other occupants of the truck. There were seven other people of various ages sitting on the benches. Six of them had the Star of David displayed on their clothing like Aaron and his grandfather. The seventh lay in the front left corner of the truck, slumped over to a point where Aaron could not tell if the man was marked as a Jew.

From the smell that came from his direction Aaron figured that the man had been drinking and had at one point vomited all over himself. Aaron wrinkled his nose and tried to bring his coat up closer to his face to help filter out the vulgar smell. It helped a little.

Four more people, all Jews, were added to the back of the truck before the tailgate was closed and the flaps from the canvas top were tucked in. Aaron was wondering where the two soldiers had gone when the engine of the massive truck groaned several times then coughed to life. The entire truck shuddered for several seconds before it began to slowly move down the street. The noise from the big diesel engine was deafening.

"Papa." Aaron whispered into Samuel's ear.

"Yes."

"Are we in trouble, Papa?"

There was a moment of silence as Samuel formulated his answer. "I don't think so, Aaron. We may have to pay a fine for being out after curfew, but I don't think it will be more than that."

"But, Papa. It was still half an hour until curfew. You told that man we still had half an hour to get home? We were not breaking the law."

Again, it was several seconds before Samuel answered. "Aaron, son, the man had no need for a watch. All he needed to know was that we were Jewish. Anything else didn't matter."

"But, Papa, we did nothing wrong."

"These days being Jewish is enough."

"Why do they-" Aaron stopped as the man in the front of the truck began to vomit on to the floor of the truck. Again Aaron pulled his coat up over his nose and leaned against his grandfather. Samuel placed his arms around Aaron's shoulders.

Aaron was unsure of how long they had been riding in the back of the truck or how far they had gone. He had only ridden in a few vehicles in his life and none for very long. He and Samuel usually walked or took the trolley when they had to go somewhere. The ride had been very uncomfortable. The canvas sides of the vehicle were stretched over thin metal ribs and offered very little protection from the wind and no protection from the cold. All along the back of the truck there were gaps between the metal and the canvas that allowed blasts of cold air to get in. Aaron and Samuel huddled together for warmth and security. Others in the back of the truck were doing the same. All, that is, except the drunk who had been lucky enough to pass out again after vomiting a second time.

The truck now began to slow and several times came to a complete stop. Aaron could hear the driver talking to someone but he couldn't make out much of the conversation. It was colder now and his body began to shake. His teeth quickly followed the example of his body and began to chatter. He felt Samuel hold him closer as the man rubbed his shoulders again.

The truck came to an abrupt stop that threw Aaron and everyone else forward on the bench. They remained stationary for several seconds as the driver tried to shift gears. For some reason the grinding noise now made by the truck frightened him. Aaron grimaced as the grinding noise continued for several more seconds until slowly the truck began moving backward. It continued backwards for several feet until it hit something with a large thump and came to a quick stop.

Instantly things began to happen. The flaps on the back of the truck were thrown open by two new soldiers who shouted at Aaron and the others to get out of the truck and line up.

"Quickly, quickly!" shouted one soldier.

"Over here- line up here!" came the commands from another.

Aaron held onto Samuel as they moved to the position where the soldier had pointed.

Aaron finally had a chance to look around as he held on tightly to Samuel's coat and waited in line. It was obvious that they were in a train station, but none that he recognized. It was small, a substation of some type. There was only the one building sitting amongst the shadows cast by the lighting from large floodlights mounted atop several poles. He could make out several men inside, soldiers, important ones, he thought. Their uniforms were different than the soldiers back at the truck. They looked to be in charge of the other men. Aaron also noticed that there was a brick wall around the back of the building. For some reason the wall caught his attention. In many ways it was the same as any other brick wall that was used to enclose a secure area except that there was something different about this one.

He studied it for several seconds before it dawned on him what made it different. The wall was actually two walls, one placed on top of the other or at least, that's what it looked like to Aaron. The first wall was probably the original wall made from an auburn colored brick. The original wall was about six feet in height. It was easy to see where someone had, later on, decided to make the original wall taller by adding on several more rows of bricks until the new height was somewhere around ten feet. The newer part of the wall was made from a lighter color of red brick, giving Aaron his first impression of the two walls, one atop the other. Aaron studied the top of the wall. There, cemented onto the top, were broken beer bottles, their sharp edges sparkling in the brilliance of the floodlights, daring anyone to try and cross.

"Next-quickly, quickly!" a man shouted almost directly into Aaron's ear.

Aaron jumped at the command trying to move in any direction that would get him away from the screaming. Aaron felt the familiar touch of his grandfather's hand.

"Come, this way, Aaron," Samuel said in a very calming tone.

Aaron and Samuel walked up to the tiny table set up at the head of the railway platform. There, a thin man wearing a coat a size too big, sat at the table busily scribbling on forms arranged very neatly on his table. The man finished writing and waved for the next person to approach. Aaron and Samuel walk up to the desk together.

"Papers."

Samuel handed the man their papers. Without looking up, the wiry little man read the identification cards.

"Samuel and Aaron Singer. . .Jews?" he asked finally looking up at Samuel.

Samuel glanced down at the identification card marked with the large black "J" designating him as a Jew. Then he looked down at his jacket where the large yellow Star of David openly proclaimed his faith.

"Yes," Samuel almost sang, "Jewish."

The man grimaced at Samuel's answer then continued. "Occupation."

"Master Jeweler." Samuel answered, "The boy is a goldsmith."

"A goldsmith?" the man asked incredulously. "How old is he?

"I'm fifteen." Aaron answered for himself.

The man looked at Aaron for several seconds then back at Samuel. Finally he made a few notes in his ledger, attached a small piece of paper to Samuel and Aaron's identification cards and handed them back to them.

"Get into the second line, over there." He said with a dismissive gesture toward the groups forming further up the platform.

Aaron was afraid to look at his identification card. "Papa, what does the piece of paper say?" he asked looking around him.

Samuel read the note as they walked toward the two groups. "It says that we are essential workers for the 3rd Reich."

"What does that mean?"

"It means that it is better to have this in your identification than not, Aaron. Hang on to it. Do not let it get away from you."

"Yes, Papa." Aaron said stuffing the card back into his coat pocket.

Aaron and Samuel joined the line as instructed and were ushered down the platform. There were four boxcars attached to a small engine on the left track. A second train was just pulling into the station on the other track.

Aaron watched as the four cars were loaded with people from the lines. Everyone that was in his group was loaded into the last two cars. Aaron stepped into the car first and then helped Samuel cross the threshold. The interior of the car was dark except for the small amount of light that came through the two tiny openings on either side of the car covered with barbed wire. Aaron directed his grandfather over to the window.

"Where are they taking us?" Aaron asked as he looked out of the window. More trucks were arriving; each carrying a dozen or more people and all seemed to be Jews. There seemed to be more military men now also. All carrying rifles and taking up positions along the platform. The new arrivals were being segregated in the same manner, as Aaron and his grandfather had been earlier. Aaron noticed a small group of men were being separated from the rest. From the looks of it they were mostly older men and a few Rabbis. After a few minutes the small group was led off in the direction of the brick station house where he had seen the other military men earlier.

"That is Professor Levinski." Samuel said looking over Aaron's shoulder.

"Where, Papa?"

"Over there, standing next to the Rabbi and the other men. I think I recognize a few of the others also. Yes, next to the short man. . .with the hat. . .see him?"

Aaron stood on his tiptoes to get a better look. "Yes, that's Mr. Cohen. . .from the newspaper."

"Yes." Samuel answered as the group continued to walk toward the station house.

"Where are they going?"

The huge door of the boxcar was slammed shut with a thunderous bang. Now the only light came from the small windows. Aaron watched as the Mr. Cohen and the others were taken into the secure area behind the double brick wall. The train started with a massive jolt that almost threw Aaron and Samuel to the ground. Others were not as lucky and were tossed to the floor.

Aaron and Samuel continued looking out the window. The train moved slowly at first, getting closer to the station. Slowly it passed the station house and gave Aaron a better view inside. The military men were still standing inside, but there was no sign of Mr. Cohen and the others. As they got just past the station, Aaron could see into the small yard enclosed by the double wall.

"There they are, Papa." He said pointing toward the courtyard.

"Yes, I see."

Aaron watched as several soldiers pushed Mr. Cohen and the others up against the far wall. Two of the men moved away from the wall, their hands outstretched toward the soldiers. Both men were roughly forced back in line with the others. Aaron watched as one man fell to his knees, hands clasped like in prayer.

"Aaron, look away." Samuel said quickly.

Aaron's eyes remained glued on the men. The soldiers moved back several feet then, to Aaron's amazement, raised their weapons.

Samuel attempted to cover Aaron's eyes with his hand, but Aaron was able to see the flashes from the barrels of the guns. Mr. Cohen was thrown back against the wall; some men crumpled to the ground. Aaron now strained to see what was happening as the train moved further down the track and his grandfather was still attempting to shield his view. Mr. Cohen was still leaning against the two-colored wall, his hands clutching his stomach. The last thing Aaron was able to see was one of the soldiers walk up to Mr. Cohen and point a pistol to his head. Aaron heard the shot that finally killed Mr. Cohen, but fortunately didn't have to witness it.

"Papa,. . ." Aaron choked.

Samuel placed his arms around Aaron from behind. "I know, son. I know."

"But Papa, how could they? What did Mr. Cohen do wrong?"

"Nothing in the eyes of God, Aaron." Samuel gently turned Aaron around so that the two now faced each other. "Aaron, pay attention to me," his grandfather said, as he raised his hand in front of Aaron's face, "Take this and hide it."

Aaron looked between his grandfather's fingers. There, clutched tightly was the ring that Aaron had given him for his birthday.

Aaron's thoughts shifted back and forth between the murders he had just witnessed and the small object in Samuel's fingers. "Papa, no, that's yours." Aaron finally answered, tears welling up in his eyes.

"Aaron, listen to me." Samuel said as he forced the ring into the palm of Aaron's hand. "Take this and hide it. If we get separated, you can use it to buy food or maybe a train ticket home."

"Papa. We won't get separated. We will stay together."

"Yes, of course," Samuel said with a conspiratorial wink, "we will stay together. This is just some insurance. You put it away now."

Aaron looked down at the ring in the palm of his hand. He picked it up and even in the darkness of the car, could read the inscription inside. Tears filled his eyes until they ran freely down his cheek. Aaron refused to cry and wiped the tears away with the sleeve of his coat. He placed the ring inside his pants pocket.

"I will hold this for you, Papa." Aaron said looking at his grandfather, "I will keep it safe until you want it back."

Samuel opened his arms wide and Aaron rushed into the safety that had always been there.

Chapter 8

As a German Officer, Klas was entitled to a private hospital room, when available. Since the war began to step up, casualties also increased forcing the private rooms to be shared. The room's other occupant had been a Captain Gilbert Funck, an infantry officer also from the 1st Panzer Division, recovering from multiple gunshot wounds. Two nights ago, shortly before lights out, Captain Funck sat straight up in his bed, looked over at Klas, blinked several times and then died. He was still sitting up, slumped slightly forward when the nurse arrived. Since that time Klas had been the room's only occupant.

Klas felt very uncomfortable lying in a clean hospital bed wearing fresh laundered cotton pajamas while his tank crew was now buried somewhere in Poland. The antitank grenade had done its intended job by disabling Klas' vehicle. In Klas' mind it had gone beyond the call of duty when it ripped the tank apart from the inside out throwing molten hot slivers of metal in every direction for sixty meters.

Klas had learned from his friend, Lieutenant Zimmermen, that all of his crew had died instantly. It was very common for tank crew members to huddle around their vehicle when off duty or resting. While he and Edel had been sitting on top of the vehicle, Otto and the other two men were sitting about ten meters away when the explosion destroyed the tank and took their lives. The tank turret had actually acted as a shield; protecting Klas somewhat from the initial blast and throwing him clear of the vehicle. Edel had not been so lucky. Zimmermen had also told him that there had been very little of Edel left to give a proper burial.

Zimmermen had told him on several occasions that he was very lucky to be alive. After all, Zimmermen had reminded him that Edel had been less than three feet away from him. Edel was now dead and he, Klas, was recovering from his wounds nicely. The field medic had told him the same thing before injecting him with morphine; the field doctor who worked on him at the battalion aid station also had reminded him. Then there was the ambulance driver, the duty nurse, and his doctor and of course, Zimmermen

It seemed that Zimmermen had suffered from the same bit of luck as Klas, receiving a coin size sliver of Klas' tank in his left upper arm, causing a fracture of the humerus. It was Zimmermen who had estimated that he was eighty meters away from Klas' tank when it exploded and he had been wounded. Klas wasn't feeling so lucky though. A large area under his left arm had been burned badly from the blast and up until recently, both of his legs felt as if they were in several pieces, causing constant pain and the casts were making it impossible to scratch the areas that were itching and demanding his constant attention. The casts had been off for a few days now and he was grateful for that, but with the removal of the cast came the physical therapy. That had not been pleasant at all. Zimmermen had been released weeks ago and was now at home with his parents on convalescent leave and Edel and the others were still dead.

The light rapping on the door managed to take Klas' mind away from his dead crew for the moment.

"Ja, kommen." Klas shouted from his bed.

The door creaked open and the orderly entered the room. He was no older than Klas, maybe younger, seventeen or eighteen, it was hard to tell. With his blond hair cropped short his ears looked like someone had left the barn doors open. The child like expression on his face told Klas that the young man had never been close to front line action. His voice was unsteady as he spoke.

"Her Lieutenant"

"Ja, what is it?"

"I have some mail for you." He stammered.

Klas didn't know what to say. The possibility of getting mail while in the hospital had never entered his mind. At the front, letters were a sought after commodity, but since his injuries, Klas had forgotten about the luxury of personal mail.

His face beamed. "Mail. . .for me? Who's it from?"

The orderly looked down at the two envelopes and began to stammer.

"I. . .I don't know Her Lieutenant. No one has ever asked me who their letters were from before. They both look official. I-"

Klas suddenly felt very foolish. His voice cracked as he put his hand out.

"I'm sorry, that was a stupid question, thank you for bringing them to me."

The orderly handed Klas the two envelopes obviously relieved at not having to guess further on the origination of the letters.

"Thank you, again. . . Merrell, right?"

"Yes, Lieutenant, it's Merrell. May I go now?"

"Oh, yes of course. Thank you again Merrell."

The Orderly had been right about the letters, they looked very official. Both were postmarked from Berlin. Klas smiled, the postmarks were over three weeks old. Obviously, whatever was in the letters was not of grave importance to the war effort. He studied the postmark again and decided to open them in correct sequence as one letter had a postmark a few days earlier than the second. Besides, the first letter was much thicker than the second one.

Klas held the letter up to the light to see where the letter sat in the envelope. He then started to tear a quarter of an inch strip from the end of the envelope, being careful not to tear the letter itself. He then pulled the letter free from the open end of the envelope. He unfolded the pages and looked them over before beginning to read. The first page, while on official letterhead, was a hand written note from his father. The second letter, also on official letterhead, was another hand written note from his Uncle. He picked up the note from his father and read it carefully.

Dearest Klas,

I continue to get good reports on your recovery. Your Mother and I are very proud of your continued personal efforts to return to active duty. Your Mother has been preparing a complete menu of all of your favorite dishes. I am just lucky that I like many of the same foods as you, or I would be forced to eat at the Officers mess during the entire time you are here. I may be a General, but your Mother is still the Commander and Chief of the family kitchen.

Klas, we pray for your continued recovery and are looking forward to seeing you here in Berlin when you are released from the hospital. Again, I am sorry that I could not make it to Frankfurt to see you, but as an Officer of the Waffen SS you can understand how important our duty is to our Führer and the Father Land. The war effort goes very well and places a huge demand on Officers like you and I. But we will make time to talk when you arrive in Berlin.

Love from your Father and Mother,

Klas wondered how he was going to tell his parents that he had no intention of visiting them in Berlin. He had already checked with the doctors and if he showed good improvement over the next week or so, they would release him back to his unit on a light duty status. Klas didn't want to sit around Berlin with his parent's friends and talk about the war. He wanted back in it. At the rate the German Army was advancing, the war could be over very soon. He did not want to hear about the end of the war from some fat adjutant in Berlin, he wanted to be there when it happened. Klas knew his Father would surely understand and support his need to be with his unit.

He put the letter down and then read the one from his Uncle, Colonel Ernest Von Reichman. Uncle Ernest had lost two sons in the Polish Campaign. Both had been highly decorated and had made the family very proud. Klas had wanted to see them while he was in Poland, but the war was moving so quickly he barely had time to keep up with his own Division. He had received notice of Bernard's death the same day he had received the Silver Panzer Battle Badge. Three days later he learned Spangler, the younger of the two, had been killed. He had written his Aunt and Uncle telling them of his sorrow. The three boys had grown up together fighting imaginary enemies in the large forest by the families' homes. During those days the three of them had never lost a battle, never been wounded and certainly never died. How things change Klas thought as he put the letter down.

Klas picked up the second letter, performed the same little ritual of opening it and slid the letter out of the envelope. This letter was an official letter from the Department of the Army. Klas read it carefully.

SS-Hauptamt - SS- HA
18 February 1940
Group A
103 Wilhelmstrasse, Berlin, Den

For: Lieutenant Klas Von Reichman, Waffen SS, Unassigned

The following information is directed to your immediate attention.

1. CHIEF OF STAFF, SS-HAUPTAMT – SS – HA, ANNOUNCES THE PRMOTION OF LIEUTENANT KLAS VON REICHMAN, WAFFEN SS TO CAPTAIN, WAFEEN SS WITH DATE OF RANK 1FEB40.
2. CHIEF OF STAFF, SS-HAUPTAMT -SS-HA ANNOUNCE THE AWARD OF THE KNIGHT'S CROSS OF THE IRON CROSS FOR ACTIONS TAKEN IN THE ASSAULT AGAINST ENEMY TROOPS ON OR ABOUT 15OCT39.
CAPTAIN VON REICHMAN DID, WITHOUT REGARD FOR HIS OWN SAFETY TAKE COMMAND OF THE 1ST AND 2ND PLATOONS, 1ST PANZER DIVISION WHEN THE COMPANY COMMANDER 'S TANK WAS DISABLED.

IT IS FURTHER NOTED THAT DURING THE SAME BATTLE, CAPTAIN VON REICHMAN ACTED IN A MANNER BEFITTING A WAFFEN SS OFFICER AND DIRECTED HIS PLATOON TO ENGAGE A SUPERIOR ENEMY FORCE IN A DIRECT ASSAULT, SPOILING THE ENEMY'S ATTEMPT OF AMBUSHING THE 1ST PANZER DIVISION. DURING THIS ENGAGEMENT CAPTAIN VON REICHMAN'S TANK PERSONALLY DESTROYED 7 OF THE ENEMY TANKS.

THE ACTION TAKEN BY CAPTAIN VON REICHMAN NOT ONLY DESTROYED A LARGER ENEMY FORCE BUT

ENSURED THE ENSUING VICTORY OF THE 1ST PANZER DIVISION.

3. CAPTAIN VON REICHMAN IS FURTHER ORDERED TO PRESENT HIMSELF IN PERSON TO REICHSFUHRER HIMMLER'S OFFICE, 103 WILHELMSTRASSE, BERLIN, DEN, FOR PRESENTATION OF THE ABOVE MENTIONED AWARD UPON RELEASE FROM THE 187TH ARMY HOSPITAL, FRANKFURT.

By direction of:

Heinrich Oberlin, Lt. Colonel, Waffen SS
Administrative Assistant to the Office of the Reichsfuhrer

Klas read the letter several times before finally putting it back in the envelope. Mixed emotions ran through him like fingers of an estuary, taking various courses through a delta. Captain, he thought. The Knights Cross, more than he would let himself ever hope for. Then the thought of Berlin, there would be no getting out of going there now. He began to think of ways to limit his time there. The less time he spent in Berlin, the quicker he could get back to his unit.

His thoughts quickly turned back to his dead tank crew. He wondered if their families would be receiving the Knights Cross posthumously. He vowed that he would find out the status of their medals when he was in Berlin and if possible, deliver them to their family personally.

Chapter 9

In the midst of all of the horror going on around him, it was the dogs that frightened Aaron the most. Aaron and his family had never owned a dog nor had any of the family's close friends. So, to have these beasts straining at the end of a leash to get to him was unnerving. Aaron watched in horror as one of the animals would be given just enough leash to nip at the heels of someone close enough; the handler laughing as he pulled the animal back.

"Men to the left! - Now! Move now! Women to the right! Move now!" shouted another guard.

Aaron had not noticed but he held onto Samuels coat with a death grip. The slightest movement made by Samuel was transferred into his right hand and Aaron would quickly move in whichever direction was dictated by Samuel.

"Quickly! Form five across. Five, you stupid Jew." The guard shouted as he struck a man close to Aaron with the butt of his rifle."

The man dropped to the ground clutching his arm, screaming in pain. Before he could regain his feet two dogs were upon him. Mercilessly they tore at the downed man's face and neck, growling between attacks. The man saved his life by rolling into a ball covering his head and upper body. The dog continued to tear at the man's clothing, taking large pieces of his outer garment and shaking back and forth. Aaron was amazed to see that the two animals were large enough to be able to actually move the man as they swung their heads back and forth snarling.

"Come, Aaron." Samuel cautioned, "Stand here next to me."

Aaron moved to the spot where Samuel had directed him, but his eyes never left the two dogs. The handlers continued to coax their animals forward. The man still attempting to keep his face and neck covered. The dogs mouths were now covered with blood, their drool was in long pink strands foaming at the corner of their mouths. It was a moment that Aaron thought he would never forget.

"Straight lines!" "Hintz, Ralph, get your dogs!"

With a sharp whistle from the two handlers both dogs immediately released the man and returned to a sitting position next to the soldiers.

"You two." The guard said, pointing to several men who had not found a place in the line yet. "Come here. Pick this man up. Get him in the line."

The two men quickly picked up the bloody man and helped him to the rear of the line.

Aaron continued to stand next to Samuel still clutching onto his coat. There were several more instances where the guards hit or beat one of the men or women trying to find a place in the two lines. Finally, everyone had managed to find a place in the two groups. Immediately, two of the guards began walking down between the columns.

"We need skilled craftsmen. Are there any skilled craftsmen in the line?" the soldier in charge would shout.

Several men raised their hands.

"What do you do? Yes, you." Asked the guard.

"I'm a tailor."

"Tailor?, Good. Go over there." He said pointing to where a small group of men and women gathered.

"Yes, you, what do you do?"

"Metal press operator." "Good, the line."

"And you."

"Carpenter."

"Very good, over there."

Aaron watched the segregation continue until the two military men were close to where he was standing. Aaron looked down at the ground not wishing to make eye contact with the men as they passed him.

"Yes, you. What do you do?" the man almost shouted in Aaron's ear.

Aaron continued to look down. All he could think of was the two dogs snapping and biting at him. He lying on the ground as the dogs tore into his coat and then his flesh. He hoped they would pass quickly.

"I'm a Master Jeweler." Samuel shouted back to the man.

Aaron looked up at Samuel in shock. There, looking at the two German guards was Samuel, his hand still in the air. "Papa!," Aaron whispered, "No, don't."

"A Master Jeweler?" The man asked, as he approached closer.

The soldier now stood so close to Aaron that he could smell the starch in his uniform.

"And what do you make, Master Jeweler?" the guard asked mockingly.

"Whatever you like. Gold rings, cuff links, earrings for your wife. I can set stones also."

"You wouldn't lie to me old man, would you?"

"No sir." Samuel answered bowing his head. "I am a very good jeweler. I owned my own shop for twenty-four years. You will like my work."

"I better." he sneered, "Or I will shoot you where you stand. Understand?"

"Yes, sir, you will be very pleased."

"All right then, go to the line."

Samuel grabbed Aaron's hand and began to walk towards the small group.

"Wait!" the guard shouted. "Not the boy. We have no need for the boy."

Samuel turned to face the man again, with his head still bowed he continued.

"The boy is a goldsmith. He is very talented."

The two men began to laugh out loud.

"This skinny little boy. . .a goldsmith. Old man, do not play games with me or I will have the dogs on you. Now go, leave the boy."

"But sir, the boy has trained in my shop for many years. He is truly gifted. Even more so than myself in some areas."

"The boy stays. Now go old man!"

Samuel returned to his place in the line next to Aaron. Aaron's heart pounded in his chest so loud he was afraid that the guards would hear.

"Papa, it's okay. Go to the line before they beat you."

The guard looked over his shoulder and noticed that Samuel was still in line. He marched back toward Aaron and Samuel.

"Are you deaf, old man! I told you to get in the other line!" the man now shouted, the veins in his neck growing large and ugly. "Go now before I have the dogs make a meal of you."

Samuel removed his hat and bowed his head. "Sir, take my Grandson instead. I am too old to be any good to you."

"Papa!" Aaron was surprised at his own outburst. "Go to the other line. I will be all right." Aaron looked down at the ground waiting for the blow that would surely follow his outburst. Painful seconds went by and still nothing.

The head guard removed his pistol from his holster. "Step out here old man! We will solve this problem quickly. "Kneel over here." He said pointing to a place on the ground.

"Lieutenant, is there a problem?"

The new man approached the group with an even stride. His uniform was well tailored and neatly pressed. Aaron could tell that this man was no guard, never had been, his demeanor spoke of someone of proper schooling. He was lean but toned, almost athletic. His face was sculpted like that of a Nordic Prince he had once seen in a storybook. His eyes were judicious, the color of doves in the spring after shedding their winter plumage. Aaron knew this man was in charge. Everyone who met him knew it.

"Why have you not completed your work?" he said evenly to the Lieutenant.

"This Jew is trying to give me trouble." The Lieutenant spat.

The man flashed a superior grin toward the Lieutenant. "Then shoot him and move on."

The Lieutenant grabbed Samuel by the collar of his coat and pulled him past Aaron. Aaron followed with the movement as he still had a tight grip on Samuel's coat.

"Papa!"

"Aaron, let go!" his grandfather commanded and Aaron released his grip.

"Now, old man! You can make jewelry for your Jew God." He rasped as he threw Samuel to the ground, freeing his hand to arm the pistol in his other.

"Halt!" commanded the tall man. He pushed the Lieutenant to one side stepping in between Samuel and the man. "What is your craft, old man?"

Samuel still held his muddy hat in his hands and he bowed his head as he answered.

"My grandson and I are jewelers, sir. I am a master jeweler and my grandson is a very gifted goldsmith, my apprentice for the last seven years."

The man affected a calming smile as he looked toward Aaron. "How old are you boy?"

Aaron removed his hat and stepped forward bowing his head. "I am seventeen, sir." he lied.

The man turned back to Samuel. "You expect me to believe that this boy is of any worth to me?"

"He is very gifted, sir." Samuel repeated looking up at Aaron. "Aaron, show him the ring. Show the General your work."

There was suppressed laughter at Samuel's reference to the man's rank. Even the tall man laughed at the remark. "Thank you for the promotion." He said turning to Aaron. "You have something to show me?"

Aaron felt betrayed by his own grandfather. It was Samuel that had told him to hide the ring and keep it safe. Now he was telling him to give it to this stranger. Aaron hesitated for a brief second before digging in the sweatband of his own hat. Even though Aaron was very uncomfortable about surrendering the ring, he would never disobey his grandfather.

"Here, sir." Aaron said as he produced the ring, "I made it for my grandfather."

The man took the ring from Aaron and closely examined it.

"You made this?"

"Yes, sir."

"How do I know that you're not lying to me? How do I know that your grandfather didn't make it?"

"The inscription, sir. I gave it to my grandfather for his birthday."

The officer turned the ring on its side and read the inscription.

"This means nothing. Anyone could have inscribed this."

"That is true, sir." Aaron said."But none the less it *is* my work."

The man looked down at the ring again and turned it in his hand, thinking. Slowly he raised his other hand, fingers outstretched and placed the ring on his small finger.

"All right, then." he said, gazing at the ring now on his finger "We will put you both to work in our jewelry shop. If you are lying it will be quickly evident and I will turn you over to Sergeant Bella."

The others laughed again, this time their laughter was not suppressed.

"After Sergeant Bella has finished with you, you will have wished that Lieutenant Kroger here would have shot you both." The tall Officer turned to the Lieutenant. "Lieutenant, put these two in the line for Sergeant Bella. I want them at 117 this afternoon.

"Yes, Commander!" he replied as he picked Samuel up with one hand throwing him back toward Aaron.

"And Lieutenant." The Commander said looking at the ring again.

"Yes, sir." The Lieutenant said coming to attention.

"Next time these Jews," he smirked and gestured vaguely at the lines of people, "give you any problems, just shoot them. I don't want to get into these petty arguments with these people. Do you understand?"

"Yes, sir!" He answered and then as an afterthought added. "I could start with these two, sir." pointing to Aaron and Samuel with his pistol.

The Commander turned and studied the two of them one more time. He held up the hand with the gold ring on it and studied it again. "No, give them to Bella. He will make sure they produce."

"As you wish, sir"

The commander walked off toward the women's line and dismissed the Lieutenant with a wave of his hand.

As soon as the Commander was gone the Lieutenant pushed Aaron and Samuel further away from the line.

"Sergeant Mannz," he shouted "take these two over to the registration desk for 117."

The stumpy sergeant walked over to Aaron and Samuel and with a flip of his fingers, motioned for them to follow him. As soon as they began to move the Lieutenant returned to his duty.

"Is there anyone here that is a skilled craftsman?" he continued to shout as Aaron and Samuel moved away.

"Grandfather, that man kept your ring." Aaron almost cried.

Samuel didn't look toward Aaron but instead, kept an eye on the Sergeant in front of him. "Yes, he kept the ring and I got to keep you. I would have given him much more, Aaron."

"But Papa!"

"Aaron, do you have the skill to make me another ring?"

"Of course."

"I, on the other hand, do not have the skill to make another you."

The sergeant led Aaron and Samuel into a small building just inside the gate. The walls were a dingy color green ending at the floor, also a dingy color green. They were led down the small hallway and into a small room off to the left.

"Two more from the Commander for 117." Is all Sergeant Mannz said to the man sitting behind the desk facing the door way.

Corporal Ingel sat waiting behind the desk for Aaron and Samuel to step forward. He was obviously in a clerical position and, like the man at the railway station, was busy filling out some type of forms. But unlike the other man at the station, his uniform fit well and was also clean and pressed. Corporal Ingel motioned for one of the two to sit down at the large desk and began writing even before Aaron had taken the seat.

"Your papers." he said flatly.

Aaron had been through the drill before and already had his papers out to hand to the man. The man placed them on the desk before him.

"Aaron Singer." He said as he wrote the name in some type of ledger before him.

"It says you are an essential worker. What do you do?"

"Goldsmith." Aaron answered.

The man looked up at Aaron and then back to the papers in front of him, then looked back at Aaron a second time.

"A goldsmith. How old are you?"

"Seventeen. . . next month" he added as an afterthought.

"And you are a goldsmith?"

"Yes," Samuel interjected, "He is my apprentice. I am a master jeweler. I am his grandfather."

The man studied Aaron for several seconds and then returned to his writing.

"Take off your coat and roll up your left sleeve."

Aaron looked over his shoulder at Samuel. Samuel nodded in agreement with the Corporal.

"You know young man," Corporal Ingel said while continuing to write in his ledger. "You will save yourself some very severe beatings if you learn to obey orders immediately instead of turning to your grandfather for permission." Corporal Ingel didn't look up from what he was doing nor did he say anything further. Aaron removed his coat and rolled up the left sleeve of his shirt as the Corporal had ordered.

"Place your left arm across the table."

Aaron followed the instructions and placed his left arm down on the table.

"Palm down."

Aaron obeyed.

Corporal Ingel removed an instrument that looked very much like the small drill Aaron had used in his grandfathers shop from a hook on the other side of the desk. With a flick of a small switch, the tool began to hum.

"I am going to put a camp registration number on your left forearm. It won't hurt very much, but you should look away. It makes the pain even less." Corporal Ingel said as he held on to Aaron's wrist. Corporal Ingel looked over at his ledger and read off a number to himself and then turned back toward Aaron.

Aaron tried to look away, but his eyes were fixed on the little drill. Corporal Ingel looked at Aaron and shook his head.

"Alright, have it your way."

Aaron watched as the small tool was placed against his skin and Corporal Ingel skillfully moved it back and forth. At first it tickled his skin as the small point moved back and forth leaving a blue-black line where it had been. By the time Corporal Ingel had written the single letter followed by the five numbers on Aaron's arm, he was almost in tears. The tickle had turned into a thousand bee stings each adding to the pain.

Corporal Ingel continued to hold Aaron's arm in place as he checked the number against the ledger. He smiled when he was sure that the two numbers were the same. He then released Aaron's arm, but then before Aaron could move it, grabbed it again.

"I almost forgot." He said, "You're going to 117."

Aaron had heard the Commander tell the sergeant to send them to 117 and he heard the Sergeant repeat it to the Corporal, but he had no idea what they had been talking about. The tears welled up in Aaron's eyes again as the Corporal again started to write on his forearm. When the man had finished this time Aaron was allowed to remove his arm from the desk.

Aaron stared at the new number on his arm for several minutes as the Corporal went back to writing in his ledger. "Does everyone get a number?" he asked looking down again to see what he had added. There, behind the letter and the 5-digit number, was a small picture of a skull and cross bones, just like the one he had noticed on all of the soldiers uniform collars or caps.

"No, not yet, but soon everyone entering the camps will have one. Your camp is amongst the first." The Corporal motioned for Aaron to get up. "OK, move and let your grandfather sit down." He ordered.

Aaron, still rubbing the tattoo, exchanged places with Samuel.

Samuel was halfway through the process when another soldier entered the room. The looks of the man frightened Aaron as soon as he walked through the door. Aaron got a good look at the man before he cast his eyes down to the floor.

He was everything the Commander wasn't. The man was short and overweight. His shoulders were massive, like that of an oarsman who could row forever. His barrel chest pulled at the buttons of his uniform while his waist did its best to push his shirt up and his trousers down, giving his huge belly the room it needed. The sidearm on his belt seemed to almost hang down to his knees.

With his trousers being pushed down by his stomach, the pant legs were all bunched at the bottom of his feet around his dirty boots. The worst part of the man was his face. It reminded Aaron of a bullfrog, the flabby double chin protruding and covering part of his fleshy neck that was covered with stubble and needing attention. His face was accented by his gourd like nose, misshapen and punctuated with a noticeable wart on the right side. His eyes were deep set and cold, covered by a ridge of curly black eyebrows. Aaron could hear him wheezing as he stood there.

"I'm leaving now, Ingel." He belched. "Why are you wasting your time with these two?" he added looking at Aaron and his grandfather.

Corporal Ingel looked up at the Sergeant and a huge smile flashed across his face as if he were going to truly receive some type of pleasure from what he was about to say.

"They're yours, Sergeant Bella."

"What," he bellowed, sounding like a wounded bear. "This old man and this pup, mine?"

"That's right, they're the last two for 117."

Sergeant Bella sucked in a breath of air, his nose wrinkling like there was a foul stench floating in the room. "Don't screw with me, Corporal, I'm in no mood for your stupid pranks."

Corporal Ingel still had his hand on Samuel's arm and raised it for Sergeant Bella to see. There, just like on Aaron's arm, was the letter and five digits followed by the small skull.

"Ah shit!" Sergeant Bella spit out. "What good are these two Jews?"

"Jewelers."

"This old man and the pup, Jewelers?"

"The Commander sent them over himself."

The anguished expression flashing across Bella's face softened at the mention of the Commander. He walked closer to Aaron and looked him over. Aaron was praying that the man could not see him shaking.

"Well, I won't have to put up with them for long. The old man will die within a month and the young one here will be a favorite with some of the queer ones. He will probably like it. This might be fun to watch." Sergeant Bella looked back at Ingel.

"You finished with them?"

"A hair cut and they're yours."

Sergeant Bella wrinkled his nose again, which forced the wart up and outward.

"Well, I'll be in the truck. Don't make me wait too long, Ingel, you prick.

"You'll make it back in time for dinner, Sergeant, I promise."

Sergeant Bella looked a bit sheepish as if Corporal Ingel had hit on his real reason for wanting to return to camp.

Bella waddled out of the room and down the hall.

Aaron's shoulders relaxed when the man was out of sight. Corporal Ingel had noticed the reaction.

"You're right to be worried about that one." Ingel said spitting out the word "that". "If you can, stay away from him. That will also keep you alive a lot longer. Now come with me."

Aaron and Samuel walked down the hall following Corporal Ingel, both unconsciously rubbing their left arms.

"Papa?"

"Yes?"

"Do you ever think about Mother?"

"Every day."

Aaron continued to walk behind the SS Corporal. "Me too." He added feeling the tears returning.

Chapter 10

Klas stood at one of the large windows located in his Father's office, looking out onto the street and the park beyond. It was early yet, but several people were out enjoying the crisp morning air. Outside the window, you would never know that there was a war going on where people were dying. Klas changed his focus slightly and was now staring at his own ghostly reflection in the large panes of glass.

His eyes stared at the black double breasted jacket he was wearing, the collar patches, shoulder straps and collar were all piped in the same rose-pink color denoting proudly his position as an SS-Panzer Officer. The silver shoulder straps now displayed his new rank of Captain. His eyes quickly fixed on the long ribbon encircling his neck, holding the Knight's Cross of the Iron Cross.

He watched the reflection as his hand moved up and touched the Iron Cross. His eyes then moved to his left breast pocket where just below his Waffen-SS tank Battle Badge was now hanging the Black Wound Badge. Klas stared at his reflection for several seconds before his thoughts turned to his new orders and his image faded from the glass.

"Father," Klas said still staring out the window, "There is a matter that I need your help with."

General Von Reichman was several inches taller than his son but they shared the same family good looks. Even at his age, the blond hair was still striking. His eyes were still sharp, clear, lightening blue in color and still held an edge that matched his commanding figure. The German uniform was made for Peter Von Reichman. He had spent all of his life since the age of seventeen in a German uniform and never had any other man made a more striking appearance. He moved away from the small table carrying two glasses of Schnaps.

"Of course, son." he said, now handing one of the glasses to his son. "Is this an official request or a personal one?"

Klas hesitated for a second as he swirled the liquid around in his glass. "Both." he finally answered.

"Then why don't we drink up and take a walk around the park." Peter said, raising his glass in a salute to his son.

The walk felt good to Klas. He had been locked up in the hospital for far too long. His legs were stiff but he was able to keep pace with his Father.

"I have my new orders."

"So soon?"

Klas picked his next words carefully. "I'm not being returned to the Panzers."

If this surprised the older Von Reichman, he did not show it.

"Well, I would imagine that your legs still require some healing and your side. . . the burns under your arm are not totally mended, Klas."

"Yes, I guess that is true. I can't imagine being knocked around in a turret of a tank right now, but there's more."

"More?" his father asked, still not showing any emotion.

Klas had rehearsed this part of his speech over and over again on the train from Frankfurt. Now that the time had come he still wasn't sure how his Father would take the news. Klas had tried to understand the orders, hell, he had even tried to get them changed, but nothing he had done was enough to get the new assignment changed. Now, for the first time in his life he would have to ask his Father not only for a personal favor, but ask him to use his position within the service to show favoritism to his son.

"Father, I'm not even being allowed to return to a combat unit."

"Klas, you shouldn't be so hard on yourself. I'm sure that whatever assignment you have been given you will serve with distinction."

Klas swallowed hard, stopped and turned to face his father. The older Von Reichman took a few additional steps before coming to a halt.

"Father I have a temporary assignment for six weeks at a school in Dachau. It's a school to become an Administrator for prisons."

"And you don't approve of your new assignment?" Peter asked studying the young Von Reichman's response.

Klas was confused at his father's question. He had thought that his Father would be outraged at the fact that a Von Reichman was being turned into a prison guard. Now new thoughts ran through his head. Did his Father feel that his disapproval with his new assignment was in some way an act unbecoming of an officer? Or, for a Von Reichman?

"Father," he said weakly, "I'm a combat officer. I can best serve the Führer at the front lines with a Panzer Group."

Klas' Father raised his left eyebrow forcing the right eye to squint slightly. "You can best serve the Führer by following your orders."

Klas' heart sank at the tone of his father's voice. He had heard it many times while growing up. It was the tone of duty and honor.

"Father, what I'm saying," Klas said trying to back pedal, "is that I think there has been a mistake in my orders. I don't believe that I was to be sent to some school to become a jailer. I'm a Combat Officer at a time when our country needs experienced combat personnel."

Klas' father's eyes narrowed. "Are you asking me to help you disobey your orders?"

"No, sir." Klas answered quickly, "I would ask only that you help me solve this problem by helping straighten out my orders. I'm sure there has been a mix up somewhere."

The older Von Reichman began to walk again. Klas noticed that his father's face had suddenly turned ashen; his eyes dull, lifeless as he began to speak.

"There is no mix up in your orders, Klas." His father said in a voice as cold as death.

"I'm sure there is, father. I can't believe-" Suddenly, Klas felt the blood drain from his face as the tone of his father's words struck him. "You knew about the assignment."

His father looked at the ground as he continued to walk. "Yes, I knew."

"But-"

Lines formed across his brow as he looked directly at Klas and began to speak. "Klas, your mother and I were afraid. . ." he stopped as the words stuck in his throat. "We don't want to see you get killed like your two cousins."

Klas staggered for several steps before he stopped. "It was you. You had my orders changed to this school."

The once composed demeanor of the older Von Reichman's face changed as a grimace of agony spread across it.

"Yes, your Uncle and I made arrangements to have you reassigned to the school."

Klas' eyes widened as the truth of what had happened settled in.

"Why?" he stammered, "Why would you do this to me?"

"Klas, we were only thinking about you."

"Me! Thinking about me?"

The older Von Reichman looked around the area to see who might be within hearing distance. Satisfied that no one could hear, he continued. "Yes, about you. Don't you understand, Klas?"

Klas began pacing back and forth in front of his father as he thought about what had happened.

"All I understand is that you have put an end to my military career. With a single stroke of your pen you have ruined everything I have worked so hard for."

"Will everything you've worked for do you any good when your guts are spread across the Eastern Front?" His father almost spat. "You're the last, the only remaining heir in our family."

Klas could feel the blood rising up in his neck and warming his face. "Bernard and Spangler were killed in the line of duty and you and Uncle Ernest think it's your duty to ruin my career?"

"And your mothers." Peter added.

"Oh, yes don't forget Mother. I'm sure she was a big influence on Reichführer Himmler."

Peter Von Reichman peered down the end of his nose at Klas. "She, as much as any of us." He stated flatly. "The orders were signed by the Reichfürer himself, Klas."

"Well, General," Klas said saluting his father, "I'm sure you will not mind if I say goodbye now. I have to go and see about getting my orders changed and catching up with my Panzer Group."

"Do what you feel you must, Klas." The older Von Reichman sighed, "The orders can only be changed by the Reichfürer or the Fürer himself and I don't think you are on a first name basis with either."

Klas finished his salute, turned and walked away from his father.

"Your mother is still expecting you for dinner," his father shouted as Klas distanced himself.

Chapter 11

Things had gone wrong from the arrival of the first train and Lt. Colonel Heinrich Oust's mood had only worsened as the day continued. It started with the train's arrival. The Jews had been herded out of the cars and quickly into the standard two lines, one for men and the other for women and children. Selections for the different work camps had been made quickly and efficiently. Then, on schedule, the remaining Jews were marched over to the holding area to have their heads shaved and to be stripped of their remaining possessions including their clothing, gold fillings, glasses, shoes and any other items they may be harboring.

At this point the normal procedure was to inform the Jews that they were going to be showered and deloused. They would then be crowded into the gas chamber where the doors were bolted shut and the gas administered through openings in the ceiling.

Normally this was accomplished with great precision and with enough time allowed for the chamber to be re-opened, aired out and the bodies removed for cremation. But this morning's group did not flow as planned. One of the prisoners assigned as a cleaning commando to remove and catalog the possessions of the newly arrived Jews recognized a friend in line. Feeling personally responsible for the young friend, the man told the woman of her upcoming fate in the gas chamber. Within seconds the word spread through the ranks like plague and a massive riot started. Over 400 Jews had to be beaten or shot before the troops regained control of the crowd. Getting the remaining Jews into the gas chamber as well as cleaning up the dead bodies had taken up precious time. 400 bodies, piled haphazardly here and there had to be removed from sight while other prisoners were put to work hosing down the area to remove the blood. The illusion of normalcy had to be maintained if Heinrich and his men were to remain in control. Heinrich and his men could handle a train containing 2,000 to 2,500 Jews in two to two and a half hours if they kept to his strict schedule.

The second train had already arrived when the troops were forcing the first group into the chamber. This meant that the lines had to be held at the railway siding until the last of the morning group had been disposed of. The third train had been forced to wait further down the tracks until Heinrich's men were back on schedule.

Heinrich had personally walked the man guilty of the breach of security over to the crematorium where the other members of the cleanup crew were made to throw the man into one of the furnaces alive. He then personally shot an additional four men as a reminder to the others not to speak to the new arrivals.

This did not help to cheer Heinrich up at all. He would receive a negative report from the Reichsbann for delaying their trains. A negative report translated into more paper work and less time to work on things that were important to him.

Col. Heinrich Oust had been well on his way to becoming an accomplished musician before the war. A graduate of the Munich Conservatory of Music, Heinrich had broken with the family tradition of entering the military and sought his fame as a pianist and maybe one day, a composer. While he pursued his career in music, Heinrich was smart enough to keep his father placated and joined the Nazi Party in December of 1932. In order to stay in his father's good grace and money, he later enlisted as a reserve officer in the Waffen-SS. Heinrich took the preparatory courses as a Reserve-Führer-Bewerber and then attended the reserve officers' candidate course. After passing his final examinations, Heinrich had hoped to go the Waffen-SS special school for Bandmasters (SS-Führer und Musikführer), but his father again intervened and Heinrich was sent to the Officer School of the Economic Administrative Service where he received training in the practical application for officers as a Waffen-SS Officer of Administration.

Heinrich was furious with his father, but being a wealthy reserve officer was much better than being a poor piano player. He had experienced the life of a poor musician and knew that the only way to the top was with plenty of talent and even more money. Heinrich knew he could not count on his father for the funds needed, at least without paying some type of price and with his father the price was always heavy. He had tried to secure the money through the banks but the Jews stopped him there. When the war broke out and he was called up for service, Heinrich knew that his dream was slipping further and further away.

Then his luck changed. His father, again meddling in his affairs, was able to use his money and influence to get him promoted. His new rank and accompanying orders sent him to Dachau Concentration Camp to learn prison administration. He found he had a hidden talent for being ruthless and he excelled at the new work and within a year was promoted a second time and sent to Poland to head up a new concentration camp there. His luck didn't stop there. With his long-standing membership in the Nazi party and the friends it provided, Heinrich quickly joined the inner-circle of the SS and became a central figure of the Economic Office of the Waffen-SS and more importantly, a member of the central financial group of the SS-Totenkkopfverbände or Death Head Unit of the SS. So now he was entrusted with the task of squeezing every ounce of money and wealth out of the Jews.

Whether it was gold, diamonds, jewelry or the sweat of their work, Heinrich was to turn it into riches for his SS brothers in black. For this purpose he had established Camp 117.

It was the intention of the SS to gather the best laborers the Jews could supply and work these people at their talents to produce the wealth needed to fulfill the needs of the SS. Heinrich and the others knew that the riches produced in this camp would be the key to their future, even if the war were to be lost. It was decided early on that Colonel Heinrich Oust was the man to run the secret operation. Other than Colonel Höss, Commander of the main Auschwitz and a few other high-ranking members of the SS, no one knew of the existence of Heinrich's hidden workshops buried within the labor camp known only as Camp 117.

The small group of special workers had been hidden within another concentration camp so as not to arouse any suspicions. It was here that Heinrich's fortune really took a turn for the better, because here, he was free to do as he pleased as long as the Jews produced. In this position he could do no wrong and it was here that he started his first orchestra made up from the Jewish population. Now, as he made the SS and himself rich off the labor of the Jews, he could also fine-tune his skills as a conductor from that same labor pool.

But at the present moment, it was this endless labor pool that was giving him the most problems.

"Lieutenant Klein," Heinrich shouted.

Klein was a well built young man no more than 19, a soccer player from one of the universities as Heinrich remembered it; still not enough hair on his face to shave. He ran as he approached Heinrich, his eyes wide and nervous. "Yes Sir,

Colonel!" he answered, as he came to a stop just in front of Heinrich.

"As soon as you get the signal from Captain Coop I want these people moved over the hill to the showers. Is that understood?"

The hill was a man-made embankment spanning over 200 meters, separating the rail yard from the East end of the camp where the building housing the gas chamber was constructed. The purpose of the earth mound was to physically separate the two portions of the camp, not allowing the people standing at the railway siding to see or hear what was happening on the other side. The construction of the embankment also allowed for two guard towers to serve double duty by being able to watch both sides of the camp. It was these two guard towers that had been most successful in stopping the morning riot. Machine gun fire from the towers had been able to stop the Jews from crossing back over the embankment when the riot started. The machine gun fire had killed almost half of the four hundred Jews and had forced the remainder to the ground, their hands stretched above their heads in surrender.

"Yes, Colonel, we are almost ready to move them now. I am just waiting for the signal from the Captain. We will be ready for the next train without a delay."

The information that they were finally back on schedule should have pleased Heinrich more, but there was something that kept him from enjoying the news.

"Is there something wrong, Colonel?" the Lieutenant asked, noticing the frown on Heinrich's face.

Heinrich looked at the young officer as he himself tried to figure out the problem, but nothing came to mind. The trains were back on schedule, Heinrich had received a report that they had picked up an additional artiste that were always in demand in 117, but something still ground at the nerves along his back and neck, something that wouldn't let go.

"No, Lieutenant, there is nothing the matter. I am just glad that we are finally back on schedule and I expect that you and Captain Coop will keep it that way.

"Yes, Colonel." Klein said, snapping to attention.

Again, Heinrich strained his brain to figure out what was irritating him so badly. With all the noise sounding the movement of the Jews, Heinrich found it impossible to concentrate. The train whistle cut into the cold winter air, leaving a cloud of steam in its wake as the train began to back out of the main yard. Guard dogs barked excessively, straining at their leashes; soldiers screaming above the noise like street merchants and the thousand other noises associated with moving 2,000 people quickly and expeditiously to their deaths.

"Colonel, there is one other matter that needs your attention." Klein interjected.

Heinrich rubbed his temple, "Yes, what is it."

"The 117 truck is getting ready to leave. Do you want the orchestra on this truck or should they continue playing until. . ."

"The orchestra?" Heinrich almost shouted.

"Yes, sir, the orchestra. You said-"

"That's it." Heinrich said under his breath.

". . . that you wanted them back at 117 by 4pm. It is almost 3:30 now." Klein continued not knowing if the Colonel was even listening.

"The orchestra," he repeated to himself again almost smiling. Now he turned his attention to the group of women chosen from the camp's main orchestra to play at the rail siding. He listened carefully as the women played Franck's Sonata A-dur. They were carrying the piece very well for only having eight musicians. As part of their duties, the orchestra was assigned the task of playing each day as the prisoners were marched off to work and again at their return in the evening. Heinrich had also instructed the orchestra to have a smaller group available to play as the trains were unloaded and the Jews were being segregated. Heinrich felt that the music would help to keep things calm, or as calm as possible while his men carried out their task quickly.

Heinrich listened again, this time shutting out all of the other noises in the rail yard. There, he thought to himself, there is the problem. The group was standing at the head of the two lines facing the new arrivals. He listened again trying to pinpoint the problem. It took several seconds before the mistake was made again.

"There!" Heinrich said out loud, "Did you hear it?"

"Sir?" Lieutenant Klein said, not knowing how to answer the Colonel's question.

Heinrich put his hand up in the air to quiet Klein and waited. It would only take a few more seconds before he would have the problem identified.

"There!" he said again this time pleased with himself for identifying the woman causing the problem.

"Sir?" Lieutenant Klein asked again.

"Wait here, Lieutenant." Heinrich ordered as he walked toward the women musicians.

Lieutenant Klein watched as Heinrich moved toward the women. When he was within five meters he removed his pistol for its holster. As he continued to close the ground between himself and the musicians, he armed it; aimed it; and fired at the back of the head of the woman to his far right. He wasn't a meter away from the woman and the shot caught the girl in the back of the head. The force of the projectile pushed the woman's head forward with such speed that Heinrich was sure he heard the woman's neck snap like a dried twig. The woman crumpled to the ground, dropping the violin.

The other women continued to play although it was several minutes before the group regained any type of composure. Heinrich stood there for several seconds before he replaced his pistol in its holster and returned to where Lieutenant Klein was standing.

"Stupid Jew!" Heinrich spat, "Didn't she think I wouldn't catch the mistakes?"

Klein did not offer an answer to his question.

"These people have to understand that I will not put up with their lies and underhandedness." Heinrich continued. "I don't have time to screen each and every one of them, but eventually I will get to hear them play and I will weed out the imposters."

"Yes, Colonel." Klein answered feeling that he needed to say something.

Chapter 12

Anna didn't know who was holding on tighter, her mother or herself. Either way neither had wanted to become separated from the other. There were hundreds of people jumping down from the rail cars being forced into lines along the side of the train by German soldiers. If it were possible, there seemed to be more confusion upon their arrival at the new camp than when they left Frankfurt.

The trip on the train had been un-bearable, the single most terrible experience Anna could ever remember, even worse than being told by Frau Klibe that she could no longer play in the orchestra. Her father had left early that morning in an attempt to get the necessary paperwork completed for the family to leave for America. The soldiers had come shortly after his leaving. Anna

and her mother had been given an hour to pack their clothing and report outside to the large truck parked in the middle of the street. It had only taken the soldiers a few hours to clear out Anna's entire neighborhood.
By 10 am she and her mother were at the rail yards where Anna's mother had to give a soldier their names for the register. Later, they were given a small piece of white chalk and made to mark their suitcases with their names. The luggage was then turned over to a young man in uniform that assured them that it would be placed in another car with the rest of the baggage. It took the young man several attempts to separate Anna from her violin case, but the youth finally won out when he promised her he would personally take care of the instrument.

By noon, she and the others were lead inside an old wooden rail car. The first thing Anna noticed was the strange musty smell that filled her nostrils upon entering. It was similar to the odor of farm animals but stronger, something totally new to Anna. Whatever the stench was it caused her to shake uncontrollably.

People were forced into the boxcar until Anna didn't think she could breathe anymore. Finally, the pushing and shoving came to a halt and Anna was glad that no one else would be entering the car. That's when another 9 people were quickly shoved into the opening and the door finally closed. Anna hoped that her violin case was being treated better than she was.

The journey was long and miserable and Anna chose to sleep as much as she could. It was the only way she could block out the pain. Sleeping worked until she began to have the nightmares.

She shuddered as she remembered the old dead lady in the boxcar with them. She had been the first to die, but more followed as the train traveled further and further away from Anna's home. Even though the train stopped several times, the doors were never opened giving them a chance to remove the dead. As more died they were gently, almost ceremoniously placed in a pile in one corner.

Anna remembered the nightmares on the train. The feeling of sleeping peacefully in her own bed until her mother would gently awake her only to open her eyes and see the old dead lady smiling wickedly at her.

"Come Anna, come lie down next to granny," She would cackle.

Anna remembered waking up screaming uncontrollably. Her mother would hold her close, rocking her, comforting her by insisting that everything would be all right. It would calm her down when her mother would reassure her that they would get through this together. Anna would then peek through her mother's arms toward the corner where they had begun to stack the dead bodies. There, the old lady seemed to be resting quietly until she invaded Anna's next dream.

Now, standing next to her mother in the blowing cold somehow felt a lot better. They had only been at the new station for less than fifteen minutes. The German soldiers had been very hateful to people, kicking them, pushing them until they were all in two lines. She, her mother and the other women were in the line closest to the now empty train on their left while the men and some younger boys were in the line to their right. German soldiers were moving up and down the lines looking for special people, skilled people to help in the camp. Some of the soldiers were shouting that skilled people would be given jobs in the new camp.

"Mother," Anna asked as the soldier past them, "are we skilled?"

Her mother only shook her head from side to side and motioned for her to remain quite.

As the men moved further down the line, Anna's attention returned to the small group of Jewish women playing in a small orchestra. The group was standing between the two lines, oblivious to what was happening around them, content in playing their music. She had been listening to them earlier, but the screaming of the soldiers had pulled her attention away. Again she listened to the small orchestra as they played Franck's Sonata A-dur. Anna was amazed at how well the small group played, most of them anyway. There were eight women, dressed in the same uniform, ranging in age from what Anna guessed to be eighteen to her mother's age. Three were playing the violin; two were on cello while the last three played the flute.

Anna's attention focused in on the three women playing the violin. Two of them seemed to be quite accomplished and from the short time Anna had been listening it seemed that they had played together for some time. The third woman was definitely struggling to keep up with the other two. She had obviously not played the violin for some time and was working at getting her rhythm back. Most of the time she played very softly, hiding under the music of the other two, but once in a while she would draw the bow incorrectly causing her instrument to cry out as if in pain.

"Mother, she's not very good." Anna said wincing at the latest mistake made by the young woman."

"Quiet, Annie," her mother whispered down to her, "These men are very dangerous."

"But, Mother. . ."

"Anna, please!"

Anna frowned as she pulled her hand away from her mother's. She wished that this lining up thing would just end so they could go to their new home and get settled in. She looked around her mother toward the other line where the men were standing. She didn't understand why the men had to stand in their own line just to get a house. There were so many people, she thought. Anna just hoped that there would be enough houses for everyone.

Suddenly, Anna's attention was drawn back to the women musicians; actually her attention was drawn toward two German soldiers standing some ten or fifteen meters behind them. The taller of the two men was definitely upset with the other man and was shouting. Anna could not make out what they were saying, but she could see that the smaller man was scared of the tall one. Anna also noticed that every time the woman musician would make a mistake it would register on the man's face. Finally, after a few more missed notes, the man turned and headed toward the woman. He knows, Anna said to herself as he continued to approach the girl.

Anna watched in disbelief as the man quickened his pace toward the woman, as if he had to reach her before she made the violin scream again. Finally, the soldier drew out his gun and pointed it at the young girl's head. The girl continued to play the violin as the man fired the gun at her. Anna stared, her eyes as large as saucers, as the young girl was shot. Anna was amazed that the expression on the woman's face never changed as her head moved forward, hit her chest, and returned to its original position. Anna watched as the girl crumpled to the ground, the violin following her.

Her eyes shifted back to the tall soldier. Now there was a smile on his face as he put his gun away and walked back toward the other man. Anna did not hear the scream escape her mother's mouth, nor did she see her mother's hands reach up to cover it before another cry escaped it. Anna became transfixed on the dead girl and the violin lying next to her. She watched as a red stream ran from under the girl's head and made its way toward the violin.

Anna's mother covered her eyes and turned her head away from the sight and in doing so missed seeing her daughter walk out of the line and over toward the girl. Anna moved as if in a trance, having to step around a passing German soldier to get closer to the dead girl. She stood staring at the woman for several more seconds just as she had at the old dead women on the train. Still not sure what she was doing, Anna bent over and picked up the violin and bow before the blood had reached it. The feel of the instrument was amazing. She had never held such a beautiful instrument in her hands. She turned the instrument and looked for any damage. Mindlessly, she wiped several small pieces of the dead women's flesh from violin with the corner of her jacket.

"Do you play?" someone asked her as she continued to care for the instrument.

"Young lady. . ." the voice asked again this time catching Anna's attention, "do you play?"

Anna looked up at the tall German Officer and noticed that he was smiling at her. She didn't notice that he had his gun out again and was holding it in a way that hid it from her view. Anna heard the question, but was unable to answer. Instead she lifted the violin to her cheek and drew the bow across the stings.

Tchaikovsky's Serenade for Strings took flight from the bow like a flock of snow geese dancing on winter's air. Anna closed her eyes and was instantly transported back to the recital hall playing for her mother and Frau Klibe. She was so entranced by her own playing that she didn't even hear the other women in the orchestra falter and then stop playing altogether. Anna continued to play as the bow waltzed across the strings.

As they regained their confidence, the other women joined in and accompanied her to the end of the piece. Anna looked down at the violin in disbelief. Never had she had the opportunity to play such a lovely instrument.

"It's beautiful, isn't it?" Heinrich asked, noticing her interest in the violin.

"Yes," Anna answered numbly, "I've never seen such a beautiful instrument before."

"It's yours if you'd like." Colonel Heinrich smiled putting his pistol away and motioning for Lieutenant Klein to approach.

Anna looked down at the instrument again. "It's so beautiful."

"Yes," Heinrich laughed, "You've already said that. What is your name young lady?"

"Anna!" her mother screamed, finally noticing that Anna had moved away from her side. Frau Mayer had not even noticed Anna walk over to the young lady lying dead in the snow, nor did she see Anna pick up the violin and begin to play. When she noticed that Anna was no longer standing right next to her, she began to look around the lines. It wasn't until she extended her search beyond the lines that she saw her talking to the SS Officer. "Come back in line. Now! Quickly!"

"Anna Mayer." she answered with a small curtsy that Frau Klibe had taught her. "You are really going to let me keep it?" Anna added as the tall officer's words had finally sunk in.

"Anna, please come back to the line." Her mother pleaded approaching as close to the officers as she dared.

Heinrich raised his hand toward Sigrid Mayer in a motion to silence her while his eyes remained on Anna. "Well, Anna, you may keep it if you join the women's orchestra here at the camp."

Anna's heart leapt. "Join the orchestra, you have an orchestra here?"

Anna's smile was contagious. Heinrich had forgotten about the morning's trouble and was smiling himself. Anna was truly a find in this den of death. "Yes, we have a very good orchestra here, but there is always room for one more player of your caliber. Where did you learn?"

"Frau Klibe, was my music teacher." Anna beamed with pride.

"Music teacher, surely you studied professionally somewhere. How old are you?"

"I am fourteen, Sir."

"Only fourteen? You look, ahhmm, older."

"Sir," Lieutenant Klein interjected, "The standing order is that no one under the age of fifteen be allowed to enter the camp."

Colonel Oust's eyes narrowed as the smile left his face. "I am well aware of the orders surrounding this camp, Lieutenant. I am also aware of a request from Berlin that is sitting on my desk right now, looking for able-bodied officers. Seems that some of the combat units are short line officers."

Lieutenant Klein paled. "Sir, I was merely suggesting that we, ah, update her paper-work to show her correct age of fifteen."

Heinrich did not bother to comment on Klein's statement, but instead returned his attention back toward Anna."

"Where were we, Anna?"

"Sir, you were asking me about my music schooling. I was still in primary school, but I had already been requested to attend the Frankfurt Conservatory for Music."

"Frankfurt Conservatory," Heinrich snorted, "And how were you going to attend the conservatory, my young Anna?"

"I was going to start working with Professor Guttmann at the Conservatory during the summers until I completed my schooling."

"Professor Guttmann! You were going to study with Professor Guttmann?"

"Yes, sir." Anna answered a little unsure why the Officer was so upset. Wasn't Professor Guttmann any good with music? "I didn't get a chance to play with him though."

Oust looked down at young Anna. "I am truly sorry that you did not get to study with Professor Guttmann, Anna. He is a wonderful musician and

Conductor. He would have done wonders for your playing."

"Yes, sir." Anna thought back to the last day at school when Frau Klibe told her about being kicked out of school. "I like nothing better than playing the violin."

"Well Anna, so you shall. I am going to have this Officer," Oust said pointing toward Klein, "Lieutenant Klein will take you to a place where you can get cleaned up and join our orchestra." Oust turned to Klein briefly, "personally get her through registration, Lieutenant," Oust said as he prepared to walk away.

"Come with me, Anna. We have to take care of some paper-work." Klein stated as he guided Anna away from the women's line.

Anna was so happy that she would be allowed to play again. Her mother could be proud once again. "Wait!" Anna blurted out, "My Mother. My Mother has to come with me."

Anna broke away from Klein and ran back into her mother's arms. "Mother, you have to come with me. They want me to play in the orchestra."

Frau Mayer grabbed Anna tightly and wept freely into Anna's coat. "Liebling."

"Anna, you must come with me now." Klein said softly although firmly.

"But, my mother must come too." Anna pleaded.

Lieutenant Klein looked over to where Colonel Oust had stopped when Anna had broken away from Klein. Oust looked at Anna for several seconds and then at her mother. Finally, Oust looked at Klein and shook his head. "Place her in the line to the right." Oust ordered.

Klein understood all too well that the right line was designated for those prisoners going directly to the gas chambers. "Anna," Klein said softly as he knelt down along-side Anna, "You mother cannot come with you right now."

"No! My mother has to come with me."

"Anna, your mother is not in the orchestra. I have to take you to register and get your uniform."

"Mother can come with me - she won't be in the way. I promise." Anna pleaded as tears welled up in her eyes.

"I'm afraid not, Anna." Colonel Oust interjected "Your mother must stay in line with the others if she is to get housing for the two of you."

Anna blinked the tears away, trying to understand what the tall officer had just said. "Mother will get us a house?"

"If she stays here in line, yes." Colonel Oust said adding a reassuring smile.

"And then I can be with her after I get my uniform?"

"Of course, Anna. So give your mother a kiss and let's get you registered. It will only take an hour or so and then, by that time, your mother should have your new house."

Anna looked up at her mother. There were tears as large as teacups running down her cheeks, but there was a smile across her lips.

"Go, Anna," She prompted, "I will stay here and take care of the housing. You go and get registered in the orchestra."

Anna released her grip on her mother's coat. "Did you see the beautiful violin the nice officer gave me?"

"Yes, it is wonderful. You must take special care of it." Her mother said fighting back the tears. "Now, go. Make me proud."

Anna gave her mother a hug and then took Klein's hand. "I won't be long, Mother. I promise. I can't wait to see our new home."

Anna continued to hold on to Lieutenant Klein with one hand and her new violin with the other. Every so often she would look back over her shoulder at her mother standing in the line and waved. For a brief moment she became angry with her father for not being able to be there and hear her play in the new orchestra at the camp, but then her thoughts warmed as she hoped he would be alright and somehow find her and mother. Then there would be plenty of time for him to hear her play.

Anna was taken to see Corporal Ingel where she received her tattoo. Anna cried when it was applied to her skin.

Her mother cried as the guards forced her into the cold mud and beat her for no apparent reason.

While Anna's beautiful dark curls were trimmed, leaving her hair just above her shoulders, her mother's head was shaved down to the bare skin.

While Anna was being fitted for the camp orchestra uniform, her mother was made to strip off all of her clothing and was ridiculed by passing guards.

While Anna was allowed to shower and remove the filth and dirt of her long ordeal, her mother was forced into an overcrowded chamber where poison gas was administered.

Anna thought about being with her mother as the warm water ran over her body draining away the filth and stink. Her mother thought about Anna and cried out for her baby, as the life was drained from hers.

Chapter 13

He could never love this place, Aaron thought as he looked around his new home. It was nothing like his home in Germany, nothing like any home he had ever visited. It was missing everything, a front porch where his mother would wait for him to come home from school, a warmly lit kitchen with the wonderful smell of the evening meal being prepared and the smell of scented soap as his mother whisked by him carrying a hot baking sheet.

Instead of front porches, there were guard towers where the guards always peered down at you over the barrel of a machine gun. The mess barracks was poorly lit serving carelessly prepared food and the entire camp had a musty smell that reminded him of rotting vegetation. He would never want to stay here one minute more than he had to. He would never want to come back if he ever had a chance to escape this awful place.

Aaron looked through the double strands of barbed wire that separated him from the outside, the concrete poles towering over him holding the electrified wire. When it rained, like now, he could actually hear the electricity racing through the wire. Sometimes, he listened to the humming of the wire as if it was calling him like the Sirens songs from the tale of Odysseus that his grandfather had read to him so many times. The Sirens of the wire called to him softly, tempting him to approach and touch, while at the same time warning him of the death that awaited him if he did. Aaron worried that one-day he might give in to the Sirens and fall victim to their trap as the ancient sailors had in the Odyssey.

Aaron blinked several times to clear his head of the wire's song. He looked left and right along the barbed wire. He glanced up at the towers where the German guards peered down upon him, guns ever ready. He gazed back at the wire and then again to the guard tower. It would be hard to say which would kill him first, he thought, the sirens of the wire or the dark angels that manned the towers.

He continued to walk toward his new home, a wooden building that he shared with 400 other men. Again, he thought of his mother and their home back in Germany. His stomach tightened with every step. Some of it was from the hunger he felt, but he knew that his returning to the barracks caused much of the sick feeling. He hated going back to the barracks more than going to work; at least at his work-station he had more room. In the barracks there was little space for 400 men to do anything. Aaron spent most of his time lying in his bunk that he shared with his Grandfather and one other man.

Aaron tried to remember the name of his other bunk mate. The previous occupant had died two days ago and his place had been quickly filled by the newcomer, his name, Aaron couldn't remember. They changed so quickly. Most of the men in the barracks worked in the stone quarry that was six miles from the camp. Every morning at 4:30 they were all rousted out of bed and made to report to morning roll call. Aaron and the other "special workers" were taken off to a separate place for their roll call. Because there were less than forty of them, their roll call only lasted a few minutes. Aaron had watched the main camp roll call take hours. There were over 6,000 prisoners in their satellite camp, approximately 4,300 men and 1,700 women. It was hard to tell the exact numbers as men and women died every day and every day new prisoners were brought in. Aaron had no way of knowing the exact count, but he knew the SS guards knew. They knew everything.

Each morning was the same. The camp orchestra would quickly assemble at the main gate and begin to play. As if on cue, the men would be marched out to the rock quarry while the women were marched toward the farming area. It didn't matter which area you were assigned to, there was death waiting at both sites. It was only the special workers like Aaron and his grandfather that had a good chance of making it through the day. Of course the orchestra also had a good chance. They were assigned to play each morning when the prisoners left for work and again in the evening for those who returned. During the rest of the day the members of the orchestra were either practicing or assigned to other tasks within the camp.

"You continue to day-dream like that and drag your feet; Bella will beat you into the ground."

Aaron jumped as he looked up at Ira, the blokowy[2] for his barracks. Ira had been in the camp for almost 7 months when Aaron and his grandfather had first arrived. Ira had an informal power in the camp, as did all of the blokowy's of the other barracks. The SS used the block leaders to maintain order among the prisoners and as long as the blokowy's kept order they had power. Within the confines of the wire, the blokowy's had freedom of movement and usually had the easier work assignments.

"I didn't know I was dragging my feet." Aaron answered defensively.

"You won't know when Bella walks up behind you and cracks open your skull with his ax handle either. You're stupid even for a zugang[3]."

Aaron's stomach lurched at the mention of Sergeant Bella's name. The man encompassed everything that Aaron had been taught was evil. Since his first encounter with Bella at the reception station, he had done his best to stay away from the man. Bella didn't need a reason to beat a prisoner; he would simply invent a reason when the need arose. Aaron shook uncontrollably

---

[2] Blokowy: The male prisoner in charge of a block or barracks. The term was used to mean "block senior," "block leader," "block supervisor," or "block elder"

[3] Zugang: German term for "new arrival" within the camp system.

at the thought of Bella's ax handle, his pet he called it. The shaft of the handle was made from the trunk of an oak tree and was almost three feet in length. Either end of the club had been blackened by either the dirt and sweat from Bella's hands or, in the case of the other end, the blood of some prisoner that had managed to fall victim to Bella's anger. Aaron had already witnessed its use on a poor man that had the nerve to attempt to fix his shoe without getting Sergeant Bella's permission.

At times Bella carried the stick proudly in his right hand as if it were the scepter of his high office and at other times he would wield the stick as gracefully as any conductor might, directing his orchestra with his baton. However he carried it, the stick was as deadly a weapon as any in the camp. Bella took great pleasure in extending the beatings he would administer with his ax handle, sometimes only poking or prodding the victim with the end of the stick while he taunted them. On one occasion he made the unfortunate man carry the handle around all morning. Following several steps behind, the man was made to carry the stick away from his body in his outstretched hands as Bella continued on his morning rounds. Finally he took the handle from the man and beat him with it, laughing the entire time. He didn't let up until the man's face could no longer be recognized. Bella then, puffing like an over worked oxen, cleaned the handle off on the dead man's clothing and went on about his business.

On other occasions, like the one with the man fixing his shoe, Aaron had seen him knock the man clean off his feet with a single blow, killing him before he hit the ground again. Bella never looked happier than when he was beating someone with the handle.

"I'm sorry, Ira, you are right." Aaron said as he hurried into the barracks.

"Of course I'm right, ass." Ira spat, "If it happens again I'll beat you myself."

Although Aaron had only been in the camp for two weeks, he understood Ira's threat. Sometimes the blokowy took the same punishment as the prisoner who had angered the SS guards. Ira would rather beat Aaron than have to share in the punishment at the hands of a guard.

"Why are you so late? Your grandfather and the others have been back for almost an hour."

"I had to stay behind and clean the work area."

"Alone?"

"Yes, alone."

Ira motioned for Aaron to come closer to him. When he was only inches away from Aaron, Ira bent in a little closer. "Never let yourself get broken away from the group like that, Aaron. Buddy up with someone and stay together. You must learn to protect yourself at all times. The SS guards are not the only threat in this camp. Understand?"

Aaron looked directly into Ira's eyes. There was wisdom there beyond Ira's outward appearance. Prior to his seven months in Camp 117, Ira had been in Auschwitz or one of the other satellite camps for two years now. In the ways of the camp he was much smarter than even his grandfather. Aaron knew that, deep down, Ira liked him; he could feel it.

"Yes," Aaron whispered, "thank you."

"Now go on." Ira said with a toss of his head.

Aaron walked into the wooden building that had become the center of his life and moved between the endless rows of bunks until he reached the one that he shared with his grandfather. His grandfather was not in the bunk, but Aaron already knew that. Samuel would be meeting with the other men in their barracks that made up the elders. Samuel was quickly brought into the fold upon arrival and had become good friends with Ira and the others. Aaron knew when to approach the men and when to stay away. He didn't know what the men talked about, but he was just as happy not to know. Around the concentration camp too much information about the wrong things could get you beaten or worse, killed.

Aaron grabbed the rim of the top bunk and placed his foot up onto the lower bunk in order to climb up into his area. He had just pulled himself up level with his bunk when the attacker moved forward from the rear for Aaron's bunk, grabbing him on the hand.

"Gotch ya!" the attacker yelled as he tightened his grip on Aaron's hand.

Air rushed out of Aaron's lungs in a steady stream of fear and desperation as he tried to figure out what to do next. His hand was frozen on the bed rail, trapped there by his assailant's hands. His eyes darted back and forth between the dark shadow of his assailant and the area where his grandfather and the other men were standing. Aaron hadn't even noticed that he had let out the scream, but when it had come to an end, the room was filled with laughter.

"I got you good, Aaron!" David said between laughs.

Aaron finally recognized the beaming face belonging to one of the other special workers in his group, David.

David had been in the camp for eleven months now and was assigned to the print and plate shop. Like him, David had come up through the apprentice system working in his father's business. David's father had been a member of the Polish militia and was called up to fight the advancing Germans. His father never returned from the battle front and David was soon arrested by the SS and placed in jail. It was David's masterful skill at engraving and printing that saved him from being taken out behind the police station and shot with the other prisoners. It was those same talents that had got him into the special work group here in the camp.

"That wasn't funny, David!" Aaron hissed as he looked over at the barrack Elders. It was obvious that they were both annoyed and amused at the prank. They quickly went back to the conversation leaving Aaron and David to themselves.

"You should have seen your face."

Aaron rubbed his hand. "You should look at your own face."

David was only sixteen, and like himself, with thick black eyebrows covering his burnt almond colored eyes. Also like Aaron, his hair had been shaved from his head giving it a slightly lopsided egg -shaped appearance. His ears were small and lay close to his head. His voice cackled as he spoke.

"If you need to go outside and clean your underwear, I'll understand."

Aaron scowled at him. "It looks like they've already been cleaned using your face."

David's smile diminished. "What's wrong with my face?"

"It's covered in black ink. Did you get any on the paper today?"

David wiped his face on the sleeve of his prison uniform. The movement only managed to smear the ink further.

"One of the presses got jammed and I had to work on it." He answered in defense.

"Well they could have used your nose as one of the rollers."

A smile broke out on David's face. "Well, at least it's honest dirt, my Dad used to say."

Now Aaron smiled. His grandfather had said almost the same words to him many times.

"What are you doing up in my bunk?"

"I was waiting to scare you, stupid. Boy it was hot up here. I thought you would never arrive."

Aaron jumped up into the bunk next to David. "Had to clean the stupid shop. Where is everyone else?"

"Ira said he heard that the men in the quarry hadn't made their quota yet. He heard Bella screaming that they would stay there all night if they didn't meet it soon."

"Bella was here?" Aaron asked trying to control his quivering.

David rolled over on his back and looked up at the ceiling. "No, Ira heard him screaming as he got into a truck headed out toward the quarry."

"That won't be good for them."

The smile on David's face vanished as he looked over at Aaron. "No. . .it won't."

Both boys knew that some of the men would not make it back from the quarry this evening; both tried not to think of whom it might be.

Chapter 14

Klas stared out of the staff car's window as the vehicle bounced down the country road. Some of the surrounding area looked familiar to him, but he was almost certain he had not been there before. His last trip to Poland had been a quick one in the turret of his Panzer. Now sitting in the backseat of the staff car everything looked different. Maybe it was the difference of the height, he thought. He had a much more commanding view from the top of his tank than he did slouched down in the rear seat.

Trees and burned out farms were the extent of the view along the road. Twice now he had seen a train pass on the tracks along-side the road. Both trains contained twenty or so cars and no guards in sight. He didn't need to guess what the cargo of either train was. The people jammed up against the small barred windows on either side of the cars told him that they were packed with prisoners headed for Auschwitz.

For some reason, at that moment, thoughts of Alfred Shone popped into his head. He hadn't thought about Alfred since school when they played on the school soccer team together. Alfred was lanky, not what one would have pictured when thinking of a soccer player, but he was one of the best players Klas had ever played with. There was even talk about Alfred playing for the national team one day. Of course his being Jewish crushed any chance of that ever happening. He wondered if Alfred might be on a train like one of these or in one of the hundreds of concentration camps being built around the Third Reich. Maybe he and his family had left Germany altogether, they had money.

He pushed the thought of Alfred and his school days out of his head and returned to his current problems. In some ways, he thought, there wasn't much difference between the train cars and the car he rode in now.

He had spent the last two weeks of his leave trying every avenue he knew to undo the damage his father had done to his career. As always, his father had been very thorough in assembling his plan. Every door Klas tried to open was either barred or quickly shut. So much so, that just two days before he was to ship out he received a telephone call from the office of Reichsführer Himmler asking if there was a problem with his orders. When Klas assured the Aid that everything was in order, the officer very politely reminded him that this assignment came directly from the

Reichsführer himself and that if he needed anything else before leaving, he should not hesitate to contact the Reichsführer's office directly. Klas did not need to be run over by a tank to understand that he had been out gunned.

He looked down at the briefcase on the seat next to him with a forced grin. Shackles come in many different forms, he thought. The orders tucked away inside the briefcase were just as confining as any barbed wire fence. He glanced up at the rearview mirror.

"How much further, Sergeant?"

The driver's eyes met his in the mirror. Just around the next stand of trees there, Captain. The main administration buildings are on the left as we enter the compound."

Klas half-heartily looked over the seat and through the windshield as they made the last turn toward the main gate. The car slowed down only momentarily as it was cleared past the checkpoint. The driver's eyes were back in the mirror.

"The house to your right there Captain is the camp commander's home. And up ahead on the right is the main guardhouse. The building on the left is the camp's administration building. That's where we're headed."

Klas looked around at the different work details consisting of all male prisoners. "How many prisoners are here?"

"I'm not sure, Sir. I've heard as many as 20,000. Maybe more by now."

The sedan started to make the turn to the left when suddenly Klas was thrown forward in his seat. "Damn!" the driver hissed as he leaned on the horn.

Klas instantly surveyed his surroundings for the cause of the trouble as any seasoned tank commander would. It was evident that the driver had failed to see a small work crew standing in the street and almost hit them.

"Move out of the way." He screamed through the windshield.

Quickly the guards assigned to the crew began to push and kick the prisoners out of the way. Those not moving quickly enough were beaten. Soon, the driver was clear of the group.

"I'm sorry for that, Captain. Are you alright?"

Klas regained his seating and adjusted his jacket. "Yes, fine." he mumbled.

"There are so many work groups around here these days it's hard not to run over one of them and I would too, except for all the paper work I would have to fill out on the damage done to the sedan. Damn Jews."

"It's OK, Sergeant. That's the most excitement I've had in several months."

The car glided into the parking slot designated for official vehicles and staff cars only. Almost before the vehicle had come to a complete stop, the driver was out opening Klas' door.

"Through there, Captain." He said pointing to the entrance of the building.

Klas grabbed his briefcase and checked around the backseat for any belongings that might have fallen to the floor after the abrupt stop.

"Are-"

"Yes, Sir. I'll be waiting right here for you."

Klas smiled and moved toward the door.

It was only a matter of seconds before Klas was standing in front of a desk manned by a portly looking corporal. The corporal awkwardly managed to get to his feet while tucking his shirt back into his trousers.

"Heil Hitler!" he said extending the proper salute.

Klas returned the salute without speaking.

"Good morning, Captain. May I help you?"

Klas studied the man for several seconds wondering if the man could ever have fitted into a turret of a Panzer. The corporal, noticing Klas' inspection of him, attempted to straighten his uniform. Klas dismissed the thought and cleared his throat.

"Yes, Corporal, Captain Von Reichman reporting for duty."

"Oh, yes, Captain, you are a little early, but we have been expecting you. If you'll have a seat over there I will inform the commandant that you are here."

"Is there a washroom where I can freshen up first?"

"I'm sorry, sir. I should have asked." the corporal answered, face flushing, "It is straight down the hall. First door on your left."

Klas turned and looked down the hall. "Thank you."

"I'll make sure the commandant knows of your arrival."

"Of course." Klas answered as he moved down the hall toward the open door.

Turning into the washroom, Klas almost ran over a small prisoner standing just inside the door. Without a moment's hesitation the man snatched the cap from a-top his head and held it in both hands in front of him. Simultaneously he lowered his head and stepped back out of the way. Klas stepped around the man and walked over to the urinal. Several times he looked over his shoulder at the man who had not attempted to move. Klas could tell from where he was standing that the man was shaking uncontrollably as if he were expecting Klas to attack him at any moment. He finished at the urinal and walked over to the washbasin and ran warm water over his hands and then his face. The shaking figure was still in the mirror, eyes gazing at the floor, cap still being held in both hands when Klas looked up. Klas looked at his uniform in the mirror and straightened up his appearance. He turned and intended to leave the room without looking at the prisoner again, but at the last second glanced over his shoulder. The man was still looking at the floor but his hands were moving toward his head, the prison cap unsteadily making its way toward the man's bald head. Klas wondered what was holding the man up.

"Captain Von Reichman?"

"Yes." Klas answered as he looked over his shoulder one more time at the little man then back at the Lieutenant standing in front of him.

"Heil Hitler!" the man saluted.

"Heil Hitler, Klas replied as he returned the salute.

"I am Lieutenant Schneller, Colonel Höss' aid. The commandant will see you now." He said as he moved away from Klas and back toward the front entrance.

Klas followed the Lieutenant back past the Corporal and into the office of the camp commandant.

"Commandant." The Lieutenant started.

Colonel Höss turned to face Klas. Klas guessed Höss to be in his late thirties; shorter than he had expected and carrying a few extra pounds, but what immediately caught Klas' attention was his eyes. There was a haunting look about them, cold and indifferent. They held a look that Klas had only seen on the battlefield. It was the look of a soldier that, one morning while shaving, had seen his own death staring back at him in his mirror. Men, who often thought they were going to die in battle, did. But Colonel Höss was different, he seemed to be a man who already knew his fate but was unsure of how to get there.

Klas caught himself and snapped to attention.

"Heil Hitler!"

Höss returned the salute half heartedly. "Lieutenant, you may leave us." Höss' voice was soft and even.

Without speaking again, the Lieutenant saluted and left the office.

"I would normally ask a new officer coming in under my command to have a seat and we would get to know each other, but that will not be the case here today, Captain."

"Colonel?" Klas asked, his forehead wrinkling slightly.

Höss raised his hand, stopping Klas from speaking further.

"Captain," Höss started again as he walked toward a large map covering one of the walls. "Up until now you have been under the impression that you were coming here to Auschwitz to work under my command."

"That is correct. Sir." Klas answered not knowing what else to say.

"I have been charged with, not only, the construction of this camp, but its administration also. The camp currently houses some 18,000 prisoners. In three to five years that will double, maybe more. Later this year I will start construction on Auschwitz II northwest of this site. It will hold another seventy to eighty thousand prisoners. As it is now, I have very little time to spend with my wife and children." He added as an after-thought.

Höss stepped closer to the map. "There are over thirty satellite camps," he continued, "covering the countryside containing work groups laboring in rock quarries, gravel pits, clinker[4] works and numerous other industries. There are another thirty that are scheduled to be built." As Colonel Höss turned to face Klas again he made a vague gesture toward the map now behind him. "All these camps report up through a system of camp administrators to me, except one."

"The one I will be assigned to." Klas volunteered.

Höss smiled weakly, his eyes unchanging. "That is correct, Captain, except the one that you have been assigned to. It looks and operates just like all of the other camps but you will not find it on the camp register, nor will you find it on any of the maps here or in Berlin. But it's out there."

"And the function of this camp."

The Colonel's eyes shot through Klas like molten steel. "I told you, Captain, it is not under my jurisdiction. What goes on at that camp is the business of Lt. Colonel Heinrich Oust and the office of the Reichsführer. My only task is to supply Colonel Oust with the prison labor he requires and *that* I have plenty of."

---

[4] Clinker works: Facility that produce bricks for construction.

"Then, Sir, why this meeting?"

"Because from time to time you will be required to visit this camp in the performance of your duties. For the rest of the morning you will be shown around the camp and will take a tour of the Birkenau facility. After lunch. . ."

"Excuse me, Sir." Klas interrupted, "Birkenau?"

"Yes, Birkenau - Auschwitz II."

"I see."

"The Lieutenant who brought you in here, Lieutenant Schneller, will be at your disposal for the rest of the morning and through lunch. After lunch your driver will take you to see Colonel Oust." Höss walked toward the door. "Is there anything else, Captain?"

"I'm sorry, Sir, but you still have not told me why I am in your office."

Colonel Höss' face became void of any expression. It was several long seconds before he began to speak again. "You will be Colonel Oust's second in command, Captain. The work force you will be in charge of will have a direct bearing on many high-ranking officials in the 3rd Reich, including myself. So let's say that I have a vested interest in you and your work."

"I see." Klas answered, knowing that he had just been told to shut up and move on.

Klas reached for the door handle and stopped just short of it when Colonel Höss' hand reached it first.

"Captain, this is my fate, here in Auschwitz. Yours is out there with Colonel Oust. I don't expect to see you in my office again. For that matter, I don't expect to see you until after the war, if at all."

Klas stared into the dead eyes one more time looking for some type of understanding; there was none. "Thank you, Colonel. You have been most kind."

Chapter 15

Either Colonel Höss had down played the size of the Auschwitz facilities or, more likely, Klas had not been able to fully grasp what the man was trying to tell him. After touring the Auschwitz I facility and then taking a tour of the construction site of Auschwitz II there was no comparison between the two. The newer facility was at least ten times as large as the camp where he had met with Höss. The thought of entire villages or towns being scraped off the face of the Earth to make way for a single concentration camp made him sick. He could only think of the amount of money and labor being wasted in what he considered non-essential to the war effort.

Klas had not shared his thoughts with Lieutenant Schneller. The man seemed very impressed with the work they were doing here and Klas saw no reason to tell him differently. It was a pity that Schneller had not had a chance to see the real German Army in action. He would have seen their project for what it truly was, a waste of military men and supplies. The tour of the camps only gave Klas more incentive to find a way back to the front. Whatever this was here in Poland, it was no longer military and the quicker he could get back to a fighting unit the happier he would be.

Klas got out of the car and walked up to the front of the administration building of Camp 117. The ride to 117 was very short, but gave him time to reflect on what he had seen and what his next steps would be when he met Colonel Oust. He had even thought of allowing himself to be busted down in rank if it would assure his transfer out of Poland.

"Captain Von Reichman reporting, Colonel." The young sergeant said as he and Klas entered the Colonel's office.

Colonel Oust was sitting at a very large desk strategically placed in the center of the room. He was busy working on a mountain of paper-work that managed to cover one end of the desk to the other. While Klas was able to quickly recognize some of the forms, others were totally foreign.

Klas stood at attention waiting for Colonel Oust to look up and acknowledge his presence. It was several minutes before he finally put his pen down and looked up at him.

"Heil Hitler!" Klas said, extending his best salute. Klas was startled at the resemblance he and Colonel Oust shared. Even seated Klas figured the Colonel to be a bit taller than himself, but the hair; eyes and facial features were very similar.

Heinrich extended his arm in a half-hearted salute. "Heil Hitler." He added as an afterthought.

Heinrich took a few seconds to look Klas over from top to bottom. Klas noticed that the Colonel took special notice of his Knight's Cross as well as his other combat awards. It hadn't taken Klas nearly as long to see that the Colonel had no combat awards on his jacket.

Heinrich finally managed a curt smile and extended his hand toward Klas. "Welcome, Captain, we have been anxiously awaiting your arrival. Reichsführer Himmler speaks highly of you."

Klas did not know if Colonel Oust was testing him. Was he trying to see if Klas knew Reichsführer Himmler personally or was he trying to see if Klas would attempt to lie about his relationship with the Reichsführer? So it was going to be a battle of wits, he thought.

"I am disappointed to have to tell you that I have never met the Reichsführer, Colonel. He was scheduled to personally award me the Knight's Cross, but was called away." Klas said feeling quite good about being able to mention the fact that he had the Knight's Cross.

"Yes," Heinrich said extending his hand again, "Congratulations on your award. I understand that the rest of your crew received theirs posthumously, is that correct?"

The smug feeling drained out of Klas faster than milk from a spilt pitcher.

"That is correct, Colonel. I was just as disappointed that I was not able to give the awards to their families in person."

Heinrich studied Klas' face for several seconds before firing the next volley. "Yes, that would have been the proper thing to do, but unfortunately, our duties keep us from performing such ceremonial tasks." Heinrich walked back to his desk and took a seat in the expensive leather chair. "You know, Captain, for a minute I thought you were going to say that you wished that you had died with your crew."

Klas' mind quickly evaluated the situation and within seconds answered Heinrich without faltering. "I would never have thought of such a thing." Klas answered smoothly, knowing that he was lying and that a hundred times he wished that he had died with his men. "They were a fine combat crew, but my death would not have added anything to their own deaths. They died as soldiers, fighting for the Fatherland. I was spared so that I may continue their fight."

Heinrich smiled as only the cleverest of foxes could. "Continue their fight from the inside of a tank or from behind a desk?"

Klas felt the blood drain from his face. There was no doubt that Colonel Oust had spoken to someone back at the Reichsführer's office if not Reichsführer Himmler himself. Klas' mind spun as he searched for possible answers to the question. After exploring numerous dead ends, he decided to answer truthfully. "I would prefer to do it from inside the turret of a tank, Colonel. That is what I was trained for. That is what I do best."

"What you do best!" Heinrich quipped, "Your men were all killed, and you were seriously wounded, almost killed. Your wounds could possibly have left you paralyzed and that is what you do best?"

"A sniper, Colonel, killed my men; he had his choice of at least four tanks to fire at. In the end it was mine that he picked as a target. I'm not angry with him for what he did was an act of war. My men died in an act of war. We did our best every day and given the chance to command a tank, I would again do my best."

"And here." Heinrich said waving his hand in an elaborate gesture, "will you do your best here, Captain?"

"I am a professional soldier, Colonel Oust, I go where I am told to go and perform the duties I am assigned. If that is what you are asking, then yes, I will do my best, but if you are asking me where I would rather be assigned, then the answer would be back to a combat armor division."

Klas stood at attention as Heinrich digested what Klas had just told him. The man showed no emotion as his mind replayed the conversation, every word Klas had said, every facial expression Klas had made. Finally, Heinrich relaxed somewhat and sighed. "You have been assigned here, Captain, because you are the best. You have shown beyond any doubt that you are a good combat soldier, but you have also shown your superiors more than that. You have shown them that you are capable of more than getting shot at in a tank."

"Sir. . .I"

Heinrich raised his hand in a peremptory fashion, "Hold your tongue, Captain. That wasn't meant in a derogatory manner. You have become an asset to the 3rd Reich and especially to the Reichsführer."

Klas wondered if Colonel Oust knew that his father had set his appointment up in order to keep him from being killed. He wondered how the Colonel would feel about him knowing that his family thought he was a bigger asset to them than to the 3rd Reich.

"I am pleased to hear that, Colonel." Klas lied.

Heinrich studied Klas' face, he wasn't sure that Klas had meant what he had just said but he decided to continue. "Your assignment here is as important as any you could have been given Captain. But let me make something very clear to you, here and now. When you walked through that door there was no turning back. You are here until you are relieved of your command duties or you die."

Klas wondered if he had really heard what the Colonel had just said. If he wanted out of this unit, it would be as a corps? He thought of asking for clarification, but decided against it. "Well, Colonel, that is very straightforward." Klas said instead, "Can I ask what my duties will be here, and if it is not a breach of security, what we are doing?"

Heinrich stood up from his desk and straightened his jacket. In doing so he took the opportunity to give Klas the once over one more time. "We will have plenty of time for that this evening, Captain. You will be dining with me and the other officers under my command at my quarters. In the meantime I will have someone show you to your quarters."

"That would be very kind of you Sir." Klas answered.

Heinrich reached out and offered Klas his hand. "Welcome to Camp 117, Captain. I am sure you will serve us well and I have no doubt that your service here will only help to enhance an already promising career."

Klas shook Heinrich's hand noticing for the first time that his hand was rough and callused, his grip matching his own. He would have thought that the Colonel's hands would have been much softer, used to the pen instead of the pick.

"Thank you, Sir." Klas said saluting, "Heil Hitler."

Heinrich returned the salute and gestured to the door.

"Oh, and Captain," he added as an after-thought.

Klas turned in the doorway. "Sir."

"Have the Lieutenant show you over to the Quartermaster's office. You will need to replace that pink piping around your shoulder straps. The proper color here is the light brown piping."

Klas face flushed at the mention of his pink piping. Ever since Officers training Klas had been proud to wear the pink piping denoting his service in the Waffen SS tank division. The Colonel's remark was meant to remind him that he was now to wear the light brown color denoting his affiliation with a unit assigned to the concentration camps.

He's just trying to castrate me one more time, Klas thought to himself as he smiled.

"Yes, Sir. I will make sure we include a stop to the Quartermaster before the day is out. Anything else, Colonel?"

Heinrich shook his head in a negative manner as he returned to his desk.

"See you at 19:30 hours for dinner, Captain."

Chapter 16

Oberfeldwebel[5] Christopher Bella, Waffen-SS, stood on the platform over-looking the morning roll call. Bella was not a tall man at 5′ 6″ nor was he in any way to be considered good looking or attractive. His massive frame came from years of stuffing his face with meats and breads, washing it all down with large tankards of beer. Before he had ever experienced the joy of killing anyone, he had turned to food to help comfort his frustration and pain. It wasn't until later on in his life that he discovered that killing was a much better way to make himself feel better although he never lost his taste for rich foods and drink.

[5] Senior Non-commissioned officer. The rank of Sergeant often held by the platoon leader.

Christopher Bella was raised in the southern town of Stuttgart, the only son of Fredrick Bella, a poor butcher, who, through hard work and a little cheating on the scales, was able to provide a miserable living for his wife, Nanna, his three daughters, Brita, Sigrid, and Trude and of course Christopher.

Not only was Christopher not planned, but also by the time he was born his Mother and Father had exhausted all of their parental assets on the other children. There was little left for him whether it was food, clothing, love or understanding. It wasn't his fault that he was the last-born nor was it his fault that he was the only boy in a household where all of the available clothing was female. Christopher had spent his first four years of life dressed in hand me downs from his three older sisters. His Mother would attempt to alter the clothing to give it the look of something that would belong to a little boy, but somehow she was never able to quite pull it off. So, when Christopher became five and began getting into fights with the other boys about his clothing, his Mother and Father were forced to start buying him boy's clothing. This of course put him in a bad light with his older sisters who were required to share what little money there was for buying new clothes with him.

Christopher had learned to hate the Jews very early in life. In his mind they gave him ample opportunity to do so. It was the Jewish kids at school, dressed in their nice clothing that made him feel out of place and poor. It was the Jewish mothers coming to his Fathers butcher shop always demanding bigger or better cuts of meat leaving only the scraps for him and his family while the Jewish bankers took away all of the money his Father and Mother worked so hard to make.

Christopher's hatred was not only directed toward the Jews, but also toward the rich and influential Germans who always seemed to direct him back down to his place anytime he tried to better himself. Then in 1922 he found a home in the National Socialist Party. He remained a member of the Nazi party even through Hitler's imprisonment in 1923 and became a member of the SA that same year. He enjoyed being an SA thug and soon got a reputation for being someone who could be depended on to advance the party's view at any cost. Of course, those opposing Christopher and the other SA men were always made to pay the price.

In 1925 things changed. With the formation of Hitler's personal guard unit, the SS, he saw the opportunity to enlist and did so. He found the SS much more disciplined than he cared for but his intense loyalty to Hitler enabled him to see his way through the training. After bouncing around several units he finally found a home in the concentration camp system. Keeping prisoners in line through the use of force was something he understood and excelled in. By 1938 he was a senior non commissioned officer in the prison system and had been assigned to Auschwitz.

Christopher had no particular love for any of the German Officers as many of them came from the same type of German families that had constantly put him down, but again his love for what he was doing and their common hatred for the Jews outweighed his dislike for them.

Now, huddled in front of him like spring lambs to the slaughter, Sergeant Bella was looking for his first kill of the day. They had been standing in formation for almost two hours now trying to straighten out the count. Bella had returned to the Mess Hall twice to get some more coffee and a little more of Sergeants Müller's apricot-cheese strudel, but now even the thought of more food didn't satisfy his urges.

Bella scanned the lines of Jews hoping that some brave soul would meet his gaze eye to eye. It would be all he needed to justify letting his trusty ax handle fly. If he didn't find a victim soon he would be forced to give the Corporal in charge of the count the nod to move on. The count had been correct for almost two hours now, but the Corporal was not allowed to announce it until Bella gave him the approval to do so and Bella was not about to give the approval until he had felt that the Jews had suffered enough. But now, time was running out and he would have to give his approval and release the work details to the rock quarries and vegetable fields.

Bella scanned the formation one last time then nodded to the Corporal of the Guard. The count quickly became correct and the Corporal blew his whistle, releasing the prisoners to their work details. Now Bella would be forced to go out to the quarry itself to quench his desires. That angered him. Whoever it is will pay dearly for making me come out to the quarry to find them, he thought. He wished there would be someone in the camp that he could select, but those remaining would only be those left to the special details. Bella wasn't stupid enough to kill one of them without good cause.

Chapter 17

"Yvette"

"What? What did you say?" Aaron asked missing his mouth with the spoonful of watery soup.

"I said," David repeated laughing, "Yvette."

"What are you talking about?"

"The girl you're staring at. Her name is Yvette."

They were only allowed twenty minutes to eat and get back to work in their respective shops and Aaron had wasted at least five minutes staring at the young woman sitting two tables over from where he and David were. Aaron had never seen a young woman quite like her before. She was different in so many ways. Her hair for one thing was cut short, very short not unlike a young boys hair. It was not like the other prisoners that had been shaved down to the nub. Prisoners working in their section had a much higher survival rate than those that worked in the fields or at the quarry. So much so that their hair actually had a chance to grow back, but hers was almost styled. The reddish-brown color reminded him of a fox. Her skin helped to accent her hair being as light as it was. It was pale compared to the other women, as white as the flowers on the magnolia tree in his garden back home.

Aaron wasn't sure if it was her personal features that drew his attention to her or the fact that she was covered in blotches and drips of multi-colored paints. There was paint on her smock. Some splattered across her neck and chin and even some visible in her hair. From the looks of her, whatever she had been painting, it got the best of her.

"I'm not looking at her." Aaron said as he continued to stare at her.

"No, you're not looking. You are staring. David chuckled.

Aaron blinked several times then shot David a searing look. "I wasn't staring. It is just she is such a mess with all of that paint on her."

"Oh, that. It probably has something to do with the fact that she is a painter, you know, an artist."

Aaron smiled nastily. "It's amazing, David that your pea brain can power such a clever mouth."

"Can I help it if I was born so gifted?"

"You know anything else about her." Aaron asked, ignoring David's last comment and finally getting a spoon-full of the soup into his mouth without spilling it down the front of him.

"Well she's French and she insists that she's not Jewish."

Aaron's eyes scanned the front of her blouse. There, partially visible under her paint covered smock was the yellow Star of David, just like David's and his.

"She's wearing the Star."

"I know, but she has told everyone that she's not Jewish. It seems that when she was picked up in Kraków she didn't have her papers with her. She was arrested with several friends who were Jewish."

"Didn't her friends vouch for her?"

"Of course, but they were Jewish so the Gestapo didn't believe them and arrested her as well."

"They were all brought here?"

"No, only Yvette. She thinks the others are in the main camp."

Aaron scanned her face again. "She looks so. . .distant. . .cold."

"Well she does have a pretty bad attitude, even for this place. She hates the Germans for putting her in here and she hates us for getting her in here."

"Us?" Aaron asked fishing for another bit of his meal.

"Yes, us, Jews. She feels that it's somehow our fault that she's here."

"Our fault? It's not even my fault that *I'm* here. She was the stupid one for being somewhere without her papers."

"Hmmm. . . maybe you should remind her of that when you introduce yourself to her." David smiled.

"I have no. . . "

Aaron didn't get to finish his sentence. Before he knew it, he was lying on the floor of the cafeteria covered in what was to be the rest of his meal. His head pounded from the blow he had received. His vision was slightly out of focus but he recognized the voice booming in his ear.

"You little pile of shit!" Bella wheezed, "That mouth of yours is to stuff food in and not to talk." Bella kicked in Aaron's direction but somehow missed him or so Aaron thought until he heard David cry out in pain.

"That goes for you too, pretty boy." he hissed, "If I had my way the two of you would be out in the quarry with the rest of the worthless, stinking Jews. I would love to have you out there for just one day."

Aaron knew better than to try and get up while Bella was standing over him. Any such move would end in more pain. He opened his eyes and was able to focus on David lying just a few feet from his position. Blood was leaking out of the corner of David's mouth forming a small puddle on the floor. One of his eyes was already beginning to swell.

"Now the two of you get your worthless asses off the floor and clean this mess you made," Bella said, as he began to walk off. "And if either of you are late in reporting back to work or, if when I return, I'm not happy with the condition of this room, I'll let my pet loose on the both of you."

Aaron knew that was only a threat. Bella was allowed to keep them in line, but he wasn't allowed to kill or seriously injure any of them. Their work was too precious to the SS, or at least that's what they all thought. He had heard of only one man from the special group that had actually been killed. He had been caught attempting to take food back into the barracks area. It was one of the few unbreakable rules enforced by the SS and the penalty for breaking the rules was always the same, death.

The work area of the camp was separated from the main barracks area. To enter the work area the prisoners were required to exit out of the main barracks area through a checkpoint at the rear of the barracks compound. They were then marched along a dirt road that led through the trees and into the work compound. Although the work compound could not be seen from the main barracks area they looked almost identical. It had the same looming guard towers overlooking the double fences of barbed wire. The main camp consisted of three rows of barracks whereas the work site was broken into two different parts. The first part was the main supply area containing three buildings used for warehouse storage. Across the grounds was a large "U" shaped building containing offices, the hospital, kitchen and cafeteria. The prisoners were allowed almost unlimited access to the main building.

A double wall of barbed wire again separated the second section of the camp from the first. It was there that another checkpoint was set up and again random checks of the prisoners were made. Here, again the prisoners were allowed free passage with the one stipulation that no work item was allowed out of the area. Any contraband found in the prisoner's possession was a violation of the rules punishable by death.

Aaron had heard the story many times of how the man was caught with the food and was immediately reported to Bella. Bella made all of the prisoners assemble just outside of the three warehouses where after a lengthy speech about stealing from the 3rd Reich, Bella proceeded to beat the man to death with the help of his "pet", the ax handle.

"He's gone, Aaron." Samuel said as he bent over and helped his grandson to his feet. Two other men were helping David up as well.

Aaron looked over at David who was wiping the corner of his mouth on his sleeve. Aaron did the same, wincing when the raw material of his jacket scraped across the cut in the corner of his mouth. He tried to swallow the lump that was hanging in his throat and was rewarded with the stale metallic taste of blood as it filled his mouth. He looked for somewhere to spit but he would then only have to scrub it up again so in the end he was forced to swallow it.

"Thanks, Papa"

"Are you alright?"

"Yes, I think so." Aaron said, "I didn't see him, Papa."

Samuel handed his grandson a small wet cloth. "Ah, well, with that one you had better have eyes in the back of your head."
Aaron looked over at David again.

"You OK?"

David's left eye was now swollen shut and discoloring quickly, the blood at the corner of his mouth had been wiped away, leaving a red streak across his cheek.

"Yes, I guess. Where did he come from?"

"Hell." Aaron answered bending over to pick up his chair.

"Well we better get this cleaned up or *hell* will be back." David stated, his face twisted in pain when he moved.

Several men and the two boys began to straighten up the area as the others filed out of the cafeteria on their way back to work. Aaron only looked up once from his work when Yvette was walking through the door. For a second, Aaron had caught her eye. In that brief moment Aaron saw what he thought was a myriad of expressions from the girl. Some was anger, some pain, but Aaron felt the blood drain from his face when he recognized that most of it was pity.

Chapter 18

Aaron crawled up into his bunk after first checking to see if David was hiding there again. David had the miserable habit of pulling the same joke over and over if he got a big enough laugh out of it the first time. Although the bed was nothing more than wooden planks nailed over a few support beams and then covered with the thinnest of straw mattresses, it felt good to Aaron's tired bones. He never imagined that Sergeant Bella could hit so hard with his bare hand. He shuddered at the thought of getting hit with Bella's ax handle.

Aaron subconsciously touched the corner of his mouth with his finger, instantly he pulled the finger away as a sharp pain made his lips spasm. He then removed his shoes and tied the two bootlaces together and then placed them under his jacket, which he always used as a pillow. What he wouldn't give for his pillow back home, he thought, or for that matter, his bed.

His thoughts quickly went from his bedroom at home to the kitchen where he had last seen his mother fourteen months ago on the day he and Samuel were arrested. Or at least that is how he remembered it. His mother is still standing in the kitchen cleaning up the dishes from the morning meal, he right there by her side, helping where he could. He missed his mother and often wondered what had happened to her. He knew she had no idea where he and his grandfather had disappeared to. He just prayed that she hadn't been arrested and put in a place like Auschwitz.

Aaron looked over to the corner where his grandfather and some of the men had gathered. It seemed like they were always talking, whispering about this or that. Aaron never could understand what could be so important in a place like this. He turned his attention back to where his grandfather was standing. Several of the men, including Ira, surrounded Samuel and Aaron could tell that they were listening very intently to what his grandfather was saying. In a way, it made him feel good to know that the other men in the barracks respected his grandfather. He had always thought that his grandfather was a very important man, but to see it in the eyes of others gave Aaron a feeling of pride.

The meeting didn't last much longer and soon Samuel made his way over toward Aaron. A warm smile filled his face for a moment then it was replaced with a concerned gaze.

"How's your mouth, Aaron?" He asked.

Aaron gently touched the corner of his mouth with his finger.

"Don't touch it," his grandfather warned, "Your hands are very dirty."

"Everything around here is dirty, Papa."

"All the same you shouldn't invite trouble into your house."

Aaron smiled at the proverbs Samuel was always using. Most of them made little sense but Aaron thought them funny just the same.

"I'm OK, Papa. How was your meeting?"

Samuel looked over his shoulder at where the meeting had been held. When he turned back to face Aaron, his eyes were hollow and the smile gone.

"Not well, Aaron. Many of the prisoners are either sick or too weak to work. The others believe that there will be another selection soon."

Aaron shuddered at the mere mention of the word. He had seen what the SS called selection already in his short time at the camp. The process would usually start out early in the morning. Both male and female prisoners were made to strip and parade in front of the SS doctors. With just a slight glance at the prisoner, the doctors would decide if the prisoner was fit for work or if they would be assigned to the M-12 barracks.

The camp had a total of eighteen wooden barracks buildings. Six of them were designated as W-1 through W-6 for the women prisoners and the other twelve were marked M-1 through M-12 for the men. Each barracks housed about 400 prisoners except for M-12, which was mostly kept empty. It was in M-12 that the unfit were sent to live, or die, or until there were enough of them to transport back to Auschwitz I. The SS had told them that the prisoners removed by selection were being sent back to the main Auschwitz facility where there were better medical facilities available. After a time in the hospital recovering, the prisoners would be reassigned to a work group.

No one believed this of course. In all of the time that the camp had been in operation, no one who ever left for Auschwitz ever returned from the trip. In all of the time they had been there, no one who had been transferred into Camp 117 ever came from the Auschwitz hospital. New workers always came from the same place, the trains.

"Do you think we are going to be included in the selection this time, Papa?"

"I would not worry about it. We are much too valuable to the Nazis. I think they would rather just work us to death."

Samuel winced as the words came out of his mouth and looking at Aaron's expression confirmed his suspicions.

"I was only making a bad joke, Aaron. We will be fine as long as we continue working in the shop."

Aaron relaxed a little, the color returning to his face.

"Papa, what do you and the other men talk about?"

Samuel thought about how he would answer the question if Aaron was ever to ask him. Now that it had happened he didn't know how to start.

"Aaron," he said, clearing this throat. "Living here in the camp is like living in a small city, understand?"

Aaron shook his head intent on hearing more of what his grandfather had to say.

"Well, like in any city there needs to be rules and an order about the place."

"Like the rules the SS have set up?"

"No, Aaron, not like the SS," Samuel said trying to think up some examples. "The SS are more like the weather."

"The weather Papa?"

"Yes, somewhat like the weather. You see back home we could not control whether it rained or didn't rain, right?" If it rained it rained. We could not stop it from raining nor could we control how much rain we received. The best we could do was either wear our rain coats and carry an umbrella or stay out of the rain altogether."

Aaron wasn't sure what his grandfather was getting at, but knew from experience that his grandfather would have the patience to explain it over and over again until he understood."

"What does the rain have to do with the SS?"

"The SS are just like the rain, Aaron. Here we cannot control what they do or when they do it. The best we can do is prepare ourselves for when something happens."

Aaron's thoughts returned to Bella. "I would much rather stay out of the SS rain altogether, Grandfather."

Samuel smiled. "Yes, so would I. Unfortunately, we don't have that luxury and must deal with what is given to us."

"So why the meetings, Papa?"

"Well son, we get together and try to predict when the SS will do something and see what we can do to minimize their actions."

"Like what?"

"Like making sure some of the sick people get the proper attention and, if possible, get some medication that will help them. For others we try to make sure they get a little more to eat."

Aaron thought about the kitchen workers. They were a group of the original prisoners sent to this camp to help build it. When the camp was completed, they were in the position to get the better jobs. Aaron also knew that none of them were Jewish and Bella and the other guards liked that. Each noon and in the evening they were in charge of rationing out the soup. Even he noticed that when one of the Jewish workers passed his bowl under the ladle, the man holding the ladle would only dip it in just far enough to get the watery mixture that lay on top of the soup. Then, when one of their friend's turn would come, they would dip the ladle all the way to the bottom where the richer portion of the soup lay. He and the other Jews would get a watery mixture with very little taste and certainly no vegetables while the others would get a much heartier mixture.

"What about the soup, Papa? How come you don't do something about the way they serve the soup?"

"We have talked about that son, but we don't know what we can do. There are some things we can do and there are others that are best left alone." Samuel looked around the room for a few seconds before continuing. When he felt that no one was watching he reached into his jacket.

"Here, eat this."

Aaron was amazed at the large piece of bread his grandfather pulled out from under his coat. It was the size of three or four portions.

"Papa," Aaron whispered while scanning the room, "You're not supposed to have that. You can get in trouble if you're caught."

"Then I will try not to get caught. Now take it."

"I will take a portion," Aaron said as he broke a small piece off, "You must eat some too."

"Yes, yes, later." Samuel said, as he hid the remaining piece back in his jacket.

"Papa," Aaron mumbled, as he stuffed the bread in his mouth, "You take too many risks. You know what the SS will do if they catch you."

Samuel reached out and ran his fingers through the stubble of what had been a head full of thick silky black curls. His face was weathered, his smile weak and insipid. "What more can they do to me Aaron? They have taken away my shop, my livelihood, and most of my family. They treat us worse than their dogs. They beat us more than they do the farm animals. They take away anything they can, but there is one thing they cannot take away."

Aaron immediately thought about the Commanding Officer and how he now wore his grandfather's ring.

"Papa, they will kill you if they catch you. You must stop."

"I am much too smart for that, son. I know how to stay one step ahead of them. I know what they want and how best not to give it to them."

Aaron frowned, his cheeks full of bread. "What are you saying, Papa."

Samuel placed his hands on the railing of the bunk and leaned against them, his face close to Aaron's.

"Aaron, do you remember when your mother would try and teach you how to dance, waltz? She would make you dance with your little cousin."

Aaron's cheeks reddened, still puffy from the bread he chewed. "Augh, Papa, you're not going to try and make me learn how to dance again, are you?"

Samuel's smile widened. "No son, no dance lessons. Well, maybe just one."

Aaron rolled his eyes at the thought of having to learn how to dance again.

"Remember, how clumsy you and your cousin were?"

Aaron shook his head.

"And remember how much it hurt when she stepped on your toes?"

"Yes, she always stepped on my toes. She weighed a ton!"

"Well it's kind of the same thing here with the SS."

"Papa?"

"Aaron you must be able to waltz with the Dark Angels without having them step on your toes. Let them believe that you are giving them what they want," Samuel continued, reaching out and placing his hand over Aaron's, "but never forget that what they truly want is your soul and that, they cannot have."

"Yes, Papa." He answered.

"Work for them, give them their little gold trinkets and shiny medals, but remember what they really want is to beat you down. Take away who you are, who we are as a people. We cannot let that happen, Aaron. If I can help others by bribing a guard for medical supplies or helping someone with what I can steal, I will do it. Someday you may have to do it. The Rabbi depends on me."

"Rabbi?" Aaron asked as his brow formed into several lines of wrinkles, "What Rabbi?"

Samuel closed his eyes and shook his head from side to side. "Nothing, Aaron, just the ramblings of an old man."

"Papa, you don't ramble. What Rabbi are you talking about?"

Samuel held his ground, "There is no Rabbi, Aaron."

Aaron shot straight up as if hit by lightening. "One of the other men is a Rabbi, isn't he? One of the elders."

Samuel looked around the barracks to make sure that no-one was in listening range. When he was satisfied, he leaned closer to Aaron. "You mustn't speak of this to anyone son, not even your friends."

"Papa, I swear." Aaron whispered, as he bent toward his grandfather.

"Almost two years ago, when the German Army invaded Poland, they were destroying every synagogue along the way. The temples were destroyed and the Rabbis taken out and shot."

"Why shoot them, Papa?" Aaron interrupted, "Why not send them to the camp like all the others?"

Samuel frowned as he spoke. "The SS didn't want anyone in the camp that could become a leader or organize the prisoners once they were in a camp, so they eliminated them before they had a chance to get on a train or end up here."

"Professor Levinski." Aaron interjected.

Samuel blinked several times. "What? Professor Levinski?"

"Yes, Grandfather, Professor Levinski, don't you remember? The guards shot him and the others the night we left on the train."

Samuel nodded. "Yes, yes, just like Professor Levinski."

"Okay," Aaron said prompting his grandfather to continue.

Samuel paused for a moment regaining his original line of thought. "Well, when Poland was over-run, this Rabbi decided that it was his duty to disguise himself as a common Polish Jew instead of being killed on the spot."

"You mean he didn't want to die." Aaron said flatly.

"No, son. He didn't think he could do anyone any good by dying. There is a difference."

"I don't see a difference."

"The difference is that he could continue helping our people both physically and spiritually if he were alive." Samuel paused and looked into Aaron's eyes, "Understand?"

Samuel could tell that many thoughts were running through Aaron's head as he continued. "So on the night that his synagogue was burnt to the ground, Rabbi Helfer became Ira Helfer."

Aaron's eyes grew to the size of small saucers. "Ira! Ira is really a Rabbi?"

Samuel motioned with his hand for Aaron to quiet his voice. "Yes, and you must promise me that you will never mention it again."

"OK, Papa." Is all Aaron managed to get out.

Samuel placed his hand on Aaron's shoulder. "So you see, son, the Rabbi spends all of his efforts helping those he can and I have pledged my help to him."

Aaron's head began to whirl, more than when Bella had knocked him off the chair. "Papa, no! We can't do that. We must stick together. You and

I are all we have left of our family. You can't throw that away for some strangers."

Chapter 19

David stirred the milky white liquid around in his bowl, every so often picking up a spoonful and carefully poured it back into the bowl again.

"There is no turnip in this stuff." He said curling his lip. "Have either of you found any turnip in your bowl?"

Aaron and Yvette continued to sip on their evening ration of soup. Neither wanted to talk about the meal sitting in front of them. It was easier to eat if you didn't talk about it.

"I can't even remember what a turnip looks like anymore." David continued. "Do you have any turnip in your bowl? I would like to see one; just to remember what they looked like."

"Shut up, David." Yvette finally answered. "There is no turnip in my bowl and there's no turnip in Aaron's bowl. There's probably no turnip in anyone's bowl in the entire room so just shut up about it."

David had finally introduced Yvette to Aaron and in the last two months the three had become close friends. Aaron couldn't help but like Yvette. There was something about her mannerisms that Aaron enjoyed. Yvette was more serious about her work than either he or David. Somehow she brought a good balance to the trio.

"Be thankful there isn't something floating around in your bowl that looks like turnip." Aaron added.

Yvette and David looked at Aaron then at each other and pushed their bowls toward the center of the table. There had been occasions where different objects had been discovered in the soup. Just yesterday, a friend of Samuel found part of a shoestring in his bowl. The man removed it with his fingers, stared at it for a few seconds then dropped it on the table and continued with his meal.

"Thanks, Aaron." David whispered.

"Thank yourself, David." Aaron shot back, dipping the last piece of his bread into the bowl. "If you would just eat the stuff without trying to find some hidden treasure, we all could get this. . .meal behind us."

Yvette moved her bowl closer and resumed eating in silence. David soon followed. The three continued to eat without another word about the meal. They always complained, but no one ever left a drop of the watery soup in the bowl.

"What was Bella so happy about this morning?" David asked changing the subject.

"I hardly ever talk to him." Yvette said, "Ask Aaron. The two of them are very close."

Aaron shot Yvette a searing look. Yvette just stared back at him until he looked away.

"What about that?" David said winking at Yvette.

"We never really speak," Aaron said, measuring each word, "our relationship is a simple one, he beats me. . .and. . .I fall down."

David and Yvette tried desperately to suppress the laughter. While Bella was gone the other guards rarely cared what they did as long as order was maintained, but it was never a good thing to be seen laughing. The guards could mistake it for laughing at them and that always ended in a beating.

"Damn you, Aaron." Yvette said, her chest vibrating as she attempted to internalize the laughter.

David, on the other hand began to cough out loud trying to expel some of the energy that way. His actions brought tears to his eyes.

Aaron felt quite smug in his reply to Yvette's badgering. With Samuel spending more and more time with the elders of the barracks and for that matter, the entire camp, Aaron had turned his attention to David and Yvette. They were both slightly older than him, but compared to the rest of the men and women in the camp, they were all very young. In the last few weeks Aaron had found out more about the two of them than he knew about anyone outside his own family.

He learned that David had been working as an apprentice in a print shop before the war. David had two very useful talents. First, he was an excellent engraver and plate maker. There was very little that David did not know about lithography, which brought about his second talent. David could make any printing machine run. His knack for digging into a press that was down and getting it up and running again was remarkable. The equipment in the workshop was far from the best, but David was able to keep it in top working condition.

Yvette was very different from David. The only thing Aaron was really sure about Yvette was that she was indeed French and she was an artist, oil paintings were her specialty. Yvette had a hard time deciding who she hated more, the Germans for putting her into the camp or the Jews for getting her there. Yvette had told him the same story she had told everyone else in the camp. She had been visiting a girlfriend in Poland when the Germans invaded.

She and the friend ran from the advancing German army and were able to stay hidden for several months, until one day they were arrested while digging through a garbage pile for food. Yvette had left all of her possessions behind when escaping. Yvette's girlfriend on the other hand, still had her papers in her possession when they were arrested. Since the girlfriend was Jewish, Yvette became Jewish through association. No matter how hard she tried to explain, she was forced to wear the Yellow Star of David and was treated as a Jew. Yvette and her friend remained together through the ghetto and on to Auschwitz. They had been separated at the main camp. Yvette was sent to camp 117 and her girlfriend remained at the main camp. Yvette had not seen or heard from her girlfriend since their first day in the camp.

"So, what are the two of you working on today?" Aaron asked.

Both David and Yvette stopped laughing. Both knew the danger involved with Aaron's question. Special prisoners were not to discuss what they did in their own workshops. It was forbidden to discuss the work so of course, it was always discussed in secret or when out of earshot of the guards.

The three no longer had smiles on their faces as they pretended to be eating.

"More of the same for me." David answered quietly, "They still have some of us working on forms. Forms for crossing the frontier, forms giving a person permission to be on Reich property, forms for ordering supplies, forms for ordering forms. The entire German Army cannot run without forms, I am convinced of it." He said shaking his head, "The others are working on propaganda posters supporting Hitler and the war effort."

"And you?" Yvette asked.

"As usual, a little bit of everything." Aaron said shrugging his shoulders in a helpless manner. "What about you, Yvette?"

"More of the same for me. . .reproducing the Masters. . .Making copies for the SS to sell to rich German Officers. Monet is very popular now." She answered, wiping her nose on her dirty coat sleeve. "I'm glad; I was getting tired of copying Rembrandts."

"They really sell them to Officers?" Aaron asked.

Yvette rolled her eyes. "Yes, of course they do. I understand next to pictures of the Fuhrer, having a copy of a famous masterpiece in your office is the thing to do these days. Of course the more important the officer, the more important the painting must be. When I first got here, they had me working on a Degas. I understand it went to someone very important, close to Hitler himself, I think."

"It's got to be better than printing propaganda pamphlets." David scowled still looking for the turnip in the bottom of his bowl.

"Well it keeps me busy." She answered.

"And alive." Aaron added.

"What do you mean?" David and Yvette asked simultaneously.

Aaron looked around the room to see if any of the guards had moved. When he was sure they were out of range he leaned forward.

"I over-heard my grandfather and some of the Elders talking the other night." He said bobbing his head up quickly to check on the guards again. "If it was not for the fact that each of us has a needed craft, we wouldn't be here right now."

"That's okay with me," Yvette said flippantly, "I'd rather be with my friends in the main camp."

Aaron swallowed deeply, "You'd be dead by now."

"Yvette's left eyebrow rose slightly, giving her face an inquisitive look, "What are you talking about?"

"He doesn't know." David added sarcastically.

Aaron's eyes grew to the size of small saucers, "No, no, I'm serious. I overheard them talking about how anyone under the age of fifteen was not being allowed into the camps unless you had a skill the SS needed. You had to be an. . .aaa...oh, what did they call it?"

"Essential worker?" Yvette volunteered.

"Yes!, he beamed, an essential worker or else."

"Or else what?" David asked, chewing on his last piece of bread.

"Or else they kill you." Aaron whispered.

Yvette and David looked at each other for several seconds then started to laugh, as softly as they could.

"That's stupid." David chuckled.

"Come on Aaron." Yvette chimed in, "your grandfather must have known you were listening. He just wanted to scare you."

Aaron shook his head solemnly, "He didn't know and I'm telling you that's what they were talking about, no one under fifteen."

"There are plenty of kids under fifteen around here." David stated.

"Like who?" Aaron quickly shot back.

David looked at Yvette for help.

"That boy in your barracks. The one with the funny looking nose." Yvette answered.

"Seventeen" Aaron answered.

Yvette looked at David for confirmation.

"He's seventeen." David said still trying to think. "What about that one girl Yvette, the real young looking one?"

"The one in the orchestra? I don't know her, but I don't think she's more than twelve or thirteen."

"There." David said triumphantly.

"She's in the orchestra." Yvette reminded him.

"There." Parroted Aaron

"That doesn't make her an essential worker."

"It does if Commandant Oust says so." Yvette answered beating Aaron to the punch.

David was about to argue the point when he fell silent. He knew that if Commandant Oust said it was an essential position, it was. There would be no arguing that. He had seen the Colonel order Bella to beat a prisoner just because he didn't think the man had been respectful enough when he had passed by. Of course Bella was pleased to follow the order. David and another man had to carry the body to the truck.

"There has to be someone." David said in frustration.

"None." Aaron answered, "I've been thinking about it ever since last night. There's not one."

"So what's your point." Yvette asked getting a little tired of the conversation.

"The point is," Aaron whispered, "if it wasn't for our jobs we would all be dead by now."

"So, we're lucky to have been born so talented. So what?" Yvette said.

"So what?" David repeated finally seeing where Aaron was going. "The so what is that the minute they don't need us we are in big trouble."

"We're going to be dead." Aaron added to further make his point.

Yvette looked down at her empty bowl, rubbing her stomach as if she were waiting for it to magically refill itself with hot soup. It was several seconds before Aaron noticed that she had dropped out of the conversation.

"Yvette, you okay?"

Yvette looked up at Aaron and gave him a weak smile. "Yes, fine."

"Then why the sick look?" David interjected, "Your soup hasn't even hit bottom yet. You can't be sick already."

The color drained from Yvette's face as David and Aaron waited for an answer.

"You're not worried about what we were just talking about, are you?" Aaron prompted.

Yvette shook her head, "No, not really. It's just that. . .well, I am a little worried."

"About what?" Aaron asked.

Yvette continued to stare at the bowl in front of her, her fingers lightly wrapping around the metal surface of the vessel moving it ever so slightly.

"It's just that when I first came here, there were fourteen people in my workshop. Everything seemed normal until you said what you did."

"What are you talking about? Did something just change?"

"No, well yes, maybe. I don't know." Yvette answered not looking up at either Aaron or David.

David looked around the room to check on the position of the guards again. He had not forgotten the last time he had failed to do so. "Yvette, this is not the time to play cat and mouse. What is wrong?"

"It's just what you two were saying. If you're not talented enough they will kill you."

It was Aaron's turn to check where the guards were. He had not forgotten Bella's attack either. "What about the fourteen people in your shop?" he prompted.

Yvette started to slowly move her head from one side to the other as if refusing to believe what she was thinking. "I never thought about it before now." She said, still shaking her head from side to side. "I just thought they were being transferred back to the main camp." She continued still speaking to her bowl.

"Who?" David asked.

"The ones who didn't do so well." She answered as her eyes began to water. "Every time we start a new project they warn us that those who don't do well will be removed from the shop. Every time we finish a new batch of paintings the pieces are checked by several men and one or two of the artists are removed from the workgroup. Remember I told you about Gretchen and Élan Levy?"

"The brother and sister who are in your workgroup?" David said.

"Yes, them. Yesterday Elan and another man were removed from the group."

"I'm sure they're just sent back to the main camp." Aaron said trying to console her.

"They were transferred to M-12 with the sick." She answered, "They went on the truck back to the main camp."

"That doesn't mean they were killed." David said

"Then why didn't they just keep them here to work in the quarries? Why would they transfer them back to the main camp when they bring in new prisoners everyday for the quarries?"

Aaron briefly looked at David, then lowered his eyes to the table. He knew Yvette had a good argument. If artists were going to be put to work at hard labor, the SS could have done that right here in this camp. There was no need to transfer them. You didn't need any special talent to work in the quarry, just a strong back and a will to make it through another day.

It was because Aaron was sitting with his back to the window that he failed to see his grandfather had been stopped at the checkpoint. Although

David and Yvette were both sitting across from Aaron and could see the checkpoint from their vantage point, neither had seen Samuel going through the random search. Both had been too caught up in their own conversation to notice that something was going wrong, something requiring the guard to signal for the Watch Commander. Unfortunately for Samuel, Colonel Oust had been speaking with the Watch Commander when he was summoned to the checkpoint.

The young SS private saluted the two Officers as they approached the checkpoint and turned over the three small pieces of gold he had found in Samuel's possession. It wasn't until Colonel Oust backhanded Samuel across the mouth; knocking the elder jeweler to the ground, did David start paying attention.

"You're probably right, Yvette." Aaron said after a few seconds.

"Aaron." David said in a low, flat tone.

"No, David." Aaron continued still thinking about what Yvette had said. "They could have just kept them here."

"Aaron." David said again, this time tapping Yvette under the table with his leg.

Yvette gave David an inquisitive look bordering on annoyance. David made a motion with his eyes for Yvette to look beyond Aaron. It only took a second for Yvette to understand completely what was happening at the checkpoint.

"Are you two listening?" Aaron asked when neither made a comment about his last statement.

David got up slowly and moved around the table to a position between Aaron and the window.

"Aaron," Yvette said interrupting.

"What?" Aaron answered, his eyes following David.

Yvette stiffened as she tried to find the words that would lessen the blow. Her eyes brimmed with tears when she quickly concluded that there would be no words available to her that could change what was unfolding at the checkpoint. "Aaron..." she stammered.

"What!" he hissed turning back to Yvette.

The first thought that went through Aaron's mind when he saw the anguished look pass across Yvette's face was that somehow Bella had managed to sneak up behind him. His muscles tightened instantly waiting for the blow that was certainly on its way by now. When the blow didn't come, he relaxed slightly, his eyes no longer squinting, his shoulders dropping to their normal position.

"What?" he asked Yvette with his eyes, the adrenalin still pumping through his body.

"Your grandfather." She was finally able to answer while staring out the window, relieved that she did not have to look Aaron directly in the eyes.

Aaron turned in his seat to look out the window. Yvette's words were still vibrating in his ears as he began to understand the scene at the checkpoint. He began to come up out of his seat as Samuel made it back to his knees. Oust leveled the pistol at Samuel's forehead as David moved forward to intercept Aaron.

Samuel looked toward the window as Yvette lunged over the table to help David stop Aaron from diving out into the yard. Samuel smiled weakly hoping to see Aaron one more time as the pistol went off.

From where Aaron was, the pistol only made a muffled popping sound, hardly anything serious enough to hurt his grandfather he thought. It wasn't until Samuel collapsed into the cold mud of the prison yard that Aaron knew that his grandfather had been killed. "Papa!" Aaron screamed as he fell under the full weight of David and Yvette. "No, Papa!" he cried as he struggled to break free from the smothering grip of his two friends, pulling them along with him as they refused to let go.

"Aaron stop!" someone shouted in his ear. "They'll kill you!" another voice added.

Aaron's body was truly pinned under the weight of his two friends. He had been immobilized, but his hand continued to stretch out, his fingers reaching, trying to touch his grandfather. Every part of him tried to reach out and touch Samuel's face, feel the soft crinkles around his eyes or run his fingers through his silver hair before he was gone. Deep inside he wanted to see one more smile or to hear Samuel call him son. Just one more time he thought, was that too much to ask?

Chapter 20

David and Yvette waited until Colonel Oust and the Watch Commander walked away before they finally let him up. Both jumped back as if they had come across a coiled cobra ready to strike, but Aaron didn't have time to strike out at either of them, his grandfather needed him. He cleared the building barely touching every other step as he leaped toward the ground. Aaron didn't feel as if he were in complete control of his legs. At times, he was not sure they were even touching the ground as he ran toward his grandfather. He knew that if he thought about them they would surely seize up and he would tumble to the ground not being able to reach Samuel.

Samuel still laid where he had fallen; his back facing Aaron, his legs slightly tucked under him.

Aaron knew that as soon as he reached Samuel he would be able to touch the man gently on the shoulder and he would wake. Everything would be fine once he was able to help Samuel up from the mud and get him back to the barracks. Samuel had friends in the camp that would help him recover.

Several meters from Samuel's body, Aaron's legs finely crossed sending him flying head first toward his grandfather. Aaron skimmed through the mud and grabbed his grandfather as he almost slid by.

"Papa?" Aaron whispered almost afraid to wake him. "Come on, Papa, we have to get you out of here. . .back to the barracks." Samuel did not move.

"Papa." Aaron said a little louder shaking the man's coat. "Please Papa. Before they come back."

Aaron sat in the mud clinging to Samuel's jacket. His eyes darted around the compound not focusing on any particular person or object. His fingers tightened on the jacket forcing the blood from them until they were deathly white. How could he tell his mother about Samuel? He thought. How could he tell her that he had failed in the one thing she had always asked him to do. 'Watch after your grandfather, Aaron', he could hear her say as his grip tightened again.

Aaron looked down at Samuel and his hand that held so tightly onto the man. Slowly he turned Samuel over, allowing his grandfather to fall into his lap. He looked at the small wound in the middle of Samuels's forehead. The wound was mercifully small, not more than a cut from the looks of it. Aaron brushed Samuel's hair out of his face and wiped the mud from his cheek.

"Oh Papa." Aaron said softly, tears racing down his cheeks. "Papa, I need you, please don't go."

Aaron reached down and gently closed Samuel's mouth. Then, cradling Samuel in his arms, Aaron closed his grandfather's eyes for the last time.

"Papa!" Aaron screamed as he tore the lapel of his muddy jacket. "Oh, Papa, please!"

Aaron wept until David and Yvette walked up to where he and Samuel were lying. He didn't recognize the two Jewish workers as they approached, nor did he see or hear the cart they pulled along with them. He did not see that both men were fighting to hold back the tears that filled the corners of their eyes. They had carried a lot of bodies to the fence where the truck would be waiting to take the body away for disposal, but today their cart would carry the body of a righteous man. The two men carefully picked up the body of Samuel Singer and gently laid it on the cart.

David placed his hands under Aaron's arms and helped him to his feet. Aaron walked over to the cart and touched his grandfather. "I will walk with you." He told the two.

The smaller of the two men looked over to where the guards were standing and watching. He turned back to Aaron and shook his head from side to side. Aaron could see that the man would have liked to grant his request, but the guards would not allow it. Then without speaking again, Aaron turned toward the barracks and walked off.

David and Yvette stood by the cart and watched Aaron carefully, making sure he entered the barracks. David turned toward the cart lowering his head and in a low tone prayed. "God who is full of compassion, dwelling on high, grant perfect peace to the soul of Samuel Singer. He rests under the wings of Your Presence."

The two men working the cart nodded in agreement then grunted in unison as the cart began to move.

Yvette reached out and touched Samuel's hand as the cart passed her. "Holy One of Blessing. Your Presence fills creation. You are the True Judge."

David was stunned. "Where did you learn that?" he asked. "I thought you weren't Jewish?"

Yvette pulled her jacket closed over her breast. "I'm not Jewish."

"But the prayer, where did you learn it?"

Yvette started toward her barracks. "It's not hard to learn something when you hear it every day."

That night, Aaron's barracks was especially quiet as the men returned from the rock quarry. The word of Samuel's death had spread through the camp faster than any news before. Men moved around the barracks without the usual moans or whimpering. Some quietly tended to their wounds or the wounds of others. The rock pit was known to lash out at a man's flesh much like a rabid dog might bite an innocent passerby. These wounds were tended to each night as well as they could be before returning to the jaws of the quarry in the morning. Tonight they were mended in silence.

Aaron lay on his back staring at the wooden roof directly above him. Many times through the early evening he had thought of the ways he could have saved his grandfather from the murderous bullet of Colonel Oust. He had played the events of the afternoon over and over in his head, each time his grandfather somehow escaping death for a brief moment only to have it catch up with him again. How swiftly thoughts of denial came to his aid, how quickly excuses filled the moments between his tears.

"Aaron." The soft voice of his grandfather echoed in his ear.

Aaron blinked several times wondering if he had dozed off. Had he dreamt that his grandfather had spoken to him? It was so real, he thought.

"Aaron." The voice spoke to him again.

Aaron spun around in his bunk, smiling dreamily toward the direction of the voice. "Papa?" he whispered hoarsely his eyes wide with anticipation.

Rabbi Helfer had approached Aaron's bunk with all the strength and knowledge his fifty-five years of life had given him, only to have it all crumbled in a single moment when Aaron had mistaken him for Samuel. Rabbi Helfer was ready for Aaron's tears, he was ready for the grief that was normal in death, but nothing could have prepared him for being mistaken for his friend, Samuel. "Rabbi Helfer." Aaron said through a thin veil of a smile.

"Have you eaten?" Rabbi Helfer asked, not knowing how else to recover.

"I'm not very hungry." He replied weakly, "What time is it?"

"After 10pm, Aaron."

Aaron felt the conversation faltering. He had spoken to Rabbi Helfer many times, but it was his grandfather who usually had the most to say to the man. So much so that Aaron was usually asked politely to find something else to do when the two men would talk. Aaron had participated in so many of these conversations that he had learned to participate in the small talk and then politely excuse himself before being asked to leave. Now, when it was just he and the Rabbi, he didn't know how to take the conversation further.

"Aaron, would you please come with me." The Rabbi asked.

Aaron slid out of the top bunk making sure that he did not step on any of the other men and made his way to the floor. He followed closely behind the Rabbi until they were close to the center of the long barracks building. When they came to a stop, Aaron looked around the room. He gawked in stunned silence at the number of people that had gathered in the room. He wasn't so much surprised at the numbers of people there, their barracks had always been over-crowded with bodies, but at the fact that all of them, men and women, were from the other barracks. Aaron's head reeled. To be caught outside of one's own barracks after curfew was punishable by death. To harbor or congregate like this was also an offense punishable by death. Aaron took several steps backwards away from the group only to back into a huge man he had never met before. The man merely smiled at him without speaking.

"Aaron," Rabbi Helfer started, "Please come over here." He continued, "Sit here on this bunk."

Aaron looked at the lower bunk where Rabbi Helfer had pointed. It was the only open space left where someone could sit. He numbly approached the open seat hoping his legs would carry him that far without his falling. When he reached the bunk he turned to Rabbi Helfer in disbelief. "Rabbi, all these people. The curfew?"

Rabbi Helfer smiled shaking his head slightly and pointing at the lower bunk. "I know, Aaron, I know, but I could not have kept them away if I had ordered them to."

Aaron slowly lowered himself to the lower bunk. "I don't understand."

"All of these people," he said with an emphatic gesture toward the group, "were friends of your grandfather."

"Friends of Papa?"

"Yes, in one way or another, he had touched all of their lives."

"I. . .I don't understand." Aaron answered looking up at all the faces. He had seen several of them, even knew a few by name, but most had been no more than faces at the morning roll calls.

"Aaron," Rabbi Helfer said kneeling closer to Aaron, "these people are here to pay their respects."

Aaron blinked several times as the words of Rabbi Helfer sunk in.

"Shiva[6]" Aaron said weakly.

---

[6] Shiva, from the Hebrew word for seven, refers to the seven days that include and follow the funeral. This is the most intense period of formal mourning. The purpose of shiva is not to make mourners feel better or to cheer them up, but to encourage them to grieve and to share their grief with others.

"Yes, Shiva." Rabbi Helfer smiled. "Even here," he gestured, "We must remember who we are. The SS can imprison us, they can beat us and they can even kill us, but Aaron, they cannot take away our faith. They cannot take away what is in here." he said pointing to his chest.

Aaron felt the tears run down his cheeks. He couldn't believe that he still had enough moisture in his entire body to squeeze out another single tear. "But Rabbi Helfer," he sobbed, "my grandfather will have no burial shroud, no casket. He will not have a proper funeral. They have taken away everything."

Rabbi Helfer's eyes began to water. "What you say is true Aaron. These things we do not have and cannot offer to Samuel, but what we do have is his memory and you, Aaron." Rabbi Helfer moved closer to Aaron and sat next to him on the bunk. "So, young Aaron, tell us of your grandfather and we will tell you of the man who touched so many lives."

Chapter 21

Aaron sat at his workbench fumbling with his tools. Between speaking with all of the people that had come to pay their respects to Samuel, his conversations with Rabbi Helfer and his frequent nightmares about his grandfather, he hadn't had very much sleep. The morning didn't bring any relief to his grief as he went through the usual routine. Everything was the same except he hadn't spoken with David or Yvette at breakfast nor did he finish his meal.

Instead, he left the cafeteria early and walked over to his workshop by himself. Now he sat there looking at the empty workbench next to his. He studied the bench top for a long time looking at the scars embedded in the wood knowing that they had been made by his grandfather. The work surface was covered with a myriad of cuts, deep impressions and burn marks. Aaron's eyes began to tear as he realized that these meaningless marks were all that he would have to remember his grandfather. His fist tightened at the thought of someone else taking over the work station. In the next day or two some other poor Jewish jeweler would be forced down from a rail car while rabid dogs strained at their leashes to tear him apart. The man would offer his talents to the SS, praying that the offer would save his life.

Aaron looked around the room trying to focus on anything that would take his mind off Samuel. Of course nothing helped. Samuel was all around him. Everywhere he looked he could see his grandfather's hand. From the redesign of the work stations to the cracked pain of glass in the window, Aaron found a reason to think of Samuel. For the first time since he had come to the camp, he wished that the workday would hurry and start. Maybe if he could just start working he could take his mind off of Samuel for a while, but he would have to wait at least another fifteen minutes before the rest of the workers started filing into the room and the SS guards would bring in the gold and silver they would be working on.

The conversations with Rabbi Helfer continued to haunt his thoughts. Aaron just couldn't believe that his grandfather had become involved with the camp's resistance group. No, not just involved, but, one of its leaders! How could he have been so blind as to miss the fact that his grandfather was one of the men who organized and ran the camp underground? He knew that Samuel was always off talking with the other elders of the camp, but

Aaron would never have believed his grandfather to be resistance leader.

No matter how hard he tried to disbelieve it, the facts remained that Samuel had organized and supported the Jewish résistance group. Over twenty people had come to see him last night, each telling of how his grandfather had in some way touched their lives. While these people had been vague about what Samuel had done to help them, Rabbi Helfer was much more informative. The Rabbi had told him how Samuel had been sneaking out small pieces of gold to help obtain more food for the hungry and medicine for the sick. Rabbi Helfer had made it very clear to Aaron that Samuel had indeed saved countless lives in the time they had been there.

Aaron's emotions were a swirling mass of confusion. At times he felt that somehow Samuel had cheated him by not confiding in him. Then just as quickly, he was happy that Samuel hadn't included him. Then there was the guilt that he was feeling. No one had been closer to his grandfather than he was. To have missed the fact that Samuel was a leader in the resistance group somehow hurt him deep inside.

Aaron rubbed his stomach as he thought of the rest of his conversation with Rabbi Helfer. The Rabbi had never actually come out and asked Aaron to take his grandfather's place, but there were enough hints given that he knew Rabbi Helfer would have accepted his offer to continue Samuel's work or, at least, continue stealing gold for the résistance group. The image of Samuel kneeling in front of Colonel Oust, the man pointing his gun at his grandfather's head brought a taste of bile to Aaron's mouth. It felt as if someone had poured hot lead down his throat as he tried to swallow. During the night he had dreamt about his grandfather's involvement. Somehow Samuel would have his pockets stuffed with gold, large pieces hanging out of his pockets as he attempted to walk past the checkpoint. The guards would point to him and laugh as he approached. Sometimes it was Colonel Oust himself standing there, laughing as he removed his pistol from it holster, waiting for Samuel to get close enough to him so that he could backhand him across the face then shoot him in the back of the head. Aaron had seen the man do it to other prisoners many times.

Then the dream would change and Aaron was now the one trying to sneak the gold past the checkpoint. The part of the dream that scared him the most was that instead of Colonel Oust, it was Bella standing there waiting for him to walk through the checkpoint. Bella would stand there, blocking the passageway with his stocky body, lightly tapping his ax handle in the palm of his hand. Aaron tried to stop his feet from bringing him closer to the waiting killer but he had no control over them. Although both of his legs felt like lead weights, he was barely able to lift one and put it in front of the other, he couldn't stop their forward momentum. Each agonizing step brought him that much closer to Bella and the ax handle. Finally, Bella would swing the handle toward Aaron's face, his eyes dancing with a devils fire, laughing through yellowing teeth at him until Aaron would jump up in his bed screaming. At first he had been worried that he might have woken some of the other prisoners, but screaming in the middle of the night in his barrack was no different than the soft hissing of one's furnace on a winter's night back home. Exhausted, sleep was the only thing the men of the quarry were interested in.

Aaron's concentration was broken as the workers began to file in. He looked down at the tool in his hand not wanting to make eye contact with any of them. Eric, a tall Polish Jew, was the first to file past his desk. Eric was what Samuel had called a gentle giant. The man towered over the other workers in the shop, but was by far the quietest person Aaron had ever met. The only time Aaron had ever heard the man join in a conversation was during one of the meals. The workers were complaining, as usual, about the poor food, the dreadful working and sleeping conditions. In the conversation one of the other men had asked Eric for his opinion. Eric studied his bowl for several seconds, his brow wrinkled, eyes narrow and focused on the watery soup. It was as if the bowl was his own private window to the universe and at any moment Eric would be given the answer to any question that he may ask of it.

Finally, slowly Eric raised his head and smiled. "It's not for an eternity" he answered softly and then continued with his meal.

Aaron could feel the huge man's presence as Eric lumbered past his workbench on the way to his own. Suddenly, Eric stopped in front of what used to be Samuel's work bench and stood there for what seemed to Aaron to be forever. Aaron shot Eric a quick look out of the corner of his eyes. Aaron was in time to see Eric pull a small stone from his pocket and place it reverently on the top of Samuels's desk. Aaron's eyes meet

Eric's as the man completed the ritual[7]. Eric smiled warmly at Aaron and nodded. Tears began to well up in Aaron's eyes as he nodded back at the gentle giant.

As usual, the man didn't say a word but moved on so that the next worker could approach the workbench. In turn each man filed past Samuel's desk and placed a small stone on the desktop. Each man in turn smiled at Aaron and nodded before he moved on. Aaron was surprised to see that the last man to file past the desk was Rabbi Helfer himself. Rabbi Helfer was not himself a jeweler but often was put on clean-up details around the camp. Aaron had no doubt that the Rabbi had used what little influence he had to make sure he would be working in the vicinity of Aaron's workshop this morning. When Rabbi Helfer heard the SS guards approaching with the little cart carrying the gold and silver, he quickly walked over to Aaron. Rabbi Helfer placed his hand on Aaron's head and, too softly for Aaron to hear mumbled a quick blessing. With a wink, the man was out of the back door before the first SS guard made his way in the front entrance.

Aaron wiped his eyes on his tattered sleeve and prepared himself for work. Many times during the day Aaron would glance over at Samuel's desk and look at the rocks lining the edge. It was during these brief moments that a wave of deep feelings would wash over him in strange and confusing combinations. It would start with an

---

[7] As customary, people visiting a grave of a departed Jew will place a small stone on top of the headstone or grave in honor of the departed.

intense bottomless sadness and feeling of deep loss. Aaron knew he would miss his grandfather and would never get over his death. Then, in the same breath, he knew that his grandfather had been preparing him of this moment. . .a time when he would have to step forward and through his own voice and his own actions, show the world what a great man his grandfather had been. From that moment on Aaron knew that Samuel would always be with him and somehow, he would make Samuel proud of him.

Chapter 22

Achtung!" Bella screamed as he entered the small work area.

Without delay Aaron, and the seven other men seated at their work benches jumped up to attention, lowering their eyes toward the floor. Just the sound of Bella's belching voice was enough to send waves of fear racing down Aaron's back coming to a final resting place somewhere between his stomach and groin.

Aaron could not see who was with Bella and he dare not glance up to look, but he could tell that several pairs of boots had entered the room. If one took the time to listen, three, no maybe four pairs of distinct footsteps could be heard. One was definitely Bella's; Aaron had heard the sound of Bella's boots lazily slapping the wooden floor until he heard them in his dreams. The other three people entering the room were not regular visitors to the workshop. Their stride was even and precise as if every step they took was measured and somehow important. Bella's footsteps on the other hand, seemed to groan under the weight of his husky build. He tortured his boots with every step.

"In here are the jewelers."

Aaron recognized the voice. It was Colonel Oust. Aaron's fist tightened instantly knowing that the man was so close, close enough to kill if he knew how. If there was one thing he dreamt of more than the death of his grandfather, it was his dreaming of the chance to kill Oust. For the last month he had wished for a chance like this and now that he had the opportunity he didn't know how to act on it.

"It is in here that we take the raw precious metals and convert them into useful items." Colonel Oust continued.

Aaron had seen the "raw precious metals" he was talking about. The SS had been stealing everything that was worth any value from the arriving prisoners. Anything gold, silver or containing precious stones was confiscated and placed in the warehouse.

Later, the gold and silver was melted down and given to the workers in Aaron's workshop. Sometimes, the precious stones were also given to them to transform into. . . What did Colonel Oust call them? Oh yes, items of value, Aaron thought.

"How many men do you employ in this shop?" another voice asked. Aaron did not recognize this voice at all.

"Currently only eight. There is room for more and of course we can go onto a second shift when it becomes necessary." Heinrich answered.

"Is this their only job?" the other voice asked.

"Yes, we work them on a fourteen hour shift, the same as the quarry and farm workers."

"They look to be in better shape."

"Yes, of course, they are only lifting a few ounces of gold all day. They have nothing to complain about."

"Are they ever assigned to other work details?"

"Some, mostly cleaning work around the offices and other buildings like the hospital. We never send them out to the quarry."

"Never?"

"No, never," Heinrich answered as he moved into the center of the room. "They are skilled workers and are never allowed to leave the camp. Essential workers like these are hard to come by."

"You told me that they are not segregated from the main prisoner group. How do you keep track of them? What is stopping them from being selected for work outside the camp?"

"That is a good question, Captain. Let me show you." "You, boy, come here."

Aaron immediately knew that Oust was speaking to him. He was the youngest worker in the workshop. He moved to the position where Oust was pointing.

"Yes, sir." Aaron answered not raising his eyes.

"Show Captain Von Reichman your arm." Heinrich ordered.

Aaron didn't have to ask which arm the Colonel was interested in. Aaron quickly raised his left arm and pulled back his sleeve exposing his tattoo. Aaron yearned for a knife or sharp tool to thrust into Oust's heart. At this distance no one would be able to stop him, not even Bella.

"There, see how they are marked."

Klas looked at the young man's arm. "It looks like all the others I've seen since I've been here." He answered.

"No, not quite the same," Heinrich said, moving closer to Klas and Aaron, "See at the end of the number, the Death head symbol?"

"Yes."

"That separates them from the common workers in the camp. Only the workers in the special part of the camp have that marking. Only prisoners with the Dead Head symbol are allowed past the final gate and," Oust added as he looked at Bella, "Only those marked with the Death Head symbol are not to be beaten in such a fashion as to deter them from their work."

"I can only assume, Colonel, that you bring that up for a reason?" Klas asked.

"Well, I only mention it in passing because sometimes some of the non-commissioned officers get a little carried away with their issuing of punishment to the essential workers. One of our engravers received an eye injury the other day that caused us to lose some precious time."

"Weren't there others to take his place?" Klas asked innocently.

"Not in this case. Many of these workers here are working on very special projects. You will learn more about them in good time. But this young man does excellent work with precious metals." Oust raised his hand. "Look at this ring."

Klas studied the ring for several seconds. "Yes, the work is excellent."

"If you like," Heinrich continued, "you can have him take some of your medals and decorations and reproduce them in either silver or gold. It's one of the ways we produce a profit from these Jews. There is a big market for all types of this work back in Germany. Everything from military decoration to cigarette cases are made here and sold back in Germany.

Aaron was staring at the medals on Klas' uniform. He had never seen so many different ones before, not on any of the SS men around the camp. He would actually like the chance to reproduce some of them. As Klas started to move away Aaron looked up at him for the first time. It was remarkable how much he and Colonel Oust looked alike. It was another bad mistake to make in front of Bella.

Aaron's world exploded in rapid flashes of light and pain as Bella hit him between the shoulder blades with the blunt end of his ax handle.

"Keep your eyes to the ground you stupid pig!" Bella shouted as Aaron fell to the floor.

Aaron hit the floor hard, his arms failing to follow his commands to reach out in front of him and break his fall. The impact from the ax handle had stunned him to the point where his normal reaction time was too slow. What little air that remained in his lungs after being hit between the shoulder blades was forced out of his lungs when he hit the rough wooden floor.

"That's better, Bella." Oust said as he started to leave the workshop. "Make them suffer for their mistakes, but don't damage them to a point where we have to get rid of them."

"Yes, sir. I will see to it that they only wish that they would die." Bella leered.

Aaron lay on the floor gasping for any tiny bit of air he could suck into his lungs. It came much too slowly. He thought that he would never get enough oxygen to ever fill his lungs again.

"Stop trying to breathe so fast." Klas commanded. "Control your breathing, slow easy breaths."

Aaron didn't know why he was listening to the SS man, but something in his voice almost made it impossible for Aaron to resist. He held his breath for a second in order to get better control. Slowly, painfully his breathing was returning to a more normal rhythm.

"That's better." Klas coached. "Now. When you finish work today I want you to come over to my office. I have some work I want you to do for me. I will tell the sentry at the gate to pass you through. Do you understand?"

"Yes, Captain." Aaron managed to squeeze out painfully.

"Good." Klas said looking around the shop. "Some of you others help him back into his chair. He can't work while he's lying on the floor."

Chapter 23

Aaron walked toward the checkpoint that separated the workshops from the rest of the work compound. He was heading toward the South wing of the main building. That is where the new Captain's office would be located. In the nine months that he and his grandfather had been in the camp, he had managed to stay away from most of the German Officers, often blending into the group around him, never wanting to draw attention to himself. Up until this morning it had worked very well. Now, he was being forced to go directly into the lion's den, but first he would have to get by Sergeant Bella's office. He was smart enough to fear that more than seeing the new

Captain. He still wore the latest cuts and bruises from his latest run-in with Bella.

Aaron only stopped briefly at the checkpoint, just long enough for one of the guards to give him a loathing glance and a curt gesture with his head, giving him permission to pass through without further search. He quickened his pace somewhat after clearing the gate. For some reason, the guards were more attentive to the prisoner's movement outside of the special work area. It was easier to draw a sour glance or a terse order from a passing guard once outside the checkpoint. It was almost as if the special work area was a sanctuary for the prisoners working there. Step past the first checkpoint and things became a little rougher. Step though the next checkpoint and it worsened. Then, once through the woods and back into the main barracks compound and you were no different than any other prisoner. Several times the fact that he wore the death head symbol on his left arm had saved him from a beating by a passing guard with a frustration to work out. Even in the colder days now he and the others tried to keep the left arm bare allowing any who cared to notice that they wore the death head mark of Colonel Oust.

He thought about Colonel Oust, how could someone hate people so much? How could he kill a prisoner for spilling water on his boot one minute and then turn around only seconds later to laugh and joke with his men. Aaron was glad that Colonel Oust spent most of his free time with the men and women of the orchestra. They received 90% of his attention and no other prisoner ever complained unless, of course, you were a member of the camp orchestra. Aaron had heard that Oust had personally killed at least three members of the orchestra for being inferior. Where a missed note would bring the wrath of the orchestra's conductor somewhere else, here it could bring death. Oust had no patience for inferior players.

Aaron continued his pace until he had reached the south entrance to the main building. He quickly glanced inside to see if the hallway was clear of any German soldiers that might be heading out the door. Many a prisoner had been thrown back through the door and kicked by soldiers that were making their way out the door. Aaron was in no hurry to make that mistake especially after being hit my Sergeant Bella earlier in the day. As a general rule, he mused, staying away from beatings by angry guards was important for any prisoner wanting to stay alive. There were plenty of beatings around without having to go looking for them.

Aaron removed his cap and entered the building. Immediately his ears were filled with the sounds of typewriters banging out memos and schedules, clerks talking on the phone trying to locate this item or another and still others talking about their wives and children. He looked down the long hall and the air escaped from of his lungs and across partially closed lips, sounding much like an automobile tire leaking air. Every single door down the hallway was open meaning a chance to either run into a soldier exiting the office or he, himself, getting sucked into an office to perform some type of manual labor.

He put his head down and continued down the hall at a pace denoting a person on a special mission. Maybe, he thought, if they see that my pace is quick and determined, they will believe that I am on a special assignment for someone. Therefore they will not want to detain me. He thought about it until he past the third door and heard the soldier inside call to him. Aaron's heart sank. To ignore the soldier would be certain punishment, but to make the new Captain wait for him would not be good either.

"Yes, sir," Aaron answered as he entered the office. "Is this the office of Captain Von Reichman?" he heard himself ask in amazement.

The Corporal inside the door was in the middle of lifting several large boxes and was totally caught off guard by Aaron's question.

"What?. . .who are you looking for?" he stammered.

"Captain Von Reichman." Aaron repeated, "Is this his office, sir?" he continued knowing it wasn't.

"I was told to report directly to the Captain, sir. Am I in the right place?"

The Corporal set the corner of the box down on the desk.

"No, no you stupid Jew." He cursed, "His is the office at the far end of the hallway. Now quit wasting time here and report to the Captain before I have to have someone beat you for your stupidity!"

"Yes, sir," Aaron said trying to look scared. Of course that part wasn't hard to do. Aaron was unsure if his legs would work when they had to. "Thank you, sir." He continued, leaving the Corporal to do his own manual labor for a change.

Aaron moved down the hall toward Captain Von Reichman's office and as he did so, drew closer to Sergeant Bella's. Aaron could feel the small hairs on the back of his neck start to itch as he approached the door, his stomach wanting to give up the watery soup he had for lunch. He slowed as he reached the door, straining his ears to hear any tell-tale sound that the man was indeed in his office. It was difficult to silence all of the other background noise but Aaron concentrated on Bella's office.

Quiet, he thought, nothing coming from the animals cave. Aaron walked briskly past the office trying to keep his eyes focused at the end of the hall, but at the last second, glanced into the office. He relaxed when there was no sign of Sergeant Bella and was a little less apprehensive about seeing the new Captain.

Aaron approached the door he had been told was the entrance to Captain Von Reichman's office. He knocked several times on the outer frame of the door.

"Yes, come in." Sergeant Bella said in his usual gruff voice.

Aaron froze with terror. Had the Corporal got the best of him, telling him that this was the new Captain's office and instead delivering him right into the hands of Bella? Aaron looked back down the hall to see if the Corporal was standing there enjoying his little joke. The hall was empty.

"I said come in." Bella repeated.

Aaron had no choice but to enter the office and take what punishment the man might deal out to him. He held his cap in both hands, lowered his eyes to the floor and entered the office.

"Ah, it's the young pup." Bella smirked, "Are you finished in the shop for the day?"

Aaron kept his eyes glued to the ground. The pain between his shoulders reminding him of the last time he broke the rule.

"Yes, sir, Sergeant Bella." Aaron tried to say without being too nervous, "I was told to report to the new Captain's office. I am sorry for disturbing you Sergeant, but I was told that the last door was the Captain's."

"You were told correctly." answered Klas, "Come in."

Aaron moved into the center of the room, eyes still focused on the wooden floorboards.

"That will be all, Sergeant." Klas said as he handed Bella back the duty roster.

"Yes, sir. I'll be next door if you need me Captain."

Aaron knew exactly what Sergeant Bella meant. He would be next-door if the Captain wanted the young Jew to be beaten.

The meaning did not slip past Klas either. "Thank you, Sergeant, but I think I will be alright. I suggest that you post this duty roster as soon as you can. The changes on there will need to be reviewed by the men as soon as possible.

"Yes, Sir." Bella answered as he walked past Aaron.

Aaron listened as the huge man's boots pounded the floor as he left, he could feel every step the Sergeant took, vibrating through the floor and up his own legs. He relaxed slightly when the man had finally cleared the door.

"The Sergeant is quite noisy when he walks, isn't he." Klas asked.

"I hadn't noticed, Captain, Sir," he answered dodging any type of answer that would earn him another beating.

"You may address me as either, Captain or Sir, both is not necessary."

"Yes, Sir."

"I was impressed with your work this morning."

"The Captain is being very kind." Aaron replied.

"Where did you learn such a skill?"

"My grandfather, Sir. He is the gentle . . .he was the prisoner working to my left in the shop before his death."

Klas studied Aaron for several seconds, sizing the young man up. Klas concluded that Aaron was young and scared, but there was an underlying strength that was either well hidden or undeveloped beneath his persona. Klas made a mental note to watch him in the future.

"Did your grandfather do as good a job as you do?"

"Much better, Sir. He had been my mentor since I was very young."

"How did your grandfather die?"

Aaron bowed his head even further. "He was caught trying to smuggle some gold out of the work area and was shot by Colonel Oust."

Klas stared at Aaron for several seconds. "Do you think your grandfather taught you well enough to be able to complete the job I have in mind?"

Aaron shifted his weight from one foot to the other. "You will be happy with my work, Captain."

Klas tried to gaze into Aaron's down cast eyes.

"You may look up." Klas commanded.

Aaron straightened somewhat still avoiding eye contact with Klas.

"Thank you, Captain. How may I be of service to you Sir?"

Klas instantly noticed that Aaron had taken some control of the conversation by asking the question. He smiled inwardly enjoying the first sign of life in the young man. Klas pointed to his Knights Cross.

"If given the proper materials, could you replicate this?"

"What materials would the Captain be talking about?" Aaron asked.

"Either silver or gold."

Aaron tried to study the medal from where he stood. It didn't appear to be anything that he couldn't handle but he felt uncomfortable about committing to its replication without closer examination.

"Come closer." Klas commanded seeing the look on Aaron's face. Klas then removed the medal from his tunic and offered it to Aaron.

"Here, take it. Get a better look at it."

Aaron held it in both hands and studied the piece. It would be simple enough to make a casting, he thought.

"It seems to be made of several parts." Aaron mused as he took a closer look at the cross. Aaron's hand went searching his upper breast pocket as he continued to examine the piece. Soon his right hand produced the jeweler's glass. "The quality is quite excellent, Captain." Aaron studied the piece under the glass. "The frame is made from about 94% pure silver. There are three pieces here. A core fitted between the two outer pieces, one obverse, and the other reverse. The seam between the obverse and reverse rims is excellently welded together and there is only the slightest trace of a hairline seam joining them to the core. The swastika and date are both very sharp and the edges, well defined." Aaron handed

Klas back the medal. "It is a beautiful piece Captain."

"Thank you." Klas said replacing the cross around his neck. "Can you reproduce it?"

Aaron thought about the job for several seconds before answering. "I would have to take the pieces apart to make a casting, Captain. It would be a shame to do that."

"What if I gave you another? One used for wear in the field."

"If the Captain didn't mind me taking it apart."

"Of course not."

Aaron thought about the work involved and how he would go about the job. It gave him a feeling of confidence to know that the other workers in the shop would be there if he needed help.

"Excuse me, Sir." Aaron asked, "But with the quality of the medal you have shown me, why would you want another?"

Klas considered his answer. "I want special ones made for some comrades of mine."

"You want more than one?" Aaron asked a little surprised.

"Yes." Klas said smiling at Aaron's apparent surprise. "I want four of them made."

"I see." Aaron thought out loud.

"And I want the core of each made out of gold, the trim in silver."

Aaron's head spun as he wondered what he had walked into.

"That's going to require a lot of material and time, Sir." Aaron stammered, "does the Captain need them by a special date?"

"Yes, I have a date in mind, but I would be willing to forego the date instead of sacrificing the quality. The most important thing here is the quality of the work. Is that understood?"

"Yes, sir." Aaron shot back as he thought about the tight controls the SS imposed on the gold they used. "You will get my best Captain, but the amount of gold needed."

"I will take care of the raw material." Klas answered flatly.

"Of. . .of course, Captain." Aaron stammered. "I will begin work as soon as I have the piece in my hands."

"Then you shall start tomorrow." Klas said standing.

Klas was shocked at the amount of pain that shot through his legs. The constant standing and walking had caused some discomfort during the day, but they had begun to feel better once he had returned to his office and was able to sit and rest them. Now as he stood there, he knew that the muscles had relaxed to a point that they no longer wanted to support his weight. Klas tried not to show any sign of his discomfort.

Aaron immediately knew something was wrong with the Captain when he stood. He felt very uncomfortable standing there watching the young Officer try and hide his pain. Aaron's mind raced as he tried to find some way to bridge the awkward moment.

"Captain," He said thinking again about the medal. "The cross, it is a very high honor to get one?"

Klas quickly regained his composure. "Yes, it is a very high honor."

"Excuse my ignorance, Captain, because I know nothing about war except what I see here."

"Don't ever confuse this," Klas shouted as he flung his arms around in a pathetic gesture, "for war! This is the furthest thing from war and the men who fight it as you can get. I don't know what this is, but it is not what I would call war."

Aaron's eyes immediately went to the floor his head bowed once again. "I'm sorry, Sir, but this is the only war I know."

"I haven't figured out what this is," Klas said trying to work it out in his head, "but I can tell you it has nothing to do with war." Klas said as he limped slightly toward the window. "The real war is out there. The real soldiers are out there. I don't know what this is."

"I am sorry, Captain," Aaron, said a second time wishing he was back in the barracks, "I only meant to say that the men who you want this made for must be very fine soldiers."

Klas turned to face Aaron, the words riding up on his bile tasting breath. "They were the finest men I have ever served with."

Aaron shook; his legs ready to fail him at any second. "Then, Captain, they will have the finest work I can give them."

Klas stared at the pitiful figure of the young Jew standing in front of him as he regained his composure. After what seemed like a lifetime for both of the young men, Klas nodded in agreement.

"You may go back to your barracks now. I will send you what you need to your work bench."

Aaron backed out of the room slowly, keeping his eyes focused on the floor until he was clear of the office.

Chapter 24

Klas returned to his quarters after having one of the longest days of his military career. He couldn't remember ever having to walk so much since he was in uniform. In some ways, the tank corps had spoiled him. Now, being assigned as a jailer, no he thought, a babysitter was more appropriate, he had to walk everywhere. The fact that his legs were still healing and were not 100% only added to the pain and misery of his new assignment.

When he left the compound he attempted not to limp. It was painful, but he thought he had carried it off fairly well. It was the last 100 meters to his quarters that gave him the most trouble. He was happy that his quarters were partially hidden from the camp and the other officer's quarters, by trees and ground cover. When building the camp

Heinrich had ordered the officers quarters to be built into the natural terrain of the forest surrounding the main camp. This allowed the officers some privacy.

Klas, being second in command, had his own private quarters. Thirty or forty meters south of his quarters, hidden from view, was Colonel Oust's home. By the same distance to the north were the other two houses containing the junior grade officer's quarters. Those quarters were shared between the four officers.

Klas managed to limp up the stairs, as large beads of sweat began forming and running down his hairline. By the time he reached the top stair, sweat was running down the sides of his face. He stopped on the front porch and leaned against the porch column. His only thoughts at the moment were dealing with getting inside before someone spotted him. He longed for the chance to splash some cold water on his face. The thought of lying down also managed to work its way to the top of the priority list.

The door swung open with a loud thud and Klas used his remaining strength to move inside the house. He managed to close the door and move through the house, using the wall for support. He entered the bathroom and quickly turned on the cold water. Immediately, he began splashing the water onto his face, running his fingers through his matted hair. He could feel the color returning to his face and it also seemed to help take his mind off the pain pumping through his legs.

Klas held onto both sides of the porcelain basin and shifted his weight to help lessen the pain. He stared down at the running water not wishing to look at himself in the mirror. 'Quite the hero now,' he thought to himself while wondering if he had remembered to bring the pain pills he had received at the hospital. He had convinced himself that he would not need them, but somehow they managed to follow him to Dachau and still remained in his toiletry bag for the trip to Auschwitz. Today was the first time that he thought seriously about taking them.

He dipped his hands under the tap and slowly brought the cool liquid to his face. The water seemed to draw the heat away from his face and eyes. He shook the excess from his hands and looked at himself in the mirror. The image of the woman standing behind him caught him completely off guard.

He hadn't seen or heard the woman standing at the door behind him. He spun around, forgetting about the pain in his legs. The sudden twisting motion in his lower hips and upper legs was all that it took to make his legs give out completely. Klas fell toward the floor his legs turning to jelly. It was his arms grabbing onto the basin that kept him from going completely to the ground.

"Who in the hell are you!" Klas shouted at the young woman.

The young woman opened her mouth to speak, but Klas blasted her with another question.

"What are you doing in my quarters? Why are you here?"

"I - I'm" she faltered looking for the best way to answer his barrage of questions, "I've been. . ."

"For God sake, woman! Speak up! Who are you!" Klas continued to shout as he tried to gracefully regain his footing.

"I've been assigned. . . Do you need some help, Captain, Sir?" the woman asked.

Klas still maintained a death grip on the basin his knuckles turning white. His eyes narrowed. "I don't need your damn help!" he bellowed ferociously, "I asked you what you are doing here."

The young woman bowed her head and looked side-to-side trying to figure out the quickest way out of her current situation.

"My name is Marta," she finally answered in broken German.

Klas managed to get his footing and was able to release his grip on the basin. He attempted to straighten out his uniform as if nothing had happened.

"I didn't ask who you were." He spat knowing that he had indeed asked her the question. "I asked you what you were doing here."

"I have been assigned to your quarters, Captain." She whispered.

"My quarters? What for?"

Marta held tightly onto one hand with the other. "For whatever the Captain might need." She quivered.

He studied the young woman's face. She was not like most of the prisoners he had seen during his inspection of the camp. She still retained much of her youthful looks, her hips round and soft, and her breast filling the thin blouse she wore loosely round her shoulders. Klas shook the thoughts from his mind and returned to his current dilemma. He was sure that he could now make it to the other room without too much trouble. He pushed past the young woman almost knocking her into the wall.

"I didn't ask for you." He spat over his shoulder. "Who sent you here?"

"Sergeant Bella told me to come here. He told me to take care of you. To give you whatever you wanted."

Klas turned back to the young woman, his face a spasm of loathe and disgust.

"I don't need you to take care of me." His lips tightly drawn with suppressed fury. "I don't need some whore gift from some fat piece of shit sergeant. Do you think I'm some cripple needing your pity? Some - some - Oh hell, get out of my way!"

Klas no longer tried to hide his limp as he made his way to the kitchen where the phone was located. He quickly rang Sergeant Bella's number and waited.

"Good evening, Sergeant Bella." came the answer.

"Sergeant, this is Captain Von Reichman." Klas started, "I'm in my quarters and there is a Polish woman here," he continued not allowing Bella to respond, "Did you send her here?"

"Yes, Sir." Bella finally was able to answer.

"Sergeant Bella, I want her gone. I want her out of here now. Get rid of her. You understand me?"

"Yes, Captain!" Bella squealed, "I will be there as soon as I can."

"Not when you can, Sergeant, now! I'm sending her out the door right now. You pick her up on the way up here, understand?"

"Yes, sir, right away."

Klas slammed the phone back into it cradle using it as a support. He looked over at the young woman. For the first time Klas noticed that the woman was sick with fear, her entire body trembling like a small animal caught in the cold. Klas closed his eyes and tried to compose himself.

"I am sorry, frauline." He said in what he hoped was a calming voice. "It's not your fault. I just don't want a . . . a house maid, understand?"

Marta shook her head in a weak response. "Yes sir, Captain."

"You may address me as Captain or Sir, but not as Captain, Sir. Understand?"
Marta nodded.

"Now, please leave. Sergeant Bella will meet you and return you to the camp."

Without whispering another word, Marta darted out of the house, closing the door behind her.

Chapter 25

Every day started out the same way for Ivan Shim, rising from the hard wooden bunk before most of the others, fighting off the chill that never seemed to leave the barracks and putting on the worn pair of leather dress shoes that didn't fit. He had lost the only pair of socks he had months ago when one of the prisoners had the audacity to remove them from his feet while he slept. Now, every morning, it would take several minutes for Ivan's feet to warm up enough to heat the cold leather to a point where he was able to walk without the shoes hurting his feet. Then a quick trip to the toilet barracks where the air was foul and suffocating.

Ivan would then meet up with Lukasz from Barracks number four and Osip from building five. Together they would start the daily chore of collecting the bodies of those who had died during the night. The three would take turns either pushing the old wooden wagon from behind or pulling it from the yoke. Today was Ivan's turn to guide the wagon and pull it from his position in the front.

Their daily routine would never change, except for the days when they would have to make more than one trip. They would start at the women's barracks and guide the wagon along the rear of the building between the barracks and the toilet buildings. There the Blokowe[8] would already have the bodies of the women who had died during the night waiting.

Without any ceremony, Ivan, Lukasz and Osip would load the bodies onto the wagon. They had long ago strangled their emotion for the dead men and women and had forgotten what reverence for the dead had meant. It had become a job, much like emptying out the garbage. After the trip behind the women's barracks was completed, they would head over to make the run between the two rows of the men's barracks. Here the members of the barracks would sometimes help the three and would lay the dead upon the wagon or, in some cases, they would be left outside the door for them to remove.

If there was still room on the wagon, they would then head over to the hospital to remove those who had passed away during the night. This was their last stop on their morning rounds before

---

[8] Blokowa: Feminine form of the word Blokowy. Polish name for the female prisoner in charge of a barracks. Blokowe is the plural form of the word.

heading to the side gate to load the bodies onto a truck to be taken to the main camp for disposal. Today's load had been light and they were able to finish in one trip. All they had to do now was load the truck. As soon as the bodies were loaded onto the truck Ivan and the other two men could go to breakfast.

It was at this point in their morning chores that Klas happened to be walking by the work group. He had spent much of the rest of his evening soaking in a hot tub of water, washing down pain pills with a very cheap tasting glass of Brandy. The pills aided by the Brandy had made it possible for him to sleep through the night and wake this morning with only a light fog hanging over him. He had managed to get up and dress without much pain at all and had even managed to muster up a decent appetite.

Where the Officers housing was located, it was much easier to enter into the compound through the side gate. It was also, to his liking, a shorter distance to walk. He had promised himself in the mirror this morning that he would keep his walking to a minimum today. He would get the necessary exercise the doctors had prescribed, but he would not over-do it as they had also warned.

As Klas passed through the gate, Ivan and the other two were busily loading the truck with the morning dead. They halted their work upon seeing his approach and took the position of respect owed to an SS Officer when passing. Klas had no interest in their gruesome task and paid them very little attention.

"Continue with your work." He commanded as he had heard Heinrich do so many times the day before during their tour of the camp. Klas continued into the compound past the two guards stationed at the gate. It wasn't until he had cleared the gate that the image he had just seen had broken though the painkiller fog in his head and registered clearly in his mind. He turned and looked back at the three prisoners loading the truck. Klas blinked several times trying to replay the last few minutes, his walk through the gate and his glancing at the men completing their work. Klas slowly walked back through the checkpoint and stood a few feet from the three. He watched for several seconds before approaching the men.

"Where are these bodies from?" he asked.

Ivan removed his cap. "They are from the barracks, Sir."

Klas felt stupid for asking the question. Where else would they be from, he thought. "There are both men and women on the truck?"

"Yes, sir. We make rounds past both the men's and women's barracks." Ivan answered.

Klas approached closer to the truck and scanned the bodies, wondering why he had stopped in the first place. They were all just shadows of the people they used to be, their skin stretching over their ribs and bones like a worn piece of cheap cloth. Their faces twisted in agony when even death could not bring peace to their souls. Whatever Klas had thought he had seen among the bodies was no longer there.

"Continue with your work." He said getting ready to leave.

Ivan and Osip picked up the nearest body to them and nervously tossed it onto the truck. To their horror, the weight of the new corpse was enough to throw the pile off balance and several of the bodies tumbled from the flatbed of the truck back onto the ground.

Klas took several steps back to avoid having the bodies fall onto his boots.

"I am so sorry," Ivan cried out as he scurried toward the body. "Forgive me, Sir. It was not intentional." he whined.

"It's OK," Klas said, reassuring Ivan that the body had not slid onto his boots, "It was an accident." He added hoping to end the incident.

Klas stood there as the three prisoners now began to pick up the fallen remains. He couldn't understand why he hadn't moved on or why he continued to watch the men work until they threw the first body back onto the truck. There, now in plain sight, was the body of a young woman, her features still quite striking even in death, her breasts no different from when he saw them last night. In contrast to last night, her face was now calm, tranquil, as if in a deep sleep instead of the frightened look of a small animal, eyes peering about wildly looking for the safest place to hide.

"Stop!" he commanded, "That girl." he said pointing to the young woman. "Where did you pick her up?"

Ivan raised his eyes and looked at the young woman. He began to shake when it dawned on him that he couldn't remember where he had picked the women up.

"It was at the hospital, Sir." Lukasz said. "She was with the ones we picked up at the hospital."

"Was she sick?" Klas asked still looking at the young woman's face.

The three men looked at the young woman as if any of them could tell if she had been sick or not. The three continued to look at the body hoping that the SS Officer would just go away and let them finish their work. If he detained them much longer they would miss breakfast.

"I asked if she was sick." Klas repeated.

Again, it was Lukasz that was able to answer the question. "No, sir . . . not sick."

"Then how did she die?"

The three men squirmed like school children being question by their teacher.

Lukasz frowned trying to force out the words that might cost him his own life. "Sir, her arm."

"Yes. . ." Klas said prompting him to go on.

"Well, Sir, she has the mark on her arm." Ivan interjected.

"What mark? What mark are you talking about?"

Ivan walked up to the dead girl's body and extended her arm for Klas to see the small black and blue mark on her forearm. "The needle mark, Sir."

Klas studied the small puncture wound on her forearm and the bruising caused by someone's careless work with a needle.

"Yes, I see it." He said, "So what does it mean?"

"Sir," Ivan continued, "It means that she was in the hospital last night and she was - was - injected with something that killed her."

"Poison?" Klas asked looking at the three of them "Are you saying she was poisoned"

"We don't know, Sir." Lukasz said. "All we know is that we often pick up people from the hospital with this kind of mark on them.

They look somewhat healthy except for the marks on their arms."

Klas looked at the young woman for several seconds as he collected his thoughts. He thought of asking more questions of the three prisoners, but decided against it when he saw the fear on their faces. He knew that the three had already told him more than they should have.

"Continue with your work." Klas said, walking away from the gruesome work detail.

Klas decided to skip breakfast and headed to his office. The image of the young girl followed him every step of the way. The image changing randomly between that of the haunted young women, eyes drawn, face etched in fear to that of an angel in restful slumber, arms spread across the pile of corpse protecting those in her charge beneath her. Klas tried to clear his head of the visions. I am too young to have so many deaths haunt my thoughts, he said to himself as he entered the building.

Klas headed directly for his office hoping to find some solace there. He dropped his full weight into the chair taking the burden off his legs. He ran his hands across the top of the wooden desk feeling the smoothness of the grain against his fingertips. Klas studied the lines in the wood trying to feel the small imperfections formed by the grain. He studied it more intently, chasing off the visions of the young girl.

"Good morning, Captain." Bella said entering the office, "I trust you slept well?"

Klas did not take his eyes of the top of the desk. "I've slept better, thank you."

"Would the Captain like a cup of coffee?" Bella wheezed.

"No thank you, Sergeant, not now."

"I'm sorry about the girl last night, Sir." Bella added.

Klas looked up at the fat Sergeant, his fingers still wandering over a small portion of the wood surface of the desk. "What are you sorry about?"

"Well, sir, I'm sorry that the young girl was not to your liking."

"It's of little matter now." Klas said, as the vision of the angel entered his thoughts again.

"I thought we had picked out someone that would be pleasing to you. Marta was an excellent worker." He added as an after-thought.

"Then you know she's dead."

"Of course, Captain. I personally brought her over to the hospital and had your orders carried out."

Klas' fingers froze to the desktop as if glued in place; his eyes took on a wounded look anticipating Bella's answer before he asked the question. "My orders? What orders are you talking about?"

Bella walked up to the desk and placed a pile of papers onto the corner. "The order to get rid of her, Sir. I could tell by your voice last night that you were very angry with her. I figured it best to get rid of her as quickly as possible. "

Klas was sure that he had just been shot through the chest, the impact taking away his last breath. He sat there motionless, wondering why he hadn't fallen yet. Klas blinked incredulously at Bella.

"You thought. . ." The words caught in his throat as the blood drained from his face. "You were. . ." Klas couldn't chase the young girls face from his mind. Her eyes begging for her life, he too wrapped up in his own discomfort and shame to recognize the plea for her life.

"Captain, are you alright?" Bella asked. "You look pale."

"Yes, I'm fine." Klas said, trying to regain his composure in front of Bella, "I didn't have anything to eat last night. The pain pill for my legs . . . my head's a little light this morning."

"I can get you something from the kitchen? Bring it here to your office."

"Would you?" Klas answered taking the opportunity to get Bella out of his office even if only for a little while.

"Some coffee with your breakfast, Sir?"

"Yes," Klas almost whispered, "black- no sugar. He continued mechanically.

"I'll have that for you right away, Captain." Bella said as he left the office.

Bella's smile grew with every step he took down the hallway. He was sure that the young pup of a Captain would have screamed at him for killing the girl, maybe even threatened him. He had planned on it, knowing exactly what to say, how to turn it back upon him, but the young piece of shit just sat there. He was a little disappointed that Klas hadn't, thrown up on his desk, but it had worked out almost as well. Bella doubted that the young war hero would even get a single swallow of coffee down before lunchtime. A quick laugh slipped out of Bella's mouth as he thought of the next part of his plan to torment Klas. He quickly looked up and down the hallway to see if anyone had heard him. Sure that no one had heard the short outburst; he almost danced the rest of the way to the kitchen.

Chapter 26

The music made its way through the trees and down toward the side gate of the camp. Even the barbed wire fences and the armed guard towers could not bar the notes from penetrating the perimeter. It was just inside the checkpoint that Klas unconsciously caught the first few notes. His head was still filled with the business of numbers. The number of guards on each shift, the number of guards on leave, the number of new prisoners and the number of dead for the day. Today, for the first time, the number of dead seemed to bother him because today, one of the dead had a name.

He had thought about Marta several times during the day. He had thought about how he had treated her in his quarters and how he had inadvertently ordered her death. He wasn't entirely sure that Sergeant Bella had not taken the opportunity to misunderstand his orders about the woman on purpose, but he knew there was nothing to be done about Bella or Marta now.

Klas casually returned the guard's salute as he exited the compound and headed toward his quarters. He had kept his promise to himself and had stayed off his legs as much as possible and with the way they hurt now, he was more than glad. It wasn't as severe as the night before, but the pain was there as a constant reminder that no matter how hard he tried to ignore it, he still walked with a slight limp. Bella had even had the nerve to ask him if he would like a cane. The thought of Bella's helpful suggestion made his blood boil. 'How dare he!' Klas thought, as he ground his way up the path. The fat pig had never seen a single day's combat and he had the nerve to offer him a crutch.

Klas feeling the anger swell inside him, shifted his thoughts away from Bella. The man had ruined his day and Klas was not going to let the pig ruin his evening. The thing that bothered him the most, even more than the pain in his legs, was the knowledge that he could not get rid of Bella. Colonel Oust kept Bella around like a pet, like one of the vicious dogs used around the compound. Yes, Klas thought, just like one of the drooling, half rabid beasts just waiting for permission to tear into some unsuspecting victim's flesh.

Enough! Klas thought and turned his attention to the trees that lined the path toward his quarters. It was then that he took note of the music echoing through the forest. Klas' quarters were separated from the other junior grade officers who were north of him by twenty-five meters of densely populated forest, just as Colonel Oust's quarters were separated from his to the south. The fact that the music was so intense told Klas that the other officers were playing their phonograph much too loud. If they didn't lower the volume by the time he made it to his quarters he would call over to them and ask them to turn it down. He was sure that they did not understand how well the music carried through the forest.

Klas continued up the path at an even pace trying not to put too much pressure on one leg over the other. That's how he got into so much trouble the night before. When one leg took on too much of the burden it would tire quickly and begin to hurt. Soon he would begin to favor that leg placing undue pressure on the other until he was in terrible pain. By taking his time and measuring each step, he had managed to reduce the pain to a tolerable level.

As he cleared the last portion of the forest that blocked his quarters from the compound, Klas figured out that the music was not coming from the other quarters, but from his own. His heart sank. Evidently some of the other Officers had come to his quarters and arranged some type of welcoming party. He was in no mood for a party or anyone's company. He had his heart set on taking a few pain pills and washing them down with the remainder of the cheap brandy. Now he would have to play host to a bunch of drunks until the liquor was gone or most of them had passed out. Either alternative was distasteful.

Klas stopped short of the last turn, caught his breath, adjusted his uniform and started out for his quarters again this time without the limp. He stopped again when he was in clear view of the house.

There were no other Officers on his front porch waiting to throw him warm salutations of welcome, nor was there a phonograph playing the music he had been listening to for the last 50 meters. Instead, Klas was looking at the back of a young woman playing the violin. He gawked at the woman for several moments as she swayed with the music. He noticed that her body moved with the rhythm of the music, her entire body swaying like a young willow tree dancing in the evening breeze, the two gently waltzing together. Nor did it escape his attention that the silhouette of the woman's body was clearly outlined under the thin cotton dress by the setting sun and that her curves while subtle were exquisite.

Klas continued to listen to the music for several minutes, forgetting everything but the enchanting melody dancing through the forest. It wasn't until the young woman, still swaying with the music she played, turned enough to see Klas standing there that he continued up the path. The sight of Klas standing there startled her and the bow in her hand skidded across the strings in a horrific ending to the piece.

The woman quickly placed the violin down on the table next to her and took the position Klas had become only too familiar with. Klas walked up to the porch forgetting the pain in his legs until he attempted to climb the few steps. In her current position, head down, hand limp by her sides it was easy for the woman to see his discomfort, but she made no move to offer him help.

"That was quite beautiful." Klas said reaching the top of the stairs.

The young woman, her head still down, answered with a silent curtsy.

Klas felt awkward in the silence. "I have heard that piece many times before, but can't remember its name."

"Vivaldi's Allegro, Sir." Anna answered weakly.

"Ah, yes, now I remember. It is one of my mother's favorites." Klas said looking down at the young woman. "Do you like Vivaldi?"

"Yes sir, Captain."

Klas noticed that the young woman was shaking ever so slightly. Klas did not know if the young woman was afraid of him or merely shivering because of the cold. Her hard nipples pressing against the thin material of her blouse were easily noticeable. He looked her in the eyes again and continued to speak to her in a softer tone. "I am personally fond of Vivaldi's Four Seasons. Do you know that piece?"

"Very well Captain, sir."

"Klas smiled, "You may address me as Captain or Sir but not both at the same time. Understand?" Klas almost choked on the last word remembering the conversation with Marta not wanting to either complete the sentence nor swallow it. "Why are you here. . .what is your name?" He asked calmly.

"Anna, Captain."

"Anna, why are you here on the front porch of my quarters?"

"I have been assigned here to work for you."

Klas closed his eyes wanting to have Anna disappear before he opened them again. "What do you mean?"

"Well, Captain, Si -" she started and caught herself "I mean, Captain - I was told to wait here for you to come home. I will be your housekeeper."

Klas moved closer to Anna and looked down at the violin. "You play in the camp orchestra?"

"Yes, Captain."

"Then how is it that you will also be my housekeeper?"

"I was told that I am to have my chores completed before roll call each morning. Then I am to report to the front gate for my duties in the orchestra. Then in the evenings I am to return here and take care of you."

Klas' eyes flared at Anna's last remark, "What do you mean, take care of me?"

Anna shook her head from side to side. "I'm not sure, Captain. I guess I'm to cook for you and make sure you are comfortable. Sergeant Bella was not very clear on my duties. He said. . ."

"Go on." Klas ordered

"He said that you would show me what was required and I was to do whatever you told me without question or hesitation. And. . ."

"Yes."

"And. . .I. . ." Anna faltered not knowing how to continue. "And. . .I was to satisfy your needs better than the last woman."

Klas fought to keep his composure as he kicked a small twig lying on the porch with the tip of his boot, knocking it several inches in one direction before pushing it back to the opposite original point. "And what do you think that means Anna. It was Anna, correct?"

Anna curtsied out of habit. "Yes Captain, Anna. I'm sorry, Sir, I don't know what that means. I can cook, my mother taught me how and I can clean and wash." She volunteered.

Klas looked closely at Anna for the first time since he stepped onto the porch. He regarded her with an icy speculation. "How old are you Anna?"

Anna bowed her head further. "Four. . .fifteen, Captain."

"How old?"

Anna's shaking became more evident; shifting her weight from one foot to the other she finally answered. "Fifteen, Sir. No one is allowed to enter the camp unless they are at least fifteen years old." She volunteered.

"And who verified your age when you entered the camp?"

"Colonel Oust did, Captain."

"I see." Klas said smiling to himself. Klas knew of Heinrich's love of music and had to admire the man for seeing the talent in this young girl. "Well, Colonel Oust is not one to make a mistake, is he?"

"No, sir."

Klas looked down at the small bundle lying next to the open violin case. "And what is that" he said pointing to it.

"It's my things, Captain."

"Your things? Am I to suppose that you will be moving into my quarters permanently then?"

A wave of acid welled up in Anna's belly as she remembered Bella's instructions. The man had always frightened her from the very first day she had seen him, but having the dirty old man stand so close that she could smell the souring food on his breath and feel the moisture of the perspiration soaking his dirty uniform had frightened her into tears. Anna stood in front of Klas licking her dry lips with an even dryer tongue. "I was told. . ."

"Yes?"

"I was told to get my things from the barracks because I would not be returning there again."

"And what if I was to tell you that you can't stay here?" Klas asked rising one eyebrow superciliously.

Anna swallowed the dry lump in her throat. "Then. . .I'm to. . ." Anna tried to wet her tongue. "Then. . .Sergeant Bella told me to report to the hospital for reassignment."

The image of Anna's lifeless young body flung across the body cart, a careless needle puncture discoloring her soft skin entered Klas' mind momentarily. The thought brought a rancid taste with it.

"And what does that mean to you." Klas asked out of curiosity.

"I think that it would mean I would lose my position in the orchestra."

The innocence of Anna's answer saddened Klas. It was obvious that she had no understanding why she was here or that her life was in danger. Her only concern was her ability to stay with the orchestra.

"Do you like your music that much?"

Klas saw Anna's answer clearly in her eyes before she ever spoke the words. "Oh, yes Sir, Captain."

The intensity of Anna's blue eyes reminded Klas of a piece of lapis lazuli his mother had purchased while in Chile. The luster of her eyes and the warmth of her answer drew some of the arrogance from his stance. He had seen his mother do it to his father many times, but now, for the first time, understood how she had managed to do it so easily.

"Well, Anna." Klas said as he started into the house, "We better find you a place to put your. . ." Klas looked down at the tattered pile of rags, "things."

Anna entered the house clutching the violin case to her chest, the small bundle of her things swinging from her arm. The first thing she noticed was that the house was warm, much warmer than anything she had felt since arriving in the camp. The second thing was that the house was sparsely decorated, most of the furniture was mismatched, but in fairly good condition. The walls were all painted white and the only picture visible was one of Adolph Hitler, the same one she had seen so many times before. The windows were covered in heavy drapes that did not allow the sun to penetrate. Several were either closed or only partially opened allowing just a few streamers of light to enter making the rooms feel dark and uninviting. Anna's shoes squeaked with each step as she timidly crossed the wooden floors. While the house and its furnishings were nothing compared to her home in Frankfurt, the quarters were a palatial château compared to her cramped quarters in the women's barracks.

"For this evening," Klas' voice boomed in the confines of the small living room, "you can sleep on the sofa."

Anna looked to the place where Klas was pointing. Her heart leaped as she eyed the soft upholstered cushions of the couch. The thought of sleeping on anything soft and warm was too wonderful to imagine. The wooden beds in the women's barracks were sparsely covered with a thin layer of straw, unfit for a mule to eat. Her clothing was more of a cushion from the hard wood than the straw was. She made a mental note to herself to make sure that whatever the Captain needed; she would do her best to supply it for him.

"I think there is an extra blanket in the armoire. I will check for you later."

Anna sighed openly causing Klas to turn and look at her. "Is there something wrong?"

"No, Captain." She answered looking down at the floor.

Klas approached her and stopped a few paces from where Anna was standing. He noticed that he had kept a larger distance between the two of them than he would if he had been talking to one of his men. "Something caused you to sigh like that."

Anna's face brightened at the thought of a warm blanket wrapped around her as she slept. "I have not had a blanket for so long now, Captain. The barracks are so cold and windy. I - I . . ."

Feeling a little embarrassed, Klas walked away before she could finish. "The kitchen is in here. Tomorrow I will see about getting you a cot or a bed and maybe you can sleep in here or possibly down in the cellar. There is running water down there and the furnace will keep you warm."

The thought of living in the cellar like some animal didn't please Anna at first, but the thought of being as far away from this SS Officer as she could brought her some comfort. If she were lucky there would be a lock on the cellar door. Anna had not seen this SS man before but she was sure that he would be no better than the others she had met, with the exception of Bella.

Chapter 27

"We can do it." Aaron insisted, his eyes moving back and forth between Yvette and David. This was his second attempt at getting the two to help him take up Samuel's work. The first attempt had failed miserably.

"You are going to get us killed." David answered flatly.

"You may die anyway." Aaron proposed.

"I will die, someday, but not here, not in this hell. The war will end and we will be out of here. All it will take is to do what the SS wants and we'll make it out of here."

"You're lying to yourself, David." Yvette interjected the vision of yet another one of her colleagues being removed from the work group just this morning and sent to M12 was still fresh in her mind. "Even if Hitler is defeated, none of us will be left alive. The SS will shoot us before the Americans or Russians ever get here."

"How do you know that?" David spat. "We have a better chance than those poor bastards out in the quarry."

"Yes, they have a very slim chance of surviving, but we have none." Yvette answered, "Don't you see that we know too much about what the SS is doing here?"

"What? What do I know that is so important that it's worth my life?" David retorted.

"Your life is worth nothing to the SS." Aaron answered, "But what you do for them is well worth your dying."

"I'm a printer. Is that so bad?"

"And what have you been printing the last few weeks?" Yvette smirked.

David looked at his two friends as he searched his brain for a good answer. A frown crossed his brow when he couldn't come up with one. "Travel documents." He finally answered, knowing the barrage of innuendoes that were to follow.

"Blank travel documents." Aaron corrected.

"What else would they be except blank?" David shot back.

"Stop it David." Yvette sighed, "They're blank passports and visas. You know better that anyone else that they have you counterfeiting foreign travel documents. Do you think they're just going to let you walk out of here with the information you have in your head?"

"Look, this is the way I see it. They have me making fake travel documents for their spies to use. Once the war is over, no more spies, no more need for fake documents and no more need to kill me."

Aaron thought about what David had said and shook his head. "Okay, David let's say you're correct. You're still a Jew. If Hitler wins, do you think you're getting out of here? Do you think he is going to personally thank you for all the hard work you've done and give you a medal?"

"If Hitler wins,' David answered, "None of us will get out of here alive."

"Then we have to pray that the Americans and British win or the Russians win." Aaron stated, "And we have to do our part to help keep as many of the prisoners alive until they do."

Yvette placed her hand on David's arm. "If we can save one life."

"There you go again, Yvette, quoting Hebrew scripture." David hissed as his eyes flared, "Don't you find it just a little bit hypocritical for someone who doesn't believe in God to be quoting scripture?"

"I never said I didn't believe in God. All I've ever said is that I'm not Jewish. And I don't think the Jews are the only ones interested in saving lives."

David drew small circles with his finger on the table. Aaron and Yvette watched as the circles got smaller and smaller. "Okay," David sighed, "but you better have a good plan. You better be able to dissolve the group if something goes wrong."

"What do you mean?" Aaron asked.

"I mean that if one of us gets caught, it can't be traced back to the others. It will have to be as if it was an act of a single individual, not a group."

"Are you that afraid of getting caught, David? Are you afraid that Aaron or I will mess up and get you killed?"

"No, not at all. If one dies the others can continue, but if we all die, there will be no one to carry on. That is what I'm afraid of. If we are going to do this, we are going to do it until the Allies come or we're all dead."

Aaron shook his head. "I agree. It must look like we acted alone. Like it did when my grandfather got caught." Aaron said weakly, choking on the last few words.

Aaron looked at his two friends. Both were nodding in agreement. "Then it's done. We will waltz with the dark angel and he will pay for the pleasure."

"Yes," David added as an after-thought, "but as your grandfather was fond of saying. "Don't let the dark angel step on your toes."

Yvette shook her head in agreement. "Then what do we do next?"

Aaron and David looked at each other as if the answer might be written on the other's face. Soon, both looked down at the table.

"This is not a good beginning." Yvette said.

"Well. . ." Aaron started, "I know I can get the gold. It will take me several days to get enough together to make it worth our while."

"Just don't make it too much." David added.

"We're not talking pounds of the stuff." Aaron scowled, "Grams, small amounts taken out a little at a time."

"How much do you think would be safe Aaron?" Yvette asked.

"I'm not sure. Something we could hide in our pockets or maybe under your tongue."

"That didn't work for your grandfather." David interjected.

Aaron's eyes narrowed as his head turned toward David.

"Sorry, Aaron. I wasn't trying to be cruel. It's just that Samuel got caught trying to take it out that way. We have to find something better."

Yvette placed her hand on Aaron's arm. "He's right, Aaron. They're even checking us closer now than before your grandfather was caught. We will have to be much more clever now."

Aaron relaxed at the touch of Yvette's hand. "I don't have an answer yet, but we have a little time to come up with something. Like I said, it will take me a while to gather enough gold. We will have two or three days to come up with something."

"Have you talked to Rabbi Helfer about some ideas?" Yvette asked.

"Yes. He didn't know anything about how Samuel got it out or where he put it once he had it in the barracks. It's like David said, each man had his own part in getting it out. No one knew anything about the operation other than the next man he was to pass it on to. My grandfather only knew the next man in the chain, no one else."

"But wouldn't the SS just have to torture the man caught to find out who his contact was and so on until they had everyone?" Yvette asked.

"Well in my grandfather's case that wasn't a problem since Colonel Oust shot him right away," Aaron said, hesitating slightly as the words forced their way out. "He was too stupid to let him live long enough to find out what he knew."

"Too stupid or too crazy." David interjected.

"Maybe, but in any case the name of my grandfather's contact died with him, but I don't think Oust will be so stupid a second time. He will torture the next person he catches."

"Then what?" David asked.

Aaron glanced down at the table. "In that case." Aaron said, the words coming slowly and softly, "Rabbi Helfer has told me that the next man in the chain would be killed before the SS had a chance to find out who he was."

"Or she." Yvette added.

Aaron looked at his two friends. "Yes. Or she."

"Wouldn't that make the SS suspicious?" David asked. "Killing the next person in the chain?"

"No." Aaron answered. "It's like hiding a tree."

"What? What does a tree have to do with it?"

Aaron shook his head. "Don't you know where the best place to hide a tree is?"

David's eyes widened. "No. I guess not."

"The best place to hide a tree is in a forest." Aaron said.

"So?" David said hunching his shoulders waiting for Aaron to continue.

"So, the best place to kill someone is in a place where people die every day. There is nothing suspicious about someone dying here."

David thought about the answer for a few seconds. "I don't want to become one of the trees."

"Then stay out of the forest." Aaron said getting up from the table. Let's talk again when we each have had some time to think about how we are going to do this."

Chapter 28

Yvette walked very slowly toward the checkpoint as she had done every day of her life for the last three years. This time she was having trouble remembering just how she had done it every day up until now. She was trying to remember what that same nonchalant stride felt like and repeat it. The walk that said she was dead on her feet after painting for the last fourteen hours and she was glad to be heading back to her thin straw bed, but now, she couldn't remember how that felt or looked. The gold she was carrying made all the difference in the world. The few grams of gold hidden on her were so light in her clothing she couldn't feel it, but so heavy in her mind that she seemed to be tripping over it.

She knew that every guard in every tower was watching her, their eyes following every stumbling step she took, waiting for her to cross through the checkpoint so that they could gun her down. It was certain that Sergeant Bella and Colonel Oust were watching her from some vantage point, waiting to pounce on her the second she crossed that invisible line taking her from the work areas into the yard of the housing area. Somewhere behind her, Aaron and David were watching every step she took. Had they noticed the awkward gait of her stride? She strained her ears to hear their pleas for her to come back. Come back, Yvette, her mind heard them calling. Quickly, they know you have the gold. Come back before they kill you!

Each step became harder to make as if glue was running through her leg muscles, hardening every time she made a move closer to the guards standing at the checkpoint.

"Halt!" the guard closest to her sneered. "Komm her!"

Yvette approached the guard without smiling.

"Komm her." He repeated and he motioned with his hand for her to step closer. Yvette noticed that the other guard also moved in closer.

The guard now stood close enough to Yvette for her to smell the stale odor from the last cigarette he smoked before coming on duty.

Yvette didn't bother to speak. There was nothing for her to say and the guard had not asked her for anything.

The older SS guard now reached toward her. "We have to search you." He said as he reached inside her painters smock.

Yvette tried to stand perfectly still as the man ran his hand across her stomach and up the side of her rib cage. She also noticed that the other guard now had his hand inside the pocket of her smock, shaking his hand slightly as he worked his way toward the bottom.

The older guard's hand finally made it's way to her breast. The man squeezed her breast for several seconds. "These are too small to hide anything." He said laughing to his partner. The thought of her stabbing the sick old man in the eye with one of her paint brushes helped to lessen her fear, but could not erase the nausea she felt as the man began to pinch her nipple through her blouse.

The second guard now grabbed her other breast and began to rub it much more softly than the first guard who still had a tight grip on her nipple. "Yes, they are small, but like tiny gems, I think. They may be worth something in a few years."

Both men were laughing as they released their grips. Yvette was able to take in a full breath of cool air as each man then bent down and began searching her shoes. They then worked their way up under her skirt until the older guard ran his hand between her legs.

"I guess this is a gem too." He said showing his crooked teeth as he pushed his fingers hard against her.

Yvette sucked in the cold evening air as the rough handling by the man brought tears to her eyes. Now she thought about stabbing the dirty pig in the groin.

"If you ask me," the older guard continued, "the gems on this one aren't enough to make a man a good pair of cufflinks."

The other guard laughed out loud as he continued to pat her down around the buttocks and then up over her smock. "Maybe not, but I bet I could make them shine if I were to polish them a little!"

"Shit!" the older guard spat, "What is this crap?" he asked, as he held his hand out and looked at it.

The man's hand was now covered in a pasty red and blue goop, blending in some places into a sticky light purple substance.

"It's paint." Yvette volunteered.

"Paint!" the older guard spit as he wiped his hand on Yvette's shoulder.

"Yes, paint. I'm a painter."

"You have it splattered all over your coat." He said as if he had just noticed it for the first time. "What do you paint?" he asked still trying to get the mess off his hand.

"You would have to ask Colonel Oust that question."

Both men unconsciously took a step back from Yvette at the mention of Colonel Oust's name. Neither was privy to what went on in the workshops and knew it to be in their best interest never to find out. As privates in the SS, they would be told what they needed to know by Sergeant Bella and Sergeant Bella had instructed them not to ask question about the special workers.

Yvette stood perfectly still as the two men now examined her visually from a respectable distance. The younger of the two guards handed the older one a handkerchief to finish wiping the paint off his fingers. The older guard stared at her wondering what he should do next. Finally, he scowled at her and gestured vaguely with his head toward the barracks. "Go!" is all he said.

She had to dig deep to find the energy to move away from the checkpoint, but it was fear, fear that they may call her back and touch her again that propelled her toward the barracks. While the two guards were groping her, Yvette promised herself that she would not cry in front of the two bastards, but now, walking away from them, she also promised herself she would have the luxury of crying in private when no one was listening.

Yvette continued toward her barracks not allowing herself to look back at the checkpoint or the two SS men. She quickly stepped into the doorway and let the door close behind her. Yvette leaned against the wall and looked around her. The barracks was dark. The workers had not returned from the fields yet and the lights would not be turned on until they did so. The construction of the barracks was so poor that in some areas there were large gaps between the wooden planks making up the walls and ceiling. When the searchlights from the towers would pass across the building, thin fingers of light would pierce the darkness and ghostly shadows would dance around the room. Because of her desire to one day sketch the dancing shadows; Yvette had memorized the entire troupe of the shadowy figures. Now, in the darkest corner of the room stood a new member of the cast of dancers, a dark shadow that, until tonight, had never been there before, one that had been waiting for her to make it through the checkpoint without alarming the guards, one that now moved toward where she was standing.

"You have something for me?" the shadow asked in a lifeless monotone.

"Who are you?" Yvette asked immediately wishing she hadn't.

"Someone who has lived long enough to know not to ask such a stupid question." The shadow quipped.

"Yes, of course." Yvette answered as she fumbled with the smock. Her hands went directly to one of the large globs of paint covering her jacket. It was the one that the guard had grabbed and had quickly pulled his hand away from when it made contact with the wet paint. Yvette grabbed hold of the gooey substance until her fingers had a firm hold on the piece of gold hidden underneath. The glue David had given her was just strong enough to hold the gold in place forcing her to tug a few times to get it to release. The paint she had applied on top of the piece of gold had been enough to dissuade the guards from checking too close.

Yvette took a small rag out of her pocket and removed the rest of the paint. It had been Aaron's idea to hide the gold in this manner after he had accidentally brushed up against Yvette one afternoon and put his hand in a blob of wet paint. He had cast the metal into pieces mimicking a large blob of paint hanging on her smock. David had come up with the method of fastening it to the smock with the glue and she of course, supplied the paint.

Yvette held out the piece of gold toward the shadow. "This is all we have this time." Yvette offered, "We will get more when we can."

"Whatever you do is appreciated," the shadow dancer whispered, as Yvette dropped the gold piece into the outstretched hand.

"What will you do with it?"

"You insist on asking questions that can come to no good young lady."

Yvette bowed her head. "I. . .I'm sorry. I shouldn't ask."

The inky figure moved further into the darkness of the room. Yvette tried to stay focused on the shadow but in a single blink it faded amongst the troupe of shadow dancers and was gone. Yvette found herself alone again. She suddenly felt physically and mentally drained as she stumbled toward her bunk. She held onto the wooden slats of the bunk with both hands for support fearing that she would not be able to make the climb.

Never had the thin straw covering the wooden slats of her bunk felt so inviting. For the first time today, she felt safe. The gold was someone else's problem now and she was secure in the darkness of her barracks.

Yvette heard the rear door of the barracks open with the faint sound of un-oiled hinges. It opened only a splinter. Yvette held her breath listening for any sound at all. The only thing she could hear was the blood pounding in her ears.

"It will be used to save a life." The darkness whispered.

Like a bolt of lightening the door opened and shut leaving Yvette alone and exhausted.

Chapter 29

Klas' heart lifted with the notes as he followed the music up to his quarters. In the last year Anna had become a permanent fixture in his home. While her cooking was not the best he had ever eaten, her hard work and soft music more than made up for it.

When it came to his quarters, Klas had never wanted for anything since Anna had arrived. Their morning schedule had become ritualistic in nature. Klas would wake to the smell of coffee boiling on the stove, his uniforms were always pressed and hanging on the armoire for his inspection. Even his ribbons and decorations were attached precisely as required by the Waffen SS handbook. Each decoration had been brought to a high order of shine and ready for any inspection. At the foot of the bed lie his boots, polished to a black mirror luster, his socks, washed, mended and rolled like pastries were seated inside the tops of each boot.

Klas would stagger into the kitchen still rubbing the sleep from his eyes to find his breakfast laid out on the kitchen table. There were usually one or two boiled eggs, a piece of cheese and if Anna was able to sweet talk him, a large piece of Sergeant Müller's apricot-cheese strudel. On occasion there would even be a portion of hot porridge or pickled herring when available.

Klas' routine would then take him over to the stove where the hot coffee would be waiting for him. In crossing the kitchen he would often glance out of the window in time to see the tiny silhouette of Anna and her violin case running down the path toward morning roll call.

Klas considered himself lucky to have Anna. The other officers all had personal servants but none of them the quality of Anna. Most were better cooks than Anna and some were even better housekeepers than Anna but, Anna brought more than order to his quarters, Klas had surmised, she brought a feeling of. . .home. He had received several requests from the other officers to barter for Anna's services, one Officer even offering to buy her outright, but Klas had refused all offers for her services.

The first few months had been difficult to adjust to. Klas had only wanted to be left alone. He had convinced himself that he could not be bothered with looking after a housekeeper let alone a young woman barely old enough to take care of herself. At first, he thought Anna to be clumsy and stupid. He had even accused her of being lazy and indifferent when it came to the care of his uniforms and boots. Klas had been stern with her, often making her cry. Several times he had considered calling Sergeant Bella to come and get her, but then would remember Marta.

But after a very rough adjustment period, Klas learned that Anna was very thorough in her chores. He found out that Anna would work hard on correcting the mistakes she had made previously and seldom made the same mistake twice. The only drawback that Klas could see was her being Jewish.

Others had warned him of the trickery and witchcraft a Jewish woman could use on a soldier. He had even heard of soldiers losing their rank or being imprisoned for giving favors or a simple hug to a Jew. Klas could not and would not let this happen to him. Since arriving at Camp 117 he had made several written requests to be transferred back to a combat division. He knew that if he could get back to a tank command his life would return to normal or at least what was normal during a war. In turn, each of the requests had been sent back disapproved. He expected to be called into Colonel Oust's office about the requests, but the Colonel had never approached him about them. Klas was hoping that he would be called in and asked about the numerous requests. He had rehearsed his speech time and time again, wanting a chance to plead his case before the Colonel, but Oust would not fall for the bait. With the war bogging Germany down and a high demand for qualified commanders at the fronts, Klas thought about going over Oust's head, but each time he drafted the letter it would end up in the wastebasket. He had been warned by the

High Command that his duty here was more important. He figured that if the High Command wanted him for his combat experience they would transfer him. To go over Oust's head after being warned by the RF-SS would be an act of career suicide.

Klas' attention returned to the music calling to him from his quarters. He knew that by now Anna had prepared the evening meal and was using the extra time to practice her music. In some ways it saddened Klas to think that the young woman's talents were being wasted in the camp, but then, wasn't his own talent being wasted as a jailer? It seemed to him that the war had played a cruel trick on him. While on the one hand it had given him the perfect chance to advance his career, it had hobbled him with the Jewish issue. If it weren't for the Jews there would not be a need for so many concentration camps and the normal riff-raff like Bella could more than handle the job. Then on top of that it had seen fit to burden him with a young Jewish girl. Anna was very talented just like him and Klas knew that neither would be allowed to leave 117.

Klas continued his climb up the gravel path towards his quarters, every step now hard and determined. His anger grew when he turned past the last stand of trees to see another young woman sitting on the porch with Anna. She was the young French woman who had been given the task of doing an oil portrait of each of the Staff Officers working in Camp 117. It was another one of Oust's efforts to bring culture to the camp. He had forgotten that he had another sitting this evening with the young artist. He was not in the mood to pose for this woman tonight or any night for that matter, but he of course, walked a thin line with Colonel Oust. He did not want to get on the wrong side of the man who could one day give him the transfer he desired.

He would sit for the young artist and immerse himself in Anna's music. Her music always made the sessions easier to handle.

Anna stopped playing as soon as Klas came into sight. She and Yvette both jumped to attention, their arms folded in front, eyes to the ground as Klas climbed the steps to the porch.

"Good evening ladies." Klas smiled, "I had forgotten that tonight, you were once again to immortalize me in oil."

"I could come back at another time, Captain if you wish." Yvette answered, her head still bowed.

"Nonsense, I understand that the National Gallery has already cleared a spot for me and are anxiously awaiting the oil."

Both girls laughed nervously at the snide comment made by Klas.

"I hear that I will be placed between a Rembrandt and a Degas. Quite an accomplishment for me and of course," Klas continued bowing toward Yvette, "the artist."

"You are too kind Monsieur." Yvette curtsied, "They will pale next to the image of such a handsome German Officer."

Klas smiled. The light bantering by the young artist helped to brighten his mood. "Of course the paints will float to the canvas on the lovely notes of our violinist." He added as he bowed and pointed toward Anna.

Anna blushed at the compliment. She had tried to please Klas ever since she had been assigned to his quarters. At first she had convinced herself that it was because she knew how lucky she was to be allowed to stay in such nice quarters. She had made her quarters in the basement of the house, close to the furnace. Since arriving, Anna had never gone to bed cold or hungry. There was always enough food left over from the Captain's meal for her and her cot was always warm. If anything, she felt guilty for living so well when she knew the other women did not. Anna knew from the first night in the house that she would never lose her job because of not performing her duties. She would fight to keep her position in the house, if necessary. She never wanted to go back to the barracks again.

"Would the Captain like to eat first?" Anna asked.

"I think not," Klas said as he tapped his stomach, "I don't want our young artist here to have to run back to the camp to get more paint just because I stuff myself."

Anna and Yvette giggled at Klas' jesting. They had commented before how Klas was somehow different from the other officers they had met. In the past several months Anna and Yvette had become best of friends. Neither girl had remembered seeing the other a year or so ago when Anna had come to the camp. She and Anna had been in different barracks and on different schedules. Anna would always get up earlier than most because of her duties with the orchestra.

Her group was already assembled by the time the whistle blew for the others to assemble. Yvette, being a member of the special work group would assemble on the north end of the assembly area while Anna and the rest of the orchestra would have already gathered on the south end close to the main gate. Yvette and the special workers would proceed north through the checkpoint leading to their workshops when the main body of the prisoners was marched south through the gate. Anna and the orchestra would play while the work details dragged their tired bodies out of the compound toward the fields and rock quarry.

The two women even ate in separate mess halls; Yvette's being in the special work area and Anna, in the main camp. Since moving into Captain Von Reichman's quarters, Anna never ate in the main camp mess hall any more.

Once they had become acquainted the young women were inseparable. Yvette had even been able to get Anna assigned to the special work area when she wasn't playing with the orchestra. Anna was very grateful for the transfer since the work usually kept her away from Sergeant Bella. Bella very seldom came into the special work area anymore. Anna and Yvette had surmised that it was difficult for him to keep his hands, or worse yet, his ax handle, off the special workers. When one day at lunch Bella crushed the hand of one of the more promising young artists Colonel Oust was furious with him. For several days there were even rumors that Bella would be transferred to a front line unit, but in the end, things seemed to quiet down and Bella made less and less visits to the special area. Now that Anna's extra duties kept her in the special work area, she hardly saw the man at all.

"Very well then, Captain." Yvette said, "Shall we go into the living room and continue with our work?"

Klas motioned toward the door. "Please, destiny awaits."

Anna and Yvette allowed Klas to enter first. Yvette went over to her easel and prepared her paints while Anna made her way toward the kitchen. "Sir, would you like some tea before I start preparing your dinner?" Anna asked.

Klas had already taken his position in front of the canvas. "That would be very nice, Anna." He shouted toward the kitchen. "Yvette, would you care for some tea?"

Yvette bowed her head. "No, thank you, Captain. You are very kind." She answered as she had every time he offered in the past.

Anna brought out a place setting for Klas and, as usual, a glass of water for Yvette. Anna looked over Yvette's shoulder as she placed the glass on the table next to her. Anna admired Yvette's skill with the paint brush. The portrait of the Captain was more than two-thirds finished and it was magnificent. Amazingly, Yvette had captured the very essence of Klas and transferred it to the canvas in front of her. He was quite a handsome man, she thought, probably one of the most handsome men she had ever remembered seeing. Almost by magic Yvette was able to enhance that on her canvas.

Anna had heard Klas remark to some of the other officers that Yvette was, in his opinion, the most gifted painter in the workshop and would certainly be in the final selection. Anna didn't understand what that meant, but assumed it was a great honor for Yvette. Anna knew the value of doing a good job around the camp. Those who did their work well and pleased the SS were much better off than the prisoners assigned to the hard labor details. She had heard rumors that the main camp was much the same. She prayed every day that her mother had somehow managed to get into a special work group, maybe in the camp's kitchen. She knew her mother was a very good cook and baker; maybe she had been assigned a job in the kitchen.

"Yvette, have you ever gone to the main camp since you've been here?" Anna suddenly asked.

The color drained from Yvette's face as she quickly looked down at her palette. Yvette thought about ignoring Anna's question as if she hadn't heard it, but knew better. Anna, in her childish innocence, would just ask it again. "Yes, I have been there a few times."

"Is it as big as they say it is?"

"I think so." Yvette answered trying not to make eye contact with Captain Von Reichman. "There is no way you can see it all in a single visit."

The tea kettle began to whistle and Anna turned and walked back into the kitchen. Yvette wasn't sure but she thought she saw a momentary look of relief in Klas' posture when Anna was called away by the tea kettle. When she looked up the next time, he had regained his composure.

Anna returned with the tea and set it on the table next to Klas. "Do you want anything else, Captain?"

Klas lowered his eyes toward the table trying not to move too much. "No, Anna, that will be fine."

"Then if the Captain is not hungry yet, may I stay and watch Yvette work?"

"Yes, unless Yvette thinks otherwise."

Anna smiled at Yvette, her eyes glowing with the question. Yvette looked at Anna and then back to the painting. She could still feel Anna's eyes on her.

"Yvette?"

Yvette looked at Anna again. "It would be fine, Anna, but please no talking tonight. I am at a difficult part and must have my concentration."

"That's right, Anna." Klas said quite seriously "I do not want to be hanging in the National Museum looking like Quasimodo!"

Laughter burst out of the two young women like that of innocent children on a playground.

Yvette was laughing so hard she had to put down her brush and wipe the tears from her eyes. "Captain, please!" Yvette managed to get out between sobs and giggles. "I can't paint while I'm laughing."

Klas laughed out loud himself. He broke his stiff pose and reached down for the tea cup. "I think this might be a good time for me to have a little tea."

Anna had both of her hands over her mouth trying to suppress her giggles. Finally, she began waving her hand in front of her face trying to suppress her laughter. "Well if you are going to take a break Yvette, let me get you a cup of tea."

Yvette's eyes darted toward Klas. He had his cup to his mouth and hadn't heard Anna's statement.

"What?" Klas asked, a little confused at first, then catching on to the conversation that must have just happened. "Yes, Yvette. You may have some tea if you like."

Yvette smiled toward Anna. "That would be nice."

Anna was happy to rush off toward the kitchen for the tea. Yvette took the opportunity to re-arrange her paints and clean a bush or two. Anna darted back into the room with the extra cup.

Yvette brought the cup to her lips and the hot liquid ran into her mouth. Yvette, being used to the camp diet of turnip soup, sour bread and moldy vegetables was shocked by the clean bite of the fresh tea. It seemed that every taste bud in her mouth fought to get a sample of the tannic brew if for no other reason than to refresh themselves after so long.

"This is wonderful." She stammered between sips, "I have not tasted anything like this in years."

Klas looked over his cup at Yvette. His gaze firm but not cruel, "And you still haven't. If you take my meaning?"

Yvette paled as she nodded her head in understanding.

Anna sat down on the sofa next to her. Klas remained in the chair where he had been sitting.

"So," Anna's voice boomed like an artillery piece, "What is the main camp like?"

Yvette coughed some of her tea back into her cup and down the front of her chin. She quickly wiped the liquid from her mouth with the sleeve of her smock.

"Anna," Klas said interceding "You are not supposed to talk about that. It is forbidden to discuss such things." he added a little more sternly.

Anna bowed her head and slowly pushed herself up off the couch. Yvette could see that the Captain's words had scolded Anna like a small schoolgirl.

"I am sorry, Captain." Anna almost pouted. "It's just that I haven't seen or heard from my mother in so long." Anna looked at Klas and then back toward Yvette. "I was just hoping to hear some news of her."

The air in the room became stale as the festive mood vanished as quickly as it had come. Yvette tried to hide her nervousness in the bottom of her teacup while Klas stared at Anna.

"I am getting a little hungry, Anna." Klas said evenly "You should prepare my meal while Yvette finishes up this session."

Anna bowed her head and slowly left the room. It wasn't until the sounds of clinking pots and pans filled the kitchen that Klas relaxed.

"You are Anna's friend?" He asked.

Yvette was busy with her paints again, "Yes Captain."

"And you have been to the main camp?"

"Yes, Captain." Yvette answered weakly.

"And you haven't found it necessary to tell her about it?"

Yvette wished desperately to be back in her studio right now. "It is forbidden, Captain."

"Don't play games with me, Yvette." Klas said

The sudden change in Klas' voice frightened her. Somehow the lighthearted jovial tone had transformed into a calm, but commanding voice that demanded a response rather than screamed for one. The voice seemed to be separate and apart from Klas.

"I am sorry, Captain, but Anna is such a wonderful musician. She has such a talent. I - I. . ."

"Yes?" he said, still waiting for the response that Yvette knew that she had no choice but to give.

Yvette finally let it out. "To tell her might crush the gift inside her."
"How do you know that?"

Yvette looked up at Klas, tears sparkling in the corner of her eyes. "Because it almost crushed me." She whimpered, as the tears raced down her cheeks and around the corners of her mouth.

Chapter 30

Things were going too well and Aaron knew it. The smuggling operation had proceeded without a hitch for the last seven months. The Germans seemed to have more gold and silver than ever before which meant larger amounts were available for smuggling.

Aaron never knew whom the gold went to or what it was used for, but that never bothered him. They had been very successful in their operation and that's what was important to him and the others. But now the Rabbi Helfer had summoned him and after all the time that had passed it couldn't be good news.

Aaron walked through the check point without incident and continued toward his barracks. His jacket pulled at his neck because of the weight of his two hands in the pockets, forcing the collar to rub the skin. Aaron ignored the irritation as he concentrated on the bigger issue at hand. Just beyond the door of the barracks, Aaron knew the Rabbi would be waiting for him. Aaron burped slightly and was rewarded with an acid taste in his mouth. Yes, he thought, things had gone too well. Now the Rabbi was going to up the anti for him and his group.

Aaron quickly went through the door and as no surprise to him, saw Rabbi Helfer sitting on the bottom bunk of the stand of bunks Aaron slept in.

"Shalom, Aaron." The Rabbi greeted him without standing.

"Hello Rabbi." Aaron answered, taking a seat next to him. "You look well."

Rabbi Helfer made a dismissive gesture toward the roof of the building. "By the grace of God."

Aaron sat looking down at the floor in front of his feet for several seconds. The silence between he and the Rabbi hung thick in the air. Aaron thought about his grandfather and how well the man could handle any conversation. As far back as Aaron could remember, Samuel always had a way with words and people. Aaron was not one for small talk. Getting directly to the matter at hand seemed to suit him the best. Pleasantries were best left to the men who knew how to handle them. That had been his grandfather's forte, not his.

"You would not have asked to see me Rabbi unless there was something wrong."

"Wrong?" Rabbi Helfer blinked, "No, no nothing wrong Aaron. Things couldn't be any better."
Aaron smiled at the candor of the older man.
"That is good to hear sir. I can think of nothing better than to be free of bad news for awhile."

"Yes, yes, bad news can weigh a man down terribly."

Aaron looked at the Rabbi. "Like they weigh you down now?"

Rabbi Helfer looked deep into Aaron's eyes. "Ah, you are not the boy I knew a year ago, Aaron."

"A lot has happened in a year, Rabbi. I have learned more in the last year than I have in my entire life before that."

Rabbi Helfer shook his head in agreement. "Truer words have never been spoken Aaron, but remember, it was your upbringing that allows you to be here today."

As it had many times before, Aaron's entire life with his grandfather flashed before him. It didn't happen often, but when it did, it always gave him a warm, loving feeling. The flash backs never included his grandfather's death. That always came separately. That always brought him back to reality.

"Which brings us to our meeting, Rabbi. What could weigh so heavily on such a light soul?"

A smile ran across Rabbi Helfer's face only to be quickly chased away by a heavy frown. "Ah, one's good luck is another's misfortune, Aaron."

Aaron sat quietly and waited to hear of the latest misfortune.

"First of all Aaron, let me tell you that what you and your group have done is remarkable. You have given us the means to save many, many lives."

"We have never doubted our worth Rabbi."

Rabbi Helfer waved his hand lightly in the air. "I know Aaron, I know. But you have never asked for proof of the results and I know how hard that must be for such an inquisitive mind."

A huge smile raced across Aaron's face. Not knowing what was happening outside of his little group had always bothered him. They had always talked about it amongst themselves but it was mostly speculation.

"What your little group has done," continued Rabbi Helfer, "has saved the lives of many men and women, Aaron. We have used the money to bribe guards, buy extra food and drinking water. We have even used the money to have people removed from the death list."

"Rabbi," Aaron interrupted, "if you are afraid that we will not continue to help. . ."

"No, never! I would never think such a thing Aaron. You have helped more than most."

"Then why the meeting?" Aaron asked, looking directly into Rabbi Helfer's eyes. Aaron thought he could see the very life draining from the man. The Rabbi's shoulders seemed to welter, his posture crumble right in front of him. Suddenly Aaron felt bad for asking such a direct question.

Rabbi Helfer looked at Aaron for several seconds and then turned away. "Because, Aaron, I must now ask more of you and your group."

The blood began to pound in Aaron's ears as if that could somehow force the Rabbi's last words out of his head. Aaron felt as if a huge hand had just ripped into his chest squeezing the breath out of his lungs, the blood out of his heart. His strength left him as if stolen by the Rabbi's last request. He was thankful that he was sitting down and prayed that the Rabbi, sitting only a few inches away, could not feel the uncontrollable shaking he was experiencing.

"Rabbi, I. . .I don't know." Aaron muttered trying to gather his thoughts into an understandable sentence while trying to find the strength to speak them intelligently. "how. . .what could...I mean..."

Rabbi Helfer placed his hand on Aaron's shoulder. Aaron was surprised to see that the man's hand was shaking. "Aaron, the SS has tightened security around the camp, more so here in this camp than even the bigger ones. We don't know why or for how long, but the added security has hurt us badly. Our sources outside the camp are afraid to come close to the camp to make contact with us. The SS has cut us off from the outside world."

"Can't you just bribe the guards with more gold?"

Rabbi Helfer shook his head slowly from side to side like a huge bell tolling a death notice. "Bribes can do only so much. The guards we are able to bribe will only take so many risks. They want to be able to live long enough to spend the money."

"Then we wait and see what happens," Aaron said proudly for thinking so clearly under pressure, "maybe in a few weeks things will be back to normal. In the meantime, we can continue to move the gold out of the shop and into your hands. You will have plenty of gold when things get better."

"We have considered that. We could wait and see how long this tightened security lasts and, like you say, we can continue to move gold out of the workshop and into secure places. But, every day we wait, people die."

"Rabbi, everyone in the camp knows of death. It is part of our daily existence."

"True, all true Aaron, but until now we have been able steal a few lives back. But now we are seeing huge outbreaks of typhus and dysentery. In some of the camps lice have reached epidemic proportions. It is bad enough that the SS beat us from the moment we rise until the second we close our eyes. They feed us swill that their own dogs wouldn't eat. I saw Sergeant Bella beat a man to death yesterday because he tried to pick up a few crumbs that the fat man had dropped on the ground."

Aaron noticed that tears now made their way down Rabbi Helfer's rutted cheeks. "For a few lousy crumbs of food, the man lost his life. And now even nature works hard at doing the SS's job. Aaron, yesterday a friend of mine told me something that I will never forget as long as I draw a breath. He told me that before the war he would wake up each morning and wonder what life would share with him. Now, he wakes up each morning and wonders what death will take away from him.

He told me, 'Rabbi, in this camp one thing is certain, every day someone will die.' Every morning I must ask myself; 'Do I ask God to spare me from death or do I ask him to give it to me and end my suffering.'

Aaron placed his arm around the Rabbi's shoulders as the man sobbed. He felt strange giving comfort to a man that had always been the strong one for him. In some ways Aaron knew that he had adopted the Rabbi as his family after Samuel had died. In a time when the SS was trying desperately to destroy Jewish families, the Jewish people turned to each other and made their own family. That was another reason why Aaron believed that the Nazis would never win.

Aaron held the man tightly as he had done so many times with Samuel. "Rabbi, you ask nothing of us that you don't give yourself. We will do what we can, when we can."

"I never doubted that, Aaron. What I doubted was my ability to ask you to do more. To do something that could put you and your friends in more danger than you have ever been before."

"Go ahead and ask Rabbi, we will do what we can."

Rabbi Helfer took several deep breaths as he gathered his thoughts. "You have a friend in the camp orchestra, Anna?"

"Yes." Aaron answered cautiously. "But she is not part of the smuggling operation. She has been able to get us some information about the war by listening to Captain Von Reichman's radio at night, but little more."

"She listens to Von Reichman's radio? Isn't that dangerous?"

"No, not really. Her quarters are in the basement close to the furnace. She says she can hear it as well as he can."

Rabbi Helfer thought about what Aaron had just said for a few moments then continued. "But she is still with the orchestra, yes?"

"Yes."

"Aaron, our contacts will not come close to the camp right now so we must go to them. The orchestra is taken out of the camp from time to time to perform for the SS and their friends, correct?"

Yes, I guess, I mean I know that Colonel Oust likes to show them off to his friends. I've heard that they play at parties and concerts."

"It will be at these concerts that Anna will be valuable to us."

"How can she help?" Aaron asked, already fearing the answer to his question.

"Our sources outside the camp have access to these functions. We must devise a way that Anna can take the gold to them and retrieve the medicines and drugs we need. You must find a way for her to do this Aaron."

Aaron knew that this was something he would have to discuss with the others before he told the Rabbi they would do it. Aaron had no doubt that they would do it; at least he hoped they all would agree. Anna added a new twist to everything. He knew he would be in for a fight with Yvette. She and Anna had become very close.

"I have to go now, Aaron," Rabbi Helfer said getting to his feet, "Please work quickly. Much depends on what we can do and how fast it can be done.

Aaron stood and extended his hand. "We will work quickly, Rabbi. Good-bye for now."

The two each headed for the opposite ends of the barracks. Aaron was almost to the front door when he turned back to face Rabbi Helfer. "Rabbi."

Rabbi Helfer released the latch on the rear door of the building. "Yes?"

"If you can, will you see about bringing Anna's mother over from the main camp?"

Rabbi Helfer turned and walked back into the room. "Aaron, what you ask would be very difficult to do."

"Everything that is asked these days is difficult to do, Rabbi."
Rabbi Helfer rubbed his chin until Aaron thought he might remove skin. "What is her name?"
"Sigrid Mayer. She is in the main Auschwitz camp we think."
Rabbi Helfer frowned for a few seconds and his eyes blinked several times as he processed the request. "I will do what I can." He said as he returned to the rear door of the barracks.

Chapter 31

Anna found it impossible to fall asleep with Klas still banging around on the main floor of the house. He had barely spoken a word to her since he had marched up the gravel walkway from the camp and charged into the house. Klas' appearance had frightened her. German Officers were known for their professional demeanor and outward presentation of military correctness. Klas had been the perfect model until now.

But this evening Klas had tossed professional demeanor and outward presentation to the wind. Each of Klas' wool tunics was a privately tailored item of high quality. The collar patches were hand-embroidered, as was the sleeve eagle. On his right collar was the SS-rune while the left bore the emblem of a Captain. Both insignia were mounted on a double underlay of light brown,

Concentration Camp, and the SS black. Klas wore the officer regulation black leather belt and highly polished buckle. All of his orders and decorations were always in a state of high polish as were his boots. Anna knew these details by heart as she had cleaned, polished and assembled them time and time again. Anna had always heard that it was the uniform that made the man, but in Klas' case it was the furthest thing from the truth. Except for Colonel Oust, no one in the camp filled out the SS uniform better than Klas.

Tonight Anna felt hurt by Klas' unruly appearance. He had come back to the quarters later than usual, stopping somewhere along the way to have several drinks with the junior officers. Somewhere between the last drink and the house, Klas had managed to unbutton his collar allowing his Knights Cross to dangle freely to one side. She had noticed that he had managed to scuff both of his boots and drop his service cap. She had surmised that in his drunken state, he had unconsciously allowed himself to favor his injured legs by shuffling them along the path and in the process, tripped over his own feet catapulting his cap into the mud.

Anna knew of his injuries and had even noticed him limp somewhat when they were alone in the house. She had never mentioned the injuries or let on that she had ever seen him limping.

The house that had seemed to be roomy and comfortable before, now, had become confining and tense as Anna found herself dodging Klas as he moved in and out of rooms talking mostly to himself. It was obvious that he was upset about his having to work in the camp. He had never hidden his dislike for the work in the camp and had often commented about being a combat soldier, not a jailer. Anna knew little of what a soldier was supposed to do or not do. The only thing Anna knew about the German Army was what she had learned in the camp, but to hear Klas rave about his wanting to go back to the armored division she thought that there must be something more to being a soldier than she saw.

She spent most of the evening avoiding any eye contact and had abandoned any thoughts that he might stop drinking long enough to eat. Finally, after several arguments with himself, Klas dismissed her and ordered her down to the basement. He had been particularly cruel to her at the end calling her a Jew. Since that time he had been stumbling around the house slamming cabinets and doors.

Anna took her violin out of its case and checked the strings and polished the wood. Playing in the camp orchestra had turned out to be hard work. Colonel Oust had been a lot stricter than Frau Klibe. He had no tolerance for those that did not perform well and on more than one occasion had sent a musician back to the main camp work detail when he decided that the musician was not of the caliber he was looking for.

When Colonel Oust was unavailable for instruction they were split into several work details. Their main duty was to play each morning and evening as the prisoners left and returned to the compound. On occasion, a group was selected to play at the main camp when Colonel Oust was there selecting new workers. She had never been picked for the main camp duty, but had hoped someday she would. The best duty was when Colonel Oust would arrange for a concert to be preformed. Most often these concerts were held in the nearby town of Oswiecim or, on special occasions, at one of the large industrial compounds in the area such as the I. G. Farben SS War Industries Complex. She especially enjoyed the concerts because of the wonderful uniforms they were required to wear during the performance. Colonel Oust had the uniforms especially made by the main camp clothing shop. It was the nicest outfit Anna now owned.

Anna was about to place her violin back into its case when she noticed that Klas had finally quieted down. She was relieved to think that the man had finally gone to bed. She made a mental note to go upstairs later on and check on him. She was also very happy that Klas was scheduled off for the next two days. It would give him a chance to get over his drinking and give her time to work on the parts of his uniform that needed attention.

Anna jumped as the sound of the piano cried out; its notes echoing off the walls and through the vents of the furnace. In the two years she had been in the house no one had ever touched the piano before. It had always sat dormant, up against the wall in the living room. Now the instrument jumped to life, the notes harsh and loud.

It had to be Klas, Anna thought, she hadn't heard anyone enter the house. She was shocked at the idea that Klas could play. He had never mentioned any musical talent before and had made no attempt to play the piano previously. Anna listened to the music drifting through the vents and also down the stairs from the kitchen.

While the music was clear and perfectly played, there was a hard tone about it, as if Klas was punishing the piano. He was not working with the instrument. It was more like he was fighting with it and had every intention to win or at least make the instrument submit to his will.

She listened while Klas bounced from Brahms to Debussy then raced into Mozart and then back to Brahms. It was hard on the ears to listen to such rambling on the keyboard. Then as quickly as it started, it stopped. Maybe he'll go to bed now, she thought, but she had no sooner made the wish than Klas started up again, this time much softer, more in control of the music and himself.

Anna shivered as he began the piece. She had played it may times for her Mother and her friends. It was Amadeus' Sonate e-moll in E minor. Without thinking she reached for her violin lying in the open case and brought it up to her chin. The feel of the smooth wood pressed up against her chin brought her comfort. She prepared and waited, listening to Klas play. Then she began to play softly not wanting him to hear her for fear that he would stop playing. She quickly got lost in the music coming from upstairs and barely breathed as she moved the bow across the strings, the music floating into the air to mix with that of the piano. Anna continued to play, the feeling and the momentum taking her away from the dimly lit basement to the Opera house in Frankfurt where her mother had taken her many times and the place where she would often dream about playing.

Anna became enveloped in her playing, the pounding of her heart keeping rhythm with the notes. Soon she found herself standing, the volume of her playing matching that of Klas'. She closed her eyes, forcing the moisture there to form into small tears, which grew until they finally, burdened by their own weight, splashed on to her cheek and ran their course down her face. Anna knew that many a tear had followed that path in the last few years, but none before tonight had flowed with the feelings she was experiencing now. She continued to play, wondering what was so different and what had brought her to this moment. The music came from where it had always come; an area deep inside her just below her heart, but the other feeling was much stronger, coming from a place much deeper inside her, racing from place to place, entangling itself with her music forcing her to play with such passion that she had not noticed that Klas had stopped playing and was now standing at the bottom of the staircase watching her.

Anna finished the piece and softly exhaled, her eyes still closed.

"That was magnificent." Klas whispered.

Anna jumped at the sound of his voice. Her eyes dashing from his to the violin and then darted around the room as if she was a small animal desperately searching for a corner to hide in. When she concluded that there was no such hiding place, she immediately dropped her eyes to the floor, the violin held closely to her chest with both hands. "Thank you, my Captain." She said softly wiping her eyes, "I'm. . ahhh.. . I'm, I'm sorry for disturbing your playing," she stammered, "but it was so beautiful - I didn't know you could play." she blurted out.

"Yes," he answered, taking note of Anna's peculiar use of the phrase 'my Captain', "It was one of my mother's requirements."

"Requirements?"

"Yes," Klas answered as he stepped down from the bottom stair and moved closer to Anna. "A German Officer is also a Gentleman." Klas mimicked in what Anna could only guess was Klas' mother's tone of voice. "There are finer things that they must learn besides the art of war."

Anna smiled sheepishly, "Yes, mothers can be that way."

Both stood there, Klas looking at Anna, Anna looking at the floor in front of her.

"No doubt." Klas laughed nervously after an awkward moment of silence.

Anna could only manage a weak smile. Klas began mindlessly to straighten his uniform or what he was still wearing. He had discarded his tunic and now wore only a long sleeved undergarment and suspenders so he ended up only being able to straighten his suspenders. "Anna I, ahhhh, would like to apologize for my behavior this evening. It was not. . . appropriate for me to. . ."

Klas stopped short on his apology when he noticed that the color had drained from Anna's face and her eyes hollow and ghostly darted manically about the room. "Is there something wrong?" he continued, "Are you feeling alright, Anna?"

"Sir," Anna answered softly, her voice quavering, "this is *your* house. You need not offer any type of apology to me."

Klas looked into Anna's eyes and found comfort there. He held up a piece of crumpled paper for her to see. "I've just been informed that my friend, Lieutenant - no sorry," he said correcting himself with a thin smile, "Major

Zimmermen was killed on the Eastern Front last month."

Klas noticed that Anna had begun to shake, her violin held tightly to her chest. Klas took another step closer to her and reached out with an open hand. "Anna, let me have the violin."

Anna's eyes shot up and caught the warm smile on his face and knew it would be alright to do so.

"Thank you." Klas said continuing to smile, "It would be a shame if you damaged this wonderful instrument," he added as he placed the violin into its case with an almost reverent ceremony. "Now," he continued, "Where was I?"

"Your friend Major. . ."

"Ahhh yes, my friend Conrad." Klas continued as he swayed from side to side the liquor still in control of his senses. "I felt it necessary to send Conrad off with a toast this evening and I got carried away. So I must apologize for my. . .rude – yes, rude behavior."

"I am sorry to hear about your friend, Captain," Anna said tenderly, "but as I said before, this is your home. You need not offer any type of apology to me."

"Ahhh," Klas started, pointing his finger into the air, "it is because this is my house that I feel the need to make an apology."

"Captain, Sir." Anna started but was quickly silenced by Klas raising his hand and gently motioning her to be quiet.

"Anna, there are things happening that you are not aware of and I cannot discuss them with you, but the war does not. . ." Klas hesitated for several seconds before continuing, "go as well as the General Staff had hoped. The notice of my friend's death could not have come at a worse time and my current assignment here is not what I had hoped it would be and sometimes, well, sometimes it is a heavy burden on me."

"If I have done anything to worsen your burden, my Captain?" the words rattled out of her mouth before she could think them through, "I will try to do better. . ."

"No, no Anna. You are wonderful. I could not ask for better. It's just that at times the burden is too much for me to just shrug off and some of my anger spills over into other areas."

"Other areas?"

"Yes, other areas," Klas answered measuring his next words carefully, "like the way I treated you this evening."

Anna blinked several times, her mind taking in every word Klas spoke. "Oh, I see, Captain. I did not know that your duties were so important - no that's not what I meant." Anna said, her face turning a bright crimson color, "What I meant, Captain is that I do not understand your duties or the burden they must bring."

Klas smiled at Anna's confusion. "Thank you for trying to understand."

Klas stood there, swaying slightly. For the first time since entering the basement he felt extremely warm as the Brandy began to pound in his ears. He looked around the small room that was Anna's quarters and listened to the metallic sounds coming from the furnace as it clicked and popped busily warming the house.

"I will take care of your uniform in the morning." Anna said breaking the silence.

"That would be good." Klas answered looking down at what little of his uniform he still had on, "You remembered that I am off duty tomorrow?"

"Yes, Captain."

"I think I will sleep in tomorrow then." Klas said as he turned and made his way back to the staircase.

"Anna had to smile at the comment. "I think that would be wise, my Captain."

Klas staggered to a stop and turned to face Anna again. He looked at the young woman for several seconds. "Anna."

"Yes, Captain."

Klas shook his head slightly as if the motion would help clear his thinking. "Anna, when we are alone, you may call me Klas. . .if you like." He quickly added.

Anna's eyes warmed at the gesture. "Yes, Captain."

Chapter 32

Having given up on trying to sleep, Aaron carefully slipped out of the bunk in such a manner as not to disturb those trying to cram in every moment of rest. He wrapped his thin coat around him and shivered at the thought of the cold weather outside. It was only early August and the nights were already turning bad. He did not understand how the men assigned to the quarries survived. Their rations were half of what he and the other special workers got. Their clothing, nothing but rags and the shoes, battered and worn, had been the home for more than a dozen pair of feet before the current owner. Some of the men wore shoes that didn't even match, taking the better shoe of two pairs and making the best of it.

Most of the men were too sick to give a real day's work, but the only way to get off the quarry detail was to go to the infirmary or to die. Everyone knew that the infirmary was just another path to death so they went out into the quarry each day instead. Often, they were still singled out during the "selections" and replaced by new, stronger workers. It seemed to Aaron that all roads for the quarry worker lead to death. He remembered what Samuel had once told him. "This camp is all about work, Aaron. The SS work the Jews in a manner that ensures that the Jews die working under their boot."

Despite this, he and the others in the underground continued to work every day at helping the camp's occupants to survive. It was a job that he and the others lost often, but it was a job that none were willing to give up. The words of Rabbi Helfer also echoed in his head. "There is no past, Aaron and no future, there is only today. It matters little whose life we saved yesterday and there's no time to worry about whose life we may save tomorrow. It is the life we save today that matters. That is what is important."

Aaron walked toward the rear of the building. For some reason it was the warmest place in the wooden barracks. He sat in the corner going over the things he would have to do once the SS guard blew the whistle for morning roll call. The list was short and distasteful. Today he would have to do something he had hoped to avoid. Something that may cause him to lose a friend in the camp; and he reminded himself that friends were worth much more than the gold he and the others had been smuggling.

The men started to move about, milling around the barracks as if each were searching for the one thing that would keep them alive. A few of the men walked past Aaron and opened the rear door leading to the toilet barracks. The cold air rushed in the opening carrying with it the foul stench of the toilet. Aaron turned his head and got up from the floor. It took him a few minutes to make his way to the front of the barracks. Many of the men would often reach out and silently touch Aaron on the shoulder. No one in the barracks was supposed to know what Aaron had been doing, which meant that everyone knew. Touching him as he passed had become their way of silently thanking him. Aaron got the feeling that some merely touched him to assure themselves that he was still there.

The guard's whistle cut through the air and signaled the start of the workday. It was still dark outside as the men quickly filed through the door and onto the assembly area for roll call. Aaron stood to one side and allowed everyone else to exit before him. It was important that the quarry workers clear the barracks first as they always had Sergeant Bella watching their every move. Bella was always watching for the straggler. Someone he could easily cull from the herd, as would a pack of wolves singling out a sick sheep.

Aaron knew that he had about three or four minutes between the time the last man made it through the door and when the SS guard would enter the barracks looking for stragglers or those too sick to make it out of their bunks. He looked around the barracks and noticed that only one man remained in his bunk. Aaron could tell from where he stood that the man would not be going to roll call this morning. Instead, he would wait for Ivan Shim and his cart.

Aaron walked out into the open area and glanced over to the raised platform where he knew Bella would be standing, supervising the morning count. There, as predictable as a good Swiss timepiece, stood Bella. His stubby legs spread about shoulder width apart supporting his massive frame. Across his shoulders lay his only friend, the ax handle. His two arms were looped over the ax handle giving Bella the appearance of a huge Ox strapped to a yoke. From where Aaron stood he could see Bella's lips curling with disgust, his dirty teeth snarling at the workers. It would be an especially hard day for the quarry workers, Aaron thought as he turned toward the North end of the camp where he and the other special workers would gather.

The special workers quickly lined up in rows of four across and waited to be counted. Aaron did not bother to look for David and Yvette. It was better to mind your own business during roll call and get it over with quickly. The quicker roll call went, the quicker they got out of the cold. Their roll call was not meant to be a form of torture as was the quarry workers. The SS guard would quickly walk down the ranks verifying the count where in the main roll call there were often miscounts meaning the workers had to stand at attention while the count was taken a second or third time. The guards at the main roll call would often yell and scream at the prisoners taking the opportunity to kick or beat them for the slightest infraction. The SS in charge of Aaron's group would rarely speak to them; getting roll call over as quick as possible. After all, Aaron and the others were of no use to the SS unless they were in their workshops.

Aaron's group was lead through the checkpoint and was directed toward the kitchen barracks for breakfast. Once through the checkpoint the SS guard would abandon them. Within seconds David had caught up with Aaron and stood by his side.

"Did you see Bella this morning?" David asked

"I see him every morning." Aaron replied, "I see him in my sleep."

"He looked really mad this morning, even for a rabid dog."

Aaron shivered slightly. "I know. It will be a long day for the workers."

"Hmmm"

"How many?" Aaron asked. It had become a daily ritual for he and David to discuss how many men had died during the night. Neither knew quite why they would discuss it, but it had become important to them. Yvette had refused to participate in their morning count and would therefore never join them in line until the discussion was over and they were inside having breakfast.

"Two, possibly three." David answered. "You?"

"Only one." Aaron answered thinking about the dead man. "One of the new arrivals."

"Have you talked with Yvette yet?" David asked.

Aaron's eyes burned into David. "When would I have had the chance?" he shot back.

"Still going to ask her to do it?"

"What choice do we have?"

"None." David answered. "I was just hoping that you would think of something else."

"There is nothing else. Nothing that fits what we need."

"Do you think that she'll help us?"

Aaron shook his head from side to side as he climbed the steps leading into the kitchen barracks. "I don't know, but if the plan doesn't work I don't know what to do next."

"Then you better convince her."

"Thank you for the advice." Aaron mumbled as he pushed the door aside and he and David entered the barracks.

It didn't take Aaron and David very long to get their ration of soup, a small cup of weak coffee and even smaller piece of hard bread. Together they moved to an open table and sat down and began to eat.

"Is it safe to sit down?" Yvette asked, as she juggled her food into a position where she could put the bowl and cup down without spilling any of the precious liquids.

"If you're asking if we finished our conversation about the morning count. The answer is yes." David smiled with malicious delight, "Would you like the final tally?"

Yvette swung her legs over the bench and rearranged the food in front of her. "No. Good morning Aaron."

Aaron briefly glanced up from his bowl. "Morning." is all he said.

"Is this going to be one of those days when I have to pull every word out of your mouth, Aaron?" Yvette asked before turning to David. "Is he in one of his moods?" she asked, gesturing emphatically toward Aaron.

"He has a solution to our little problem." David said grinning like a Cheshire cat.

"David!" Aaron hissed under his breath.

Yvette looked back and forth at the two boys. "Well, what is it?"

"Aaron has it all worked out." David shot back before Aaron could respond.

Yvette looked at Aaron and waited for several seconds. "Well? Are you going to wait and have David put it into print for publishing or are you going to tell me?"

Aaron looked around the room to see exactly where the guards were standing. As had become the norm lately, they were both standing close to the kitchen holding cups of coffee. "I'm not sure it will work."

"Well, tell us." Yvette said patiently, "That way we can all be unsure together."

Aaron's nose wrinkled up in a manner that made him squint as he stared at Yvette. As always, Yvette continued to stare right back at him until he broke eye contact with her. "It's very dangerous." He said.

Yvette became impatient quickly. "Enough with the doubt and warning, Aaron. Do you have a plan or not?"

David giggled at the exchange.

"Shut up." Aaron and Yvette spat simultaneously.

All three looked up to see if the guards had become alarmed by their conversation. When they were satisfied that the guards had not overheard them, they continued with their meal.

Aaron wasn't sure where to take the conversation. "We have to be able to get the items out of the camp and into the hands of our friends."

Both David and Yvette knew that the "items" Aaron was talking about was the gold. They always referred to the gold as "items" or "gear", but never as just gold. Talking about gold brought too many ears into the conversation.

"Yes." Yvette prompted.

"Then," Aaron continued, "we have to exchange the items for items of similar value." Both knew that in this case, "items of similar value," meant medicine.

"We know all of this." Yvette said evenly, "Where are you leading us?"

Aaron's eyes met hers. "Well the trick is to get the items out to a place where they can be exchanged and new items brought back to us." Aaron waited for the words to sink in. "That means it has to be taken out and returned by someone we trust."

David and Yvette continued to eat but both shook their head in agreement.

Aaron took a deep breath before continuing. "I know of only two groups that are allowed to leave the compound and return without going through a search. And of the two groups, I only know of one that could have contact with our friends on the outside without drawing too much attention from the SS guards."

David cocked his head slightly as he thought about what Aaron had just said. "Well, the work groups leave and return every day, but what is the other one?"

Aaron eyed his two companions. "The orchestra."

Both remained silent for a moment as Aaron's words sank in. Yvette's eyes widened in horror and spoke first. "No, Aaron. I won't let you."

Aaron's eyes met hers. This time the stare was cold, his eyes the color of blue steel. "Give me an alternative."

Yvette's voice was shaky, her eyes wandering. "We walk away from this one."

"There is no walking away."

"I don't see how." David said.

Yvette's eyes began to water as she desperately looked around the room as if the answer was written on a nearby wall for her to find. "You can't make her - she doesn't have to do it. She doesn't understand."

David's eyes widened, "No one has to do it. We do it because it's the right thing to do."

Aaron ignored David's input. "She can be properly motivated."

"Motivated? You mean tricked." Yvette answered, wiping the tears from her eyes.

Aaron shook his head. "It's no trick, Yvette. They killed her mother just like they killed my grandfather."

"You don't know that!" Yvette shot back.

The guard standing closest to the tables brought his rifle off the floor several inches and let it drop back to the floor with a loud thud. "Enough talking!" he shouted, "Finish your food and get to work!"

The three buried their faces into their bowls. Aaron was glad for the break in the conversation. It was David who broke the silence. "Who do you have in mind, Aaron?"

Yvette gave Aaron a cold, shallow glance. "Anna. He wants Anna to do it."

David's mind raced as he began to fill in the blanks of the previous conversation between

Aaron and Yvette. "Anna's mother is dead? You know that?

Aaron shook his head. "Yes. I had the Rabbi check."

"You were planning this all along, weren't you?" Yvette hissed.

"No, never. A few weeks ago I asked the Rabbi to make inquiries about Anna's mother.

"Why?" Yvette asked.

"Because I felt it might help Anna to finally know that her mother was OK."

"The Rabbi told you she was dead?" David asked

"No, he didn't tell me she was dead."

Yvette checked on the guard's position before turning back to Aaron. "Then how do you know she's dead?"

"I don't know exactly, but she is not registered on the camp's rolls."

The color in Yvette's face drained as she took in the meaning of Aaron's words. David, seeing that Aaron's statement had some type of meaning, spoke next. "So she's not registered. . .so what?"

Yvette answered the question; there was no life in her words, "David, everyone who enters the camp is given a number and it is written down in the camps rolls. The only ones that the SS don't bother registering are the ones that are sent to the death chambers directly from the trains."

David stared blankly at Yvette so she continued with her explanation. "If Anna's mother was not on the rolls, she never made it into the camp. She was killed within hours of arriving."

David did not bother to speak. Although he had never witnessed it himself, he knew Yvette had made several trips to the main camp. He never knew Yvette to exaggerate or lie.

"So how do you propose to tell her about her mother?" Yvette asked, looking down into her bowl.

Aaron was silent for a moment. It felt like Yvette had opened a trap door at the bottom of his stomach. He had rehearsed this part of the conversation a hundred times, but was never quite sure of how he would handle it when the time came. As he began to speak, what little stamina he had mustered up until now suddenly left him.

"I don't think she would believe me if I told her what I found out from the Rabbi, I don't even think she would believe you Yvette."

"Good," Yvette shot back, "I will not be the one to break the news to her."

Aaron looked at David hoping to find some encouragement in his friend's eyes. All he received for his effort was a despairing look from the young printer. Aaron swallowed trying to force the lump in his throat down far enough for him to continue. "I think the only way to get her to understand that her mother is dead is for Anna to see the Auschwitz main camp and what they do there for herself."

Yvette's head shot up from the bowl, soup dribbled down her chin as the words began to swell inside her. "And how do you plan on that happening? She mouthed, spitting soup in Aaron's direction.

Aaron didn't have the nerve to wipe the small droplets of spittle from his face. Instead, he gawked at Yvette waiting for the words to come out of his mouth. "Most of the women in the orchestra are in your barracks." He managed to get out without much feeling behind the words. "You will have to. . .convince them to make the switch at the last moment and make sure Anna gets on the bus going to Auschwitz." He said as he reached out and touched her hand. "Yvette. . ."

Yvette stiffened at his touch and pulled her hand out of his reach. "You bastard!" she gasped. "You've become a cold hearted bastard just like the rest of them. Haven't you?"

"Yvette, please. . .this is not easy. . .

Yvette looked around the table. Quickly she began to gather up her utensils, placing the smaller items in her bowl. Both of the boys noticed that Yvette had very little control over her movements as she shook violently. It took her several seconds to gain enough strength to stand and gather her things. "I'm out. I don't want to talk to either of you again - ever!"

Aaron and David sat quietly as they watched Yvette wildly make her way to the door. Aaron had hoped that she would at least look back one more time before going through the door, but was disappointed as the door slammed behind her.

"That went better than I expected." David said still watching Yvette march away.

"She was right." Aaron sulked, "We are bastards."

David's eyes widened. "No, my friend, she called you the bastard. Not me."

Aaron looked David directly in the eyes as he gathered his belongings and stood up. "That's right; I'm the bastard for coming up with the plan." he said as he paused for a moment. "But, you will be the bastard for convincing her to do it." Aaron stated as he walked away from the table.

Chapter 33

It was one of those rare early winter days in Poland when the sun shone brightly and it would make a person squint in discomfort if they were to look at the bleached white snow too long. It had snowed all night and had only stopped shortly before four in the morning. Sergeant Bella had already had several Jewish work details shoveling the paths to the camp from the Officers quarters when Klas had made his way down to the security gate. In the snow that had not been removed by the Jews yet, Klas did notice that there was only one set of footprints other than his own. The small pair of prints snaked their way down the path sinking no more than a few inches in the fresh snow. An image of Anna hugging her violin case close to her chest as she made her way down the path had entered Klas' thoughts.

Now, in the evening, as he walked up the road toward his quarters, there was nothing left to remind him of his morning trip. The freshly fallen snow had been scraped away by Jewish shovels, leaving the gravel path running up the hill like a crusty ash colored scar. The sun had retreated behind the ever-gray clouds leaving the bitter sting of winters wind stinging his face.

Klas was instantly aware that either the wind had swallowed the sound of Anna's violin or the young woman was busying herself in the kitchen and had lost track of the time. While Klas had never ordered Anna to play on his return from work, he had nonetheless come to expect the evening serenade. Anna was a dutiful servant and had always had the house in order and Klas' dinner prepared to a point where she could take the time to practice her music. The lack of her music combined with the moaning of the cold wind dampened his sprit. Klas tucked his chin into his shoulder and quickened his pace up the hill. As Klas made the last turn through the trees he was surprised to see that the house was mostly dark and uninviting. He made another mental note to the fact that Anna had always made his quarters warm and inviting.

By the time he had reached the front porch, it had finally come to him that Colonel Oust had apparently detained Anna and the other members of the orchestra for more practice. His obsession with the orchestra had been growing over the last few months to a point where Klas was no longer sure if the man had his priorities straight anymore.

What Klas saw when he entered the house immediately crushed his theory of Oust's detaining

Anna. As soon as he entered the house he noticed Anna's winter coat lying on the living room floor just a few meters from the door. The sudden fear and confusion he had experienced during his injury on the tank retook his body. Klas could only gape in disbelief at the scene that unfolded as he entered the kitchen.

Broken dishes littered the floor along with several pieces of cookware and eating utensils. Droplets of fresh blood were flung across the room; some landing on the walls and cabinet where they splattered into star like patterns or just slithered down toward the floor. A single kitchen chair lay on its side pushed up against the wall and Klas stiffened as he noticed Anna's violin case lying beneath it.

It was the trail of blood leading down into the basement and the muffled whimpering that made Klas reach for his pistol. Blind fear pushed him down the stairs, but his keen military training was still sharp enough to guide him with caution. Klas' eyes darted methodically about the room as he picked out objects in the dim lighting, his pistol pointing the way. He slowly moved down the steps, his back against the wall wishing that the blood pounding in his ears would stop long enough for him to listen to the sounds coming out of the darkness.

The muffled whimpering gave way to the faint crying that Klas knew to be Anna's. A sudden uprising of emotion flooded Klas' senses; it was a strange combination – genuine heart pounding grief, the kind he felt at the loss of his tank crew mixed with the unparalleled desire and hope to find Anna unharmed and whole. The feelings were of immense complexity all forming around the well-being of Anna.

Klas burst into Anna's room, his pistol looking for a target. Suddenly the butterflies raced through his stomach, the small hairs rose on his neck as he recognized his mistake. Klas spun around, beads of perspiration flying from his face as he dropped to one knee, his pistol pointing into the darkness. There, not knowing what else to do, he waited for Anna's assailant to charge him from the darkness. Nauseating amounts of adrenaline pumped through his body as he was torn between waiting for the attack and turning to help Anna. Again, it was Klas' training that persevered. Slowly, Klas re-entered the main portion of the basement feeling stupid for allowing the dim light of Anna's room to clearly outline his silhouette. He cursed himself for becoming so sloppy. He made his way over to the light hanging in the center of the room and pulled the chain. He relaxed slightly when he felt sure that he was the only person in the basement besides Anna.

Klas slid his pistol back into its holster and moved back towards Anna's room. He entered the room quickly at first, slowing as he approached the small figure curled up in fetal position between the furnace and the foot of the bed. He studied the young women for several seconds trying to ascertain her injuries before moving her. Klas grimaced when he noticed that her white blouse was ripped in several places, several of which were stained by the blood seeping from the cuts beneath. Anna's hands were balled into tight fists held tightly to her chest. Dried blood filled the cracks between her fingers. Anna's small frame shook as she sobbed uncontrollably.

Klas knelt down next to Anna, his hand reaching out to touch her.

"Anna?" Klas almost whispered. "Anna, are you alright?"

Anna turned her head toward Klas as if she had only just now noticed that he had entered the room. She blinked several times looking about wildly until her eyes suddenly narrowed, focusing her full attention on Klas. Anna sucked in several short, choppy gulps of air, her entire body shaking with each gasp. "Get. . .get away from me." She choked, her eyes turning cold and vacant.

"Anna, are you hurt?" Klas persisted.

"Stay away from me." She answered her voice growing harder.

Klas looked her over again, assuring himself that Anna was not more seriously injured. "Anna, let's get you up off the floor."

Anna knocked Klas' hand away. "Why bother." She spat, "you're just going to kill me like you did my mother."

Klas slowly pulled his hand back astonished at Anna's remark. He thought about trying to refute the statement, but could see that Anna was clear in her resolve and any denial on his part would send her into a rage of anger. Klas sighed slightly and looked at Anna. "How do you know this?"

"I was there. I saw them - the ones to be murdered like my mother."

Klas shook his head. "What are you talking about. . .saw them?"

"Yes." Anna answered her eyes narrow and full of contempt, "In the main camp. I saw them get off the train like my mother and I did. Watched as they were marched over that small hill; just like my mother was marched. The other women in the orchestra told me what was going to happen to them."

"In the main camp?" Klas asked, "When were you at the main camp?"

"Today. I was. . ."

"How did you get there?" Klas fired at her forgetting that she had already told him.

"With the orchestra." She repeated, "I played at the rail siding today. I watched the SS murder all of those people just like you did to my - my mother!" Anna crumpled, her face to the floor, crying uncontrollably.

"Anna." Klas started softly.

"Leave me alone. Just go. . .go murder someone else if it makes you feel better, but leave me alone."

"Anna I haven't murdered anyone since. . ."

"You liar!" Anna screamed hysterically, "You bastard! You SS bastard, you killed my Mother. You and all your friends. You kill us and then laugh about it. I've seen you do it."

"Anna, you must listen!"

"No, no more lies." Anna screamed as she swung her fist at Klas connecting with his cheek. He attempted to move out of her range. "I hate you!" she spat again, missing him with her seconded attempt.

If he felt the blow he didn't show it. Klas looked around the room not knowing how to approach her. "Anna, I want to help you." He blurted out.

"Get away from me." Her voice becoming hoarse, "I'll kill myself before I let you or that pig Bella touch me."

"Anna, I am nothing like Sergeant Bella." Klas protested in self-defense.

Anna laughed as she cried, "There is no difference between one SS killer and the next. At least he doesn't hide behind his honor."

Klas stood, taking several steps backward. He stared at Anna for several seconds, his arms limp at his side. Finally, he backed out of the room and turned to head up the stairs.

Anna's voice had degenerated into a guttural rasp, "Yes - go fetch the pig. Let him do your dirty work. I'll be dead before he ever has a chance to touch me."

Klas re-entered the kitchen, kicking the overturned chair out of his way. The glass crackled under his boots as he crossed the room and picked up the phone.

"Yes, this is Captain Von Reichman." He said sternly into the mouthpiece, "Get me the Guard Commander, now!"

The door to Yvette's barracks flew open, crashing against the wall supporting it. Two SS guards immediately entered the large quarters followed by a young SS Lieutenant. The angelic faced boy marched past the two guards and looked around the room.

"Yvette Cantrell!" he shouted venomously and waited for a reply.

Yvette leaned against the triple bunk and forced her knees together hoping that her actions would keep her from collapsing to the floor. A thousand things ran through her mind, none of them very pleasant. She was amazed that they had found out about her part in switching Anna into the Auschwitz work party so quickly. Yvette knew that she must answer the young Officer or others in the barracks would suffer. Twice she opened her mouth to speak and twice nothing came out.

"Yvette Cantrell!" The young Lieutenant shouted, his impatience scarlet on his face.

Yvette managed to stand up straight and raise her hand slightly. She wondered if the two guards with the rifles would shoot her where she stood or bother to take her outside first.

The other women began to move away from her now that she had identified herself to the Officer. Everyone knew that standing too close to a person marked for death could lead to her own demise. The SS rifles were very indiscriminate about which Jew they killed. After all, the SS never cared if a few extra Jews were killed when a person was being punished.

"Yvette -" he started a third time when he noticed Yvette raising her hand. The Young Officer's eyes narrowed with contempt as he made a curt motion with his hand and the two guards advanced on Yvette. They quickly closed the distance and seized her with their free hands. With very little ceremony they marched Yvette to a spot a few meters in front of the Lieutenant. He smiled wickedly as his eyes looked her over. "You are Yvette Cantrell?" he asked, more for procedure than any interest in her.

The two guards held Yvette between them, her shoes barely touching the floor. Yvette lowered her eyes. "Yes, Sir." She answered weakly.

The lieutenant's eyes raked the room once more before he looked back at Yvette. She feared that the young Officer was trying to decide if he wanted to shoot her there, in front of the others or take her elsewhere. He glared at her one more time then turned and walked out of the door.

Within seconds the guards had pushed her out into the cold, the three of them following closely behind the Lieutenant.

It was bitter cold, light snow flakes were falling over the camp as the small detail walked the few hundred meters from her barracks to the side gate. Without speaking, the party was waved through the gate and Yvette then knew that she would die alone in the forest. She wondered if they would leave her body there in the snow or have one of the work details bury her in the morning. She wondered if they would be kind and kill her quickly.

The further down the path they walked, the lighter the grip of the two guards became. Yvette began to think that she might be able to break free and run for the trees. With luck she may make the tree line before she was shot in the back. After all, she thought, it was cold and dark, the guards with the rifles may be terrible shots or the cold could affect their aim just enough to give her all the advantage she would need to escape. As if they had read her mind, the guards tightened their grip and continued to move her forward.

Suddenly they stopped without a word. Yvette closed her eyes trying to muster up all of her strength. She was determined not to cry or beg for her life. She had seen too many prisoners in the camp plead for their lives only to die. She would not give them the satisfaction of hearing her cry for something that they had already decided was no longer hers.

"Cantrell." The Lieutenant spat.

Yvette kept her eyes closed. She did not want to look at the gun when he fired it.

The pain shot through her cheek and into her mouth while flashes of light filled her vision.

"Pay attention when I talk to you Bitch!" the officer screamed in her ears as he backhanded her.

Yvette opened her eyes to see the young man smiling darkly. He stared at her for a few seconds and motioned with his head for the guards to release her. Yvette almost fell to the ground.

"Yvette Cantrell," the Lieutenant stated, "As you ordered Captain Von Reichman."

Yvette looked up to see Klas standing a few meters in front of her. The look on his face frightened her more than the young Lieutenant's.

"Thank you, Lieutenant." Klas stated coldly. "I will take her from here."

"Yes, sir." The Lieutenant answered snapping to attention. "Will the Captain need us to return later on this evening to retrieve the prisoner?"

Klas stared at Yvette for a while mulling over his response. "No, that won't be necessary, Lieutenant. She will be helping my maid clean most of the evening. I will return her in the morning."

"Very well, Sir." He answered, "Heil Hitler!"

Klas raised his arm at the elbow. "Heil Hitler."

Klas watched the three soldiers move back down the path until they were fifty or sixty meters away. He then turned his attention back to Yvette. "Where is your coat?"

"I wasn't given any time to collect it before leaving." She chattered.

Klas rubbed his chin. "I see. Well let's get you out of the cold then." He said as he turned and walked the last thirty meters up to his quarters.

Yvette stood silently, her mouth open as she looked around the kitchen. Klas had left the mess as he had found it. "What has happened?" Yvette asked in shock even to the point where she forgot to address Klas as Captain.

"Anna did this." Klas said as he gestured vaguely at the mess.

"But. . .why, Captain?" Yvette asked already knowing the answer.

"Somehow she was put on the morning detail going to the main camp. She spent the day playing at the rail siding."

Yvette decided to continue to act innocent. "This is a very strong response even for that."

Klas walked over to the fallen chair and moved it aside far enough to pick up Anna's violin case and placed it on the counter. "I believe that while she was there she somehow found out about her mother's death."

To Yvette's surprise tears welled up in her eyes at hearing Klas' statement. She thought that she had cried these tears many nights ago, but obviously, there were more to be shed. Or, she wondered, was it because of the obvious pain she detected in Captain Von Reichman's tone that touched her. Yvette wiped her face. "Poor Anna," is all she could muster as an answer at first then she noticed the blood. "Oh, God, did she try to kill herself?"

"No, I don't think so. It looks as if she inadvertently slipped and cut herself in her rage."

"Yvette's gut tightened at the thought of Anna purposely injuring herself. "Is she alright?" she sniffled.

Klas stepped closer to Yvette. "She is in her room, downstairs." Klas dropped his eyes to the floor, "She needs attention, but she won't let me get near her."

In the four years that Yvette had been in the camp she had never seen an ounce of kindness or consideration shown to any of the prisoners especially the Jews. Now, watching Klas' actions; hearing his concern for another; feeling his compassion, she wondered.

Yvette smiled at Klas as if to thank him for being so kind then quickly disappeared down the steps. She could hear Anna crying as she entered the room. Yvette dropped to the ground next to her trying to figure the best way to touch her and let Anna know that she was there.

Anna looked up, her eyes blazing murderously at Yvette until they softened with a few blinks when Anna recognized Yvette. Then they quickly melted into pools of unbridled sorrow as tears cascaded down her cheeks. "Oh, Yvette," she choked, "they killed my mother. They –they -my mama's gone!" she cried. "She's gone!"

"Oh, Anna." Yvette wept as she reached out for her.

Anna leaped into the warm embrace of Yvette's open arms. Yvette held her close, the two sobbing as one.

Klas stood close to the door, but at such an angle that Anna could not see him. He carefully pushed the bowl of warm water within Yvette's reach. Careful not to move Anna too much, Yvette grabbed the cloth in the bowl, squeezed it out and then began to wipe Anna's face and hands.
Klas then tapped his fingers lightly on the doorframe to get Yvette's attention. He then pushed a small tray holding a glass of water and a single white pill into the room. Yvette looked at

him confused. Klas made a motion with his hands up to his face to show her that the pill would help Anna sleep. Yvette nodded and motioned for Klas to return to the kitchen. Klas stared at the two of them holding each other tightly, gently rocking back and forth. When he was satisfied in his own mind that Anna would be alright, he quietly backed away from the door.

It was an hour before Yvette came back up the stairs into the kitchen. Yvette noticed that Klas had cleaned up the mess on the floor and was wiping the dried blood off the woodwork.

Yvette ran her fingers through the little hair she had. "She is asleep, Captain."

Klas continued to wash down the wall. "Thank you, Yvette. You are a good friend."

"I am not your friend, Captain." She spat before thinking, "I did it for Anna."

Klas' gaze could have cut her in half if it were a knife. Then almost as quickly as his eyes flared, they softened. "I meant you are a good friend to Anna."

"I am sorry, Captain." Yvette whispered. "I did not mean to over step my place."

Klas stood and looked around the room. When he was satisfied that he had done a good job of cleaning he walked over to the back door, opened it and tossed the water from the bucket outside.

"It is alright." He answered not looking at Yvette, "It has been a trying night."

"Yes, Sir." She answered.

He finally looked at Yvette. "You may sleep on the couch tonight, Yvette. I will take you back to the camp in the morning."

Yvette wrapped her arms around herself. "If you don't mind, Captain, I will go back down stairs and sleep with Anna. I don't think she should be alone when she wakes up."

"Yes, that would be better." He answered.

Yvette smiled at him. "Thank you for asking me to help." She turned and headed back down the steps.

"Oh, Yvette."

"Yes, Sir."

"Tomorrow I will find out how this mess happened and someone will be made to suffer for it."

Yvette could only stare at Klas. "Yes, Sir." she said softly as she headed down the stairs, "I'm sure someone will suffer a long time for it." she whispered to herself.

Chapter 34

It had taken a lot of time and gold to set up the operation. There were guards to be bribed and the few that couldn't be bribed had to be removed. Removal wasn't that difficult. An auto accident on the way to town or a vegetable cart losing a wheel causing a certain SS guard to be placed in the hospital with a broken leg and several fractured ribs was all it took. Information was not that hard to come by either. After all Colonel Oust was an arrogant man when it came to his music and finding the location of the next recital was easy. The part Aaron was having difficulty with was Yvette and Anna.

It had taken David three weeks to finally convince Yvette that there was no other way to get the medicine into the camp and then another four weeks to get Anna to a point where she was well enough to be approached with the idea. From that point it took another two weeks to convince her to do it.

Yvette had kept her word and had not spoken to Aaron since the day he told her about his plan. All communications between Aaron and Yvette were now passed through David. Yvette had quit sitting with Aaron and David during meals and when Aaron attempted to talk directly to her she would simply walk away. Aaron had not known how much he had cared for her until she walked out of his life. He thought that next to his grandfather being murdered, the loss of Yvette's friendship was the worst pain he had experienced since entering the camp, that is, until he saw Anna for the first time since her trip to the main camp.

Anna had stayed at Captain Von Reichman's quarters for almost three weeks, never leaving the house. When Von Reichman informed Colonel Oust about the incident the Colonel was furious and took out his anger on the prisoners. The next day after Von Reichman had explained what had happened; Oust went to the main camp with the same group of women that had played the day before. In the evening the truck returned with only the orchestra's instruments. It was Aaron who found out that after playing all day at the rail siding Colonel Oust had the women included in the last group of Jews headed for the gas chamber.

Colonel Oust also blamed Captain Von Reichman for the incident and had informed him that he was personally responsible for getting Anna back to normal and back to playing with the main orchestra. To that end Von Reichman had a woman prisoner spend the entire day with Anna while in the evenings, Yvette would return to his quarters and sit with her. He had an extra cot moved into the room for Yvette.

For almost a month Anna would not pick up her violin even at the request of Yvette. Aaron had not known it at the time, but after almost four weeks, Colonel Oust had gone to Von Reichman quarters and threatened Yvette with death if Anna did not come around soon. Yvette later had told David that it was that very threat that had brought Anna around. She had told David that Anna had overheard the conversation through the heating vents as she had done so many times before. After Colonel Oust had left the house, Anna came up from the basement and retrieved the violin. She had promised Yvette that the two of them would live long enough to see Colonel Oust and the others surrender their own lives for their crimes.

Anna's first trip back to the compound was in the morning for breakfast. Yvette had convinced her that it was time to return to her duties and accompany her to the camp for breakfast. Anna agreed and with Von Reichman's permission, the two women proceeded to the camp. After trying to eat the horrid food, Anna informed Yvette that they would, from now on, eat only at the Von Reichman's' quarters. Yvette was only too glad to comply.

Aaron gazed open mouthed at the two as they entered the kitchen barracks. The first thing Aaron noticed was the waxy color of Anna's skin, her face hollow, and her demeanor, cadaverous. Her eyes were deep-set, lacking any signs of the sparkle that was once there. Her hair was neatly brushed, but Aaron knew that was Yvette's doing.

Suddenly it hit him. Aaron was now looking at a young woman who, in a single day, had her childhood innocence burned away. Anna had become like the rest of them and it was his fault.

Aaron pinched his nose and rubbed the excess moisture from his eyes. He had to stop thinking of the last six or eight weeks and focus on the up-coming mission. He did not know what he would do if things fell apart and Anna was killed and the best way to make sure that didn't happen was to concentrate on what he was doing.

Aaron looked over David's shoulder as he removed the bottom-lining of Anna's violin case and secured the thin strips of gold. There was more than enough room in the bottom of the case since the Rabbi had one of the carpenters re-work it. The man had been masterful in his work. When David had finished securing the thin gold plates he re-inserted the false bottom. It was impossible to see that it had ever been removed.

"The men at the recital hall will know what to do?" Aaron asked for a third time.

"Yes." Rabbi Helfer replied, this time adding additional information to help calm Aaron. "The instrument cases will be left in a room behind the stage. The SS could possibly lock the door to the room so our contacts have made sure that they have access into the room through the ceiling if necessary. They will enter the room, locate the case and remove the gold. Then they will replace the gold with the medicine we have requested and reseal the case."

"What does Anna have to do?" David asked.

"Nothing really. After playing she merely has to go to the room, replace her violin in the case and return to the camp."

"If it's that easy." David asked, "Why do I feel so nervous about it?"

"Because," Aaron interjected, "with the SS nothing is ever easy."

"But what could go wrong?" David asked as he handed the violin case to the Rabbi.

Aaron shook his head at the question. "Lots of things, David. The SS could catch our contacts either removing the gold or putting the medicine in the case. If that happened it would point right to Anna."

"She could deny any knowledge of what was going on." David insisted.

"David, she would be turned over to the Gestapo for questioning. How long do you think she could last under their interrogation methods?"

David rubbed his chin as he contemplated the problem. "Wouldn't it have been better not to tell her at all then?"

Rabbi Helfer checked the case one more time and handed it to another man whom Aaron and David did not know. "We cannot place that type of a burden on someone who has no knowledge of what we are doing." he said.

"Yes, but if she had no knowledge of the gold," David persisted, "the Gestapo would quickly find that out when they interrogated Anna."

Rabbi Helfer shook his head. "David, if the Gestapo discovers the gold, I'm afraid that Anna and many others would loose their lives."

Aaron watched the man carrying the violin case leave the room. "This is going to be a long night." he sighed

The man carrying Anna's violin case hadn't been gone more than a few minutes when Yvette entered the barracks. Aaron knew Yvette well enough to know there was trouble.

"What's the matter?" he asked her as he ran to meet her.

Yvette hesitated for a moment looking around the room. To anyone else, it would have looked like Yvette was checking the room to see if it were alright to speak openly, but Aaron knew that she was searching for someone else to speak to other than him. Yvette ran up to Rabbi Helfer, the fear in her eyes obvious. "Rabbi, something bad has just happened at the main camp."

Rabbi Helfer squinted as he often did when trying to listen. "What has happened child? What do you know?"

"I was up at Captain Von Reichman's quarters with Anna when he received a call. Anna and I listened to the conversation from downstairs."

"What did you hear?" Aaron asked.

Yvette directed her answer to the Rabbi. "There's been some type of prisoner uprising at the main camp. The workers in crematorium IV have rioted and blown up some of the ovens."

Rabbi Helfer sat on the edge of the bunk. "Are you sure?"

"Yes, Rabbi. I heard the conversation quite clearly. There is going to be a major lock down in a few minutes."

"In a few minutes?" David interjected.

"Yes. When Anna and I heard the information she went upstairs to try and delay Von Reichman. I was able to sneak out of the house and come here."

Rabbi Helfer stood, his eyes blinking as he digested Yvette's words. "Everyone return to your own barracks, quickly before they announce the lockdown."

Quickly the room began to empty of its few occupants. Aaron grabbed Rabbi Helfer by the shoulder. "What about Anna and the gold?" What are we going to do?"

"We do nothing, Aaron." Rabbi Helfer said quickly, "We wait and see what happens. No one knows of the gold or the plan. If the concert is still on then we continue with the plan. If there is a lockdown then we wait."

"But there will be more guards now. They will increase their searches." Aaron persisted as he trotted along-side the Rabbi.

"Aaron, we must trust in God. Now stay here. Time is running out."

As if the Rabbi's words were a signal, the camp sirens began to wail, low at first and gaining volume quickly. Rabbi Helfer leaped through the door and disappeared between the buildings. Aaron stood at the door and watched as the SS guards began to run through the camp, shouting at the few prisoners in the compound. Aaron closed the door and returned to his bunk. He sat on his bunk and put his hands over his ears trying to block out the sirens. It helped a little. He then forced his fingers deeper into his ears and shut his eyes this time hoping to block out everything.

Anna approached the door of the bus with the other musicians. She wasn't sure if she could tell that her violin case now carried more than just her violin. It did feel heavier, but she wasn't sure. The camp lock down had caused a huge delay in loading the bus. Klas had left her at the house with instructions not to leave unless either he came back for her or he sent a guard to get her. It was just under an hour when the guard came to the house, knocked politely and instructed Anna to follow him. She had hesitated for a moment until the young Private told her that Captain Von Reichman had ordered him to retrieve her. The SS Private had even offered to carry Anna's violin, but she had declined.

When they entered the gate, security was much stricter than usual. The guard searched Anna and even asked her to open the violin case. Anna had been so nervous that she immediately complied forgetting about the gold hidden in the case. She relaxed when the guard gave the case a cursory search. The camp seemed deserted. There was no sign of any of the prisoners and the air was still. The only sound that could be heard came from one of the roving patrols with the dogs.

Anna had been escorted to the main assembly area where the camp bus was sitting. The other musicians had already been retrieved from their barracks and were standing around waiting for the order to board the bus. Anna quickly joined them. That is when Sergeant Bella arrived.

Sergeant Bella puffed his way up to the bus, stopping only once to clear his throat and spit. Anna noticed that he was not carrying his ax handle. She did notice that for the first time since arriving at the camp Bella was carrying a pistol. He looked uncomfortable, the shiny black belt cutting through his gut.

Bella barked orders to the guards and the bus was quickly searched. Then in turn, each of the musicians was required to line up and have their person and instruments searched. Bella stood at the door and would randomly check some of the orchestra members before allowing them to board the bus. Anna began to shake as she approached the front of the line. The guards were being much more thorough in their inspection this time including a complete search of the instruments. She didn't know if she or her case could stand up to the search.

"Next." Bella grunted his face showing the usual hatred.

Anna froze momentarily not wanting to move any closer to Bella or the awaiting inspection.

"Come on Princess." Bella hissed sarcastically, "There's no special line for Royalty."

Anna stepped forward her violin case being stripped from her arms by one of the guards. The middle-aged man placed the case on the small folding table and began to inspect the top of the case, removing the bow and rosin, then sliding his hand all the way into the bottom of the pouch. Anna was distracted from the case when the other guard began to pat her down.

"Don't be such a sissy." Bella said as he moved forward and pushed the guard aside. "That's no way to search her." He continued as he began to grab her.

Anna swallowed hard as Bella continued to press and grope her. Anna turned her attention back to the man searching her violin case to try and take her mind off of what Bella was doing. Briefly she thought of telling Klas what the slob was doing to her, but that was quickly forgotten when the guard roughly grabbed her violin by the neck and yanked it out of the case.

Anna let out a loud gasp not knowing if it was because of Bella's hands defiling her body or the ignorant guard defiling her violin, but in either case it was loud enough to make both men stop immediately.

"Damn worthless Jew, what's the matter?" Bella demanded with a snarl.

"I'm...I'm sorry Sergeant." Anna explained, "but the instrument is a Stradivarius and very expensive."

Bella glared at Anna and reached for the violin intending to hit her across the face with it.

"And," Anna continued her voice quivering, "It belongs to Colonel Oust's personal collection."

Bella stopped short, pulling his hand away from the instrument. He studied Anna's face trying to discern if the young Jew was telling the truth.

Anna, knowing what must be racing through his mind continued in a low tone. "The Colonel threatened me with death if I was to damage the instrument in any way." She continued lowering her eyes to the ground, "Maybe he will be kinder with you."

"I doubt it." Klas stated as he walked up behind Sergeant Bella having heard most of the conversation. "But Sergeant," he smiled, "if you're not worried about it, please continue. I understand that they are looking for a few volunteers to clear mine fields in Russia." Klas stopped for a second and looked directly into Bella's eyes. "The Jew might be worthless, but that violin is worth a small fortune."

Bella looked at Klas, his eyes blank as his little mind tried to process the information Klas had just given him.

"Are you any good with mines, Sergeant?" Klas asked.

"No sir." He stammered not knowing what else to say.

"I bet you are less gifted with a violin." Klas stated and he began to walk toward the staff car waiting for him, "I would give the violin back to the Jew, or read up on the Army's manual for disarming Russian mines."

Bella's attention was divided between watching Klas enter the staff car and how the guard was holding Anna's violin. Finally, he motioned for the guard to give the instrument back to Anna. Anna then, for their sake, very gently and ceremoniously replaced the violin back into the case and entered the bus.

The concert went as well as any Anna had played in since arriving at the camp. As always, the orchestra was allowed to take two bows and then they hurried off the stage. In the small area behind the stage, she and the others waited until the guard unlocked the door to the room holding their cases and winter coats. Anna carefully placed the violin back into the case and closed it. She hurried with her coat and picked up her violin and walked to the rear door of the hall to wait for the bus.

"Your playing was excellent tonight." Colonel Oust said as he approached her.

Anna turned to accept the compliment and noticed that Captain Von Reichman had accompanied the Colonel.

"The Colonel is right Anna." Klas added. "If you cooked as well as you play the violin I would have to be watching my waist."

Oust laughed lightly at Klas' statement.

"If you're playing continues to improve as it has so far," Colonel Oust smiled, "you will never have to worry about cooking young lady."

Anna curtsied, "The two of you are most kind."

"Sir," Klas said addressing Oust, "With your permission I would like to return to the camp straight away. There are several things I must go over before morning."

Colonel Oust shook his head. "Of course, Captain. You may go. Please be attentive to the air raid sirens."

"Thank you, Sir. I will." Klas said as he turned to say good night to Anna.

"Why don't you take Anna with you Captain?" Oust interjected before Klas could speak.

"Sir?"

Oust motioned toward Anna. "Yes, yes, take her back with you. She is ready to go and it will be a while before the bus is ready to return."

"As you wish, Colonel." Klas said coming to attention. "I will just have to inform Sergeant Bella so that he can get an accurate count for the bus."

Oust waved his hand in front of his face. "I will take care of that. You just get this young lady out of the cold."

Anna curtsied toward Colonel Oust a second time. "You are very kind, Colonel."

"Please, your performance tonight was excellent."

Klas came to attention, raising his arm in the proper salute, "Then Colonel, with your permission, we will leave. Heil Hitler."

Oust raised his arm in a very relaxed salute. "Good night."

Klas opened the door allowing the bitter cold air to rush into the room. Anna quickly squeezed out of the opening making sure not to hit the violin case on the partially opened door.

As she left the building she heard Sergeant Bella shouting orders to the SS guards.

"I want every piece of equipment checked before we get on the bus. Be careful with the instruments, but be thorough in your search."

Chapter 35

As full winter set in there were fewer and fewer concerts held outside of the compound. Allied air raids had increased forcing the camp into pitch-black darkness at night and sent everyone diving for cover during the day. Several times during the day Aaron and the others were able to see Allied bombers flying overhead racing toward some military target. Although the chances to leave the compound were diminishing, Aaron and the others made the best of each trip. Anna was continuing to bring in the desperately needed drugs.

Secretly, Aaron was glad to see the opportunities diminish. With every mission, it seemed that Anna took bigger and more dangerous chances. Aaron and David both thought that Anna was inwardly trying to get caught. It was still obvious that Anna had little regard for life after learning about her mother. It was to a point where Aaron thought she might actually be trying to commit suicide, forcing him to ask David to speak with Yvette about it.

Aaron and the others had much to hope for these days. They knew that the war was going badly for their captors. This was reinforced in Aaron and David's work groups as the complexity of the work changed drastically.

Aaron and the other jewelers were no longer designing such elaborate pieces of jewelry anymore. Aaron and Eric were both assigned to working pieces of gold either into small ingots or into thin flat strips, which, they both knew from their own smuggling operations, would be easier to conceal within the lining of a jacket or coat.

David was busy drawing up foreign travel documents for Countries in North and South America as well as other parts of the world. He was amazed at the ability of the SS to get their hands on so many different visas and travel documents. He was impressed with his own ability to copy the documents to a point where even he had a difficult time telling the original from the counterfeit.

Aaron hated the fact that Yvette had distanced herself even further from him and spent most of her time with Anna. He was pleased to see that Yvette was looking after Anna, but he couldn't shake his own personal feeling of the loss of their friendship.

Any information Aaron received about Yvette now came through David and even David had expressed concern over these changes.

It was cold enough to force Aaron to push his hands deep into the pockets of his coat. The bottom of the pocket lining had been so thread worn that a few days ago he had unintentionally managed to push his fingers through the bottom. Now, as he walked toward the kitchen barracks, he could feel the cold air rush up between his pants and coat and nip at his fingers.

"She won't tell me a thing, Aaron." David complained as the two walked side by side.

Aaron let David's words sink in before speaking. "Is she angry with you?"

"No, I don't think so. It's just that she doesn't seem to want to talk about her work." David said adjusting his collar.

"There aren't many people left in her group, are there?

David shook his head. "No, just Yvette the Levy girl and one other I think. The rest have been. . .removed."

"Talk to her at breakfast, David. See if she thinks they will do away with the rest of them."

"What do you mean?"

Aaron shook involuntarily. It seemed colder now than it had been all winter. "See if she thinks she and the others are in danger of being removed from the work force."

"Why would the SS close that group down?"

"Because they have nothing to offer any more unless Yvette can paint travel documents as well as you can print them."

"I believe she could." David answered pulling his coat tighter around him.

"You and I are valuable because they still need what we make." Aaron continued as if he hadn't heard David's comment. "If they lose the war they will need your travel documents and my gold to escape. Paintings are too big and clumsy and will be useless to them."

David walked with Aaron for several steps in silence thinking about what Aaron had just said. "What happens to us if the SS suddenly decide to leave?" he asked, hoping Aaron's answer would be better than what he was thinking.

Aaron did not hesitate with his answer. "They will kill us."

David looked at Aaron, his eyes hard, his face, cold and emotionless. "Then we better get out of here before that happens."

Aaron shook his head in agreement. "I'm working on it."

David stopped. "Working on it?" he asked, having to trot a few steps to catch up with Aaron who had continued walking. "When were you going to tell me?"

Aaron had to smile. "On the way out of course."

"I thought we were a team." David huffed.

"We are a team and we will leave as a team." Aaron answered, "The four of us."

"Well, you had better give Anna some advance warning. She's not likely to go anywhere without her violin."

It was Aaron's turn to stop. David stumbled a step or two before stopping.

"When was the last time you saw her without it?" Aaron asked.

"Good point." David laughed.

Quickly the two looked around to see if the guards had heard the laughter. In the past few months the guards had become complacent in their duties, but laughing was still not a good thing to do and if anything, Sergeant Bella got worse with each passing day. Bella had been stalking the group as if he could sense that they were up to something. It seemed as if David had become his new favorite, giving Aaron some much-needed breathing room.

Aaron and David walked through the door to the Kitchen Barracks side by side. The usual stench of breakfast assaulted their nostrils. It took several seconds for Aaron to notice that things were not normal. Once inside the door the two were ushered around to the right toward the table area instead of to the left to wait in line. The other special workers who had entered before them were also gathered in the table area and Aaron noticed that no one had gone through the soup line. Aaron and David made their way into the room and waited with the others. Aaron's heart sank as Sergeant Bella came out of the kitchen holding his ax handle in one hand and wiping his mouth on his other sleeve.

"Listen up!" He croaked. "You will quickly go through the line and get your breakfast. Each person will be given an extra piece of bread and a sausage with their soup."

The group began to talk amongst themselves, happy for the extra rations. The festive mood quickly came to an end when Bella swung his ax handle, striking the wall with a thunderous bang. "Shut up you pigs!" he shouted, as he attempted to dislodge the ax handle from the hole in the wall where the head had hit. "This is not some damn Jewish Barmitzvah. You are <u>not</u> to eat the extra rations with your breakfast. You will save it for later; when I tell you to eat it. Is that understood?"

Bella waited until most of the workers were nodding their head in agreement. "It will be saved for later;" he repeated, "for your lunch." He added, thinking he needed to clarify the first statement.

David looked at Aaron, his facial expression asking a thousand questions all at once. Aaron shook his head ever so slightly, not wanting to draw Bella's attention.

"Now quickly go through the food line, eat and get to your work stations." He said pointing toward the kitchen with the ax handle. "And," he added, the poison dripping from his words. "If I catch just one word; one damn Yiddish syllable. The man uttering it will not have the opportunity to eat again."

The group of workers stood silently as if glued to their positions. Aaron wanted to look at David but decided against it.

"What are you waiting for!" Bella shouted. "Move! Now!"

Aaron followed the man in front of him until he got in the line. Somehow, David had ended up several positions in front of him and already had his food and was seated before Aaron came looking for a place to sit. The seat next to David was empty but Aaron walked past it and headed for another table. He hoped that David understood that by splitting up there was less chance of the two of them getting in trouble. Instead, Aaron moved to a table where he knew he would not have a problem with talking. He placed his food on the table and slid onto the bench directly across from Yvette. There he sat and ate in silence. Aaron thought he felt Yvette's leg rub up against his own but was too afraid to look up at her.

Sergeant Bella was walking up and down the rows of tables, his ax handle anxious for the opportunity to strike. Aaron dismissed Yvette's touch as unintentional until she made contact the second time. This time, she left her leg pressed against his. Aaron could feel her shaking as the two of them tried to force down their meal.

Bella continued to pace up and down the rows. "You've had enough," he yelled at one man, "Get your rations together and get out of here. Take your friend with you." He hissed.

Aaron could see Bella make the turn down his row of seats and decided to get going before the man reached him. Yvette quickly followed Aaron's lead and got up from the table.

"That's right little one." Bella chuckled, "Get to your work shop and take that little French harlot of yours with you."

Aaron could still hear the fat man laughing as he burst out the door, Yvette on his heels.
"What's going on, Aaron?" Yvette asked, as she caught up with him.

Aaron didn't slow his pace. He wasn't sure if he was hurrying to get away from Bella or to find out the answer to Yvette's question. "I don't know." He wheezed, condensation billowing from his mouth as he spoke. "Something's up."

"Maybe a selection for the special workers?" Yvette suggested.

"They don't give you a noon day ration for a selection."

Yvette slowed her pace. "Aaron, look."

Aaron looked toward where Yvette was pointing. Starting at the end of the Kitchen building Aaron noticed that there were SS guards posted everywhere. There was a small opening between the two lines of guards where the other workers were leaving the kitchen building. The lines of guards lead around the first workshop, housing the print shop, toward Aaron's building. Aaron's knees weakened at the thought of being marched between the two buildings with the other workers and shot. It wasn't until he remembered what he had told Yvette about the rations did he begin to feel a little better.

"Aaron." Yvette said weakly.

"Just keep walking." Is all he could think to say.

As he and Yvette turned the corner of the building things became more confusing. Sitting between the buildings were several large military transport trucks. In the area between where Aaron and Yvette now stood, and the first truck, sat a portable table and chair. An SS Corporal occupied the chair busy asking questions of each of the prisoners as they approached.

"Name!" the man too old to be a Corporal yelled at a prisoner.

"Helmut Kohn." The man replied.

"Kohn, Kohn. . ." the Corporal repeated as his finger moved down the list. "Ah, yes. . .Kohn, Helmut Kohn. Truck number 2." He continued making a vague gesture over his shoulder toward the waiting trucks. "Next, next!"

Yvette walked up to the front of the table. "Yvette Cantrell." She volunteered before she was asked.

"Cantrell. . ." he repeated, his finger sliding down the page. "No, no Cantrell. Step over there with that group."

Yvette hesitated for a second not knowing what to do next. "I'm sure I'm on the list." She said, deciding that being on a list was always better than not.

The Corporal looked up at her, his eyes narrowing. "Who do you think you are, bitch?" He spat.

Yvette did not hesitate. "I am on the special art project for Colonel Oust." She shot back, "Yvette Cantrell."

The Corporal stared at her for several seconds. Yvette continued to stare into the man's eyes, not blinking as she had done to Aaron so many times in the past. Finally, the Corporal glanced back at the list, his finger moving down the page one more time. "I don't see your name here." He insisted.

"And the second page?" Yvette almost sang.

David leaned close to Aaron. "She sounded very Jewish. We must be wearing off on her." Aaron could only manage a timid smile.

The Corporal blushed as he flipped the first page up. "Cantrell." He repeated, "Truck number 1."

Aaron quickly approached the desk. "Aaron Singer" he proclaimed. The incident brought back the memory of the first time he and his grandfather had faced an SS man sitting at a folding table much like the one he was now standing in front of. The memory brought with it mixed emotions. It was a time when Samuel was always there for him, protecting, guiding and loving. It was a time when Samuel was still alive.

"Truck number 3." The man shouted, "Next, quickly!"

Aaron trotted up to the back of the huge green truck and climbed up into the back. There were already eight or nine men in the back of the truck and Aaron took a seat at the rear of the truck on one of the benches lining either side of the truck bed. Soon there wasn't any room on the benches and the remaining men were made to sit on the floor.

Aaron watched as the Corporal continued to segregate the workers as they approached the table. He held his breath as he watched David approach the table. Like many of the others, Aaron didn't know if it was better to be selected for the trucks or to be placed with the group standing around in the assembly area. David stood there for what seemed to Aaron like a long time. Finally, David was directed to one of the other trucks. As he passed, the two smiled at each other. The worried look on David's face told Aaron that he too was unsure whether the seat on the truck meant life or death.

Suddenly the area became deathly silent. There were no more workers to be segregated by the Corporal so the man stood up and began to collect his things. A young Private walked over to the Corporal and folded the table and chair and together the two soldiers walked back toward the Kitchen building. The sound of a shrill whistle cutting through the cold morning air and the immediate grinding, clacking noise of the truck engines turning over, shattered the stillness of the moment. One by one, each of the trucks started adding to the deafening roar echoing between the buildings. Aaron's truck started to move with some hesitation causing the men in the back of the truck to be jolted back and forth. The man seated next to him grabbed hold of Aaron's coat probably preventing him from falling out of the back of the truck. Aaron looked at the man and he smiled sheepishly and nodded his thanks.

Aaron watched the group of workers left behind. It was clear to him that each of them was experiencing the same confusion as to their fate. Just before Aaron's truck reached the corner of the building and began its turn toward the main gate, the question was answered. A large group of guards lead by Sergeant Bella approached the workers in the assembly area. Immediately, the guards forced the workers into a single line and began to remove the extra rations from each of the prisoners as they passed by Bella. Once they had relinquished the rations they were directed toward the checkpoint leading back into the main camp.

Aaron's truck rounded the building and he could no longer see Bella or the workers. The truck bounced around for a few more minutes until it reached the main assembly area of the camp and was directed through the main gate. Aaron could now see the main camp prisoners standing at attention waiting for the count to be completed and verified. Aaron also noticed that the special workers forced to stay behind were now rounding the barracks building and being forced to join the main body of the camp workers. There was no doubt now that whatever his fate was, it would be better than those forced to work in the quarries.

It gave Aaron a small measure of comfort to have been selected for the trucks. He had a large piece of bread and an equally impressive piece of sausage tucked under his shirt. Things could be worse, he thought. They were lucky to be in the trucks.

Aaron continued to watch the morning roll call as his truck slowly made its way toward the main gate. It wasn't until they reached the gate that the music coming from the small group close by, became loud enough to demand his attention. A chill ran down the center of Aaron's spine as he leaned out of the back of the truck in order to get a better view as they drove by. He could feel the man's hand holding onto his coat again as he pushed the limits of still being in the truck.

Aaron's eyes sifted desperately through the musicians praying that Anna was not among the small group. His hand reached out involuntary toward the group as he passed by.

"Anna!" he yelled as the truck bounced down the road.

"No!" he cried as he spotted her half hidden by the larger members of the orchestra. Anna, her violin tucked gently under her chin, her eyes closed, and her tiny hand drawing the bow across the strings continued to play oblivious to Aaron's cries.

Chapter 36

After clearing the camp, the trucks headed down a small two-lane road that lead past the main Auschwitz facilities. Aaron was amazed at the size of the camps. The only time he had seen anything of the camp was when he and Samuel had arrived over four years ago. Since that time the camp had grown into an enormous complex stretching as far as Aaron could see from his viewpoint. He was used to seeing the two dozen barracks at his small camp, not the hundreds that now zipped by in a blur.

At one point the trucks slowed and then eventually stopped at what Aaron assumed was the far side of the camp. Aaron's hands became clammy as he wondered if they would be turning into the main entrance of the camp. Suddenly he had visions of some SS Guard taking away his extra rations and pushing him into a line with the other workers in Camp I.

"Why have we stopped?" came the question from somewhere in the front of the truck.

Aaron leaned out to look around the side of the truck. He could see three trucks in front of his and another two behind him. They had all stopped.

"I don't know." Aaron said toward the front of the truck, "All the trucks have stopped." Aaron stuck his head out around the corner again. This time he was finally able to see what had brought the small convoy to a halt. Just ahead of the first truck he could see a railroad car make it's way across the road. Slowly another and another followed the single railroad car. One by one the cars made their way across the road moving ever so slowly toward the main complex. Aaron could see faces pressed up against the small openings on either end of the railcar. He didn't need to see any more. His own trip in a railcar still haunted his dreams. He remembered quite clearly when his face had been pressed up against the small opening, his grandfather standing directly behind him, his large hand resting on Aaron's shoulder. Instinctively Aaron moved his cheek over to touch his shoulder as if Samuel's hand was still there.

"What do you see?" someone in the front asked impatiently.

Aaron blinked several times. "It's more prisoners." He said weakly. "A train full of new prisoners coming across the road." He repeated.

Nothing else was said while the train finished crossing the road.

Aaron thought about Anna again. He felt stupid in telling David that he was working on a plan to get them out, all of them. He had been talking with Rabbi Helfer about an escape plan when the time came, but he had not counted on the SS removing them from the camp. He had not counted on being separated from Anna. Aaron's thoughts turned to Rabbi Helfer. While the man had managed to get himself assigned to the special work area as a janitor, he did not have a talent that the SS needed. In fact, if they knew he had been a Rabbi, they would have sent him directly to the gas chambers when he arrived at the main camp. Aaron remembered seeing the Rabbi at breakfast, but he did not remember seeing him at the assembly area. By now the man was probably knee deep in cold mud, knocking chunks of stone out of the quarry wall. Aaron doubted the Rabbi would last very long in the quarry. Aaron truly liked the old man even if he had the tendency to use people to get what he wanted.

The truck jumped forward, but this time Aaron was ready and grabbed onto one of the ribs of steel holding up the canvas canopy covering the rear of the truck. Aaron looked at the man seated next to him and smiled.

"They said you were a quick learner." he smiled back. "Grigori Petrov" the man said, offering an open hand to Aaron.

"Aaron Singer." Aaron replied taking the man's hand.

"Yes, I know. Shalom."

"Shalom." Aaron answered, "You know me?" he added as an after-thought.

The man smiled a large toothless grin. "I know of you." He said, "I have not had the pleasure of having known you."

"I see. . . What do you know?"

The man waved his finger back and forth in front of Aaron's face. "No no," he grinned. "do not ask me what I have sworn to God not to tell anyone."

Aaron smiled and shook his head in agreement. "Alright, Mr. Petrov. I will not speak of it again. Can you tell me what work you do?"

The man sat up, almost beaming. "I'm a tailor." He said proudly. "I worked in the tailor shop making custom uniforms and insignia for the German High Command." The man looked around the truck and bent closer to Aaron as if the information he was offering might be of some military importance. "I even made a custom uniform for RF Himmler." He beamed, "His staff gave it to him for his birthday two years ago."

"You must be very talented." Aaron offered.

"They tell me my garments are the best." He nodded with a great deal of satisfaction. "So much so, that they now have me making civilian clothing for some of the officers."

"Civilian clothing?"

"For when they're off duty, I guess." The tailor added.

Aaron absorbed the information. "Yes, of course." He said going over the information again and again. "Have you made a lot of civilian clothing?"

The Tailor's head bobbed up and down like one of the needles on his sewing machines. "Lately that's all I've been doing."

Aaron looked at the old Tailor and smiled. "Obviously they know quality when they see it."

The old Tailor's grin spread from ear to ear as he shook his head in agreement.

Aaron turned his attention back to the passing countryside and the more serious problem of where they were being taken. He convinced himself that the SS had no intention of shooting them, at least not in the near future. They could easily have disposed of them at the Auschwitz main camp or, for that matter, driven a few miles out into the wooded countryside. Too many things lead him to believe that he had seen the last of Camp 117.

Suddenly Aaron felt alone. This is the first time he had been out of the camp in over four years. This was the first time he had gone anywhere without Samuel. Aaron rubbed his stomach and belched. Within a very short time span his world had been turned upside down again. In the camp he had become used to the daily routine and the boundaries of his existence. He had become proficient in working within the system set up by the SS. Now, everything was changed. Now he knew nothing about what was to happen to him. Would they put him in another camp? Would he ever see David and Yvette?

Aaron inhaled a deep breath of air and exhaled, wrinkling up his nose, looking out the back of the truck. Something strange had happened, something that he couldn't put his finger on. He breathed deeply again, this time through his mouth. The air rushed into his mouth over his tongue and down into his lungs leaving a sweet taste dancing in his senses. He didn't know what the sensation was but he liked it and took another deep breath.

The Tailor tapped him on the shoulder. "I bet you never would have guessed that fresh air could taste so good."

That's it, Aaron thought. The air is so clean and fresh. Aaron leaned in toward the old Tailor. "I never knew air had any taste at all until now."

"That's because you never had it taken away from your before." He laughed.

Aaron felt much better, his mood changing with the wind, so to speak. They had been driving for most of the morning and his butt began to ache from sitting on the hard wooden bench. He stretched his legs and looked at the passing scenery in an attempt to get his mind off the long trip. Small patches of snow still clung to the ground, hiding in the shadows of trees and the rocks. Wherever the sun shone directly on it, the ground had given up its winter coat and was now soaking up as much sunshine as possible. Aaron knew that the fields would soon be covered with wild flowers.

He began to believe that wherever the SS was taking them; it would be better than the Auschwitz camps. He was happy to be away from Sergeant Bella and Colonel Oust. Away from Oust! Panic gripped him for the first time in hours. If Oust was gone, he would have no chance of avenging Samuel's death. He hadn't thought of Colonel Oust being out of his life. He had always thought that Colonel Oust would be captured by the English or Americans and hung for killing Samuel and the others. He had always thought that he would be there to see it. To look into Colonel Oust's eyes one last time and yell, "You killed my grandfather!" Aaron had dreamt it a thousand times in the past three years. On several occasions he had even had darker dreams. Dreams where he, himself, would take Colonel

Oust's life; shooting the man as he had done to Samuel.

The truck hit a huge pothole in the road pushing Aaron several inches off the bench and throwing him on top of another man sitting on the floor. Several of the men began laughing out loud at the incident. Even the man who Aaron had landed on began to laugh. The blood raced through Aaron's body at the exhileration of his short ride into the air. He too began to laugh as he felt the blood race to his face in a momentary feeling of embarrassment. He looked up at the old Tailor, he was laughing as hard as the others.

Aaron took his seat on the bench again "That was kind of fun." he shouted at the men in the back of the truck.

With that they laughed harder and Aaron laughed right along with them. It was good to see people laughing he thought. He couldn't remember the last time he had seen someone enjoying a good, deep laugh. It was easy to see that the men's spirits were at a high they had not known for several years.

Suddenly the truck began to brake, pushing everyone toward the front of the truck bed. Instantly the smiles and laughter died and the look of fear reclaimed their faces. The driver down shifted again; gears grinding beneath the truck as it quickly made a sharp turn to the right. Again, everyone was pitched around the back of the truck, as if they were a child's marbles rattling around in an old cigar box.

Aaron was finally able to reclaim his seat and get a look outside the back of the truck. They had obviously pulled off the main highway and were now on a narrow road. Another turn to the left and they had left the road and were travelling on bare ground. Soon the open field gave way to the cover of large trees. Aaron looked up through their branches, the sunlight shooting through the dense foliage at every opportunity.

The truck slowed again and started a slow turn to the right. Soon Aaron was able to see that the trucks were forming a circle in a clearing in the forest. Several motorcycles carrying a driver and a guard with a machine gun in the sidecar made their way through the trucks and took up positions in-between each vehicle. From somewhere beyond Aaron's field of vision came the SS guards slowly moving toward the back of each truck.

The tailgate was released with a metallic bang and the guards started shouting for Aaron and the others to get out of the back. Aaron held on to his bread and sausage and jumped down, his knees almost giving out as his feet hit the soft mud.

"Into the center." The SS Private shouted motioning with his rifle.

Aaron moved with the others toward the large open area formed by the truck. It had only taken a few moments for all of the trucks to be emptied and the workers to loosely form in the middle. Then a middle-aged SS officer made his way over to one of the trucks and climbed up on its bumper so that he could be seen by all of the prisoners.

Aaron recognized the man. It was Lieutenant Klein, one of the Officers from Camp 117. "Listen up." He commanded, scanning the prisoner-assembly before him. "We will be staying here for a few hours. During this time you may eat some of your rations and relieve yourselves over there." He pointed, "Do not eat all of your rations. They will also be your supper tonight. Is that understood?"

The crowd of men and women murmured their understanding.

"Also," Lieutenant Klein continued. "on the side of this truck and that one over there" he said pointing, "will be some water."

Lieutenant Klein looked at the assembly for several seconds as if trying to choose his words carefully before speaking again. "You will notice that there are guards posted around the perimeter and between the trucks. Do not approach them or try and get past them. You will be shot!"

The prisoners were silent. It was nothing they hadn't heard a thousand times before.

"And if any of you feel that you can escape, I have two other reasons why you should forget the notion." Again Lieutenant Klein paused for the effect it would have on the prisoners. "First there are several of my men scattered out there in the forest, hiding. You will not see them until it is too late. They will not bother bringing you back here. They have orders to shoot you on sight." Again he let the words sink in before continuing. "And second, this evening when we get back in the trucks there will be a roll call and headcount. For every prisoner that is missing at the roll call, three others will be shot."

Aaron had no doubt that several of the prisoners had been thinking about trying to escape. He himself had thought about finding David and Yvette and escaping, but now he had pushed the plan from his head. He hoped anyone else thinking about escape had done the same.

Lieutenant Klein looked around the group once more. "Enjoy your lunch" he said before jumping down from the front of the truck.

Aaron and the other prisoners stood frozen in place wondering what to do next. Lieutenant Klein hadn't really dismissed them. He just told them to enjoy their lunch. Would someone else step up on the truck and dismiss them? The ranks held firm until Lieutenant Klein climbed back up on to the truck. He sheepishly smiled at the workers. "Dismissed." He yelled.

Aaron quickly began making his way through the prisoners looking for David and Yvette. It was Yvette who found him first.

"Here Aaron" she cried out, obviously looking for David and him.

"Yvette." It made him feel good to see that she was actually looking for him and not trying to avoid him anymore. "Have you seen David?"

"Right here." David said walking up from behind the two.

The three stood there looking about the group. Finally Yvette pulled her metal cup out of her pocket and pointed to the water. Let's get some water and then we can find a place to sit and talk."

The ground wasn't much softer than the wooden bench he had spent most of the day on, but at least he could stretch his legs. The three sat in silence as they ate their meal. Aaron ate less than half of his bread and less of the sausage wanting them to last as long as possible. He noticed that David and Yvette had done the same.

"Where do you think we are?" David finally asked.

"Aaron looked around the forest. "I don't know. We could be anywhere."

"I think we're in Germany." Yvette said quite confidently.

"Germany." David shot back sarcastically, "How do you know we're in Germany? I didn't see any road signs, Aaron did you?"

Aaron shook his head back and forth and then looked over at Yvette. "What makes you think we're in Germany, Yvette?"

Yvette sat up. "Did either of you have a seat where you could look out?"

"I did" Aaron answered as David just shook his head.

"Didn't you notice?"

"Notice what." The two boys chimed in together.

"The sun, the position of the sun."

Aaron and David looked blankly at each other for several second, both shrugging their shoulders.

"Honestly," Yvette sighed, "The sun was behind the truck all morning; moving generally to our left and overhead."

"And?" David prompted.

"And, stupid," Yvette quipped, "it rises in the East and sets in the West. That means the East was behind us all day making our direction of travel West or Southwest."

Aaron thought hard about what Yvette was saying. "Heading southwest out of Auschwitz would eventually bring us back into Germany."

"We're back in Germany?" David asked becoming excited.

"If not, we will be soon." Yvette answered.

"Where do you think they're taking us?" Aaron asked

"Yes," David added "and what's going to happen once we get there?"

Yvette's shoulders sagged slightly. "I don't know."

Aaron thought more about the morning trying to figure out what had happened to them. "You noticed that they didn't take all of the special workers."

"Hmmm" David replied picking at the grass.

"They left about half of them back in the camp. By now the others are in one of the rock quarries. I don't think we will be going back to Auschwitz any time soon."

"I don't think they have any intention of taking us back there." Yvette added, "I saw a detail loading up some of the equipment as we pulled out."

"I think you're right." David said, "Rabbi Helfer thinks they're moving us further away from the Russians."

Aaron shot up. "Rabbi Helfer? When did you talk with him?"

David sat up puzzled at Aaron's excitement. "Well, most of the day. He's on my truck."

Aaron stood looking around the scattered groups of prisoners, searching for the Rabbi. "Where, where is he?"

David stood and began to look around. "Over there." He pointed, "See. . . not far from the water truck."

"Wait here." Aaron commanded as he headed toward the Rabbi.

Aaron slowed his pace as he reached the group where Rabbi Helfer was seated. He didn't want to attract any attention to himself or the Rabbi by charging up upon him.

"Ah, Aaron." Rabbi Helfer smiled "Good to see you. How was your meal?"

Aaron stood there not knowing what to do next. "Fine." he sputtered.

Rabbi Helfer smiled again understanding Aaron's confusion, "Sit down, Aaron. You are amongst friends here."

Aaron slowly lowered himself to the ground. It was with mixed emotions that he looked upon the Rabbi. The man was not supposed to be on the trucks, Aaron was sure of that, but for some reason he was sitting in front of him and that made Aaron happy.

"I'm happy to see you too." The Rabbi smiled knowing what Aaron was broadcasting across his face. "Did you have a good seat?"

"Yes, in the back of the truck."

"Good, good for you." Rabbi Helfer said rubbing his back, "I had to sit on the floor most of the trip. That floor was very cold and hard on my back."

"How..." Aaron started to say and stopped.

"It seems that somehow my documents were altered to show that I was a printing press operator and therefore an essential worker."

Aaron looked at the old man as he winked at him and smiled.

"Yes," Aaron added, speaking in a very serious tone, "That has been known to happen."

"Ah God works in mysterious ways. Who knew?"

"I was happy to hear that you were here with us."

Rabbi Helfer looked over the rims of his glasses, "No more than I was, son."

The two laughed for a moment before the Rabbi spoke again. "So where do you think we are, Aaron?"

"Germany." He quickly shot back, "If not in Germany now, we will be tonight or tomorrow morning."

Rabbi Helfer looked around at the other men seated with him. Several of the men shook their heads in agreement.

"You see," Rabbi Helfer stated, "the boy is very smart. Smarter than some of you, I think."

Aaron blushed at the remark and felt guilty for not telling him that it was Yvette who had figured out where they were. "Do you know where we are going?" he asked the Rabbi.

"Hmmm, I'm not sure." The man mused, "What is your guess, Aaron."

Aaron rubbed his chin as if contemplating his answer. Actually he was trying to remember what the Rabbi had told David earlier. "I'm not sure where we are going in Germany." Aaron said slowly, "but I think it will be as far from the Russians as they can get us."

Again the Rabbi smiled, as he looked around at the others. Aaron noticed that the small group were now nodding in agreement with his statement.

"Yes, we think so too."

"Aaron looked round at the different men and then back at the Rabbi. "But why keep us away from the Russians?"

The smile left the Rabbi's face. "Isn't that obvious?"

Aaron shook his head back and forth.

Rabbi Helfer looked over to where Lieutenant Klein and a few of the SS soldiers were standing and then back at Aaron. "They're not finished with us yet." he answered solemnly.

Chapter 37

The rest of the afternoon was quite pleasant for Aaron and the others. It was the first day since his arrival that he didn't have to work. They were able to catch up with what was happening in each of their workshops, but most of the discussion was of the future and what little they knew about it. Aaron spent time telling Yvette and David what he had learned from the Rabbi, which wasn't much. The Rabbi had found out that the Russians were winning the war on the Eastern front and the same was surmised about the British and Americans on the Western front. The SS had been afraid that the Russians would soon over-run their positions in Poland including the Auschwitz compounds. It wouldn't be today or tomorrow, but by the way that some of the SS Guards were talking, it would happen soon.

"Then what about the train you saw this morning?" David asked. "It doesn't make sense to bring new prisoners in when you're taking some of the old ones out."

Aaron looked down at the ground for a few seconds then up at David. "I don't think the trains will stop until the Russians stop them. You forget, we have value, those prisoners I saw this morning don't,"

"What do you mean." Yvette asked.

"With people like Colonel Oust and Sergeant Bella back there running things, they will continue killing Jews at Auschwitz until they have to leave or fear being captured by the Russians themselves."

"Well," David said stretching out on a small patch of grass, "It is much better that we left them behind. I don't care if I never see Oust or Bella again."

Yvette wrapped her coat around herself pulling her knees up to her chin and wrapping her arms around them. "I will see them in my dreams for a long time to come."

Aaron's expression became cold and hard, "I want to see them pay for what they did to my grandfather and the others. I want to be there when they are made to explain their reasoning for all the beatings and murders."

"Men like them are never made to pay." Yvette huffed.

"They will pay." Aaron almost whispered. "They have to pay."

"I will be satisfied to know that they will rot in the ground for what they have done." David added.

Yvette drew a small figure of a woman's face in the mud with a stick. Aaron was amazed at how good the picture looked. "Aaron," Yvette asked mindlessly as she continued to draw. "Do you think things will be better now?"

"Better?"

"Well, yes. Better now that we are away from Auschwitz."

Aaron did not take his eyes off the figure Yvette was drawing. "Rabbi Helfer said that there were hundreds of concentration camps all over the 3rd Reich. We're probably being moved to one of them. Somewhere further away from the Russians that's all."

"And away from Oust and Bella." Yvette reminded Aaron.

Aaron shook his head. "I'm afraid that whichever camp they send us to they will have their own Oust and Bella."

"Well," David said laughing, "We can at least hope that the new "Bella" won't smell like rancid animal fat."

All three laughed in whispered tones.

Aaron didn't know if he was the first one to hear the sound of trucks approaching, but he was the first to stand up and point. "Look," he said, "more vehicles coming off the road."

The three stood, as did many of the other prisoners, and watched the small convoy as it approached. The new convoy was actually only three vehicles. The procession was lead by an SS staff car followed by a large truck identical to the one they had traveled in. Behind the truck was a single motorcycle with a sidecar identical to the ones guarding them. The group of vehicles did not join the circle of trucks, but parked about 50 meters away.

"It's Captain Von Reichman." Yvette said before the car came to a complete stop.

Aaron didn't get a good look at the passenger, but didn't doubt what Yvette had just said. Von Reichman had been in charge of the special work group since the day he had arrived at the camp. It made sense that he would still be in charge now.

"I wonder who's in the truck?" David asked, as he moved around Yvette to get a better look.

"Maybe more guards." Yvette offered.

"No," Aaron said softly, "not with an armed motorcycle bringing up the rear like that. It's got to be more prisoners."

"Maybe prisoners from one of the other camps." David said, "Maybe from the main camp or something."

"That could be." Aaron agreed, "They emptied out our camp of the people they wanted to keep. I'm sure they're doing the same in the other camps."

The three watched as Lieutenant Klein and two of the guards approached the small group. Klein and Von Reichman exchanged salutes and began talking while the armed guards moved around to the back of the truck and dropped the tailgate. Slowly prisoners started jumping down from the back of the truck.

"I don't recognize any of them." David volunteered, "Do either of you?"

Aaron watched as the men and women continued to file off the back of the truck. "No, I've never seen any of them."

Yvette was about to add her affirmation when her face lit up. "That one," she exclaimed, "the last to hop down, isn't that Krista from the orchestra?"

"Krista?" Aaron asked as he took a better look at the woman.

Yvette's hands jumped to her lips as if they could catch the words coming from her mouth. "Anna! Aaron, there's Anna."

Aaron didn't hear Yvette. His eyes had been fixed on Anna's small frame from the second she had come into view. He had wanted to shout out, wanted to say her name, but the tears that had quickly filled his eyes somehow had cut off the words. Aaron dragged his sleeve across his face. "Where?" he said, hoping his voice hadn't betrayed him.

"Right there." David said pointing. "How could you miss her?"

Other member of the orchestra continued filing off the truck until most of them were accounted for.

"Where are the rest?" Yvette asked as the guards motioned the group toward the holding area between the trucks.

Aaron also was taking a mental head count. "They're probably in the same place as the special workers who weren't on the trucks with us."

Yvette turned to look at Aaron, "You mean the quarries?"

"I would think so." Aaron said as his eyes followed Anna.

"Oh, Aaron," Yvette sighed, "those people won't survive the quarries."

"I think that is Colonel Oust's intention." David said, as he started moving in a direction that would intercept Anna as she entered the circle of trucks. Aaron and Yvette followed close behind David slowly making their way through the small groups of prisoners.

The three stopped just short of the space where the new prisoners entered into the inner circle between the trucks. The new arrivals quickly began to disperse amongst the other prisoners, hugging friends if there were any. Some of the prisoners headed directly for the water trucks obviously having been told of their existence.

Yvette pushed in front of Aaron and David. "Anna, here!" she called out waving her hand timidly above her head.

Anna pushed her way over to Yvette, a huge smile covering most of her face. The two women embraced. "Yvette!" Anna cried, "I was afraid I'd never see you again."

Yvette hugged Anna tightly. "We thought you were left behind."

"Almost!" Anna half-laughed. "I was so frightened when I saw the trucks pulling out and then, later on, I found out that the special workgroups had been disbanded."

"Well at least now we know we're not going back to Auschwitz." David said as he approached Anna with his arms opened wide.

Anna released Yvette and hugged David. "No, no more Auschwitz." She said looking toward Aaron.

"It's good to see you, Anna." Aaron smiled placing his hand on her shoulder.

Anna made a move to hug Aaron, but David held her firmly. "I'll take his hug, Anna." David teased, "Aaron didn't care if you stayed or not."

Anna gently pushed David back and went to Aaron, giving him a big hug before she turned back to the others. "That's not true." she said, looking at Aaron again. "I heard you screaming my name as you went out the gate, Aaron. Thank you for your concern."

"You never told us you were screaming at her as we left" David prodded, as Aaron's cheeks began to take on a rosy color.

"I must have forgotten." Aaron said blushing even more "Anna, have you eaten?"

"I'm more thirsty than hungry, but I can definitely eat."

Aaron nodded to David. "Why don't you get her some water and meet us back where we were sitting before."

"Sure." David answered as he moved toward the water truck, the others toward the area where the three of them had been sitting.

For a small woman, Anna had quite the appetite, eating a little more than half her bread and sausage.

"Colonel Oust wasn't going to let us come with you." She chewed.

"Then what happened" Yvette asked, holding Anna's water cup while the girl bit off another piece of bread.

"Umm, I'm not sure." She said still chewing, "All I know is that Captain Von Reichman talked with him and a little later a couple of new prisoners were brought to the camp and loaded on the truck. Then we were told to take our instruments and get on the truck."

"Your violin," David asked looking around the area. "where is it?"

Anna's mouth was still too full for her to talk so she pointed toward the small convoy. "It's in the trunk of Captain Von Reichman's car." she muttered.

Aaron looked over to where Captain Von Reichman and Lieutenant Klein were standing. The two Officers were looking at some paper spread across the fender of one of the trucks and talking. "Did you hear where we are going?" He asked her.

Anna shook her head. "No. All I know is that it's somewhere in Germany."

"How do you know that?" Aaron pressed.

"I heard the Captain talking with our driver. He told him that we were going to meet up with some additional trucks later on in the day; because the Allied planes were patrolling the skies in Germany so heavily; we would have to wait for the cover of darkness before moving further south. He said this was about as far as we dare go in the daytime."

"The Allied plans are patrolling the German skies?" Aaron repeated.

"That's what the Captain said." Anna answered between sips of water. "He said that there wasn't enough of the German Air force left to knock a sick bird out of the sky let alone the American fighters. He said that the reports he had received showed that this was about as far as we dare go without getting shot at."

"Anna," Yvette asked taking the water cup back from her, "He didn't mention where we were heading."

Anna shook her head from side to side. "No. That's all I heard."

As if on cue, a sharp whistle cut through the air. "Attention!" shouted one of the SS guards.

Get into ranks starting here." He commanded, pointing at a spot a few meters in front of him.

"I'll see you all later." Aaron said as the prisoners began to line up.

Anna and Yvette stood up brushing the loose grass from their coats. "Where is he off to?" Anna asked.

"Where else," David answered standing, "he's off to talk with the Rabbi."

Chapter 38

Light was beginning to filter through some of the holes in the canvas covering the rear of the truck as they turned off the major road. Aaron was happy to see the rays of sunshine streaming through the holes for a change. During the night the holes had only allowed the cold air to rush in making it that much more uncomfortable. The back of the truck had become drafty and the air extremely cold as soon as the sun had gone down. It had been nice to have a seat at the rear of the truck during the day when it was warmer and there was plenty to see, but now he wished he had been on the floor letting others block the wind for him. Aaron tried to stretch as best he could without making any of the others uncomfortable. The muscles in his legs and back seemed to tear and burn as he extended them.

The small convoy had stopped one time during the night for refueling, but no one was allowed out of the trucks. The ride had become cold and boring and because he could not get comfortable or warm it had become miserable. The long ride gave Aaron too much time to think and his mood made it easy to hate Colonel Oust all the more. He was very happy to be out of Auschwitz but he had always figured on getting even with the Colonel before he left. Now he felt miserable for not trying to kill the man when he had the chance. Somehow he felt that he had let Samuel down or, maybe he thought, he had let himself down. Which ever it was, it just made him feel worse. The war was coming to an end and there was a good chance that the Colonel was going to be either killed or captured by the Russians. What Aaron feared more than the Colonel's capture or death was the possibility that he could escape back into Germany maybe even getting away without having to pay at all for what he had done.

The truck swayed from one side to the other as it crept down the road seeming to find every pothole along the way. Aaron frowned as he thought about their smuggling operation. He wished he could have done more, hurt the SS more. As it was, Colonel Oust would never know what he and the others had done. He would never feel the rage of finding out that a group of young children had in a small way, beaten him. It angered Aaron to think that the man would never know that he and the others had out smarted him, the SS and the great 3rd Reich.

Maybe, Aaron thought, they could set the operation up again once they were relocated. With his team still intact and Rabbi Helfer there, it could be done. After all, a change in location wouldn't be that hard to overcome. He decided to talk to the Rabbi at the first opportunity.

The gears beneath the vehicles began to grind out the usual tune as the driver downshifted, slowing the vehicle. As had become the norm, without notice the truck made a sharp turn to the left forcing its occupants to hold on to something solid or be thrown about. Aaron and the others had become quite proficient in maintaining their balance with little or no intrusion into someone else's space.

The truck made several jerks forward as the driver tapped the brakes bringing them to a halt. They still could not see where they were, but Aaron knew that they had pulled alongside another truck as he could hear the other vehicle's engine and the sound of soldiers moving about. Very quickly another truck pulled up on the other side of their vehicle. Now he could hear soldiers all around them as the engines of the trucks were being shut down. The rear flap was lifted and the morning sun burst in making everyone squint.

"Out!" one of the soldiers shouted before the tailgate had even been lowered, "Out quickly - line up."

Aaron and the others quickly followed the soldiers' orders and began moving toward an area already occupied by some of their fellow prisoners. His head began to bob up and down, looking over the group trying to find any of the others. He was finally able to spot Yvette before he moved into one of the rows now forming.

Aaron looked around the area as the final two trucks pulled up and the prisoners began to file out. The first thing that he noticed was the large single building looming just beyond the vehicles.

It was some type of factory he thought, but there were no clues as to what might have been manufactured there. He faced one of the ends of the building and could not get a very good idea how long it might be. The structure was the height of a three story building. At the end where he was standing there was a massive set of metal doors dominating the entire side. Located several meters to the right was a smaller entrance much like any normal door. Captain Von Reichman stood together with Lieutenant Klein just in front of the door, talking.

The second thing that Aaron noticed was the familiar barbed wire fence surrounding the complex. It was different than the concentration camp in that there was only a single fence of wire constructed much like the one at the concentration camp, but what was missing was the second fence around the outer perimeter of the first. He had also noticed that the fence was not electrified. There would be no sirens of the wire singing to him to jump into their arms here. Amazingly, Aaron did not see a single guard tower or the guard dogs patrolling outside the wire. He began to wonder if this was only to be their work area and not include their housing. Maybe they would be marched to a camp a few miles away for their meals and quarters.

"Alright! Pay attention you Jewish pigs!" the voice screamed.

Aaron's knees almost gave out as his heart began to pump wildly. His head shot around looking toward the area where the familiar voice had come. Small electric chills ran throughout his body as his eyes drew a bead on the fat sergeant standing in front of the group.

"Yes," Sergeant Bella said laughing out loud, "It's good to see you again too." Bella held up his ax handle and waved it slightly. "We've missed you, but I'm sure we will have plenty of time to get reacquainted in the near future."

Aaron swallowed hard as he tried to catch his breath. He wanted to rub his eyes in hopes that Bella would disappear, but that type of movement would only attract the man's attention. Aaron never wanted to be the object of Bella's attention again.

"There will be a roll call." Bella continued, "As your name is called you will enter the building through that small door over there." He said, pointing to the door where the Captain and Lieutenant had been standing moments before. "This will be your new home and work area. One and the same."

Well, Aaron thought, so much for marching off to a camp somewhere. He looked at the wire and began wondering how easy it would be for four people to escape one night.

"As your small minds are probably wondering how easy it would be to escape through the wire at night, I will tell you now. No one will escape. An attempt to do so will bring death to those around you."

Aaron shuddered at the thought of Bella being able to read his thoughts.

"If you're captured alive," Bella continued, grinning like an animal waiting for the hunt to begin, "you will have the opportunity to see your friends die just before you are put to death." Bella stopped and allowed his words to sink in before continuing. "So, please, be my guest." He taunted examining his ax handle "We look forward to your stupid attempts."

Bella looked through the ranks for several seconds. Aaron thought he saw the man focus on him briefly and smiled. Aaron knew that Bella was more dangerous now than ever before. The man's appetite for killing was growing, Aaron thought. With the war closing in on them, the SS was becoming desperate and Aaron wondered what affect that would have on a man like Bella who had been desperate most of his life.

The head count went smoothly and within a few minutes Aaron and the others were standing inside their new home. The old factory smelled heavily of diesel and oil and the floor, a poured concrete slab, showed years of heavy use. It was easy to see where heavy objects and been dragged across the floor leaving deep gashes in the surface. As Aaron looked around he noticed that the building had been gutted of its original equipment. Large equidistant blocks of concrete rose from the floor; each having several metal bolts jutting out of the top. From the size and configuration of the footings Aaron guessed that there had been some type of large metal working equipment in here at one time. There were no signs or clues as to what had previously occupied the building.

In one corner of the structure stood several wooden crates marked with the SS insignia. In the opposite corner of the work area Aaron recognized his group's equipment haphazardly piled into several stacks. Across from his group's equipment sat the printing presses to be used by David and the other printers.

The second floor had an area designed for offices. There were half-a-dozen doors along the one wall leading out onto a walkway. Several of the offices had large windows that could be used to overlook the workshop floor.

Bella moved inside the building and walked toward the stairs leading up to the mezzanine housing all of the offices. His feet pounded the stairs like massive jack-hammers until he reached the top. He was breathing heavily when he finally made it to the top and moved a few meters down the walkway.

"This is where you will work." He said pointing ambiguously out at the open shop floor. "Through that door is the plant kitchen where your meals will be served. There is a door on the other side of the kitchen leading outside to several buildings. Two of these buildings have been set up as dormitories. You will notice that there are several smaller buildings just past the dormitories that house your wash facilities and bathrooms. It will be your responsibility to keep them clean."

Bella paused at the point where Aaron would have expected the man to ask if anyone had any questions, but Aaron knew Bella didn't care if the Jews had questions or not.

"Find your equipment and begin setting it up. Bella ordered. "There will be no meals until the machinery is set up and ready to start working first thing in the morning.

Chapter 39

As Hanukkah came and went the workdays in the new camp grew longer. Aaron and the others were forced out of bed at four in the morning and worked steadily until seven or eight in the evening. The only benefit to the long days was that Sergeant Bella was never seen before 7am and rarely after 5pm in the evening. This meant that the prisoners were under the direction of a Corporal Schnider, who did his job with a lot less enthusiasm than Sergeant Bella. Schnider very seldom bothered the prisoners and the guards under his command followed his lead. So much so that on one occasion, when Aaron had fallen asleep at his work station, a passing guard gently nudged him. Aaron awoke with a fright, looking up at the guard expecting a beating. Instead the guard simply winked at him and motioned for

Aaron to continue. Aaron knew that he could not have expected the same treatment if Sergeant Bella had been the one to discover him asleep.

Bella had continued to make life difficult for the prisoners, beating them at every opportunity. When they had first arrived at the new camp in late September, Bella had managed to kill two prisoners within a week. This action had displeased Captain Von Reichman to the point where the young Captain had called him on his actions. Bella had been reminded that they, the SS, now had a limited supply of specialized labor at their disposal and that he should not squander any more of their resources. Since that time Sergeant Bella had refrained from killing anyone, but severe beatings were the new order of the day.

Anna and the remaining members of the orchestra were put to work in the kitchen and attending to any other housekeeping chores that came up. Anna still kept Captain Von Reichman's quarters, which were not much more than two rooms and definitely smaller than the previous house. However, she still maintained a small cot in the corner of the kitchen.

David insisted that the Captain was making unwanted advances toward Anna, but when Yvette questioned Anna on the matter, she was assured that the Captain had never taken any steps in that direction.

The bunks in the dormitory were more to the military standard of being two high instead of the three or four they had been forced to sleep on in the Auschwitz camp. There was even a thin mattress on the bed and the musicians now working in the laundry supplied fresh linens once a week.

Aaron lay in his bunk, his mind racing wildly as his body quivered with exhaustion. Every time he forced his eyes shut they somehow found themselves open again staring at the peeling ceiling above him. Winter was quickly coming to an end but with very little heat in the barracks, the large room was extremely cold. Aaron turned on his side, bringing his threadbare blanket up around his neck.

"David, are you awake?" Aaron asked softly toward the bottom bunk where David slept.

"Yes." David answered through chattering teeth. "It's too damn cold to sleep."

"I didn't hear the car come back yet, did you?" Aaron asked.

David knew what Aaron was really asking was whether or not Yvette had been returned to the women's dormitory. Yvette and the other painter, Jacob, were the only two prisoners left in Yvette's group and they did not work in the compound. Every morning they were placed in the back of Captain Von Reichman's staff car and driven to their job somewhere off site. Aaron and David knew that Yvette had returned each night when they heard the staff car pull into the compound.

"No, nothing yet. It seems like it's getting later and later when the car comes back."

Aaron and David would usually stay awake until Yvette's return. After Jacob had entered the building and settled in for the night, the two of them would leave the barracks and make their way to the latrine building where Yvette was usually waiting for them. The only reason that the group now knew that the factory complex they were in was located in the small town of Merkers, Germany, was because of Yvette's ability to leave the compound.

Yvette would not discuss where she worked or what she and Jacob were doing any more. Aaron had pushed her on the issue with no success. Even David's attempts had failed. Yvette insisted in the secrecy saying that it was to protect all of them from being shot. She would tell them the things she had over-heard each day and that seemed to satisfy everyone.

Aaron's ears pricked up when he heard the familiar sound of the gasoline engine of the Captain's staff car. It was easy to pick out from the noisier diesel driven trucks.

"She's back." David said unnecessarily.

Within a few seconds the door to the men's dormitory opened and Jacob entered the room. Aaron could hear the man making his way between the rows of bunks. He closed his eyes pretending to be asleep. He listened as the man shuffled his feet across the floor suddenly stopping right in front of his bunk. Aaron kept his eyes closed until he felt the man nudge him lightly. "Aaron." Jacob whispered.

"I'm awake." Aaron replied without moving.

Jacob moved closer to the bed. "Yvette says you must meet her right now. She said not to wait."

Aaron and David both sat up in their beds. Aaron lightly hopped down to the floor. "What's the matter?'" he asked Jacob.

Jacob shook his head back and forth. "She didn't tell me, but I know she is very upset."

Aaron shot David a pensive look. David's face showed the same concern.

"Is there trouble?" David asked.

Jacob shook his head again as he pushed the two toward the door. "Please - I don't know. She said to hurry."

Aaron and David both ran to the rear door of the room, stopping briefly to peek out before continuing. The two dashed across the small alleyway and through the door of the latrine building. Yvette sat in her usual place waiting for them to arrive. She jumped up at their arrival and met them halfway across the room.

"Aaron." She almost wept as she reached them. "We have big trouble."

Aaron grabbed her and hugged her close to him trying to calm the woman down. "What's wrong, Yvette? What's happened?"

She moved away from the two and sat at the edge of the latrines. Yvette looked around the dimly lit room, her eyes desperately trying to bat away the tears. "They're going to kill us."

"What!" David exploded, forcing the three of them to cower and look around the room. "What are you talking about?" David asked again, this time much softer.

Yvette looked at the two of them before continuing. Where I work there are a lot of SS soldiers coming and going. It's quite normal to see them all the time, but tonight there were a lot of Officers there. High ranking officers. Some in civilian clothing."

Aaron and David waited several seconds for Yvette to continue.

"And." Aaron prompted.

Yvette looked at him, her eyes vacant and cold. "Colonel Oust was there too."

Now it was Aaron's turn to become loud. "Oust - Oust was there?" Aaron heard himself saying as his mind reeled with all the possibilities of getting even.

"Yes, he and several others." She continued. "They were having a meeting and I was able to sneak close enough to hear a lot of what they were saying."

"And they are going to kill us?" David interjected, "When?"

"Soon - really soon."

Aaron sat down next to her, his mind still working on the idea of getting to Colonel Oust. "Why would they kill us now?" he asked.

Yvette twisted her hand in an emphatic gesture. "One of them was saying that the Allied Armies had taken Cologne and they were crossing the Rhine River. The Americans are very close now." Yvette ran her hand through her hair, "He also stated that the Russians had liberated Auschwitz and were heading this way. They expect the Soviets will capture Danzig any day now."

"So they are going to run and want us dead?" David interjected solemnly.

Yvette shook her head. "Yes...no witnesses."

Aaron tried to remain calm. "When do they plan to do this?"

"In the next few day. . . I don't know exactly when but I heard the Colonel talking with Von Reichman. The two argued over it."

"Argued?" Aaron thought aloud, "What was there to argue about?"

Yvette slipped her hand into Aaron's molding the two together. "Von Reichman doesn't see the need to kill anyone. He thinks they should just leave and let us stay in the camp until the Americans find us."

Aaron squeezed her hand. "And Oust thinks that we should be killed as soon as possible."

Yvette looked down at the floor. "Yes. After the Captain left the area Colonel Oust summoned Sergeant Bella."

"God, Bella too." David whined.

Yvette's head bobbed up and down. "Yes. Oust told him that he was ordering him to personally see to the destruction of the prisoners."

"What if Von Reichman wouldn't allow it?" Aaron asked quite smugly.

"Then Bella is to shoot him too." She whispered. "Oust was clear on that point."

Aaron quietly sat next to Yvette for several minutes before speaking again. "In which direction are the Americans coming from?"

"The west. . .Frankfurt. The Officer giving the briefing said that the last information he had showed that the Americans were in Frankfurt and heading this way."

"Frankfurt!" Aaron said standing. "That's less than a hundred miles from here."

David sat next to Yvette placing his arm around her shoulder. "You think we should head toward Frankfurt?"

Aaron began to pace back and forth as he devised a plan for their escape. "Yes," he finally answered, "We head for Frankfurt - tonight."

"Now?" David asked jumping to his feet. "You want to leave right now? The American's are still a hundred miles away."

"Yes, but if they are heading toward us and we toward them, the distance is certainly to be cut almost in half."

"Fifty miles is still a long way to go, Aaron." Yvette said as she stood and joined them. "There are still plenty of German soldiers out there."

"That's true and we will have to avoid them if possible, but I think with the Americans coming most of the soldiers will be worrying about their own lives, not ours."

"Unless they're like Bella." David threw in.

Aaron's eyes caught David's. "Yes, if they're like Bella, we will have to be very careful."

"What do we do then?" Yvette asked.

Aaron continued to pace. "We have to get to Anna and get her away from the Captain." Aaron thought aloud.

"And?" David asked prompting him.

Aaron stopped and looked back and forth at the two of them. "And while you're getting Anna," he said to David, "Yvette and I will be talking to the Rabbi and the other prisoners."

"You're going to tell everybody?" David asked quickly raising his hand, "I know, I know, everyone has the same right to live."

"Yes, exactly."

The words died in mid-sentence as a high-pitched whistling sound filled the air ending in a massive explosion knocking the three to the ground. All three were attempting to get to their feet when the second and third explosions erupted somewhere in the compound. Aaron staggered to his feet and went to the door of the latrine. It had been knocked crooked on it hinges by the explosion. Aaron forced it open.

Aaron gasped at the sight of the dormitory. The rear third of the building was almost gone. The bodies of two men lay at his feet, both twisted into gross poses. Aaron fell several steps backwards at the sight of the two. He knew they were prisoners, but could not make out their features in order to identify them.

"What are you waiting for." David shouted at him from behind. "Let's get out of here."

Aaron forced himself through the door knowing that David and Yvette would be right behind him. Once clear of the building he turned to the others and was almost run over by them. Explosions were dancing across the compound and the surrounding area outside the camp. He could see figures running in the dark as the explosions briefly lit the area. He couldn't make out if they were prisoners or SS men. Everyone was running for his or her life.

Aaron was deafened by the noise and leaned close to David and Yvette to speak. "David!" Aaron shouted not realizing he had a death grip on David's coat. "Can you still go and get Anna?"

David looked over his shoulder toward Captain Von Reichman's quarters. He simply shook his head in agreement, words failing him.

"Good!" Aaron screamed over the explosions. "Yvette and I will stay here and try to help the others. We will meet you by the back fence, up the hill between the two out-buildings as soon as we can, understand?"

David grabbed Aaron on the shoulder and grinned. "Don't be late or Anna and I will leave you."

Before Aaron could say another word David raced off toward Von Reichman's quarters diving behind a stack of metal as another bomb went off. Aaron grabbed Yvette by the hand and the two raced toward the dormitories. He was astonished at the damage done to the building. He then realized that a second bomb must have hit the building bringing a large portion of the roof structure down. The main factory had suffered a direct hit also and large flames were now leaping out of the windows. Sparks and fiery ashes were being caught in the hot updrafts and were being propelled skyward.

Aaron entered what was left of the dormitory being careful where he stepped. Heavy dark smoke filled the large room, which made it hard for him to find his way. He reached back and grabbed Yvette's hand. She had a firm grip on the back of his coat. Satisfied that she was still with him, Aaron made his way between the splintered wood and metal bunks that had been tossed around like a school child's toys. Several bodies of the prisoners were thrown about the floor. He thought about checking to see if they were alive but it was easy to see that they were dead. He continued toward the back of the room where David and his bunk had been. The further he moved into the building the harder it was to move around. He finally stopped when he reached the edge of what was now a large crater in the middle of the floor. On the other side he could see the latrine building.

"Aaron, look." Yvette shouted as she pulled on the back of his jacket.

Aaron quickly looked in the direction of Yvette's finger. There laying on the floor was the body of Grigori Petrov, the old tailor from the truck. The man looked as if he was still sleeping, eyes shut and a pleasant look to his face as if the man were enjoying a peaceful dream.

Aaron started to move toward the old tailor until the bombs started dropping faster.

"Aaron - please let's get out of here." Yvette begged as she pulled him away from the body.

Aaron grabbed her by the hand and hastily made their way out of the building. Once clear they ran along the perimeter fence and followed it up a gently rising hill. Several weeks before, David and he had been put on a work detail clearing the weeds and brush away from the fence. It was then that they discovered the weak area in the fence. They planned to use it when it became time to escape.

Aaron and Yvette were the first ones to reach the rendezvous point. They lay low in the grass hiding from any SS guard.

"Where are they?" Yvette asked impatiently.

Aaron kept a watch out for David and Anna. He knew the most direct route would be between the two outbuildings and that's where he concentrated his attention.

"There!" He shouted to Yvette pointing between the buildings.

Yvette looked to where Aaron was pointing. "I don't see anything."

Aaron pointed again. "There in the shadow of the building on the right."

As if to augment his instructions, another bomb hit close to the left building lighting up the area for a split second.

"Yes - yes!" Yvette screamed, "I see them!"

Aaron kept his eyes on the two figures lurking in the shadows as they slowly made their way along the building.

"Aaron!" Yvette said shaking him. "Aaron - look."

Aaron brushed her hand aside. "I see them. Get ready."

"Oh God, Aaron no. Look further to the right!"

Nauseating spurts of adrenaline shot though Aaron's body at the sight of Sergeant Bella making his way along the back of the right building toward the corner where David and Anna would soon emerge. Even at their present distance from the butcher, Aaron and Yvette were able to make out the pistol that Bella carried in his left hand and the hideous outline of the ax handle in his right.

The two watched with numbing fear, as David and Anna grew closer to the corner of the building where they would soon run into Bella.

Aaron jumped to his feet, his eyes widened in alarm. "David!" he shouted, waving his hands in the air. "No, David!" he continued to shout as he danced up and down waving.

"Anna!" Yvette cried out as she too had joined Aaron in trying to shout over the bomb blasts and the long distance that separated them.

They watched in horror as Bella slowly inched his way along the back wall, his ax handle cocked across his body and ready to strike. Aaron finally began to run down the hill toward the SS butcher. He hadn't taken more than a dozen steps before his legs went out from under him and he fell, tumbling in the deep grass.

"Aaron." He heard Yvette shouting in his ear. "You can't go down there." She pleaded. "He has a gun and will only kill you too."

Aaron was stunned to figure out that Yvette had tackled him from behind, causing him to fall. "Are you crazy?" he shouted at her, his eyes filled with alarm. "He'll kill them!"

Yvette held on to him, almost sitting on top of him. "He'll kill us all if we go down there."

Aaron pushed her aside and stood up. Yvette grabbed hold of him and used his counter weight to pull herself up. The two got back to their feet just in time to see David come around the corner of the building right into Bella's ax handle coming the other way.

The ax handle hit him squarely in the chest forcing him backward, knocking Anna to the ground in the process. Now Bella stood over them, ax handle raised in the air, his gun pointed at David.

Trembling, Aaron pushed Yvette backward, forcing her to the ground. "Go back – run!" he shouted to her as he continued down the hill.

He had only taken a few steps when David rose from the ground, lunging at Bella. Aaron saw the flash from the barrel of Bella's pistol before he heard the report a split second later. David gripped his chest as he staggered back falling into Anna's arms. Tears began to blur Aaron's vision as Yvette ran into the back of him. He could hear Yvette crying over the explosions.

Aaron stood there for what seemed a lifetime to him, watching the interaction of the three. Slowly he pushed Yvette back toward the fence as he turned toward her. "We must go." He almost cried as the tears raced down his face.

Yvette could only nod in agreement as they turned and ran back toward the fence. Aaron raised the bottom of the fence and allowed Yvette to crawl under. Once clear, she held the fence for him. Aaron looked at Yvette hesitating, looking back down the hill where Bella and Anna were. Anna was still holding David's lifeless body.

"Come on, Aaron." Yvette pleaded, "You're the only friend I have left. Please."

Aaron went to the ground and wriggled his way under the fence. Together they began to run away from the compound. They were less than seventy meters away from the fence when Yvette suddenly stopped. "Oh, God, Aaron." She cried, her hands coming up to her mouth. "He's going to rape her!" she screamed.

"Rape?" Aaron said, his face twisted in confusion.

Yvette began to pull him back toward the fence. "Anna – he's going to rape her!" she cried.

Aaron's mouth dropped open as Yvette's words began to register. "God!" His voice exploded in sudden horror. "Come on!"

The two raced back toward the fence. They were still several meters away when they heard Bella's pistol bark again. Once - twice, then it fell silent.

Yvette dropped to the ground. "Oh God, no." she cried. "Please. . .haven't you made us suffer enough!" she shouted toward the sky. "What do you want from us?"

Aaron forcibly picked her up and carried her away from the fence. After a few meters Aaron could feel that Yvette was again under her own power and the two ran further away from the compound. The artillery shells continued to fall in the area. Within a hundred yards they became worse forcing Aaron and Yvette to dive into a ditch. Closer they came moving across the open area toward the ditch. Bam, Bam, Bam! They screamed in the night, looking for their next victim. Aaron lay flat on his stomach; his head buried in the mud, his fingers digging into the palms of his hands.

Bam, Bam, Bam! They thundered.

Bam, bam, bam! Came the knock on Aaron's door as he jumped, blinking away his thoughts.

"Commander!" came the shout through the closed door. "Are you there?"

Aaron looked up from his desk toward the door. He blinked several times before he looked down at his closed fist. Slowly he opened his hand to see his grandfather's ring; a deep red circle imprinted into his palm.

Bam, bam, bam came the knock on the door again. "Commander?" Ms. Levy called.

"Come." Aaron said in what he hoped was a commanding voice.

Ms. Levy opened the door and was quickly followed into the office by another man. "We have him." She said not making it to the front of Aaron's desk before she spoke.

Aaron stared at the two agents standing before him. "What? What are you talking about?"

"Oust." Levy almost shouted, "We have him. He's in Uruguay."

Aaron couldn't believe what he was hearing. "Oust, arrested?" he asked.

"No sir." The young agent stated as he stood behind and to one side of Ms Levy. "We have him under surveillance. He is at a small beach resort outside Montevideo. Our agents there inform us that he is scheduled to stay there another two weeks."

Aaron's eyes shifted from Levy to the other agent and back.

"Your plane is being fueled as we speak, Commander." Levy smiled, "I've made sure that your clothing is on board."

Aaron looked down into the palm of his hand. The red impression of the ring was fading now, the gold ring lay there alone on his sweaty palm. Aaron slowly rose from behind his desk placing the ring on his finger.

"Ms. Levy."

"Yes, sir." She answered.

"You will be going with me on this one." He stated as he walked out from behind the desk.

"My personal effects are already on their way to the airport, sir. Your car is waiting at the front entrance." She answered, as she and the other agent followed Aaron out of the office.

Chapter 40

Aaron's plane had taken them as far as Rome, Italy, where he and Ms. Levy had reservations on a commercial flight from Rome to Buenos Aires. Once in Buenos Aires, locally assigned agents drove them by car to the town of La Plato, Argentina. In La Plato they boarded a private yacht and crossed the 125-mile wide mouth of the river Plate over into Uruguay.

On the boat Aaron was briefed by his agent-in-charge of the Buenos Aires office. In surveillance work there is a great deal of pride in the hunt. Agents are trained in searching for information where there isn't any. They are trained in the techniques of surveillance without being discovered. Sometimes long hours and mountains of bits and pieces of information are carefully put together to glean enough information to move to the next level. Then there is another factor, the factor of pure luck. Luck was the card this time that tipped Oust's hand for the next two weeks. It seemed that a Jewish storekeeper in the small town of La Plato had spotted Heinrich Oust while the man was shopping in his store. The shopkeeper had recognized him from one of the pictures he had received. Oust, while purchasing some clothing, was overheard to say that he and his wife would be spending the next few weeks at a small resort outside Montevideo. Oust purchased several shirts and two pairs of pants that would need alterations.

When Oust asked the shopkeeper if he could hold them until he returned from his holiday, the man informed him that if he purchased the shirts and both pairs of pants he would have them delivered to him in Montevideo. Oust then commended the man on his level of service, paid cash for the items and left the address where the shop keeper could deliver the pants. It was a simple matter for the local agent to verify Oust's address in Montevideo and obtain a positive ID on the man. Now, after fifteen years, Aaron would again be face to face with Colonel Oust.

Estancia del Sol, while meek in appearance, was a favorite destination resort for many families living in Buenos Aires. It consisted of fifteen self-sufficient bungalows nestled among the trees along 300 meters of beach. The Estancia was an easy drive from Montevideo, but the more influential guest would either arrive by private boat or one of the many charters that were available. Privacy was of the utmost importance at the Estancia as many of the guests went there because of the value the owner placed on solitude and, more importantly, discretion. Not all of the guests at the Estancia del Sol were vacationing with their husband or wife.

Aaron and Levy followed the local agent to the far end of the resort away from the water. They moved through the woods until a young man not more than twenty-two, met them. Levy noticed immediately that the young man was heavily armed.

"Good evening, Commander." The young man said politely as if they were simply meeting for dinner.

"Good evening, Agent Mann." Aaron said in return. "What is the situation?"

The young man pointed through the woods to a small house that was barely visible from their vantage point. "The suspect and his wife are in the bungalow just beyond the trees. We have four agents guarding the perimeter of the building."

"I see." Aaron said looking beyond the agent toward the house. "Security?" he asked.

"We've made a sweep of the area Commander, they are alone, no guards." The young agent stated. "We were able to rent the bungalow forty meters to the left of the subjects, but the closest one on the right has been rented for a month."

"Have you checked out the occupants?" Levy asked.

"Yes, an older couple from Buenos Aires, a Lawyer and his wife. They checked out okay."

"What about the approach?" Aaron asked.

"We can approach from the rear of the cabin. The woods offer great cover," the young man replied as he shifted his automatic rifle from one hand to the other. "They're playing music in the house. . .quite loud, actually. It will help cover our approach."

"Do they have any weapons?" Levy asked, looking down at the young agent's rifle.

"No," he smiled. "We had two agents enter the cabin this morning while the occupants were out. There were no weapons of any kind other than a few kitchen knives."

Aaron was proud of the efficiency of his men. He had always instructed his agents that force was not the only way to solve situations. More often than not, an agent who has carefully worked out the problem before making a move, is the one that will succeed without risking the life of his men or his own. "Very good work." Aaron said as he patted the young agent on the shoulder. If you are ready we can proceed."

The young man smiled. "We are more than ready, Commander."

"Do you have the field file on Oust?" Levy asked.

"Yes, Agent Ross has it."

Aaron nodded. "Then let us proceed."

The agent led them through the woods to within thirty meters of the back door, he had been correct about the loud music. They probably could have driven a car up to the house without much trouble Aaron thought.

Aaron had gone over this scenario a thousand times in his life. What would he say to Oust when he was finally face to face with the man. Could he control the anger he had been harboring for this man since the day he watched him murder his grandfather? What would he say to Oust? There were a million things he wanted to say to the ex-

SS Colonel, but could he put all of that into one or two sentences?

Aaron reached over with his left hand and touched the ring on his right. The ring began to warm to his touch as he gently moved it around his finger. Aaron then moved his hand into the left side of his jacket and felt the Beretta hanging there in its holster. He started to un-holster the weapon, but stopped, removing his hand from the jacket. Aaron wasn't sure that approaching Oust with a gun in his hand was the smart thing to do. Time and time again his dreams had taken him to a place where he finally confronted Oust. In many of these dreams Aaron had simply approached the man pulling out his weapon and firing until the clip was empty and Oust lay on the floor, dead.

Aaron again placed his hand on the butt of his gun, but stopped short of pulling it out when Levy placed her hand on his shoulder. She was so close to him that he could feel her breath on the back of his neck. "Let the team handle this, Commander." She whispered into his ear.

Aaron released the weapon then reached up and patted Levy's hand. He then looked over at Agent Mann. The young man looked around the area one more time before looking back at Aaron and nodding that everything was ready.

Aaron gave him a single nod and the young man began his move toward the house. Within three meters of the back door a second agent, Ross, joined them from the shadows of the house making theirs a four person team. Aaron knew the drill. The two field agents would enter first followed by him then Levy. Both of the agents had their weapons drawn, safeties removed.

The agent slowly turned the handle of the rear door and it opened without resistance. Quietly they moved through the kitchen toward the music in the front room. Just shy of the living room, Mann raised his left hand and the four stopped. Within seconds two agents came through the front door weapons at the ready. Instantly, Mann and Ross moved through the doorway leading from the kitchen into the living room.

"No one move!" Mann stated in Spanish, then again in German, the whole time keeping his machine-pistol pointed at the two figures, one sitting in the chair by the fireplace, the other standing close-by. The violin made an ugly sound as the bow scratched across the strings.

The agents were quick and proficient in their work. One of the agents who had entered through the front door quickly searched the rest of the small house and returned to the living room where he too pointed his weapon in the direction of the two suspects. The other quickly closed all of the drapes on the windows and took up a position by the front door. Ross, who had entered with Mann, handed Levy the field file on Oust and returned to the kitchen to stand guard at the rear door.

When the house was secured Aaron stepped into the room with Levy close behind.

"Aaron!" Levy almost shouted in his ear. "My God. . ."

Aaron's hand quickly shot into the air cutting Levy off in mid sentence and almost hitting her in the face at the same time.

"Heinrich Oust," Agent Mann said in Spanish "Place your hands out where we can see them."

The man seated next to the woman slowly raised his hands out in front of him. The woman did likewise holding the violin in one hand and the bow in the other.

"I'm sorry," he said in Spanish, "but my name is not Heinrich Oust."

Aaron did not speak Spanish and looked toward Mann for the translation.

"He says that he is not Heinrich Oust, Commander." The young agent sneered.

Aaron paused for a moment. "Have the woman show us her hands also."

Not waiting for the translation into Spanish, the woman standing next to Oust placed her violin gently on the floor and raised her hands.

"Do you speak German?" the young agent asked.

"Yes." both of them answered in German,

"But not so well." The man added.

Aaron was afraid that the young agents in the room could see his legs shaking. He prayed that his voice would hold out. "Stand and turn slowly; facing me." He ordered in German.

The couple turned as ordered, keeping their hands out in front of them.

Aaron looked at the woman then back at the man standing in front of him. His hands felt wet and clammy. "This is not Heinrich Oust." He stated flatly to the agents in the room.

Agent Mann was dumfounded at the statement. "It is." He almost shouted, "It has to be."

Aaron shook his head in disagreement. "It's not." he said flatly.

Before the agent could speak again Levy stepped forward. "We will go through the field dossier on Oust?" she said flatly as she opened the file.

The agent blinked several times, almost speaking then he stopped. "Yes." Was all he could say.

"We will check him against the medical in the dossier." She ordered, flipping the pages until she got to the medical section.

Agent Mann circled around the two suspects and looked over Levy's shoulder at the file

"Colonel Heinrich Oust," she started, "Height, 183 centimeters."

The agent took out the portable tape measure from his pocket." Stand up straight." He ordered as he walked up to the suspect and dropped the one end of the tape to the ground. "Stand on this." He commanded and the man complied. Agent Mann stared at the tape for several seconds. "179 centimeters." He said solemnly.

"He could have shrunk with age." Aaron heard himself say.

"Blue eyes and blond hair." Levy continued.

"His eyes are a light blue." Mann stated as he ran his fingers through the man's hair. "The hair is too gray to say."

"Identifying marks." Levy continued not commenting on the remark. "SS tattoo and ID number under his left arm.

The man began to unbutton his shirt without being asked. In a few seconds he had stripped down to his waist.

"Raise your left arm." Mann commanded.

Even without raising his arm, it was easy to see the large scarring that started on the edge of his shoulder blade and continued up under his left arm.

"No tattoo." Mann commented "but there is massive scaring. Looks like a very bad burn. It could have been done to remove the tattoo."

"That's true." Aaron stated, "Others have been known to have their tattoos removed or covered up before, but I've never seen anyone go to so much trouble." Aaron said looking the man directly in the eyes. That wound must have been very painful.

"Yes." He answered, "A very painful burn."

"How did you get it?" Aaron asked motioning for the man to lower his arm. In a tank battle maybe?"

"I'm a grape farmer." He answered, showing no emotion to Aarons statement, "I got it many years ago when my father's tractor turned over on me. It caught on fire while I was trapped underneath."

"A grape farmer in Germany?" Aaron asked.

"No, in Mendoza, Argentina. My family moved there right after the First World War."

"He should have a scar approximately six centimeters long on his right side" Levy quoted from the dossier, "Oust received it while fencing at the University of Munich in 1929."

"While fencing?" Mann asked.

Levy looked back down at the file in front of her. "Yes. He and another student got drunk and decided to test their skills with real blades. For his part, Oust ended up with a six centimeters long scar across his lower ribs. . .seven stitches."

Mann moved around to the man's right side and looked for the scar. "Nothing here." He said sounding quite dejected.

"This is not Colonel Oust." Aaron repeated.

"But Commander." Mann protested, "We should bring him in for further questioning."

Aaron looked at Mann and smiled. "On what grounds, Captain?"

Mann looked around the room at the other agents trying to solicit their comments. No one volunteered his or her comments.

"Sir," Mann said almost whining, "But he's obviously German."

Aaron moved to within a few inches from Mann's face, his eyes flaring at the remark. "Yes, maybe," He spat, "but before I went to Israel, I was German too. Should I be brought in for questioning also?"

Agent Mann fell back a few steps. "Sir. . .I'm sorry. I didn't mean to offend you."

"You didn't offend me, Captain." Aaron said, his voice rising to an angered pitch. "What you have offended is the very thing we fight for. We are not the Nazis or the SS." He was shouting now. "We don't take people away in the middle of the night without probable cause, Captain."

Levy placed her hand on Aaron's shoulder trying to calm him. Aaron shrugged off her touch and continued. "And we certainly don't arrest a person because of his nationality or religion. That is what the SS did, Captain." He said pointing his shaking finger at the young Agent, "That is why we must never forget what they did. If for no other reason than to never repeat it."

The room fell silent as Aaron continued to stare at the young agent. Aaron hadn't noticed before, but he was panting heavily. By the look on the young man's face, it was obvious to Aaron that he may have over reacted. Aaron took a deep breath before continuing. "Captain, I spent four years under the boot of Colonel Oust. The man murdered my grandfather right in front of me. I would not be standing here defending this man if I weren't entirely sure that he is not Oust."

Agent Mann tried to recompose himself. "I understand, Commander. I may have been a little zealous in my approach."

"Being zealous" Aaron said making a vague gesture in the air. "is expected in young agents." Aaron said as he looked at Levy and the two suspects. "But it is the job of their Commander to offer an apology when the young agent becomes overzealous."

"Sir." Mann started, but was waved off by Aaron.

"Take your men out, Captain." Aaron said in a soft voice, but still ringing with authority. "Wait for us by the car. I will make the appropriate apologies and join you shortly."

Agent Mann nodded at the others and they quietly left the house. Aaron, Levy and the two suspects stood there looking at each other for several seconds. Silently Aaron walked over to a wooden chair standing against the wall of the room and sat down. He looked up at the woman suspect for the first time since the interrogation of her husband had started. The woman had been crying the entire time without letting out a whimper.

Levy started toward the women then hesitated before rushing forward.

"Anna," she cried embracing her.

The two women began crying. "Yvette," Anna sniffled, kissing her old friend on the cheek.

"Oh, Anna. We thought you were dead." Yvette managed to get out, still not letting go of her friend. "We saw Bella kill David." Yvette whimpered, "When we started back to get you we heard two more shots." Yvette looked at Anna, "Oh Anna, we thought you were dead. Can you ever forgive us for not coming back?"

"The two shots were from my pistol." Klas finally said as he walked up and put his arm on Anna's shoulder. "I was just a few seconds behind Sergeant Bella." Klas looked over at Aaron. "I was too late to save David. I'm sorry."

Yvette bent over and reverently picked up the violin and bow offering them to Anna.

"In the midst of all the shelling that night," Klas chuckled, "Anna wouldn't leave with me until I had retrieved her violin.

Yvette looked at Klas "Thank you, Captain. Thank you for her life."

Klas raised his hands and smiled. "I'm no longer a Captain, Yvette. My commission ran out years ago." he said half laughing. Klas turned to Aaron. "And I see you are no longer a Jeweler." Aaron shrugged without answering.

"What I told you about being a farmer in Mendoza is true."

Aaron pushed himself out of his chair suddenly feeling very old. The adrenalin rush he was on when he thought he might actually arrest Oust was gone leaving him feeling weak. "What happened after you killed Bella?"

Anna released Yvette and approached Aaron. "We escaped the shelling together, Klas and I. We also escaped the Americans and made our way into Spain." She walked closer to Aaron. "Aaron, we were married in Spain. I never told you. . .couldn't tell you, but I fell in love with Klas long before we left Auschwitz."

Aaron stood looking into Anna's eyes. "Anna, I. . ." the rest of the words were lost somewhere in Aaron's throat.

Anna waited for Aaron to compose himself. "Anna," he started again, "I am sorry we didn't come back for you. We. . .I was scared that Bella would kill us too."

Anna shook her head as she put out her arms to Aaron. "My darling Aaron," She said as the two came together, "My only hopes that night were that you and Yvette made it out safely and you did. I loved you both so much. And. . ." she cried on his shoulder, "I loved David also, but there was nothing any of us could have done."

The two held each other for several minutes before moving apart. Aaron wiped the tears from his eyes as Anna looked back at Yvette. "Did I hear them call you, Levy?" Anna asked.

Yvette smiled and shook her head. "Yes. After the war I returned to France for a few years and married a very nice Jewish artist. We were only married about two years when he suddenly passed away. After his loss I found myself drifting." Yvette said looking up at Anna. "I drifted to Israel and found Aaron."

Anna walked over and put her arm under Klas'. "We have three boys." she beamed, "they are becoming good farmers like their father."

Aaron looked at Klas for several seconds as the wheels in his head cranked out the detail of the failed mission. "There is something all wrong about this." he finally said.

Klas looked at him flatly. "What do you mean?"

Aaron suddenly felt cold and moved closer to the fire. "We came here tonight fully expecting to catch Oust."

"Yes?" Anna chimed in.

Aaron looked at the three of them. "Well, we bust into the cabin tonight expecting to find Oust and instead we find another German Officer that resembles Oust very closely."

"I see what you mean." Klas stated.

"Well, I don't" Yvette said.

"Neither do I." Anna added.

Aaron looked at Anna. "I think you were set up tonight, Anna. I think Oust planed the whole thing."

Anna blinked several times, her mouth open. "I don't understand what you're saying. Set up? By Oust?"

"Yes, who do you think we were looking for?" Yvette said, finally catching on to where Aaron was leading them.

Anna gasped, her hands flying to her mouth. "Oust, here!"

Aaron shook his head in agreement. "Of course it was Oust." Aaron rubbed his hands in front of the fire watching the warm glow of the flames dance along the cuts in Samuels ring. "Our agents in Buenos Aires almost caught up with the real Heinrich Oust." Aaron held up the hand with Samuels ring on it. "That is how I got my grandfather's ring back."

A large grin ran across Klas' face. "That Bastard!" he laughed.

"Anna touched Klas on the hand. "What is it, Klas?"

Klas was still laughing. "It's the old fox and hounds game."

Now Aaron and Yvette looked just as puzzled as Anna. Klas could tell by the faces that they didn't understand.

"Obviously none of you grew up in a family who hunted fox."

They all shook their head back and forth waiting for Klas to continue. "It's quite simple. When the hounds are chasing a fox, the fox will often run across the burrow or path of another fox hoping that the hounds will lose his trail and follow that of the other fox."

"Ahhh" Yvette squealed, as she came to understand Klas' meaning. "Oust knew we were closing in on him so he crossed paths with you, setting you up to take the fall."

Klas nodded in agreement. "Oust would never have expected you and Aaron to be on the team of agents sent here to capture him. Outside of Anna, you two are the only ones who could still identify him and I doubt if he even knows you're still alive."

Aaron sat on the edge of the chair facing the fire. "It looks like we've all been set up."

Anna went to the chair and carefully laid her violin down. "I hate that man."

Aaron looked at Klas. "There's something I don't understand though, Klas.

"What's that?"

"How did he know where to find you?"

The grin faded from Klas' face like the sun fades away on a cold winter day. Klas looked thoughtfully at Anna.

Anna knew the look. "What is it, Klas?"

It was Klas' turn to sit in the chair next to Aaron. "There is something that I have not spoken about in fifteen years, not even to Anna."

"Go on." Aaron prompted.

"I swore to myself that I would not have anything to do with them when Anna and I were married in Spain."

"You're talking about the SS." Aaron added.

Klas looked into the flames of the fire, his thoughts going back to a time he'd rather forget. "It was what Camp 117 was all about. You all were unwilling participants back then. Even I had very little control of what was happening."

"We know that we were being used by the SS to enhance their wealth." Aaron volunteered. "We also know that David and the other printers were producing false documents for the SS. These documents were used to aid in their escape from justice."

Klas didn't bother to look up from the fire. "Everything you say is true, Aaron. Himmler and the rest of the SS knew that Hitler was doomed to fail. They used him as much as they used you."

"Continue." Aaron said.

"They used Camp 117 and you to produce what they needed to survive after the war was lost, wealth and a means of escape."

"You're talking about the Odessa Project." Yvette interjected.

Klas shot Yvette a quick look. "Yes, the Odessa Project. Heinrich was one of the men on the inside."

"You weren't?" Aaron asked.

Klas looked directly into Aaron's eyes. "No. I was used as much as you were. For running the special work groups I was given a set of documents and enough money to get out of Germany if necessary, but the big money was with Heinrich and the others."

Anna walked over and placed her arm on her husband. "Aaron you have to understand that Klas did help us in the camp."

Aaron nodded. "I know that, Anna. Even for a child of my age back then, I could see that Klas was running some interference for us."

Anna laughed, "You don't know the half of it."

"What do you mean, Anna?" Yvette asked.

"Klas caught me with the medicine in my violin case on my second attempt to bring them into the camp. He didn't turn me in nor did he ask me who I was working with." Anna squeezed Klas' shoulder. "He did try to get me to quit, but I couldn't and he accepted it. From then on he helped where he could."

"I would never have guessed." Yvette exclaimed.

"You weren't supposed to." Klas added.

Aaron turned to Klas. "Well he's obviously still keeping tabs on you. Do you know where Oust is?"

Klas looked at Aaron for several seconds and then at his wife, Anna. "No." he said slowly, "But there are ways to find him."

Epilogue

Ramleh Prison, Israel, May 1960

Aaron and Yvette walked out of the Prison toward the area where their car was waiting. Neither had spoken since Heinrich Oust's hanging. There was nothing to say at that point.

The trial had sapped an enormous amount of energy from Aaron, Yvette and Anna. Day by day accounts were recorded and each of them was forced to relive a part of their lives that for the last fifteen years had only haunted their dreams. More than once they had each broken down on the witness stand and the trial had to be momentarily halted.

Two months into the trial Aaron fell ill and was hospitalized. He spent a week in the hospital for exhaustion and was released under the condition that he only be allowed to attend the hearings for no more than an hour a day. In the evenings Yvette would come to his home and fill him in on the days proceedings, often leaving out the more disturbing testimony. They continued this daily ritual for another month until Aaron, no longer interested in what his doctor had to say, spent the entire last three weeks at the trial.

Aaron sat between Yvette and Anna, each of them holding on to his hands as the guilty verdict was read. Two days later the scene was repeated when the Israeli Court sentenced Heinrich Oust to death by hanging. Heinrich Oust did not appeal his conviction.

The Israeli Courts reviewed Captain Klas Von Reichman's case. In doing so it was determined that:

1. Captain Von Reichman had voluntarily surrendered to the Israeli authorities.
2. Personally helped in the locating of Heinrich Oust, a most wanted criminal.
3. Supplied testimony against the former SS Colonel and,
4. Shown to have extended assistance and aid to Jewish prisoners during his time at Camp 117.

He was released from custody and allowed to return to Argentina. The Israeli Government did condemn him for belonging to an illegal organization, the SS, and informed him that he would not be welcome to return to Israel.

Aaron reached down and took Yvette's hand in his. "Anna was not there today."

Yvette didn't bother to look over at Aaron. "No. She said she had no need to see the man hang. She left this morning with Klas."

"Back to Argentina?"

"Of course. They have a farm and three healthy sons to go back to."

The two walked hand in hand for a few more steps.

"They didn't say goodbye." Aaron noted.

Yvette smiled. "No they didn't. Anna said in Argentina they say "Until we meet again", not goodbye."

"I see." Aaron said.

"She also said that if we ever wanted to see them, we were welcome to visit them at their home."

"That was nice of them."

Yvette stopped walking, forcing Aaron to stop with her. "Aaron, what's wrong? Is it just the hanging that's got you down?"

Aaron looked at his oldest and dearest friend. "Yvette, I'm going to hand in my resignation tomorrow. I'm through."

"But why?"

"Because of hate and revenge, Yvette."

Yvette looked into the sorrowful eyes of her best friend. "I don't understand, Aaron. What do you mean?"

"Yvette, for the last fifteen years my life has been fueled by hatred and revenge for one man. Every day of my life has been in the pursuit of that goal and twenty minutes ago that reason for living was hung. I have no more energy to go on.

"What about Adolf Eichmann? He's still out there." She said.

"No he's not, Yvette."

"What- what are you saying?"

"Eichmann was captured yesterday." Aaron stated flatly. He looked back at the prison complex. "In another twenty-four hours Eichmann will be behind those walls. Probably be placed in the same cell as Oust was."

"When were you going to tell me this?" Yvette asked acidly.

Aaron pointed to the car in front of them, "In the car. I just found out myself less than an hour ago."

The two finished their walk to the car and climbed in the back. They rode in silence for almost an hour, neither bothering to look at the other, finally Yvette reached over and pushed the lever to raise the glass partition between them and the driver. She knew the glass was sound proof. "Aaron I understand that you have now cleansed yourself of your life at Auschwitz. I somehow knew that's what had to be done and I was glad to help, but now I must ask a favor of you."

Aaron looked over at Yvette as soon as he detected the strain in her voice and now he could see it in her face. "What is it?" he said, taking her hand again. "Whatever I can do." he assured her.

Yvette shook her head, laughing. "You shouldn't offer such blind assistance until you've heard what I have to ask."

"Go on then."

Yvette took a deep breath and released it slowly. "You may have cleansed yourself of Camp 117, but I haven't." she said pausing for a moment. "There is something that I must do or try to do."

Aaron stared into her eyes. Yvette returned the stare unflinching for several seconds until she finally looked away.

"You know, that may be the first time I have ever won a staring contest against you." Aaron smiled.

"It is." Yvette smiled back it him.

"Then, this is serious." he said, "How can I help?"

Yvette moved closer to Aaron, laying her head on his shoulder. Aaron placed his arm around her and gently kissed her on the top of her head.

"You know what I did at the camp."

"Of course." he said, gently kissing her on the forehead.

"Remember that each day Jacob and I were driven away from the main camp in Merkers?"

"Yes, David and I. . ." the words caught in his throat. "We always worried about you; feared that you wouldn't come back one night."

"That was always a possibility and probably would have eventually happened if it wasn't for the Allied bombing."

"I often thought the same." He added thinking back.

"Aaron, they would take Jacob and I to an old salt mine just outside of town. At the bottom of the mine we were. . ." Yvette's words became strained, "finishing up on our project."

"Copying art." Aaron interjected.

"Not copying, Aaron; recreating the masters."

Aaron nodded, "Yes so they could be sold."

Yvette took a deep breath, "That's how we started, back at Camp 117. Copying art to sell, but it was also a selection process."

Aaron looked down at her. Yvette didn't raise her eyes. "Selection process?"

Yvette lifted her head off his shoulder. "Don't you remember how they kept removing artists from our group?"

"Of course, until there was no one left but you and Jacob."

Yvette nodded in agreement. "Yes, until they had the two best, the very best."

"So what was wrong with that? It saved your life."

"Like I said, Aaron," she whispered, not able to meet his eyes, "We weren't copying the masters. We were creating new masters, nearly flawless in every way."

"Forgeries?" he said sitting up. "You were making forgeries?"

Yvette squeezed his hand tightly, "Yes, perfect reproductions. . .forgeries."

She had Aaron's full attention. "Whatever for?"

"Think about it, Aaron. You get someone to make a perfect copy. You hide them in the bottom of a salt mine with all kinds of other stolen goods. The Americans over run the town; find the goods."

"And believe," He continued for her, "they have all of the real paintings while the SS has removed them and put them somewhere else."

Aaron shook his head in disbelief. "And they got away with it?"

Yvette's eyes narrowed, "Have you heard anything about anyone discovering they are forgeries?"

"No," he answered still trying to comprehend the depth of the deception, "Are you sure they are the copies you made?"

Yvette shuddered involuntarily, "Yes, they removed the originals three days before the

Americans attacked. That is why Jacob and I knew our lives would soon end."

"How many?

"Thirteen." She answered. Most of them were painted by Monet, Rembrandt, and Van Gogh.

"All near perfect copies?" he asked deep in thought.

"Aaron, we had unlimited access to the originals for over two years." she confessed, "I don't think that anyone but the original artist could tell the difference."

Aaron looked deep into her eyes. "If I didn't know you and your talent, I would say that you were bragging, but. . ."

"I guess I should say 'Thank You', but I only feel shame."

Aaron pretended he did not see the single tear that escaped the corner of Yvette's eye as she leaned against his shoulder. "There is a way to tell," She added as they continued down the road.